Royal Hearts

LOVE AT THE LAKE BOOK TWO

MARGARET ROSE

ROYAL HEARTS

MARGARET ROSE

For all the tough cookies with fragile hearts.

One

CAT

There's glitter in my eye. I try to blink, blink, blink it away but it's lodged in there good.

While pulling at an eyelash I struggle to call out, "Keep going," to the small but competent production team sweating right along with me on the downtown L.A. sidewalk.

The offending piece of confetti is infuriating. Add that to the fact this prima ballerina doesn't know how to sell a lifestyle ad to save *her* life, and you've got a PR nightmare.

I check my slim black watch. My time to salvage this project before I board a plane is dwindling. It got delayed two hours this morning. I never thought I'd be grateful for a delay but I am now.

We need to get this shot.

"You twirl around the bench, see?" I do a janky spin in chunky Prada loafers with one eye open, the other still watering with my hand over it like a pirate's patch.

"This is ridiculous," the ballerina mutters.

I hold back a four-letter expletive. I've got two hours left of my workday to get this girl's tulle-swaddled ass in gear. As a content manager for a full-service branding agency, time is everything.

Mercifully, the glitter disappears on my nine-millionth blink and I slide my sunnies back into place. Allyn, the fierce woman who founded Brand Hub when she was twenty, has taught me everything I know about marketing and utilizing social media to implement big brand strategy. But often, keeping clients and collaborators happy—especially sassy ones covered in Pepto Bismol pink—is the hardest part of my job.

"How can I help you through this?" I ask, employing my most delicate tone. It's a stretch.

"Need an extra?" A man walking by with an armload of groceries hollers.

"Keep walking, buddy!" I toss back, without taking my eyes off Sabrina.

"Show me again?" she asks, definitely messing with me.

I twirl again to the best of my ability and botch my landing, twisting my uncoordinated ankle in a crack of concrete. With a grimace, I power through, snatching a cup from our barista who's kindly volunteered to be in the video while on the clock.

My eye on the prize, I take a sip while managing to sashay toward the camera.

"And when you hit your mark," I point with my loafer at a weird blue stain in the sidewalk we've noted as her end spot, "you deliver the tagline, and take a sip."

A few cars honk on the street, some sort of tailgating argument ensuing at a stoplight through lowered windows. I hope they get it out of their system now. I'd like to use some natural background noise in the shot but I don't need two yahoos exchanging pot-shots in my audio.

That's not the vibe.

"Must I?" she yawns. Her ballerina bun is pulled so tight, it must be cutting off the oxygen to her brain.

I plaster on a tight smile because Beanie's is depending on me and speak through my teeth, "You've already cashed the first check, Sabrina. No going back now."

I'm a reluctant cheerleader, a project manager, and a brand rep who's worked her way up from interning at the company after college, all so I can be married to my smartphone and stress over batching content. Allyn has been dangling the co-owner carrot for a while now, but even with that motivation I've been wearing a lot of hats for our women-owned-and-operated marketing agency.

Today they're feeling quite heavy.

With no warning, the ballerina shrugs as she pushes up on her toes. I signal the camera to film as she twirls around an old bench outside Beanie's coffee, and plucks a to-go cup off the barista's tray while lifting her leg in arabesque.

The sun highlights the shimmer in her tights and she looks almost magical. The visual is exactly what I imagined in my head. Luxe, but approachable.

"Now the tagline! Keep going, Sabrina!"

I wave for our camera-woman to pull in tight with the gimbal to capture her pretty pink lips as she utters the words I worked weeks to come up with.

"Beanie's Beans, keeping things bold since 1999." Another glitter cannon explodes and rains down around us.

So, it's not Shakespeare, or even a memorable McDonald's *I'm loving it* tagline. If this was Nike, I'd be fired for sure.

"That's it," I yell. "Cut."

"Thank God," she huffs, pulling a sweater over her shoulders. "Next time just shoot me."

The feeling is mutual, babe. "Don't forget to hashtag when you post."

Her assistant unties the ribbons of her toe shoes while she perches on a sidewalk table, then saunters to her waiting car in moon boots even though L.A.'s temperatures are still in the 80s despite the November date.

"Thanks, Hil," I say to our sweet camera-woman who works a la carte for Brand Hub when I'm in town. "You'll get Allyn's check in the mail per usual."

"No worries, she's always prompt with payment. Sure you don't want some help cleaning all this shit up?" Though offering to help, her tone is anything but voluntary. It's full of pity, and rightfully so.

"I got it, thanks." I grab a dustpan and broom that Beanie's was nice enough to supply when we got here. The first glitter cannon blew up before its cue and sent a young, motivated manager scurrying out sputtering about clean-up being included in the contract with Brand Hub.

Of course, cleanup is included. So is editing and graphics, securing and keeping the talent happy, and holding them to post dates and hashtag requirements. Thankfully, we've got a small team to help, but a lot of it is executed by yours truly.

I deserve that co-owner carrot.

The owners, the Rushmores, who I've known for years, waddle over in all their post-middle-age, cable-knit glory.

"Thanks for letting us watch the magic happen." Mr. Rushmore is excited, rosy-cheeked with a white beard that shines in the sun. You'd think this video was scheduled to air during a Super Bowl. "Did you get the shot you were hoping for?"

"We did. It's going to be a great campaign." I tick off a list of planned content to calm him. "All your socials are covered with new logos and branding, we've got local micro-influencers posting, and a new mailer circulating your surrounding zip codes for the over-sixty crowd."

"You are such a dear. I'm going to tell your parents that next time I have a call with your mom," Mrs. Rushmore adds. "I'm glad she reminded me this is what you do for a living. All grown up. You always were a responsible girl."

"Hardest working ten-year-old I've ever seen. I still remember you running around your dad's shop with a tag gun, marking all his latest finds. What was your family's store called again?"

"Cotton Candy Carnie, but they sold and retired. They're traveling the world now, sampling Mai Tais across the globe." Dad knew my sister and I weren't passionate about the carnival games business. It's a niche crowd and you really gotta love scrubbing decades of grime from old dunk tanks.

Growing up working in the family business came with some perks. We were the fun family in the neighborhood with all the vintage games at our disposal and a cotton candy machine my dad pulled out every Sunday, but I also worked every Saturday, and often the household chores fell to me. The oldest, next to my baby sister, Frannie, who didn't inherit the workaholic gene quite like I did.

"And so creative. I love the ballerina. Pretty, had a 'tude though, didn't she?" Mrs. Rushmore adds.

I came up with the ballerina angle, something unique to go along with the cozy fall-girl vibe and big pumpkin energy. Gourds I hauled here from a farm off the interstate this morning litter the sidewalk. The glitter cannon was because . . .

Who doesn't love glitter?

"Last month's video really increased foot traffic." Mr. Rushmore pats his wife's hand.

Ah, the one where I recruited a hockey team to drink from Beanie's cups while standing in a row on the ice, no shirts, sticks in hand. The cups were steaming and the men were just as hot. That was a good one.

"You are a talent," Mrs. Rushmore smiles at me. She knows I'm holding out on the hugs but she's going to kill me with kindness anyway.

"Tough cookie, too," Mr. Rushmore chimes in. He can also read my discomfort, I think.

I attempt to school my features into whatever nice girls generally look like, trying to emulate the sugary smile my sister Frannie effortlessly wears, or the approachable likability our best friend Willow has in spades.

"Marketing is a tough job, especially these days, but I like what I do." There, that was believable, and at least half true.

They both nod heartedly. I watched my parents struggle for years to hold their small business together. It's become a passion, and a creative outlet, to help other small companies do the same.

"You certainly are driven, for such a young thing," Mrs. Rushmore appraises me. I like her, and I really want to see them succeed with this coffee shop in their golden years.

"I'll get your socials functioning where they need to be. This video should get a lot of traction. A lot of likes and comments."

"And we want likes and comments, right? That will sell coffee?" Mr. Rushmore asks. He can't wrap his mind around a video on the internet drawing customers.

"You do. It will," I assure them, hoping my mask of black mascara and red lipstick hides my fear.

You've got to have some armor if you want to compete in this business. Because the dinging, buzzing, and constant content pings can be overwhelming. It's not too far from feeling like you're selling your soul when you're schmoozing influencers, posting content to stay relevant, and trying to keep up with every trend. I have to keep my personal socials on point for business, or clients won't believe I can produce the same for them.

I try to keep my guard up, but it always feels personal.

What are you worth in this industry? Is it your hard work, grit, and determination that speak for you? Or the little number at the top of every social account?

Truthfully, I'm jealous of the Rushmores with their wrinkles and their un-fried-by-the-internet brains. How long can I last hustling like this?

"Hang in there, kid," Mr. Rushmore says, thankfully pulling me from my spiral. "You're doing the Lord's work."

He pats me on the back and they both head into their shop

while I pull my phone from my pocket, swiping at some glitter still stuck it my hair. It sticks to my fingertips as I snap a selfie with Beanie's door in the background.

After a quick story post that I hope drives traffic their way, I sweep all the glitter sparkling on the sidewalk and dump it into a metal trashcan on Olvera Street.

My phone buzzes and if it weren't for my paralyzing fear that I'll miss something important from one of my clients, I wouldn't drop everything to pick it up.

It's an email from Allyn.

Cat-

Emergency meeting in my office this afternoon. Let me know when you land.

Don't be nervous, it's just the rest of your life on the line (evil monster emoji).

We've got an offer from Streamflix.

Allyn

My phone buzzes again as I'm reading Allyn's last line. *Streamflix?*

What could a streaming company possibly want from us? We're tiny. There's no way we could handle their PR. Maybe for a small project, but surely they have in-house people for that.

She knows she's messing with me only giving half the information. She enjoys it, and if I didn't respect the hell out of her I'd never allow it.

My phone buzzes a third time, impatient for my attention —always.

When I minimize one screen to open another, I have a blaring red, emergency notice that my delayed flight has been moved *back up.*

I have forty minutes to fight with GPS, drop my rental car, and board my plane.

Two

WINTER

Extra oxygen is pumped into the gym so I can maximize my workout with clean, fresh air. My trainer sent me a new set accompanied by his standard brand of encouragement. He's more of a life coach, foisted upon me in my twenties by my parents to keep me in line. I've kept him around the last ten-plus years because he's damn good at weight training too, an unexpected bonus. When he met me, he didn't even ask about the dark nail polish I wear from time to time on my middle finger, right hand, or how often I use it to flip him off when he's being especially cruel.

My phone buzzes in the pocket of my black mesh shorts and I check it immediately. It's a text from my mother, or rather, her assistant. *Your demands are childish but actionable.*

I pick up a pair of weights and get down to it, watching my form in the mirror, chewing on my mom's cold words, and desperately wanting to spit them out.

Free weights are my favorite form of torture and the routine Stephen sent me is monstrous, the perfect pain to focus on. The simplicity combined with the agony of never-ending repetition feels like a damn good metaphor for my life. Smile for the camera, smile at the banquet, smile for crown and country—and never show how much it hurts.

The endorphin release along with my love of my hometown of Skagen with all its culture and beauty, is what's kept me going since I was a kid. If my arms are strong enough to endure, if I can bench my weight and deadlift the equivalent of a horse, then I can survive anything.

Even another photo op with my fame-hungry family, or worse, their newest requirement of me: reality show heartthrob for the American juggernaut, Streamflix.

My pulse quickens just thinking about it, so I up my speed with the reps, relishing the sweat and mental clarity it brings.

God only knows who approached them with the idea in the first place. The only reason I'm entertaining it is because I love my people and supposedly they want to see more of me. My memories of my country are the only roots I've got, and everyone involved is convinced this will make the Danes happy. I've been told my lack of a love life is *depressing for the country.*

My middle finger twitches. Though my parents aren't here yet to witness it, I flip off the mirror while still curling a dumbbell for good measure. Why is it that I must find a wife so publicly? Why can't I win the Danes over in my own time, in my own way? Why does everything have to be pre-plotted and fake right down to the holiday photo we'll be snapping today for press?

If my life wasn't good, truly, and royally fucked up before, it is now.

"Excuse me Winter, you have a guest. Mr. Green is parking up top now." Annie's firm voice interrupts the surround sound I've got blasting admittedly emo music.

After lowering the volume, I press a button and speak through a monitor. "Send him down." Then add, "Thanks, Annie. Has Lola had her lunch?"

My girl barks in the background and Annie shushes her. "Yes, grilled salmon, carrots, brown rice."

Sweat rolls down my spine. "You're one of a kind. We'd never make it without you."

There's no answer, and before I know it, there's a knock at the gym door. "You're also faster than you look," I say when I open it to find Annie, five foot four, in an apron embroidered with Christmas holly, covered in flour and grimacing. How she made it from the kitchen all the way down here, I don't want to know. It probably involves help from the elves and goblins she's told me stories about since I was a kid.

"That dog eats better than I do," she says.

"Is this about me not showing at dinner last night?"

Annie set the table with tapered candles and formal settings with all the cutlery for the photo shoot today, and she wanted to take it for a spin last night. She loves fancy things and anything to do with Christmas. Now that the holidays are upon us, she's already added fresh greenery with fat black bows around Vikingstrong, she's baking, and she's ordered more decorations than I know what to do with from late-night TV.

Half the time I'm snoring in a chair next to her.

She sniffs. "You're not looking forward to the photo, I know, so I'm making Friekadeller tonight."

The mention of classic Danish meatballs makes my stomach rumble. "I promise I'll be there. And not because it's my favorite. I am sorry I didn't come down last night, I . . ." I let my words drift for a moment. "What they're asking of me, this ridiculous, very public, and very American dating show . . ."

She nods. "You'll do fine, if you choose to. It would be good for you to find someone. And don't work yourself too hard." She nods toward all the machines behind me.

"I won't."

"And don't forget to wash up."

"I won't," I say, already losing my patience.

"And don't forget—"

"Annie," I groan, letting my head fall back. "I'm starting to feel as if I'm back in Skagen with a butler and security breathing down my neck."

"Psh. You complain too much, and if you got serious about looking for someone else to eat your dinners with, you could be whining at her instead of me." My housekeeper is more of a mother than the woman who birthed me ever was and she's not afraid to put me in my place. She's after me to find a wife for completely different reasons than my self-serving parents.

"I want you to be cared for, and not just by me," she says, an argument I've heard many times over a cup of Earl Grey.

I prop my hands on my hips and stare down at her. "And you think I'll find the right woman on an American TV show? Galivanting about, throwing sweet nothings around like a deranged love-puppet?"

Eyeing my nail polish she says, "Stranger things have happened. And call your cousin, Elias has resorted to emailing me to get to you."

Annie never gives into my pity parties and I scowl. She might be right. But my entire childhood was wear this, say that, be here by this time and don't forget to's. I'm not looking for anyone or anything to answer to.

Moments later, Logan Green's smirk reflects in the mirrors as he enters, and I slowly finish hammer curling. "Just in time. Spot me?" I nod toward a bench press in the middle of the room.

He grunts as I drop onto the padded seat. "Nice to see you, too, buddy. Did you stock your bar? I saw a keg of Guinness on my way in that was never there before."

Settled with my back on the bench, hands braced on the bar, I wince as I test the weight I've upped to today. "I know it's your favorite, and after the last party I threw I'd rather install another draft pull than watch your ass sip water all night."

"Makes sense. Your lower level functions like a nightclub."

My dungeon parties are epic, but Logan is the most stubborn man I've ever met. And every time it's, *I'll have a Guinness or nothing*. "What's got you crawling out of your log cabin before noon today?"

"You know why I'm here. Boggs is out of town with Frannie, Holiday had to open the bait shop, Wagner and Jack are moving new furniture into Revival, and that leaves little 'ol me."

John Boggs, Ben Holiday, Jack, and Wagner make up our men's group in our small lake town. It's complete with a lake committee that reports Spirit Lake news like a knitting circle, busy-body shopkeepers on Main Street, and gossip-hungry school moms who constantly jog Stateline just waiting to fuel town rivalries between Clover, California, and Novel, Nevada.

"Spot me?" I ask again, knowing I've only got to wear him down.

He leans over my weight bench and smirks. "I don't train for free." Damn grumpy smirker. "And I gotta remind you, working out is not therapy."

"Chatting over a beer after is?" I ask.

He ignores me. "John's worried about you."

"John's head over ass in love and shopping for antiques right now. He's got better things to worry about. I need you. Other than Stephan, who's on holiday, you're the best in the business."

Stephan would quit if he heard me tell the truth: Logan is the best physical fitness guru in the state, probably the country, but he refuses to lean into marketing and social media to exploit it, which I admire. He's got a degree in sports medicine, psychology, and something in bio-science I can never name.

"You think I came over here to train your spoiled ass?" he asks, but places his hands on the bar and helps me start my reps anyway.

"I know why you're here," I say, grunting as I lower the weight and then push it back up.

Why did I up my weight again?

"You ready for today? You're seeing your parents, right? The lake committee is going to have a fit, they always do when the royals are in town."

Oh yeah, that's why.

"I made my choice. Between leaving everything I love here to live in a royal cage now, or buying myself some time and playing their game, I chose time. I need more time to figure things out."

Logan continues to spot me. "You sure? That's an awfully big ask on their part."

"Hell, it's the ask of a lifetime. I thought they were kidding for weeks. It wasn't until they started forwarding contracts for me to review that I realized they're serious."

I dig deep and push for the last rep, my chest and arms screaming, but that's what I wanted. The bar clangs back in place and I sit up, reaching for a chilled towel infused with lavender that Annie keeps ready for me.

"Have you officially agreed?"

I wipe my face and inhale the calming lavender. "Nothing's signed yet, but they'll be here in about thirty minutes to snap a photo for the annual card. 'Merry Christmas and Happy New Year from Vikingstrong.' What a crock," I spit.

When we sold the land to the state of California generations ago, we should have thrown in this old castle instead of donating the first floor as a museum. But it has been my refuge, and for that, I'm grateful. "They're expecting an answer. But—"

"But—"

"I have a request, and they've been made aware. So really, the ball's in their court. They deliver and I'm on board."

"Are you trying to draw this out like a Disney villain? What's the request? What could make you agree to a reality show?" Logan follows me out of the gym and down a wide hall leading to a steam shower and sauna that are calling my name. Too bad there's not time to soak in the hot tub today. "This is everything you hate: the spotlight, the fame. Isn't that why you left Denmark?" he calls from the hall as I jump in the shower.

By the time I'm washed and dressed in a t-shirt and a pullover that is not going to impress my parents, Logan has heard my plan. The part where I agreed to hear them out if they adhered to my demands. Today, I find out if Anker, the Crown's PR, is going to relinquish control.

"Your mind is a scary place, but I'm not following the devious plot I know you're hatching." We both stomp up the stairs to the main floor of the house which is commonly referred to as a castle, but is really more rustic chalet. My bare feet smack against the smooth wood treads, his steel-toed boots the size of compact cars following close behind. "What's in it for you? Dumb it down."

Logan is not dumb. He's quite astute, he just doesn't like people to know. "I'm asking them to put their muscle where their mouth is—no," I snap my fingers. "It's money. Put their money where their mouth is, right? Or is it put your money where your muscles are?" I flex for show.

He ignores my obsession with American slang and gives me a look that says, *am I supposed to be following all of this?*

I roll my eyes dramatically and lead him through the main kitchen, with high hundred-year-old beams and soapstone countertops, into the dining room. This past summer, our best friend fell for a woman with a sister. A sister in PR. A sister who used my name to pull off a harebrained stunt at a charity baseball game. This is payback.

"I have them looking into Cat Bloomfield. Fran's sister, Cat."

"Now, why would you do that?"

Light catches on a silver spoon on the dining table covered in berry red linens with china settings passed down from my ancestors.

I can still see her, speaking into the ears of the representatives at the charity pitch baseball game last summer. She was so charming, so beautiful, so engaging. They nodded eagerly, she laughed and laughed. Before I could wonder what the beguiling woman was doing to enchant them, her ass was being escorted onto the field. Her friend was with her, and now I know of course, they were stalling the game on purpose. And wouldn't you know, she used my name to get that job done. Told them she worked for me and I'd cleared her making a special announcement on my behalf.

Her dark hair was shiny in the sun that day, but I saw her for exactly what she was, nothing but another climber, a snake like Anker. Using me to pave her way.

"She's a self-absorbed, fame-seeking weasel who used *my name*, and told them she was *my assistant*, to get on the field for Boggs' game. Well, it's time to pay the piper."

"You actually used that one right," he laughs.

"Good to know."

Logan wanders the smallish room that doesn't quite accommodate his stature. You'd think an old Danish castle nestled in the forest of California over a hundred years ago, built to be a respite for the royal family, would be stuffy and cold, but this place was built to be cozy and welcoming.

"You need to let that shit go, man," he says calmly. "That game was a whirlwind. We were all there, we knew you were donating to the Children's Hospital when they double-checked the pronunciation of your name for the announcement."

Annie comes bustling in with boxes full of Patty's Pastries, the best you can get on Main Street. "What's all this?" I ask.

"Your parents' *people* requested that *your people*, me, provide props for the photo to make it appear as if you're enjoying breakfast," she responds, on task and giving me no attention. "But they're not getting my snegl. That dough takes hours to rise."

"Edible props?" Logan asks, rubbing his stomach like he's ready to eat everything in sight.

Annie's known him, all the guys, for years and she can't say no to any of us. "Oh go ahead, but keep the plates clean and pretty for the photo. You need a napkin? You use your shirt." She gestures to his hunter-green t-shirt and he shrugs in easy agreement.

At least I've got these two as a buffer today between me and the people I should love most in the world but sadly, I fear them as if I were still a little boy in Denmark. Annie pats my arm, staying quiet and continuing to bustle around the room.

The warmth of her reassuring hand stays with me as I barrel on about how much I hate Cat Bloomfield. "She lied about working for me to get on the field, to advance her own image and open doors, and I loathe people who use, who take, who think they're entitled to step on whomever to get to the top."

"And you feel she stepped on you?" It's at least something to think about other than my parents, and I can't help myself, the woman is still under my skin.

"Didn't she? You were there. She used my name. She had no right."

"But it didn't really hurt you. What's the big deal?" He pulls on his suspenders, a habbit of his, and holds my stare.

"What's the big deal?" I yell about two octaves higher than my natural tone. All those childhood memories of being pushed and prodded by dignitaries who wanted a photo of me to get them in the papers or an invitation to a party come flooding back with full force.

Never again.

He holds up his hands while holding his ground. "Listen, I'm always gonna shoot you straight."

"You think I'm overreacting?" I complain, fully expecting him to say no and explain himself.

"I do."

I clutch my heart, half serious, half deflecting with humor. "I can't believe you'd say that to me."

"Winter, man, come on—"

I push my hands through my hair, combing it away from my

face so I can think clearly. "No, she made a deal with the devil and now she's going to see exactly what that entails."

"It's that serious to you? You're going full on 'deal with the devil'?"

"Abso-fucking-lutely." He's trying to talk sense, be reasonable. I get that. I really do. Still, I'm not the grumpy, gentle giant with a heart made of sage and kumbayas like he is.

I'm royally pissed at Cat Bloomfield. At everyone in my life who's taken advantage of me, and today she's at the top of that list.

The front door bell rings out with a loud gong fitting for a home built for royalty. It only pisses me off more. But while my anger builds, something else inside pulls at my gut, making me feel almost sick to my stomach.

There was a time when I was small and weak, a time when I still lived in Denmark that I'll never shake, when I let my family use me. As the only heir to the Danish throne, everyone used me, and not just for the benefit of the country I love. It was all for themselves, all political, all greed and entitlement. I was never a son to them, I was a thing. A jewel in the crown. But I'm glad for it. Because that memory only serves to keep me from slipping.

My parents enter the room. Queen Mary and King Frederik. I often call him Freddy and he hates it.

Annie welcomes them, offers tea, and when they decline a steady stream of people, including Anker, follow through the door all speaking in hushed voices about imagery, light, and placement for the royal Christmas card that will come out looking like they have for the past twenty-plus years.

"Is that what you've chosen to wear?" my mom asks, stoic and calm, her hair in a twist. "Anker, is this going to work?"

He smiles from across the table, a fig leaf in his hand that Annie had already placed painfully precisely. "We can make it work."

"Perhaps I need a personal assistant to dress me," I suggest, laying the groundwork.

"Did you read over the Streamflix contract?" my father demands, taking a seat at the head of the table. Both my parents are wearing their usual combination of black, navy, and tweed.

No time for pleasantries, per usual.

"A little. Did Anker receive my request?" I will not work with this man, I won't even speak to him. He's somehow convinced my parents that this is a good idea, how, we'll never know. But I'll not let him near me again.

"Your communication was forwarded appropriately," Anker responds from the end of the table.

My father blusters, "Your demands are outside anything the Crown has allowed. We have Anker to manage the brand, and we've let you play small-town-boy long enough. It's time for you to get on board with what you owe this family."

I lower my voice and level with my dad. "I will not work with Anker. He has no place in my private business. I made you an offer. If it's so important for me to participate in this ridiculous publicity stunt that tells me two things: The Crown is in much more trouble as a brand than I thought, and Anker has sold you a load of horseshit. If he's in, I'm out."

My father considers me for a long moment, seeming to weigh the truth of my words as we ignore the continuous flash of the camera. Finally, he nods and turns back to the photographer, fake smile plastered on his face once more. "We read your request, and spoke to the agency ourselves. They'll agree to your terms," he relents.

I can't quite believe it worked.

"Anker, is this Streamflix deal really so important?" my mom asks.

"Yes." Dad answers for him. "If that's what it takes to get him to settle down." He eyes me directly as he continues, "Allyn something or other, and her protégé Catherine Bloomfield will be in the meeting with Streamflix tomorrow."

"Anker?" my mother demands again.

"This show will reinvigorate the romance of the Crown," Anker replies smoothly. "It will boost our people's morale and lighten the somewhat dark image of the prince."

The dark image of the prince.

What they mean is, the image of a kid who was never naturally equipped to deal with the world of the Crown. A kid who never got the hang of giving speeches and shaking hands. A kid who just wanted life to be quiet.

The man who never once showed me kindness as a child turns his beady eyes on me and nods in agreement. "Backing out of the deal now would be bad form. No telling how Streamflix would handle it. Could be very bad press for the Crown. My original reasoning for the show holds true, however without my guidance during filming, there's no telling what we'll get out of him." He's sold them a bill of goods, so much so that he can't back out now even if I've out-maneuvered him from the deal himself.

"Frederik?" my mother asks. "Perhaps we can give him more time?"

"The meeting is tomorrow. I'll expect everyone in attendance. Anker, you're dismissed from the project."

A saccharine smile arcs across my face, and the camera flashes again.

Three

CAT

The halls of Brand Hub are tight, full of labyrinth-style twists and turns in a nondescript strip mall in San Francisco. Professional content creation and branding is not as glamorous as the internet would have you believe. A few co-workers nod their hellos. None of them look up from their phones, mind you, but they do nod.

I pop my head in Allyn's assistant's office. "She ready for me?"

"There you are!" she says as if I've been taking a nap under my desk.

Sloan knows good and well I've been traveling all day, also not glamorous, but she makes it sound like I've been chugging lattes over sushi trays while having a mani-pedi.

"How are the Rushmores' socials tracking?" I ask.

"Good. You did a nice job with them. Over budget, which I'm assuming—"

"I'll figure it out."

"You've got to stop doing that. Allyn doesn't like it," she sing-songs, holding her natural inclination to follow rules over me.

"Which is why she needs me to come on board as the *nice* owner. I want that pro-bono arm of the company up and running by the end of the year."

"Who would have thought you'd be the nice one?"

"Hey!" But, true.

She nods to the right and motions for me to continue down the hall to the last office—Allyn's. "She's ready for you."

"Thanks."

I lug my shiny black suitcase down the hall behind me, dreaming of the moment this day is finally over and I can go home to unpack and decompress. The thin wood door echoes as I knock while examining a stain in the ceiling that I've always thought looked like a banana.

"I'm back," I say, pushing through and dumping my suitcase into a corner. I plop in a chair across from her desk. "Miss me? I know I'm over on the Rushmores' budget but—"

She waves a hand. "Fine, fine. We need to talk."

Oh no. Not good. While Allyn is my boss, I also consider her a friend. But she's got her business hat on right now, nary a girl-friend in sight. Whatever she has to say, it's serious.

"The Streamflix deal is demanding, urgent, and going to take some serious dedication to pull off."

Sitting tall, I wait for more as she eyes me head to toe. Always plotting, this one. Finally, I break. "Thanks for the cryptic email, by the way."

"You're welcome. This deal hit my desk days ago, and I'm afraid you may not like the fine print. But I'm prepared to sweeten the pot."

"How sweet we talking?"

"I'm ready to make you a partner."

I hold in a gasp and keep a straight face. "Sounds like there's a big, fat 'but' coming. What does Streamflix want? What's the project? Who's the client?"

She opens her laptop and begins pecking at the keys, squinting slightly at her screen. "It's confidential. There will be NDAs to sign. I need a PA on site for two months."

I scoff. "I haven't PA'd since college. Get someone else."

"They want you."

"Can't," I cross one leg over the other and settle in for a debate, "that's over Christmas. I'm going to visit my sister."

"Even with partnership on the table?" She glances up. "Cat, keep an open mind," she says, holding a hand up to stop me before I can barrel on about how I'll be tied to my phone and will work through the holiday anyway. At least I can do it while opening presents with Frannie.

"My client list is full, Allyn. Ask someone else." Then I add, "But still give me the partnership, because you know I'm ready."

She nods, not enjoying the fact I'm sparring with her, but she's the one who taught me how to stay strong and know your worth in business. "They requested you. By name. It's primarily to PA, though you'll be asked to manage him in general for the duration of the Streamflix contract. He's refused to work with anyone on their team—or on his own."

"Who is this demanding, entitled little man?" I cross my arms. "And who would ask for me by name?"

"NDA," she repeats. "I'm working the kinks out now. Say yes."

I pull a cold bottle of water from a fridge next to her desk and take a deep pull, wiping my mouth with the back of my hand. "You're seriously not going to tell me? That high-brow, huh?"

I am intrigued.

While I'd rather have a shot of caffeine, the water brings me back to life. I needed the water. *I've got to remember to drink more water.*

"The highest. And a boon for the agency. A jewel, actually."

She leans in over her desk, and I mirror her. We're eye to eye, hers twinkle, mine narrow. "It would change *everything*, Cat."

"That's good to hear, because I want everything. Co-owner, and the pro-bono budget I've been asking for."

"Nothing would make me happier." She stacks some papers on her desk, refusing to give me any positive reinforcement for basically accepting an offer to take ten steps backward in my career and work as a grunt over the holidays.

"I didn't think you'd cave that easily." I think quickly, adding to my deal if I'm going to give up Christmas with Frannie. "I want a raise and a company car, too."

"Done. Are you ready to leave your friends, your family? Not only for this client, but in general? I don't have to tell you, Cat. It can be a lonely life, working for yourself. I don't regret it, but you've seen the way I live."

"Impeccably, minus these shitty offices."

"We'll upgrade the offices together. Something bougie in the Bay. If we secure this client, everything will change."

"If?" It sounded like a done deal in her email.

"There's still a meeting with Streamflix, where you'll both have to agree to the somewhat creative aspects of the project."

Her twisting of words doesn't scare me, if that's what she's trying to do.

"Fine." We both knew I'd say yes. My work life balance has always skewed heavily to favor work. "Tell me where and when."

I'm already pulling my luggage to the door. One thing about Allyn: she keeps her meetings tight and I can sense my dismissal.

"I'll send them our official acceptance and email you details when I'm allowed to share. Sloan will send you a travel itinerary this evening. This whole situation is moving fast."

"When we're co-owners, we'll both be privy to deals like this. You'll always keep our line of communication open, right? No secrets." I do not like being left in the dark.

"Cat, I don't plan to work forever. I will hand you the keys to castle." She's got a real funny smirk on her face as if she's just told a joke, but I'm not privy to the punchline. "Patience, grasshopper. For now, go home. Shower. Prepare."

Now I have to figure out how to tell Frannie and Willow I won't be with either of them for Christmas. Who knows where I'll be? Streamflix could be shooting in any number of locations, from Dubai to the Dakotas.

I accept a high five from Sloan on my way out and tell myself to breathe through the exhaustion I don't have time for. There will be surprises to come over the next twenty-four hours as the details of my new job come through. There'll be hard days, and a demanding client from what little I've heard, but there will also be excitement, creativity, and growth.

This is the job.

A little pink dollhouse in the heart of the marina district sits pretty on a sherbet-dotted row-house street.

My car drops me unceremoniously at the curb, and I lug my bags down the sidewalk. I've lived here for years with my two best friends, one being my sister, but she's moved to a small lake town with an annoyingly perfect-for-her-man. We'd decided to celebrate Christmas on Spirit Lake, a place we visited multiple times as kids, after she talked up pastries on Main Street, and comfy blankets, and lounging in Adirondack chairs with mugs full of spiked cider.

So much for that little fantasy.

Trudging up the stairs with layers of airplane ick on me, I'm looking forward to throwing the door open and seeing the smiling face of my last roommate standing. Though, I don't know how I'm going to tell her she's on her own for Christmas.

Inside our cozy apartment, I expect Willow to be curled up in her spot on the end of our lumpy couch near her beloved bookshelf.

But the place is silent. Willow is nowhere to be seen.

I drop my keys in a heart-shaped dish on the entry table. Frannie found the rickety thing a few years ago on the side of the road, hammered in a few extra nails, and spray-painted it a fresh white. My sister has a real eye for turning trash into treasure. I kinda like to think I do the same, only with entrepreneurs and their unfortunate choice in brand colors.

Huffing, I leave my things by the door and proceed to peel my clothes from my body. At least when I'm home alone, I can live like a thirty-year-old single woman and walk around naked in my own house. A glimpse in a mirror over our fireplace reveals truly puffy-from-exhaustion eyes, my blunt below the chin bob hanging limp. However, the black lace set of French lingerie lends a glimmer of hope.

I'd still give me a go despite a love life being the last thing on my mind.

A shower and a vigorously applied lavender sugar scrub have me feeling much better, and I decide to have tea and frozen pizza for dinner. Not a combo I'm proud of, but it's kinda been a shit day. I'm exhausted, and that deserves a shit dinner.

Willow pops through the door just as I'm getting worried.

"Hey, where have you been?" I ask, muting the bad reality dating show I was watching and turning to greet her over the back of the couch. "I made crappy pizza, help yourself."

"Thanks," she says, a non-gooey, fake cheese slice with cardboard pepperoni already in her hand. "Long day. Also, I quit my job."

"You quit?" I sit up straighter in a blood-red sweat set so dark it may as well be black. This is me branching out.

"Yup. The sub I had last week when I was out for surgery was looking for full-time, and we've only been back to school for a month. So, I went in to chat with administration and ran the idea by them. They were sad to see me go, but happy to offer the spot to Mrs. Sanderson. And now I'm a professional spinster."

"Don't start—"

"Past my prime," she laments like an overacting daytime TV star, "tea and cardboard for dinner, living with my best friend who's as dateless as I am. Total spinster material."

"You're not a spinster!"

"Because that would make *you* a spinster." She grins, kicking off a pair of wedges she borrowed from me and never gave back.

I don't mind being the butt of her humor and winding her up if it makes her smile—but this I can't stand for. "We're not spinsters. Spinsters don't exist. The patriarchy invented them to make confident single women feel less than. I think even your hero, Austen, would agree with that."

She hammers me with bright blue eyes which, when paired with her strawberry hair, is truly commanding when she wants it to be. "So why ya watching *One Night Stand Wedding* again?"

I punch the power button on the remote and the TV goes dark. "It was background noise, I'm working." I wiggle my phone at her as proof.

"You love that show, admit it. Singles thrusting themselves at other singles, hoping to couple up—*the romance*." Now, she's poking her fingers in those pretty eyes, removing contacts at the kitchen counter which is a bad habit after a long day.

Two contacts drop into a water glass and I make a mental note not to dump it in the dishwasher later. The girl is going to get an infection one of these days.

"Fine, I'll admit it, but only because you have a wall of the same thing in book form." I point to the shelves of novels to her right. You'd think they'd be tattered and torn with how many times I've witnessed her reading them, but no, they're pristine. Virginal and untouched to the untrained eye because she never, ever cracks a spine.

"Those are different, as I've explained to you many times in detail." She plops into her spot on the couch, folding her petite, curvy frame up like a pretzel in a baggy shirtdress and cardigan.

"Your romance novels are the same unhinged, flirty ridiculousness I watch."

She rummages around in a side table and produces one of her many pairs of thick glasses and the book she's currently reading. These are tortoise and my personal favorite. "Those books," here she goes, pointing to her trophy wall. "Those books are filled with trials, tribulations, expectations, wounded souls, healing, and the list goes on! Reality dating shows are quick and dirty. I'm not saying that's a bad thing, to each his own, but there's nothing solid or grown-up or evolved in anything on that show. It's lust on top of exhibition in very questionable jacuzzi water."

I chew on my bottom lip. Even though I don't read the kind of books she does, I do love a 90s romcom, and the junk on TV cannot compare. "I hate it when you're right. You should have been a lawyer."

"I should have been a great many things, Mr. Mayer."

"A quote?" Despite my lack of interest in anything remotely literary, I'm always intrigued when Willow talks bookish to me.

"Little Women." A small smile crosses her face. I should have known. She's made us watch every version of film adaptation since we were kids at Christmas, and I don't hate it.

"So, what's your plan for the rest of your life?" I kick my feet up and try not to look at my phone screen.

"Geez, Bloomfield, *my life*?"

My phone buzzes, and I give in, discreetly checking it. It's from Allyn, but I drag my eyes back to Willow. "Okay, not your life, but your future?"

Willow's been hinting at quitting teaching for a while, so I'm not totally surprised, but I don't think she's got much of a plan either. Out of the three of us, she's been the most uncertain about what she wants to do with her future.

She toys with a bookmark in the novel in her lap. "You are a dog with a bone."

"Translation: best friend who cares," I laugh at my quirky little friend. "Well?" I prompt her. I hate that I'm so attached to my phone, but I have to read the email from Allyn. I open it discreetly, planning to skim while focusing on my conversation with Willow.

Cat,

Your new client is high-profile and European. You'll have to sign an NDA before I can share more. This project is an extended on-site position on a new reality show. Pack for two months and travel details will hit your inbox this evening.

Your experience over the past five years has teed you up to execute this client's expectations and needs, all while keeping directors and producers happy.

Along with the NDA, there will be papers for you to sign to become a partner in Brand Hub. Merry Christmas, early.

Allyn

I'm an owner!

Wait, I'm working on a reality show?

I glance at Willow and my head swims thinking of B-list celebrity men I might be chained to for the next three months. It's a sacrifice for sure, but I've already agreed to the meeting and I'm finally getting papers to sign for Brand Hub. And a raise. And a car. Allyn and I will officially be partners.

Brand Hub will be my life. As if it wasn't already.

"Hey, you asked me a question and now you're reading your phone," Willow says. She huffs and opens her book.

"I'm sorry, I am listening. It's work."

"It's always work. Okay, so I was thinking . . ." Her voice fades out as my mind spins, though I am still listening. I've spent years training my brain to split into two and multi-task.

First, Frannie left for what she promised was a summer sabbatical which turned into a whirlwind relocation, and now

I'm leaving, too? Leaving Willow alone for the holidays is especially gut-wrenching. Not to mention, if this client is as demanding as Allyn has alluded, I might not even get a Christmas. I'll be stuck spending my favorite time of the year on a beach with a bunch of production people in God-knows-where-ville.

"Dog grooming."

I blink at her, no idea how to respond. Surely, I didn't hear her right. "Wait, what?" I ask, trying to process Allyn's written words and what Willow is saying to me.

She can tell my attention is elsewhere and grimaces. "Washing, brushing—cuddling I'm sure is part of it— dogs. For a living."

A few times a year, the girls usually have a sit down with me about my phone addiction, which is really corporate co-dependence. At least I'm aware. "But you've never owned a dog." I'm trying to be supportive, but since when has Willow wanted to be a dog groomer?

"Yeah, but working with animals and not working with people sounds great. I'm maxed out on kiddos and adults are just as scary," she laughs. "I can wear headphones while I do it, I bet. Think of all the audiobooks I could get through."

"You've never once mentioned wanting to be a dog groomer," I say, trying to keep my tone even. I press the pad of my thumb into pizza crumbs on my plate while trying to come up with a way to tell her I'm leaving tomorrow without breaking her heart. "Skate in the Ice Capades, yes. Own your own bookstore, obviously. But dogs? Wills, are you okay?"

If she's not, I can stay. If this is some sort of crisis, I can turn the job down. Allyn will understand, and if she doesn't . . .

Maybe this is your chance to get out of the rat race? I mentally shush my subconscious. I love the rat race, I do.

Physically, I wedge my phone under my thigh, almost sitting on it, so I don't break focus on the friend in front of me.

"I'm fine. Time to put the boatload of money my parents gave me to good use and figure out what I really want to do in life. Unfortunately, teaching fourth grade is not it. I need some quiet."

"Believe me, I understand that. Work is very loud right now."

"So, you get it. And because I can, I'm going to give myself a minute to figure it out."

"While grooming dogs? Shaving butts?" My phone buzzes beneath me and I jump.

"Stop," she laughs. At least I did that, made her laugh.

Time to break the news.

"Okay, I like this for you. And maybe you can come visit me over the holiday." I hold my breath and wait for her answer, hoping wherever I end up, it at least has a beach bar with unlimited margaritas.

"Where are you going?" She puts her book down in earnest and eyes me over the top of her glasses. "To see Frannie? A cozy lakeside Christmas? This is perfect, I'd love—"

"No, not to see Frannie." My face falls. "I don't know yet, but I got assigned a new client and I'm leaving tomorrow-ish. Still waiting on Allyn for the details."

"Oh, that's short notice. You just got back." Willow leans on Frannie and me, she always has, and I hate leaving her. "Need help packing? Want me to do a drugstore run?"

"I'm working on location for two months, Wills."

"Oh." She shifts, pulling at a piece of hair that's fallen over her shoulder. "So you're both missing Christmas here . . ."

"Yeah. It's the worst part of this whole thing, not being with you or Frannie."

"But it's for your job, and it's what you love."

God, she's a good friend. "You're not mad?"

"Of course, I'm not mad, and yes, I'll come visit. I'll help you with whatever I can. Don't forget: when your tripod's broken and you need someone to hold your phone at odd angles for all your experimental content, I'm always your girl."

Something tells me I won't be holding tripods for Streamflix.

"Willow, you are a sweetheart, you know that? You don't need to run errands or help with anything, just hang with me tonight. I'm going to miss you. And Frannie. I can't believe we're not going to be together for Christmas this year."

"The band really did break up, didn't we?" We were all worried when Fran moved out that it was the end of an era, and we all lied to ourselves and pretended it wasn't. She looks around our apartment, most remnants of Frannie already gone.

I nod and hum, feeling somber. For years, the three of us rented this house together and now, who knows if we'll ever even live near each other again. It feels like we're scattering.

"Should we sublet?" I hold her gaze, this is a hard conversation. "You want new roommates?"

"Nah. I'll wait for you to come back."

"Money bags," I scoff, but I'm glad she has options.

My phone buzzes beneath me again and I give in to the obsession to check it, but it's just a news notification.

Do I feel like a one-trick pony, living on the internet, social media post after post to keep up with trends so I can be an asset to my clients? Sure do. But I'm good at my job and that makes up for it. Do I feel like a heel for leaving Willow here alone on Christmas? Also, yes, absolutely I do.

Willow settles in with her book in the crook of her arm and I reheat my tea, then stretch my legs and put my stupid reality show back on while I doom scroll—*for work.*

Another buzz interrupts me as I'm watching a man trying to flirt with three women on the TV with one eye, and a viral video with a new dance on my phone with the other. This time it's another email.

It's from Sloan, the first few details of my travel itinerary coming in as fast as she can book them, I'm sure.

Tomorrow, per her instructions, I'm headed to Little Star Lodge in Garland, California.

Wait . . . Garland rings a bell, I think I almost booked a ski trip there once but then something for work came up. There's always something for work coming up.

I do a search and sure enough, Garland isn't far from here, about a four-hour drive into the mountains. It's a teeny, tiny ski town and Little Star Lodge looks like it's been plucked Mary Poppins-style straight out of a coffee table book on Danish architecture. The town boasts towering trees layered with twinkle lights, and holiday festivals with patrons walking cobblestone streets holding steaming drinks. If I could make a wish, this is where I'd want us all to be for Christmas.

And— *oh my God*— my fingers fly across the screen, in my sister's new backyard.

Four

WINTER

"What's on the itinerary today?" Annie asks.

"You know what," I say around a piece of toast spread frugally with marmalade, exactly the way I like it. Not too sweet.

Various boxes of Christmas decorations are littered around the main kitchen of Vikingstrong. Annie's on a stepladder wearing reindeer antlers, and I'm trying not to hold my breath while gauging our distance.

If she goes down, how quickly can I get to her while navigating the millions of boxes under our feet?

"Remind me?" she teases, verbally poking at me.

"Hmm," I rub my chin and play along. "Not sure I recall the details."

Participating in a reality show is the furthest thing from my idea of fun, but in addition to buying myself some time before dear old Dad puts his foot down and demands I return home, I'm going to give Cat Bloomfield the shock of her life.

When I requested Brand Hub PR be my representation for the show, I never expected them to say yes. It was a farce, a revenge fantasy. I even requested PA services. It never occurred to me my parents would accept my terms, Anker would skulk back to Denmark where he belongs, and I'd be meeting Cat and her boss face to face in mere hours.

Annie loops a garland around her shoulder, teetering on the ladder. "How are we feeling about becoming an American heart-throb—is what I meant to ask."

Ah, hell. Now she's making me nervous.

"I've been in bigger spotlights than this. Talked to Elias last night and he's a fan of the idea. Like you, he thinks it might be good for me. But what does that kid know, right?"

"He's your cousin, only a few years your junior, and second in line for the crown. He might know something about the life you're living."

"You need help with that?" I gesture to her as she stretches for a hook I know is in the rafters somewhere, because I put it there years ago for her garlands, and lights, and bows.

"You still have a choice in the matter, and no, I don't need help, thank you very much. I've been decking these halls since you were gangly and running around here like a lake rat with your pack of hooligan friends."

"We were a bunch of hooligans weren't we?"

"Of the best sort."

"But you're wrong about my having a choice," I toss back.

"Oh, you have a choice here. You chose to make this about that girl, Fran's sister. You could walk away, my dear."

"From the crown?" I ask, knowing this is what she means but wondering why it feels more like she's telling me to walk away from Cat. But I have nothing to do with Cat, nothing to walk away from. And after I make her job a nightmare until she either quits or I fire her, we'll be nothing to each other again.

We're nothing to each other now.

Except enemies.

I could walk away from the crown, abdication is a thing, but then what would I be? All grown up. A guy in a big house. My identity is tied up in Denmark even though I want nothing to do with my family.

Instead I say, "What about the people? They deserve a leader. And after Dad's reign, I'd truly like to turn things around in parliament. Give a different view and guidance, still strong, but a different brand of strength than they've had these past few decades with him."

"You owe them nothing, that's all I'm saying."

"But how can you say that? You love our little fishing village in Skagen, Marselisborg Palace with your favorite gardens in the spring, the cups of tea and the fairytales, it's who we are."

"Oh dear." Her eyes turn misty, and she gently lays a shiny blue ornament back in a box.

"What?" I look at her, perplexed. "Do you need more lights?"

She's wrapped them around the garlands swathed through the house; why I thought the kitchen would be spared is beyond me.

I guess I'm not as excited for the season this year because I know it's not going to be filled with reading by the fire, mugs of hot tea, Annie and I chatting on walks around the lake, or riding horses in still mornings across fresh snow.

"No, dear, I don't need more lights, but I do miss home."

"Will you stop with the *dears*, Annie?" My voice cracks, the pressure getting to me and constricting my throat. I'm at a loss here. I want it all and none of it at the same time. I want my crown and my people to be happy and prosperous. I just wish that had nothing to do with me leading a country. With photo ops, sound bites, and press tours. I'm not cutout for it. Never was. "I'm sorry," I add. Even though my words had zero bite to them, they were still out of line. She's trying to help.

She steps off the ladder and comes to stand beside me, her hair so platinum it's nearly white and in the same cheery bob she's styled since I was crawling across hand-knotted royal carpets back in Denmark. "I'm on your side. I only want you to be happy."

"I'm happy." We both know it's a bald-faced lie. I pull it off most of the time with the guys, but Annie sees right through me.

"You could be." She gives my back a few supportive pats, not overly affectionate, but there nonetheless. "Cup of tea?" And there it is. The real way a Scandinavian woman, or at least this one, shows love, with something warm in the belly.

"I'd love some. Thanks."

My arms are still sore from my workout the next day as I grasp the reins, taking Daylight up to a trot by squeezing my thighs and pushing my heels into her sides. She knows what I want, and I post in the sleek English saddle while we take in the winding mountain road.

This time of year, when things are a little more quiet and calm, is my favorite.

"Hey there Mr. Troutwine," I yell across a dirt path riddled with orange and red leaves, some with hot pink centers.

Fall swept through the lake towns of Clover and Novel like a hungry teen at a Thanksgiving table. For years, the guys and I crashed Thanksgiving at Ben Holiday's house, the only buddy with a big family who cooked, and believe me, I've seen teen boys inhale turkey. Mrs. Holiday's stuffing is pure American goodness and my stomach rumbles thinking about it. I'm looking forward to sitting at that table in a few weeks, hopefully without a camera crew in tow.

The skiers who know about our cozy lake towns with the

mountain only minutes away flock here every holiday season, especially for Christmas. In the distance, they're already cutting down the tops of snowcapped mountains which are sure to see fresh powder soon instead of the manmade snow the Lodge makes for pre-season. The lifts from Little Star Lodge will be packed with down coats, ski bunnies, and shredding boarders soon.

Mr. Troutwine tips his beanie, "Winter. What brings *you* to Garland?" The mayor of Clover grouches.

"Just a ride up to the lodge, you know my heart is still in Clover." Eh, I'll win him over sooner or later. He isn't a huge Larsen fan—something about the Danes and our cozy hygge culture puts him off, though how anyone can hate what it stands for bewilders me.

Still, it makes me itch when people don't like me.

Up at the lodge, I dismount and tie Daylight's reins to a post they keep for mountain riders and waltz through the automatic doors, careful to kick the mud off my riding boots because manners count. I saunter up to the desk and ring a little brass bell.

"Winter, you're here!" Darcy, longtime manager of Little Star Lodge, greets me cheerily.

Leaning easily against the counter and watching her fiddle with desk accessories, I say, "Lead me to the slaughter."

"Shoot. Your mom and dad aren't that bad."

Aren't that bad? *Mom and Dad?*

I push my hair back from my face, making sure it's smooth after the ride, and level with her. "Hate to tell you this, but they're only nice to you because you always hold the good room for them when they're in town."

Brutal but true. But Darcy doesn't buy it, she's one of those optimists I keep hearing about, people who obsessively see the cup half-full. I don't trust them.

"Follow me, they're in The Elk Room with production. I can't believe they're filming a Christmas-themed dating show at the lodge."

Time to play the game, I put on my poker face, of which I have many. This one says, *I've changed my ways and I'm here to make all your Prince Charming dreams come true, dear family.*

The door swings wide and I'm introduced to a bunch of suits in a room. My father stands, grasps my hand and pats my shoulder, turning for Anker to snap a photo then scurry out of the room.

"Freddy, I thought we had a deal?" I glare.

He waves me off with a grimace. "He's getting on a plane now —had to have something for when this hits the media."

My mom appears at my side and grasps my elbow. "The country needs to see this as much as they need to see you acting like an adult and finding a wife to settle down with."

"Will that make you happy, Mom?" I ask through my smile, still glad-handing my dad while he keeps his grip firm. Streamflix reps watch out of the corner of their eyes.

She startles. "Yes, it will make me immensely happy to see my only son settled in life."

"You've bought yourself some time," my father grates, "In exchange for returning with a wife."

"Which equals stability in your mind."

"It's a step in the right direction. Maybe some real responsibility will force you to find some pride and do your duty. Be a man, Winter. Stop acting like a sniveling child."

I stand tall, push my shoulders back, and pretend his words mean nothing.

Five

CAT

My head is a little spiny from being on multiple planes in as many days. Brand Hub flew me out here despite the fact I could have made the drive in pretty good time. Allyn wanted me to arrive fresh and ready for anything.

Apparently, this *big fish* has made even her nervous.

The doors to Little Star Lodge slide open automatically. The place is nice, like nicer than nice, made of stacked wood logs that go a few stories high and nestle into the trees and the mountains behind. Inside, it's rustic but soft and understated, pine scented candles permeating the air.

The warmth of the place is almost palpable.

I march straight up to a polished mahogany desk with my carry-on dragging behind me, and ring a quaint brass bell with an intentionally strong poke, *ping!*

Nobody comes. The place is deserted. The mile-long bar with leather high-back chairs and brass footrests is ominously empty, not a soul stands in the lobby stuffed with luxurious mallard-print pillows. A fire burns in a massive grate surrounded by river rock, the only indication that I'm not alone.

Finally, a woman with a knit pumpkin sweater and a matching pumpkin beanie pops out of a maintenance closet off the entry. "Thank you for waiting," she says, tipping her head as she smiles. "I was digging the holiday paperclips out of storage." She shakes a can with little candy canes attached to clips as she makes her way to the desk. "I'm Darcy," she adds. "Are we expecting you?"

"Yes, the reservation is probably under Catherine Bloomfield."

She taps on a sleek tablet, bringing the device alive with light. "Oh right, you're with Brand Hub, correct?"

"That's right."

"Great." She taps a few times on the tablet. "I've got you right here. Let me call a bellman to stow your bags and I'll take you straight back. Your meeting is in The Elk Room. They're expecting you."

Figures. No time to freshen up, but Allyn said the meeting would be quick, a formality we're all entertaining because of the elite client—the elite client she's still told me nothing about who is solely responsible for requesting me by name to work on the Streamflix show.

Who could it be? A musician I'm friendly with on socials? A handsome politico I've met during my years of networking? I'm trying not to let my nerves get to me but the fact they've requested me personally is really throwing me off.

Darcy catches me staring at her hat. "Oh, this," she says, reaching up to lightly pull at the green stem of the gourd on her head, stick straight blonde hair popping out the bottom. "Our local grade school is here on a field trip. We plant a pumpkin patch every year near the entrance to the lodge. Got a ton leftover from the Halloween carving contest and even with saving some for Thanksgiving centerpieces, we're overrun with gourds. So, now they're out there blowing them up for science experiments."

"Cute," I say, passing my bag to her while she shoves it into the maintenance closet. "My favorite science experiments in school were the ones where we blew things up."

She smiles kindly as if she knows she looks ridiculous but she's owning it. "Today is the last day I can wear it. Tomorrow is officially gingerbread, nutcracker, fresh powder, and tree decorating season around here. We host a lovely Thanksgiving dinner, but we go big for Christmas."

"Ski season," I reply knowingly. "I grew up in ski club, but we never came here."

"We're a little off the map and do zero marketing. Somehow, we're always booked."

"Nice problem to have, but I can tell why. It's a beautiful inn. I can't wait to see your decorations. I'm a big fan of the Christmas season."

"If I can put fake snow or a handful of tinsel on something, I will." She gives me a wink. "Follow me. The lodge is pretty quiet right now, but that's all about to change. In the next few days we'll creep up to capacity and stay there for the rest of the holiday season. I'm glad you booked early since you're staying through Christmas."

"I got the call from my boss yesterday," I shrug. "And here I am."

"I'm sure it has something to do with the prince." She wiggles her eyebrows. "He's a smokeshow, isn't he? And so down to earth, even though he tries not to show it."

"The prince?" I ask as my chest tightens. My heart begins to race at an explosive pace.

I think I'm having a heart attack? Are my limbs going numb? I can't tell.

Allyn careens around a corner in a flash of cream silk, shushing Darcy, "Bupp, bupp, bupp—thank you, Darcy. I need a few moments with Catherine before we join the others." She grabs me by the hand and tugs me toward the bar, dropping her act in a flash.

Winter Larsen's face explodes across my mind's eye, causing my stomach to bottom out. The client, *the prince*, cannot be the man I'm thinking of.

My sister's boyfriend's best friend, my arch nemesis for the past six months, cannot possibly be the prince she's talking about. But what if it is? If he's the one who requested me by name? I remember how much he hated me after I said I was his assistant at the baseball game I went to for my sister, and how he berated me in the stands afterward. And how every time we spoke after that, sparring over a video call when he'd inevitably yank the phone away from Frannie while we were on a chat, his lips hardened and my eyes narrowed in response.

Why would he request Brand Hub?

He hates me.

Tore up my business card in front of my own two eyes when I tried to apologize for any inconvenience.

He should be thanking me. I did what he clearly can't do himself—I made him look good, delivering a great speech on his behalf that day. Of course, I've researched him. He's been living a quiet life in America for years and has an absolute trash reputation from his younger days as a temperamental tween who didn't want to play ball with the media in Denmark. Winter Larsen, prince, in line for the Danish throne no matter how long he hides out in the US.

"Cat, are you listening to me?"

I look up. "Yes?"

"Cat," Allyn snaps her fingers in front of my wide eyes and I blink. "Focus!"

"What's going on, Allyn? You've never been this dodgy about a client, and we've had our fair share of massive celebrities with quirky demands," I hedge, bracing myself for whatever's coming next.

"This job had to stay under wraps."

Oh no.

"We couldn't risk an international leak before the official announcement."

Oh, shit.

"Like I'd be a leak! Allyn! You're not yourself."

Please don't say the client is who I think it is, I'm mentally praying on my knees right now. Please let it be a sheikh from Dubai or something.

"We've been booked by the Prince of Denmark."

I blink at her, hearing what she's saying but refusing to believe it. "Who?"

"The Danish royals!" She breathes in my ear, expensive perfume invading my senses and making me feel even more ill. "The ones with the castle at the bottom of the mountain in Paradise Bay, the only castle in California? It's part museum, did you know that? Ring any bells?"

"Oh, God." I shake my head because too many bells are, in fact, ringing. The second she said 'prince,' I knew. Only, I really, really didn't want to believe it. "I know him, Allyn. I can't work for him." This is worst-case scenario.

"You're here, Cat, and you've already agreed. We discussed this. They're waiting . . ."

"That's when I thought he was a sheikh from Dubai!"

"I know you two had some sort of conflict last summer, but it's a reality show, Cat. This deal will seal our reputation in the industry. We'll officially be a sought-after boutique PR agency to the stars. *To the royals.*"

"Winter Larsen is a fancy pants man-brat. Allyn—he hates me."

"You must be mistaken, otherwise, why would he request you? Ownership is a sacrifice. I'm sorry you have a personal issue, but that needs to be put aside. If you can't make this choice . . ."

She doesn't have to say it. If I can't put the company first and do this job, maybe I'm not partner material. I'm disappointed in myself already for appearing so weak.

"Can't we use someone else? I have a lot of clients, Allyn. To move here for months, and do what? Babysit him? Save him from himself on TV?" The first glimmer of hope settles my racing pulse, just a little. "I'll swap jobs with Sloan. Let her take him on. She's been wanting to move up. I'll happily be *your* assistant."

But Allyn shakes her head. "He wanted *you specifically* for his PA." She emphasizes her words as if she can melt them into my brain. As if her enunciation alone will make it all okay.

Fire heats my cheeks, my pride swelling to the point of blowing like a bomb. "I haven't PA'd since I interned for you. How am I supposed to be a partner in Brand Hub and a PA at the same time, Allyn? What will the execs at Streamflix think?"

"They'll think you're damn dedicated like I will. You've got me to hold the fort down till you get back. And when you get back, we go shopping for a new office space. We print your name real pretty on the front of a shiny glass door. And our business booms."

This woman knows how to close a deal. "What exactly do his demands entail?" I ask, feeling my anger slowly dissolve into spite.

The nerve of him to request me by name. He knows exactly what he's doing by putting me in this position.

"They've pitched a new idea. Everyone is filmed so the viewer feels immersed in the action. It's reality, in real time. The last episode is filmed, a fancy finale proposal, I think. They've optioned a honeymoon special."

Allyn is more excited than I've seen her since we worked on a campaign for a viral YouTuber's body shaper line. Having a royal on our PR list would set our company apart. But Winter Larsen is my sworn enemy. I'd rather eat grass than follow him and his unfortunate new wife-to-be around all day. I'll definitely puke if I have to watch anyone get cozy with a narcissistic playboy like him.

Oh God, get the visual out of my mind!

"Allyn, I'm telling you, the history I've got with this guy is not the good kind."

I've been a professional who can put personal issues in a box, compartmentalize, and do my job. Now, I'm not so sure. And I hate that he's the one making me question the bedrock of my work ethic.

"Shh." She hushes me as if we're already being filmed.

I look around. *Wait, are we?*

Quitting isn't in my DNA, so I argue with the last few options I've got, even though the realistic side of me knows it's a losing battle. "I don't think I'm cut out for reality TV. I still think there's someone better at Brand Hub for the job. Maybe I can speak to him and pitch a few of our people. We can explain I'm an owner now."

But she's checking her watch and fluffing her hair. "No time." She pulls a compact from her purse and double-checks her impeccable lipstick. "We can't keep them waiting. I'm sorry to put you in this position, but this is our break, honey."

I start to protest but she stops me with a hand waving in my face, stacks of expensive bracelets almost blind me. "And we both know you're close to burnt out. Think of this as a vacation."

It's so ridiculous a thought I choke on a laugh. "Allyn, you're a good saleswoman, but you're not that good."

"Sure, you're working twenty-four hours a day and you have to agree to appear on camera, but you're also in the sweetest little spot for Christmas." She gestures around us at the towering windows and all the brass and wood that is admittedly cozy and chic as hell.

"Me? On camera?"

"They're filming everything organically, but I'm sure you won't be a focal point, just background. I'll insist you get time off for Christmas. They won't shoot on the actual day. Take your skis for a spin. Detox, or drink yourself silly in your room and watch cheesy Christmas movies. Whatever makes you happy."

Nervous energy rolls through me. "This is not going to make

me happy. Being Winter Larsen's beck-and-call girl is most definitely going to make me miserable."

"Be that as it may, a break from the usual grind is needed, Cat. Your well of creativity will run out, and that's the most precious asset you can protect in this business. The only way I've made it this long is by taking breaks before I'm broken beyond repair."

Her words hit home, and they hit hard. I have watched her over the years, she's my mentor, and she's been more than honest about her struggles with burnout. She's giving me *A Christmas Carol* advice right now minus the ghosts of Christmas Future and the visiting all my past mistakes.

I should take it.

Switch things up.

I can handle him.

I deflate and drop onto a barstool. My shoulders slump as if Allyn talking about burnout has immediately taken away my ability to try and hide it. "What is he up to?"

"Up, up, up." She pulls me off the stool by the arm and drags me down the length of the bar, through the spacious lobby, and toward double doors that are at least two stories tall. "No time to think. We're already late."

A plaque on the wall reads 'The Elk Room' in stately gold, and the doors open wide.

Six

WINTER

Her eyes squint as her boss pulls her into the conference room. She's clad head to toe in black with red lips—chin up.

I stand, and her gaze snaps to me.

"You," she breathes quietly, letting the words fall mostly on my ears as I round the conference room table toward her.

"Bloom," I respond. I've come so close our breath almost mingles and I take a step back while simultaneously reaching to shake her hand.

Prince Charming, at your service.

But she refuses to take my hand, and I pin her with a slight glare, letting my facade slip a touch.

Oh. So it's going to be like that, then.

I haven't spoken to her since stealing her sister's cell a few months back when they were video chatting and our group was having dinner at the Tipsy Taco, a charming place in town despite

48

heavy-handed dancing condiment decor. She was applying makeup and wearing black silk then. My mind flips back to that image unbidden. The robe split open, exposing a sliver of creamy skin.

Is her hand as cold as the ice she's throwing my way now?

Chatter and pleasantries surround us with the chaos of people standing up for royalty even though this isn't my hometown where formalities are still in regular practice for a decorative, at best, monarchy. These TV people have been educated by the team my parents employ, including Anker, lovingly nicknamed The Crown.

They also know their entire project depends on Cat signing on as my assistant, for real this time. Funny how life works, isn't it? She's going to get exactly what she asked for, and she's not going to like it. My parents know I won't do the show without her, Streamflix knows I won't do the show without her, and her boss Allyn knows my name on their client roster will change the trajectory of their company the second it's announced.

And judging by the look in her eyes, Cat is beginning to realize all of this, too.

"This is a mistake," she says, low and firm so only I can hear. She can't meet my eyes as I relentlessly stare at her. I'm making her more uncomfortable by the minute.

Good. Exactly what I'm aiming for.

"Quite the opposite," I reply, tailoring my response to counter her hard-won collectedness as I take a seat across from her. My ease is making her more dodgy, she seems very much like a trapped animal, which gives me pause despite my intentions. "This is exactly what you wanted, to be my assistant. You've already made use of the title."

Everyone sits, but Cat stays standing as if she's an unbroken stallion about to bolt.

So, I test the waters and give her a command she's not going to like. "Have a seat, Cathy," I toss across the table, the rest of the room engrossed in another round of pleasantries.

She doesn't budge, and those eyes heat as they narrow into slits.

It's an effort to conceal my grin.

"Cat," Allyn whisper-shouts, patting the chair next to her while she smiles around the room.

Cat sits, reluctantly. It kills her, and I watch every delicate move as she crosses her legs under the table, still refusing to meet my eyes.

The room continues to titter, Streamflix reps gesturing and making introductions between Cat and me. A producer, a director, and a showrunner bend over backward to make us acquainted, but I know her. And she knows me.

My parents feign interest, they're ready to board their jet now that they've gotten me in the room, and most likely will do exactly that the second Cat signs on to the show.

Cat tucks her hair behind her ears and attempts composure. I can tell it's an effort, clad in a turtleneck so tight it's second skin. She still wants to run. Her eyes keep flitting to the door. It's like that day on the baseball field, she instantly hated me, and still hates me now.

I marvel at how deeply brown her eyes are. How epically pink her cheeks are turning as I refuse to give her a moment's break from my assessment.

Prior to her posing as my PA, I met her months ago in a discotheque, of all places, and we watched her sister and my best friend hit it off on the dance floor. At first, I thought we might hit it off as well. She is beautiful, with strong cheekbones, a determined brow, and heart-shaped lips that snagged my attention. But after quickly coming to know her, that beauty has soured if not in my eyes, then absolutely in my opinion. She makes a career out of embodying everything I hate.

It's annoying that I still find her exquisite to look at.

"Now that we've all been introduced," her boss, Allyn says in a striking suit. "Moving right along to logistics." She motions to the producer whose name I don't remember.

I push back from the table and lean in my chair, resting an ankle on my knee. A strategic smile around the table and a dashing hand through my hair puts them at ease and me in their good graces.

Everyone grins back at the good guy, and my confidence falters for only a second. All eyes on me is not comfortable, but I've had years of grooming to deal with it.

My mother smoothes flyaways from her elegant French twist. "Where do we begin?"

Allyn gestures to a perky-looking young man at the head of the table. "Marco, can you bring us up to speed? Due to your strict instruction to keep information iron-clad, Cat hasn't heard the pitch. And I'm not sure how much Mr. Larsen has been made privy—"

I wave my hand nonchalantly. "I know I'm being married off to better my reputation and that's about all I need to know."

Marco stands, looking like a determined squirrel in royal headlights. "As the head producer for *Royal Hearts*—"

"*Royal Hearts*? You've got to be kidding me," Cat bursts out as if she's finally processed what we've been saying. She seems to be in shock, 'poor dear' as Annie would say, and I feel like the Grinch as my smile twists in her direction.

The room stills again, silent as a dewy morning in a barn before I head out for a ride. All eyes shift to her as she continues. "That title screams romance, chivalry, love and passion." She meets my eyes for the first time since she sat at this table. "That's going to be a stretch, for you."

"Did you think they'd want to feature me baking cakes, Bloom?" I chuckle. She ignores me.

"Thoughts?" Allyn asks, ignoring Cat's remarks and probably hoping the rest of the room does the same. Her face is neutral, but there are nerves in her tone, trying to help her protege recover.

What she really said was, *pull it together Bloomfield, and say something magnanimous in front of the people who will be paying us a large amount of money for this deal.*

Cat hesitates. "The royal aspect is a unique twist. Dating shows are bingeable but the general *boy-picks-from-a-football-teams-worth-of-women* has run its course. Playing up the Crown, the heritage, and the general wealth of the Prince is a good angle. What's the timeframe? The stakes?"

Well played, Bloom.

While I do respect the recovery and no-nonsense attitude, I stick to my mission. "It's nice to have your opinion," I say, purely for the people in the room, "but we don't need your take on the premise of my show."

I look to Marco and wait for the producer's confirmation. As much as it pains me to shut down savvy feedback, I'm not twisting my heritage, my family, my secrets, and my pride into a pretzel she can sell for profit. She is not running this show and I'll be the one to say how much of the prince they're going to get.

"Well, she has recently signed on as a partner at Brand Hub," Allyn says. "Taking this deal, as you've laid out some very specific terms, is up to Cat. She'll have to put the rest of her clients on hold to meet your demands. We still stand to walk away if it's not a good fit."

"That's not what we discussed—" I turn in my chair to debate. Per Allyn's email, I have an agreement that Cat will sign on as my brand manager today. And because I've requested it, she'll also act as PA while on set.

"What you discussed? Why wasn't I part of a discussion about my involvement?" Cat asks.

"That's a moot point," I say, glancing at my PA-to-be. "The deal is done, per my requirements."

Her head swivels from me, to Marco, to Allyn, she wasn't expecting my involvement in this process, I guess. "Your requirements?"

"Yes."

"What else is on your laundry list, sire?" she asks flippantly. Definitely a spoiled first child, entitled and full of pride even when she hasn't the slightest clue what she's getting into.

I must say, I admire her guts and guile in speaking to me this way in front of my parents, though.

It's impossible not to chuckle. "You're not here to have an opinion. You're here to forecast my needs and execute any necessities I require while going through this godforsaken process of exhibition." My lips twist with delight. I'm going to run her ragged with demands.

"Now, wait a minute," Cat taps a finger on the table to get my attention. Little does she know, she's already got it. All of it. And she's going to regret it. "I haven't signed the deal."

Allyn tenses beside her but she reclines in her chair, toying with a pen, the epitome of playing it cool. Cat's eyes slide in her direction, they make eye contact and seem to have an entire conversation. These women respect each other. And because they seem to care about their company deeply, I know I've got Cat Bloomfield on the hook.

"If you think I'm going to grovel and memorize your coffee order, you need to wipe that delusion clean from your brain now," she says, calling me directly on my unspoken plans.

Allyn smiles, and I'm pretty sure my mom lets a chuckle slip from her prim lips.

"That's a yes." I click the pen in my hand, ready to sign on the line even though I don't have any papers in front of me yet.

"Ahem," Allyn clears her throat. "She gets a real Christmas, at least a few days while you break from filming, or we're out."

Nice balls, Allyn.

I can concede to that, this whole charade balances on Cat being involved. Otherwise, what am I doing here other than buying time until I have to sign my life away and give up everything I love? At least enacting payback with Cat makes it interesting.

"Fine," I relent.

"Sign the contract, both of you." Allyn pushes a stack of papers toward Cat with a *do not mess this up for me* look. Then she pushes a matching stack my way. I respect her directness, even with me.

"We'll be going." My dad stands, taking my mom by the arm.

"Clean up your reputation," she says to me, "And for heaven's sake, pick someone suitable. Anker says this is our last resort with you, it has to work.

"And might I add," Allyn says, focusing on Marco and my parents, "we're thrilled to have been chosen for this project."

Cat's narrow eyes which are quite the embodiment of her namesake slide to me as she clicks her pen. "I'll figure out what game you're playing and when I do, you're going to regret it," she whispers.

"I can't wait to see you try," I whisper back. "And I can't wait to watch you quit. Or perhaps I'll fire you first?"

She drops her pen. "I'm doing this for my company. There's nothing you can do to make me quit, and if I'm the perfect assistant, you can't fire me. Which I will be. You're just another client."

I bite down a little too hard. "I know how much you wish that were true."

The papers lay in waiting on the table as the meeting progresses, both of us picking up our pens, putting them down, click, unclick. I'm not even sure what game we're playing, it feels ironically a lot like foreplay.

Who will make the first move?

Marco explains the show will air in real time with little to no editing which means everyone needs to be camera aware and no one is safe from public humiliation. A lot of red tape regarding security, production value, and expectations get tossed around the room.

"Phones in the basket please." Marco pushes a basket down the table. The social media ban is comical for me since the few pages I do have only contain photos of all my animals.

I drop my cell phone in the basket without ceremony.

Cat's face turns white as she turns to Allyn. "No."

I bite back a grin, pick up my pen, and sign my name on the contract with a few quick slashes.

"You're all being filmed and you'll be mic'd," Marco says, "We can't afford a slip-up online. Fans will be watching in real time. It's a sacrifice everyone agreed to make for the integrity of the show."

"I have to be connected. I have clients to look after."

She has her followers to appease with pretty pictures of her face smiling up at the sun under the arched gate of Little Star Lodge. She posted the second she arrived on the property. I've got her alerts set on my phone.

Marco holds up a hand, stopping her mid-protest. "You can check your phones before filming each day. This is a move of good faith for us to know you'll adhere to your contracts and stay offline for the duration of the shoot. You can check in with family, pay bills, and stay in contact with the necessities of your lives. But that's it."

I think for sure we've lost her and I'll have to come up with another way to diabolically enact payback. But then, with a flourish of black ink, she signs the contract, tosses her phone into the basket, and walks out of the room.

Everyone stands, the Streamflix reps looking thrilled this circus is finally over and they've officially signed their leading man, despite his odd demands.

Cat Bloomfield might be even more formidable than I thought, she's going to keep me on my toes, I can admit that. Too bad she'll end up on her knees, begging to be rid of me.

Seven

CAT

Allyn flies through the double doors of The Elk Room to follow me into the main sitting room of the lodge.

"What do you think you're doing?" she demands, surprisingly not breathless. She bikes religiously in her office, stripping down to her bra, and taking meetings via earbuds.

"I can't believe I just agreed to this, Allyn." My stomach is a ball of nerves. I think I just agreed to be Winter Larsen's PA out of sheer spite.

"You can do this, Catherine."

I pace in front of the crackling fireplace. "I can't believe he's gone to these lengths—"

Allyn raises her eyebrow at my uncharacteristic complaining. "You haven't even seen his trailer, yet."

"I don't have to. I remember my days as a lowly PA on photo shoots and production sets, and I know what this is about."

"Where is the take no prisoners, I can get the job done, relentless Cat Bloomfield I've been working with for over five years? I can't believe you're not dancing on the ceiling right now."

I flop into a scrumptious leather side chair and hug a mallard print pillow, letting my head fall between my knees. "She's exhausted, Allyn," I groan to the burgundy carpet under my feet. "The fighting, the clawing my way up. I'm spent. All I want is to use our powers for good, for the little guy. An agency like ours would have saved my parents endless nights of fighting over a marketing plan neither of them understood, *if they could have afforded us.*"

"You know, you're a bleeding heart under that hard black shell of yours. And honestly, you're in the wrong business, but right now I'm counting on that heart you try so hard to hide. You're doing something out of your comfort zone, that's a good thing."

I look into the fire and dig deep, soul-searching, but I'm interrupted by large hands grasping the arms of the chair I'm sitting in on either side of me. Winter leans over and suddenly, I'm trapped in a bubble of smoky clove and citrus cologne.

"Come on, Bloom. It's not gonna be that bad, I promise." His breath is in my ear and I shiver. He's curved himself around me, cocooned me, and caged me in.

I shoot up from the chair, nearly knocking his head with mine in my haste to escape. "Stop encroaching on my personal space, pretty man." I'd rather do the job of a thousand PAs than feel his hands on me.

"Easy, I won't bite." He holds his palms up, chuckling at the rise he so clearly wanted to get out of me. I straighten the collar on my turtleneck and pull at my cuffs, refusing to let him see me ruffled.

"Oh," I scoff, "I'm sorry, I forgot. Mr. Royal Highness is entitled to everything. And now you think because we sort of know each other—"

"My best friend is going to marry your sister."

"I know that! Don't think you know that and I don't." *What was I saying?* I wave my hands between us. "But that doesn't make us anything."

"Well, you did sign the NDA. We're something, and now at least I know you can't sell a story to a gossip blog."

As if I would, but that's beside the point. "If I'm doing this, I have ground rules."

Allyn, wise woman that she is, excuses herself quietly saying to me that she'll be in touch. She disappears through the entry doors of the lodge, out into the sunlight and snowcapped mountaintops while I'm left with this mess.

I'm on my own now, but the feeling is nothing new.

Still, losing Allyn as my backup stings and I lift my chin so it doesn't show. I can handle him. My heart starts to pound in my ears as I realize, I'm all in.

"Go on." Winter gracefully settles his body in the chair across from the one I was just sitting in. He's tall, taller than I wish he was and laced with fine-tuned muscle under a sweater and appropriate princely-looking equestrian pants. He's wearing black boots that go up to his knees and he looks every bit the royal rake the show is surely going to trot him out to be.

I settle slowly back into my chair. "I have . . . stipulations."

"I have . . . no doubt."

"Under no circumstances are you allowed to enter my personal space. We don't know each other, you and I. We're not friends." He scoffs as if I'm wrong and I barrel on, determined, incredulous. "Just because we've got a tiny bit of history—"

"You know, the night our friends met, I thought we liked each other."

"What on earth gave you that impression?" The night we met he was on a bachelor party and looking for trouble, trying to rile me up while hollering at me from a bus as I simply tried to watch over my sister while she talked to his friend—the friend she's probably going to marry. "You know what, don't answer that. My stipulations are the following. Number one: no touching, joking around, acting like we're familiar, because we're not. You want me, no," I clarify, "you *need* me to keep your image clean, to make you loveable, to sell your crown, and that's what I'll do because I love my job."

"What a sad little life you must live."

I love my job, I love my job, I love my job, I tell myself, so that I don't break my own rule ten seconds in and fly across this coffee table to strangle him. This is going to be a long two months. I can't believe my sister fell for this guy's best friend. I can't believe this guy *has* friends. He's so, *so smug,* sitting there in his tight, form-fitting pants with a cheeky *I own the room* smile painted on his pretty face.

He runs a hand through dashing sandy brown hair, casually waiting me out as if irritating me is the only item on his itinerary for the day.

"Number two—"

"Oh good, we're counting," he mocks.

Is everything a game to him?

"No unreasonable requests. I've PA'd for a handful of celebrities while I interned for Brand Hub, and I didn't let Styles push me around. I won't let you, either. You want the full-service, boutique agency treatment? You want a Brand manager, a PA, and PR all rolled into one? It's going to cost you, and that means keeping demands reasonable and doing as I say."

"You PA'd for Harry?"

I let my face drop into my hands and groan. "The one and only."

"He's a good dude. Gets a bad rap sometimes, but damn, do you not love him in spandex?"

When I peek through a crack in my fingers, wondering for the billionth time how I ended up in this situation, he's playing with a tassel on a pillow, rolling it between two fingers and I find myself mesmerized until he coughs and my gaze shoots back to his.

I clear my throat. "I worked for him in the early days, anyway .

. .” I shake my head. I don't care if Harry is Winter's BFF and they have slumber parties every weekend in the castle down the mountain in Clover. He's not throwing me off my train of thought. "When we're on set, we keep it professional. When we're off set, *I don't know you.*"

"Ouch, Bloom." He covers his heart with his hand and makes a pained face. Then laughs at my non-reaction, running a hand again through his gravity-defying and somehow perfect hair. "Are you always so gracious to people who are saving your ass?"

"My ass? What could you possibly be talking about? None of this is for me, I still don't know how you managed to make this happen."

"I didn't make this happen. My parents are forcing the show on me." The words leave his lips in earnest, but his eyes tell a different story. There's fire there, determination, and a sadness I can't ignore.

Do not squirm in your seat. I've been in meetings with powerful clients with more intense gazes than this.

"This is you getting your rocks off while someone grovels for your royal glance—admit it."

"*Or,* this is me helping your floundering company while also getting a bit of revenge."

"Don't you worry about my company." He's trying to throw me off and I won't let that happen. "Which is why I'm setting boundaries. No funny business," I finish, vaulting my words at him with everything I've ever learned about negotiation laced into my tone and the set of my shoulders.

He leans forward. "Noted, Bloom. Well." He slaps his knees and stands, "now that's done."

"Where do you think you're going?" I demand, standing to mirror him.

"Sad to see me leave?" he asks over his shoulder, already walking away. "Don't worry, we're going to have plenty of time together, Bloom."

He's laughing at me, baiting me, and it makes heat rise in my cheeks because I immediately want to chase him. The alarming part is, I have no idea why.

"No, I'm not sad," I sputter, tripping over my own feet to follow, "I haven't finished with my rules."

His nerve is unbelievable.

"Rules are for children. I'm a prince. And while I don't like to play that card often—see ya, Darcy—" he adds as he passes the front desk.

Darcy is carefully untangling a ball of tinsel from a shopping bag and laying it lovingly piece by piece across the desk. "Bye, Winter. All my love to Lola."

I makeshift wave as I follow Winter toward the front doors.

Who's Lola?

He goes on, a self-obsessed actor mid-monologue, "I moved from my home country to get away from all of it. But you're working for me. And I'm leaving. Perhaps we circle back to number three another day."

I might puke right here in the entryway. "Wait."

Despite the fact I hate myself for it, and that I know I shouldn't continue to chase him, I can't let him have the last word.

He saunters through the doors. It's unfortunate for me that I notice his broad shoulders, slender waist, and strong thighs high-lighted perfectly in those damn riding pants and boots.

I swear to hate him for all eternity, but I will him to turn around with my eyes burning into his back so I'm not forced to go after him. But he doesn't.

"Dammit," I whisper to myself. "Who's Lola?" I yell, chasing after him.

Outside in the crisp mountain breeze, he fits a boot in a stirrup and mounts a stunning grey horse dappled with black spots. Then takes hold of black leather reins and makes a clicking sound with his mouth. "Easy girl," he murmurs as the horse stomps.

Of course, he came here on horseback. Fucking hell. "I said, who's Lola? As your manager, or whatever, I need to know if you're going on a dating show with a girlfriend and about to blow up your image for good!"

No man, or horse, is going to intimidate me, and to prove it, I march right up to him waiting for an answer.

He pulls back on the reins while his horse snorts and dances beneath him.

"She's my dog—watch your toes," he commands.

I hop a little, trying not to get stomped on but my feet get all tangled up. Suddenly, I'm way too close to this horse.

He swings a leg over the side of the horse and drops to his feet, gripping me and putting himself between my body and the enormous animal, pressing his back against its round middle which immediately causes retreat. When he's put at least three feet between me and the horse, he seems appeased.

"Are you always this needy?" he breathes, removing his hands from my upper arms and turning to stroke the horse's neck as if I did something wrong.

"One more rule."

He mounts the horse again in one quick movement, and my gaze tracks up his black boot, up his thigh flexing in the saddle, until I meet his arrogant smirk. Blue eyes delighted, which only makes me angrier and more thrown off.

"I, I," I stammer. He's literally sitting on his high horse and I hate that the sight affects me.

He leans over to scrub the horse with rough but loving pats. "Yes?"

"Next time, let me get stomped on."

He tips his head back and roars with laughter. "Sure, Bloom. Whatever you say."

"I mean it, and remember, off hours are *off hours*. Don't even think of sending me a request in the middle of the night."

"How *are* we going to communicate? Without our phones?"

he muses, one hand on his hip, the other scratching his head to make fun of me.

He's dropped his reins and for a flash, I dream of smacking the horse on the ass and watching Winter Larsen get tossed onto the cobblestones.

"Exactly. We won't. If you must get in touch with me, you can leave me a note at the front desk."

"Charming. Just when I thought the art of letter writing was dead."

At the front desk, I ring the bell.

Darcy pops up in a flutter of papers, pens, and twinkle lights. "Oh I'm sorry, I didn't see you there. Are you ready for your key? I'll walk you up."

We make our way up a wide staircase, the wooden treads covered in plaid carpet. My hand glides over an ornate, dark wood banister carved intricately with flora and fauna as we climb, Darcy humming a holiday tune under her breath.

"So, they'll be filming the show here? At the lodge?"

"That's right," I sigh. "Offsite too, I'm sure."

"It's exciting, but it's going to cause a lot of commotion. Our little ski village doesn't get many celebrity sightings, we're something of a secret up here. Off the map with our own post office, market, and shops. Novel and Clover, the two towns butted up against each other at the bottom of the mountain, get most of the traffic."

"My sister just moved to Clover, actually."

"You mean Frannie?"

"Yes, you know her?" We hit the top of the landing and I peek over the edge at the lodge below, filled with a few patrons and staff. I was beginning to think poor Darcy was a one-woman show.

"I met her at the re-opening of Boggs' Bar and Grill last

summer, best boat-up restaurant on the lake. They make a mean cocktail and I like to go there to watch the water. We're a close-knit community around here."

We come to the end of a gold leaf-papered hallway and stop at the last door. "Is this me?"

"Yep, I gave you a good room. Figured if you're here for the winter season, you deserve to see Garland at its finest." She opens the door wide and ushers me in.

I quite literally lose my breath.

"Darcy, this is . . ." I trail off, gulping. "There's a fire!" My fingers glide over a sleek black marble mantle with garlands, a warm fire crackling merrily in the hearth.

It's everything I could have wished for. The holidays are my absolute favorite. Maybe because that's the only time my parents ever slowed down when we were kids, maybe because of the presents, or maybe because I like cozy socks and warm fires.

Probably all of the above.

"You like it?" She putters around the room fluffing pillows and then pulls back a thick, blue velvet curtain from a frost-tinted window. The view is of the mountain, down below workers are hauling a Rockefeller-worthy tree to the center of a square, hefting it up as others unpack boxes. There's a huge golden star that three people are pulling off the back of a truck and I wonder if I've accidentally wandered into Whoville.

"I love this time of year," I say with a long exhale.

"Figured you could use a warm soak in a bath, a fire, a good night's sleep." Darcy is an angel. A layer of stress I've been carrying around this past year slides off my shoulders. This job will be over soon. And I get to spend Christmas living in the beautiful lodge, and with my sister. Everything is going to be fine.

"Thank you. For the room and the warm welcome. If the show becomes too intrusive on the lodge, or if you have any problems with production, let me know."

"I'm not against the show being here, but I do hope we can

keep our little slice of peace and happy intact. What's the director's name, again?"

"Marco," I supply.

"Yes, him. He promised to keep the crew small so our regular guests aren't overwhelmed. He said he'd work with a small team in exchange for the lodge getting waivers signed by all guests when they check in."

Nothing says 'happy holidays' like a reality show, I grimace. "We'll do our best." A small crew means pitching in wherever needed. Visions of dusting off my rusty ski skills slip away.

She smiles apologetically, perhaps reading my disappointment. "I'll be downstairs if you need me, and we've got a night concierge as well. Just ring."

After getting acquainted with my room and stowing my things, I check on the tree decoration progress out my window. It's up, the star officially placed at the top. Ornaments litter the scene in variations of size and color. I have a feeling by the time I wake up tomorrow morning, that giant pine tree will have turned into pure magic.

And the show will begin.

Eight

CAT

A production schedule for the day slips under my door as I'm stepping out of a steamy cranberry-infused shower. I scoff at the irony of resorting to paper communication since most of us have relinquished our phones as I dab lavender oil behind my ears.

In the extensive welcome section of our brief, it says *Royal Hearts* will stream live on select days with a rerun aired during primetime each night. The show will conclude roughly eight weeks from now. The location is TBD, though they're floating two ideas in parentheses: at the top of the mountain with a heart set aflame, and a sleigh ride with a just married sign and old-fashioned cans tied to the back (the prince driving the sleigh).

"Of course, he can drive a sleigh," I murmur to my four-poster bed, tossing the schedule on a nearby desk with a mirror so it also functions as a vanity.

After a blow-dry, I tame my short hair with a few loose curls and tuck a lock behind my ear. Rose tones, deep berry reds, and emerald greens make up the fluffy plaid feather duvet I slept like a baby in last night, the fire crackling in my grate as it slowly burned out.

I want to jump right back in that bed and stay here forever instead of facing whatever this day holds for me.

Boxwood wreaths and bows adorn every window in the room, and the thick carpet tickles my toes. Even the bathroom is in the holiday spirit with a pine and berry centerpiece on the marble counter. A deep clawfoot tub I plan to soak in tonight after a no doubt gruesome first day working with Winter Larsen, is decked out with a thick slab of polished, raw-edge wood and a gingerbread sugar scrub.

I could certainly get used to this.

Once I'm dressed in jeans and a thin sweater with a black belt bag that leaves my hands free for working on set, I decide to grab breakfast in the cozy dining room I noticed yesterday off the bar, The Nook.

Candy Cane, an instrumental I recognize from The Nutcracker, is filtering through the hallway as I pass lodge employees lugging life-size nutcrackers by the necks, and when I round the corner and step onto the landing to head downstairs, I'm gobsmacked.

As my eyes roam the Christmas chaos below, I reach for my phone so I can send a picture to Frannie and Willow, but then I remember, I don't have my phone. Which is a real shame because they'd both love this wonderland.

Below, the long bar is littered with red poinsettia in sparkling pots. Six-foot Santas fill almost every corner, and there's a pine tree in the center of the room that rivals the one outside. As I make my way downstairs, swaths of garland wrap the banister, flocked with white and tied up with velvet ribbons and rustic bells. Employees buzz and run from every visible corner of the lobby. They holler for nails as wreaths are hung above windows, pulling more and more decorations out of the boxes littering the inn floor as if rabbits from a magician's hat.

"Excuse me, miss," a dashing young bellhop says. He tips his Little Star Lodge bellman cap as if he's been plucked straight from a movie set, skirting around me to be on his merry way. Marco's going to love getting a shot of him for B-roll.

At the bottom of the stairs, I step over a box filled with glittery snowflakes the size of my palm, and walk down the length of the bar watching my reflection in the mirrored backsplash. All my black clashes with the bright motif, but my Christmas red lips match perfectly.

A hostess smiles from the arched entry to The Nook. "Good morning, Ms. Bloomfield. Sleep well?" A charming sprig of mistletoe hangs over her head, and she's grinning so big, I almost expect her to kiss me.

One would think, from my exterior, sure, and from my dedication to my job no matter the holiday, that I'm a Grinch. I am not. I adore this time of year, I'm just not always good at showing it. "Yes, perfect. One please." I work to push my lips into a warm smile.

"Glad to hear it. Breakfast menu? Coffee?"

"Yes, and yes." I tuck a chunk of hair behind my ear. "I've got some reading to catch up on."

"I'll put you in our coziest little corner. No one will find you."

"Sounds like heaven."

She does just that, and I settle into a stuffed chair by a frosted window that faces the same direction as my bedroom window. Outside the mountains are topped with snow and skiers are flying down like ants in a hurry. The tree is fully decorated, sparkling with charming ornaments, and at least one hundred feet tall.

A cup of coffee magically appears in front of me in a clay mug, and a silver pitcher lands on the table.

"What'll it be?" He's tall, gangly, surly, and probably mid-twenties wearing a slightly wrinkled white button-down and black tie, a hint of a tattoo peeking out from his shirt collar. He's got a notebook folded in half in his back pocket, and a pencil behind his ear.

I look up. "I haven't seen a menu, yet."

"It's riddled with typos," he huffs, and begins to rattle off a list via memory. "Waffles, omelets, scalloped eggs—though I would not recommend—a Benedict that will make you feel as if you've died and gone to Middle-earth, an assortment of juices—"

I raise my hand to stop him. Seems I've met another human who values time and has a slight attitude problem, like me. "You had me at Benedict. Black coffee is fine. And thanks . . ."

"Liam."

"Thanks, Liam."

He nods, then adds, "You working on that reality show they're filming here?"

"What gave me away?"

"The jacket." He nods at the leather jacket draped over the back of my chair. "And all the black. Christmas sweaters are the staple around here this time of year. We don't see a lot of black leather biker jackets. Also, you're holding letterhead with the word Streamflix emblazoned across the top in a font so large I could read it from the kitchen."

"I'm Cat." I stick out my hand.

"Okay." He walks away muttering to himself about Holly-wood and I think I hear the words *reality show, hacks,* and *real art.*

Breakfast in the snug little corner with the best eggs Benedict I've ever had and scant conversation with Liam is exactly what I needed to mentally prepare for my first day as Winter Larsen's PR, PA, and all-around lackey on the set of *Royal Hearts.* God. That show title makes me want to puke a little. It's so pompous. Entitled. Tone deaf. It's so Winter Larsen.

But we do what we must. All night I sweat through the loss of my cell before crashing into the deepest sleep of my life. I never realized how many times I checked my phone until I reached for it every other minute last night, and it wasn't there. And when I started to feel physically ill from the withdrawal, I realized, I have a problem—in addition to a nervous tummy.

Allyn was right, I might have needed this change of pace so I don't burn out. This is step one, and I flip through my show schedule to see what's ahead. Today, Winter is scheduled to shoot B-roll for the opening credits of the show, and in the afternoon, we'll shoot his 'get to know the prince' interview.

B-roll will involve sweeping panoramas of Winter with the mountains and the lake in the background, and a lot of skin, I'm sure. Selling his face won't be hard, he is a stunning man, like a perfume ad where the model's eyes are so piercing you believe he might leap off the page. He's got that certain something that makes you either want to be him or be with him. No, making viewers fall in love with him is the least of my worries. But I shudder to think of the hoops he's going to make me jump through.

"Here's your check," Liam says. "Twenty percent gratuity included."

Fair enough.

I look up. "Hey, you wouldn't happen to be—"

"You need a to-go coffee?" he demands.

"No. Are you a writer, by chance?"

His face brightens. "Screenplays. How did you—"

I motion to his back pocket. "The notebook, the mumbling about Hollywood sellouts, Tolkien references, the blue blockers resting on your head . . ."

"Ah." He scratches at the arm of the glasses resting behind an ear. I think I've earned a little respect. He clocked me, and I clocked him right back.

"Listen, I'll keep you in mind if we need extras."

"I'm not an actor," he scoffs.

"Believe me, writers have done more with less to break in."

"Are you?" He gestures at me as if we're comrades.

"No, no. I work in PR, which means I've seen it all. I could always, you know, make an introduction. I don't know much about the writing side, but Streamflix is a ladder and you gotta start somewhere, right?"

"That would be," he hesitates, a writer searching for words, "really solid of you. Thanks."

"I'll be in touch." I toss a few extra bills on the table because I believe in supporting struggling artists, and gather my things. Liam gives me a salute and walks away, a hushed *yes*! falling from his lips. And that makes me grin.

After extricating myself from the charming holiday hoopla happening inside the lodge, I step outside into a brisk, sunny fall day where workers on ladders are hanging strings of lights from the rooftops. Mountains crowd the little lodge, surrounding it on three sides with ski runs and lifts in motion. A handful of production crew, equipment, and a van are ready and waiting on the circle drive. Today's shoot is off-site at the castle in Paradise Bay on Spirit Lake, down the mountain in Clover.

"How long's the ride?" I ask a man firing up the van. Equipment is loaded in the back and an assortment of production people hop inside. Marco comes out of the lodge, an overflowing box in his hands, and nods at him.

"Less than ten minutes. Gets a little bumpy at the end of town when we go through the pass."

Marco slaps me on the back. "Ready Ms. Bloomfield?"

"Call me Cat."

He winks. "Will do. Ready for day one? I brought some things you might need for today."

That was nice. "What sort of things? I've got a few essentials from working on content shoots that I've learned come in handy over the years." I pat my little black fanny pack.

"Oh, but these are reality show essentials. Mainly, oil. You'd be surprised how often we need it. And blotting tissue, for when there's oil we don't want showing on camera. A few other things."

"So, it's all about the oil?"

"Yes ma'am."

"Thank you." I load most of the things in my bag and zip it tight.

"Today, we convince everyone to fall in love with Prince Charming. It's vital fans adore him. They'll chop up the B-roll of Winter living daily life and mix it with his first big interview. That'll run as advertising for most of the season. We have to get this right. Part of selling this show is selling—"

"The pretty man. Got it. I'm uh, a fan of some of these shows. I get how it works."

"Good. You keep him happy, keep him all polished up and shiny—good shiny."

"Got it." I nod.

"Did you know I used to work on *The Bachelor*?"

"Um, no?" I'm not sure if I'm supposed to pump up his ego right now and pretend I know who he is when I don't. But Marco doesn't come off like a standard industry guy, maybe one of the good ones. "We usually get them all on a teeth whitening regimen, but I think he's good in that department."

His teeth are perfect, and it's oddly maddening.

I rub my temples, I'm still tired. Guess I need a few more nights of deep sleep in my four-poster feather bed. I'm already looking forward to snuggling in with a Christmas movie.

"I'm sorry, I didn't mean to sound dismissive," Marco adds, picking up on my exhaustion already. *Definitely one of the good ones.* "I got in a few years ago because I was one of the Kardashian's stylists—can't say which, NDA and all—but I did my job well, kept my client happy, met the right people, and here I am."

"I'll remember that when I'm shining his boots. I heard the crew is thin on set and they were caked in mud yesterday, assuming that's my job now. If we work the whole equestrian, Prince William on a polo field angel— and we should because honestly, he's nailing it on his own— we'll need shiny boots."

"That's the angle. Will he comply? I couldn't quite tell if he's on board. In the meeting yesterday, it was cold on my end of the table. The royal Danes, his immediate family at least, aren't exactly known for warmth."

"Oh, he'll love it. Trust me. He likes the spotlight."

"You know him? Personally, I mean?"

No? Kind of? "We're acquainted, but believe me, that doesn't mean he's going to take it easy on me."

Marco barks a laugh as the van shifts gears and the back doors slide closed. "Oh honey, you don't want to know what I did to claw my way to the top. The amount of salads I had to shake for that family and how many wigs I brushed out."

I smile at him, the comradery of having to attend to rich, powerful, and beautiful people brewing between us. At least I've got the director on my side, keeping Mr. Pretty Man happy is not going to be easy, I know that for sure. Because Winter Larsen has already promised to make my life a living hell.

We pull up in a circle drive ten minutes later. A sign tells us this is public parking for Paradise Bay, and while the van is being unpacked, I take in the view. Ombre water shines in the sun as far as my eyes can see, and the castle sits in the center of a crescent beach. The parking lot is carved into a hill, and I lean over the edge of a rock wall to look down on Vikingstrong.

I've seen it before, looked it up, of course, and my sister told me about it. But it's an entirely different monster when you see it in person: all turrets and stone, Juliet balconies, and soldered windowpanes. There are workers on ladders here, too, decking the halls with holiday wreaths on every window.

We all truck down the winding hill because other than a tiny lift we found in the woods that takes a code to operate, there's no other way to get there. The crew, including me, hand-carry boom mics, cameras, tubs full of tools, and trunks full of wardrobe options.

My eyes travel up expansive stone walls and steepled rooftops after we drop our supplies on the soft sand of the crescent-shaped beach. It's a public beach but it's not tourist season for Spirit Lake, dusted with clouds in the sky and brusque breeze, only a few onlookers stare wondering what the hell this army dressed mostly in black is doing.

We look like a band of thieves in broad daylight.

The structure is made mostly of smooth stone, three stories high with a turret on each side. Giant dragon heads, carved intricately with scrolling necks, delicate scales, and cold eyes. Mouths open breathing fire over the entry, crossing at the necks.

A stunned laugh escapes me as I make my way to the doorstep. Of course, *of course,* it's an enigmatic castle that's as welcoming and rustic as a lakeside chalet. I knew this. Winter is a Danish prince. This is information I've already processed. But for some reason, the weight of it hasn't sunk in until this very moment. My hand travels the iron handle of the door, warm to the touch by the sun even in the almost winter chill.

Before I can knock or ring a bell, the door pulls open, out of my grasp, and he's there. Standing in riding pants and a white t-shirt, a black helmet under one arm, messy hair standing in all directions on his head, and barefoot. There's a crest on the pocket of his shirt, a dragon breathing fire with a scrolling L.

"Bloom. You're a sight to see on my doorstep this morning." One corner of his mouth tips up as his eyes assess me head to toe.

Unceremoniously, I drop the fat microphone cord coiled around my shoulder. The thing weighs a ton. "You're a real prince," I gush, my words floating in the air between us.

Dammit! Cat, don't inflate his ego with your awe. Reel it in!

He looks down at his feet, then drags his gaze up. "You got me."

"I mean," I reach for words that will erase the wonder in my voice, "do you have any idea what we had to do to haul equipment down here? But you just *had* to shoot at home, I suppose."

"This wasn't my—" he starts to protest, but I won't hear it.

"Spare me," I say, and look up to see two carved dragon heads curled to meet each other in architectural detail in the rafters, almost as if they're kissing. "I still don't understand how we got here. Why do you demand I be involved? I could be happily living my normal life right now with my roommate who I feel really bad about leaving, and my office, and my phone."

I'm embarrassed, and I'm annoyed: with his laziness, with my situation, and the fact I'm tethered to him for the duration of this show, probably longer if my sister ends up marrying his best friend. I yearn to run screaming for the mountaintops.

I eye him while waiting for an answer. *Leaving Winter Larsen hanging would be a pleasure.*

His jaw ticks as he bites down, and I don't think he's going to respond, but he surprises me and says, "This isn't my idea of a good time, either."

"You're the center of attention. This is all for you," I gesture behind me. "Forgive me if I don't believe you. You signed on to this show for a reason."

"Yes, despite loathing being in any kind of spotlight, I did."

That gives me pause. He does live as quietly as he possibly can, off the grid and away from it all. He hides out here in this castle that almost no one knows about unless they stumble upon it while hiking or visiting the beach.

"Cat got your tongue?" he chides, tossing his helmet onto a chair inside.

"Pompous, coddled, little prince," I growl, to remind myself exactly what he is.

"Do me a favor, as my assistant," he looks over my shoulder at the crew on the beach, "and try to keep my audience at a minimum. I . . . I get a bit uneasy with a camera on me."

"Who would have thought you'd have stage fright?" I scoff.

"More like PTSD," he says under his breath.

"But you're always so," I wave my arms around grandly, "big. You have a big personality." When I search his face for calculation, for any kind of joke or taunt, all I see is genuine fear. He's not looking forward to today. I sober. "I'll do what I can, but you orchestrated this circus. You made your bed and now you've got to lie in it. Might teach you a lesson about messing with people as if they're mere playthings."

His jaw ticks as his lips form a hard line. "Let me know when you're ready," he says, moving to close the door in my face, but he hesitates. "Wait, first I want a green smoothie from Smooth Operators. My buddy Ben Holiday recently opened it and they're running a two-for-one special."

"Green smoothies are my favor—"

"Make sure you bring the extra back for Annie. And you might want to find a cooler and some ice to tote them in, I don't want a lukewarm smoothie. It's in Novel, by Mr. Bear's Toys. You'll find it." He nods to the mountain I'll have to climb to get to the van. "Extra greens in mine, Annie is allergic to lemon."

"You can't be serious," I say, already reaching for my phone wondering if I can call it in but I don't have a phone!

"I know, right? It's the damnedest thing. Can't even have a lemon in the house. If she looks at the color yellow, I swear her throat swells up."

My eyes meet his and I hold in every single detail about how far I want him to shove it. "As you wish, pretty man," I seethe.

"And Bloom," he adds.

But I'm staring up the hill. I'll have to borrow the keys to the van, find this damn smoothie place in a town I'm unfamiliar with, and hustle back down here to get him dressed and ready to shoot.

Do they have Walmarts in this area? Where am I going to find a mini-cooler?

"What?" I grit back without turning to face him.

"Don't make me wait too long."

I make him speak to my back. Whatever game we're playing, it's point one Larsen, counterpoint, Bloom.

Nine

WINTER

When Cat returns with my smoothie that I know good and well was a pain in the ass for her to procure, she's sweating. But she is toting a cooler with the tag still attached from Holiday Bait, Boat, and Tackle and I'm impressed, despite my trying not to be.

Serves her right. She deserves it. Not only is this payback for the stunt she pulled months ago, but she's a pill. A flippant, judgy, stuck-up pill. She must be obsessed with herself to post the way she does on social media, to bask in strangers fawning over her with likes and comments. Last night when I got back to my apartment above the main floor of the castle, I fell into my laptop and searched Catherine Bloomfield.

Yes, I signed a contract to stay offline for the duration of the show. They can sue me if they find out. And anyway, I'm stealthy, I'm not stupid enough to leave any sort of footprint.

The recent comments on her posts are enough to make me

want to jump in the lake—the way they fawn over her. Her bio boasts of career accomplishments with Brand Hub, and highlights a family business with pictures of her in baggy shorts and band t-shirts in a warehouse filled with toys and games. There are pictures of her as a teen in braces with her parents, a tag gun in her hand, and a few with her sister next to her on rollerblades. Frannie grins ear to ear while Cat's got her hands perched on her hips, a *get this over with* look on her face.

Her followers love her. They trip over themselves complimenting her, and yes, there are so many *men* in addition to a bunch of small businesses who cheer her on when she posts about local mom-and-pops—probably charging them an arm and a leg.

It doesn't matter to me what she does in her free time, but this sort of glutton for fame is exactly what I hate. It's the exact opposite of who I am and what I want—I ran from it the second I could leave Skagen, and enrolled myself in school here. I met the dudes, my band of brothers who saved me, and never looked back.

"They're ready for you," Annie says as she moves through the kitchen. She's making a grocery list, one for my personal kitchen upstairs and one for the main kitchen with things she uses.

Annie's the only reason I've been able to live this life away from the monarchy and my parents. When I begged to leave Denmark as a kid, they said no. When I kicked up a royal fuss and made headlines with absolutely horrific behavior, they sent me to the castle in California with Annie, under the guise of American liaison. I'm supposed to show up for the tours now and then, and when I do, I mostly enjoy it, but something about putting on a show for oglers makes my stomach turn. My family still owns the castle, built to be a grand but rustic lakeside mountain retreat, but we donated the land and the main floor to the state long ago as a historical landmark. Hence, I reluctantly live like Quasimodo.

And the rest, as they say, is history.

"Thanks." I drain the last of my smoothie dry and toss the cup in the bin.

Cat's cheeks were glistening when she delivered it, tendrils of hair falling into her face. Brown eyes blazing with heat and loathing, for me.

Exactly how I want it. My plan is working perfectly.

I make my way down the front lawn onto the beach. The day has turned sunny and if I were betting, one of the last we're going to see for a while. Winter is coming and while it's semi-mild on the lake, up on the mountain copious snow will fall and temperatures will drastically drop.

I hope she freezes her ass off in that flimsy leather jacket she's wearing.

"No, no, no, no," Marco says as I approach him. There's a camera set up on a gimbal, I'm guessing, to follow me on a walk down the beach.

What a cliché. "Marco, good morning."

"Why aren't you in wardrobe?" He stomps a dad-sneakered foot.

I shrug and yawn. "No one's told me anything about wardrobe. Isn't that my peon's job?"

"Cat!" Marco bellows. The entire crew pauses to watch Cat cross the beach to meet us. Marco speaks softly instead of ripping into her and everyone gets back to whatever they were doing. Nice guy. "Why is Mr. Larsen not in wardrobe?"

"Got it right here." She pulls a pair of jeans from her shoulder.

"I'm not wearing those."

"*But this is wardrobe,*" they both say in unison.

I eye them and almost ask if they'd planned to double-team me. "I don't do denim."

"But I spent an hour poring over options with the stylists. I picked these specifically for the wash and slightly frayed edges, and the button fly." Her eyes jolt to my crotch when she says *fly*, and her cheeks turn berry red.

"But are frayed edges the image we want to project?" I muse, rubbing my chin. "What does a button fly say about me?"

Her eyes narrow and her lips purse. It's fun getting under her skin.

"Fine, would you like me to bring back some different options?" She is determined.

Yes, exactly right Bloom. I am here to make your job absolutely and delightfully impossible. True, denim isn't high on my list, though I would wear it, but it's so much more fun making trouble for her.

Marco surprises us both when he pipes up. "The fitted khakis are a nod to nineties, preppy-boy-chic, anyway." I look down at myself. Is that what I look like? I throw on breeches and my riding gear most mornings and think nothing of it. "But lose the shirt."

"Are you okay with that?" Cat asks. Her words are tight, forced, but I have to award her points for doing her job and asking her client what they're comfortable with.

"Fine with me."

Marco turns to Cat. "Oil him up, and . . ." he surveys me head to toe like a cut of Wagyu on a restaurant cart, "roll the pants at the ankle. Slouch them down on the hips."

I gesture at my hips. "They are slouched, I rode for three hours this morning."

"*More*," Marco says, "Show a little boxer. Cat, you've got options?"

"I've got three different waistband options. We were prepared for the 'model in a designer label' angle."

I have no idea what that means, but the word 'model' can't be too bad.

Marco nods. "That, or you can always default to plaid. The unofficial theme of this whole production is plaid. You've got five."

Time to argue. "Seriously? I'll look like an imbecile." Cat sniffs, looking away to hide a smirk. "Do you have a problem?" I ask, any points for her professionalism lost.

Try me, Bloom.

"Wardrobe can't fix the problem I have," she says under her

breath and a tiny part of me, deep down, balks. It really bothers me when people don't like me. *Hell.* I guess I'll have to deal with her loathing me since I've sworn to make her life miserable.

Marco takes control of the uncomfortable silence between us. "We need the shirt off. The sun is still shining and there's a winter warning coming in for all of next week. This is our last chance to get the shirtless beach footage, and we *need* the shirtless beach footage."

"We can't, you know, go for snuggly sweater footage? In Danish culture there's a term we use called *hygge*—"

"Could you get any more high maintenance?" Cat asks, tipping her chin up as if she's got better things to do. "You said you were fine with it."

Truth be told, I'm fucking freezing already in bare feet and short sleeves, though the sun is warming my skin and Logan's always telling me I need to get out of the gym and more vitamin D.

"Let me enunciate a little more clearly," Marco says, clearing his voice. "Shirt-less."

"You heard him," Cat says, pulling a bottle of golden oil from a bag wrapped around her hips. It almost looks obscene in her hand, like something she'd pull from her nightstand, but I squash that ridiculous thought real quick.

"Must I?" I groan, rubbing my forearms to try and build up some heat first.

"Skin sells. Hand over the Hanes."

She juts a demanding hand in my direction and despite my best efforts, a laugh escapes me. "You're certainly eager."

When in Rome. I pull at the neck of my shirt and toss it over her shoulder on top of the offending jeans. And yeah, she can't take her eyes off me.

I flex, just a little, and when my pecs jump, she jumps.

Interesting.

"Here," she launches the oil at me and I catch it easily, "put your own oil on."

I launch it right back at her and she catches it, but barely. "And do your job for you?"

"Are you trying to make my life hell on this job, because we're two hours in and you're nailing it."

All I do is smile because yes, she's getting a taste of what she's in for. "Aw, you're not going to quit, are you?"

"I would *never* give you the satisfaction, or risk Brand Hub's future, or my own. I'm not doing this here," she grits out, looking around as her cheeks turn crimson.

Rubbing me down with body oil is apparently abhorrent to her. It's not like I want her hands on me either. The crew continues with their tasks on the beach, but more than a few sets of eyes cut our way and I instantly tense up.

"We're rolling on set. Mics are hot," Marco yells, tromping through the sand and stepping over piles of equipment.

A tall Black man with a mohawk hoists a camera to his shoulder and it tracks my way. My mouth goes dry and I swallow, remembering all the cameras in my face as a kid and how much it made me wish I could disappear.

So we're doing this, my glance says when I meet Cat's eyes again. I take a deep breath and let it out long and slow through my nose. As much as I've geared up for this, it's going to take a toll. Doing the royal song and dance always does.

"What's wrong?" she asks.

Her change in tone, from cold to concerned, puts me on guard. *What is she playing at?* "Being served like a meal to the camera has never been my favorite part of the job. Not as a kid, and not now."

She looks right, looks left, surveying our audience of production crew who aren't outright staring at me, but clocking my movements nonetheless through downshifted gazes. "Follow me, *please*," she says, her voice low.

It's the unexpected concern on her face that keeps me from fighting her. Instead, I follow her to the edge of a clearing to some tall pines off the side of Vikingstrong. The camera is still trained on me but keeps its distance. Must have a damn good lens; it gives a false sense of privacy that I know isn't there.

"What are we doing?" I huff.

"I'm getting you ready without an audience." She drops to her knees and looks up at me. "Okay?"

I tense and look down, suddenly bewildered. "Okay."

With the lightest touch, she gently rolls up the hem of one of my pant legs. It's unnerving to have her kneeling before me, as is the chill I feel when she moves to roll up the other pant leg, grazing my ankle with her fingertips.

"Ouch," she mutters, shifting her weight from one knee to another. Sticks and rocks are scattered throughout the borders of the forest, not the best place to stop and kneel for a while.

"You alright?" Her concern must be contagious.

She huffs a laugh. "If you were hoping to make me miserable, you've more than succeeded."

"You don't need to do this." The words slip from my mouth unbidden as my hand almost automatically reaches out to help her up.

It has nothing to do with her, *specifically*. I don't want to be the cause of anyone experiencing actual pain, no matter what they've done to me.

"I'm fine." She leans back on her heels, rubbing a little at her knees and assessing her handiwork. "Being a royal kid . . . Not easy, I take it?"

"Not my cup of cream, no." She snorts a laugh. "What?"

"Cup of cream? I've only heard the saying 'cup of tea'."

"Oh."

"I don't think they're even, but are we going for even?" she muses while eyeing my pant legs, mostly to herself.

Thank God I have nice feet. I almost can't take her scrutiny of my ankles.

"They're good." I shift in the brush, causing her fingers to graze my skin again. I'm ready to get back to the beach and get this over with.

"No, I think one's a little higher." Back on her knees, wincing, she reaches out but lets out a, *hey*! when I grasp her under both arms and haul her to her feet.

She wobbles, and I grip her by the elbows until she finds her footing. "They're fine," I say again, firmer. "I didn't realize you were such a perfectionist."

I want her to grovel. I want her to pay for the stunt she pulled a few months ago, but not on her knees. Watching her in even the slightest pain feels wrong and uncomfortable, even though I couldn't say why.

Our eyes pin together. *What are you doing?* she asks with her gaze.

I have no fucking clue.

"I like to get things right," she says slowly, pulling from the grasp I have on her.

Surprisingly, she didn't protest my touch this time. It must be because she's clearly going to have to get over the no touching rule —because, oil.

She zeroes in on my chest, assessing what she sees up close and personal. I can smell her, all berries and lavender mixed with the pine trees around us. And I know exactly what she's going to ask. "What does that say?"

"Nothing." I gulp and look past her shoulder at the camera on the beach.

"What language is it? Not English."

I cover the tattoo with a hand over my ribcage under my left pec, feeling very conspicuous while inches from her with no shirt. "Danish. Let's get this over with, Bloom."

Her head snaps up to meet my gaze, and there's a bit of hurt in her eyes. I've seen nothing but fierceness from this woman since the night we met in a nightclub months ago. There was attraction then, of course, but the flippant dance club kind that immediately dissolved once I got to know her. After she used me to get what she wanted.

"Fine." She opens the bottle of oil and pours a generous amount into her palms. "Hold this," she says, handing the bottle to me.

Uncertain where to start, she hesitates, and I suck in a breath. Why the fuck does her hesitation make me nervous?

Rubbing her hands together, her eyes traverse my body slowly. My shoulders, my chest, down one arm and up the other. I'm not sure if she's drawing this out on purpose or doesn't know where to start. Her gaze roams until she stops on my stomach, then slides down to my waist where my pants already sit low from riding in them all morning, a hint of red plaid boxers peeking out.

"Well, I think wardrobe is fine." She's still reluctant to begin her task, hands covered in oil. My chest moves rapidly, the anticipation speeding up my breathing as I gulp for air.

I'm afraid she's going to notice.

I take her by the wrist, unable to wait any longer. "Start here," I rasp, then place her palm right over the words wrapped around my ribcage in ink, the mantra I've repeated every night when I can't bear to wake up and begin another day—trapped.

Her palm is warm, small, and fitted against my side in such a way, I can't stop staring at it. An electric current races straight down my center.

She gasps, looking everywhere but at my face.

What the fuck is happening?

She moves and I flinch, gritting my teeth and rolling my eyes skyward while she drags her hand tentatively down my side, then more confidently up my stomach, and over my shoulders.

I stretch my neck long like Lola does when she really wants a pet, allowing her as much space as she needs until sure enough, her fingertips float all the way to my jaw.

She pauses and I hold my breath, covered in slick oil and standing barefoot in the woods.

Gripping my jaw, her eyes seem to ask a thousand questions when she forces me to look at her. She's struggling for control right now, but she also has no idea where to go next.

"Jesus, Bloom," I say on an exhale, grabbing her other wrist.

She looks down when I unfurl her fisted fingers and place her other palm on my stomach. My muscles flex and jump but not because I mean to show off this time—it's my body reacting to her touch.

Out of my control and unsteady.

With both her hands on me now, unmoving, she's a rabbit caught on a winding lake road. Paralyzed with no idea which way to go. I've never seen this woman unsure, and nowhere near timid. She's usually hollering at me, calling me 'pretty man,' and threatening me.

Finally, her gaze shifts, and I can tell she's back to herself. Back in control when she moves around my body, dragging both her hands across my delts, and down my spine to distribute the oil and make me nice and shiny for showtime.

"I need more," she whispers, her breath warm on my shoulder blades, my own chest still heaving as I suck in breath after breath.

After another pour, she doesn't hesitate, dropping her hands to my shoulders and massaging the oil deep into my traps where I carry a lot of tension.

It feels so good, and I moan a little despite myself while trying to focus on the massive tree trunk in front of me. And old polo stats. And my family creed, written by my forefathers that I was made to memorize at five years old to recite at royal functions.

This cannot be turning me on.

She cannot be affecting me like this.

But it is, and *she* is. Intentionally, I think.

She doesn't laugh. She doesn't taunt me. Instead, she increases the pressure, kneading into knots of tension I exercise vigorously to abate. I'm softening, leaning into her touch. I'm fucking melting, and if I could stop it, I don't even know that I would.

When she's finished with my back, she steps around me again.

"Oops," she says, much more in control of herself now. That makes one of us. "Missed a spot." Her hands glide up my front again, feather soft over my pecs, my collarbones, and up my neck. She holds my jaw in place again with her thumbs. A ghost of a smile on her lips. "Perfect."

"Excuse me?" I husk, my chest still pumping as her gaze holds mine. Anxiety builds in my stomach, and I don't know what's happening.

What is she saying, exactly? She likes what she sees? Does she actually like something about me?

"All done, pretty man." Both her hands land against my pecs with a loud smack that sounds like a crack of lightning echoing off the trees.

"Dammit, Bloom, that hurt," I yelp, rubbing at red welts on my skin.

She laughs the whole way back to the beach, where the camera waits for me by the water.

 Ten

WINTER

The morning progresses exactly as expected after that with cameras in my face, up my armpits, and way too close to my junk. The cameraman is doing his due diligence and getting all the skin shots they could ever want. At this point, America is going to know how many moles I have.

"More walking," Marco shouts. "Robbie, get him at an angle, too."

My mohawked shadow nods.

I've been walking up and down this beach for an hour. Any originally curious onlookers have long forgotten the cameras and ignore us. Robbie, the handsome man with the blue-tipped mohawk, is my personal tail. A few other cameras seem to be focusing on everything else around us, even the crew.

"Are we done yet?" I can't help but whine as I rub my chest, baby soft now after the oil treatment, and still a little sensitive after

Cat's smack. I do a few knee-high jumps to try and warm up. "I'm a fucking icicle."

"I am starting to pick up goosebumps," Robbie says as if it's a dire situation.

"Cat, warm him up!" Marco shouts. "We need a few taglines from him, then we can move inside and get ready for the formal interview."

She runs at me with a sleeping bag flowing behind her like a massive kite she's trying to launch, throws it around my shoulders, and pushes up on her tiptoes to rub at me vigorously.

"Cat got your tongue?" I ask when she says nothing about having to be my personal warmer.

"I hate it when people ask me that."

I huff. "Enjoying being my assistant that much, huh? You're in a lovely mood, Bloom." Ever since what happened in the trees, her face has been hard as stone when I look her way.

"I don't know what I did to deserve this hellish situation, but no, I don't have to like it. Right now, I have to get rid of your goosebumps."

She's still working me over with the sleeping bag like a mom drying their kids on the beach while the crew mills around and waits for my ass to dethaw. If I'd had a comforting mom, if I'd had anything like the picturesque childhood portrayed in the American reruns I watched with Annie growing up, this would be a charming moment.

My mouth forms a hard line. "You know exactly what you did."

She ignores me and says, "Why are you an ice block right now? It's not that cold out."

If she really wanted to warm me up, I know what would do it. The words are on the tip of my tongue: another oil session like we had in the trees. I hate to admit that I felt fire in my chest when her hands were on me. Normally, I'd joke about it. I'd ask her to dinner. I'd certainly acknowledge the fact we both felt something.

But I can't, not with Cat. For so many reasons, but most importantly, because this whole charade is about getting even, not *getting turned on.*

My emotions jumble as I will myself not to react now to her touch. With her close like this, her arms around my shoulders, I can admire the cupid's bow in her top lip. It's so pronounced. Thoroughly lick-able—when she's not grimacing. And she's not grimacing now, she's panting a little from the workout of rubbing me down as if her life depended on it. Her bossy mouth is popped open as she continues to breathe hard, and I want to trace that divot in her lip with my finger.

"Can you sit? You're too tall," she grouches.

I grin down at her. She's attractive when she's grumpy. I can despise her while still admitting that.

We move to a spot on the beach with a few chairs assembled in a circle as a makeshift break room, strewn with equipment and a green cooler full of water bottles. I plop on a folding chair and debate this miserable turn my life has taken. Just when I thought I was a run-of-the-mill, needy only child and reluctant prince, now it appears I'm a masochist who's attracted to my enemy, too.

A black knit beanie flashes in front of my face, pulled from her back pocket, I think, before she shoves it on my head and moves between my legs to continue rubbing at the blanket like I'm a wet dog.

My senses fill with lavender, and *her.*

I shake my head and try to think of something else. I could be in Ibiza on a yacht right now, surrounded by women who don't hate me. But then, I'd be surrounded by people who couldn't care less about me other than my useless title. At least here, I pay my dues when my parents demand it, but I get to live with a small group of friends who enjoy my company, in a town that has always sheltered me and ignored where I came from.

But what am I going to do about Cat Bloomfield?

"You're staring," she says.

"So?"

With all her physical effort to warm me, her sweater has slipped a little, and an intricate lace strap demands my attention. So does the dainty curve of her exposed shoulder.

She clocks my gaze and keeps rubbing. "Don't."

"You really shouldn't show your cards, Bloom." I'm not the only one physically reacting to our proximity, I'm just not trying to hide it. What's the point? But Cat is, and she has no game, breathing heavily, pupils blown. I'm a thirty-four-year-old man who enjoys the company of women. I can read the signs.

When I'm about to explain that we can hate each other and still feel physical attraction, that we're human and it's perfectly normal, she looks down at me. I look up. "Why are you doing this to me?"

My heart stutters in my chest, and I turn my head toward the water and the little island in Paradise Bay. When I was a kid, the guys and I used to swim out there and play pirates all day until Annie called us back for sodas and bowls of hot soup.

"Winter?" she prods.

I turn back to her. "I hate people like you. People who want power and fame. People who will do anything to get it. People who think they're entitled to take. People who step on others to get what they want." What I'm doing right now is reminding myself that I don't want anything to do with her.

I don't.

She takes a step back. "That's what you think of me?"

I hold her gaze and after a moment I reluctantly answer, "That's what I know about you."

She steps back further, her expression full of disdain. "He's all yours, Marco," she shouts, turning in the sand on the heel of her boot.

It seems we can't touch each other without fire and ice clashing to make a Molotov cocktail of emotions inside me. An unexpected kink in my plan, for sure.

I already knew she hated me, but she really hates me now that I've told her exactly what I think of her. It's for the best. Now, I can focus on getting through this ridiculous show, and move on with my life.

Cat Bloomfield hates me. So, what?

That was the point.

We shoot for another twenty minutes while Cat and Marco shout taglines at me. I have to say things like *I'm a prince, just looking for my princess* about a hundred times over.

When the sun hits the horizon, I'm hoarse and desperately need a shirt, and socks, and shoes. I never knew my feet could hurt from cold.

"Okay, Mr. Shivers, let's get you to the barn." Cat hauls a duffle bag to her shoulder. "Marco gave me your interview questions."

"*The barn?*" I protest, dropping my head and feeling seriously sorry for myself. I want a fire, an enormous blanket, and my bed—though, I wouldn't mind checking in on the horses.

Cat shakes her head at me. "Keep the theatrics up. I've dealt with worse, pretty man."

We make our way across the property but most of the crew stays behind. It's me, Robbie, Cat, and one assistant Cat calls to come with us toting a small basket.

Once inside, I take them on a tour of the space. "These are my horses." I gesture down the aisle of stalls, "The arena is off the side of the barn."

"How many?" Robbie switches lenses and hangs back, trying to give us some space.

"Six. Four of them are draft horses for sleigh pulling. And this is Daylight and her new baby, Destiny. Your sister was here when she was born."

"I heard about that." She follows me down the long hall with stable doors on either side, chandeliers lit up overhead, and the smell of straw and oats in the air.

She gets me settled in a mucked-out stall filled with fresh bedding next to my horse Daylight, one foot propped up on a haybale as if this would ever happen naturally in a horse barn, and begins reading questions off a piece of paper.

I look ridiculous.

"Okay, Winter, answer honestly. Stay relaxed," Cat says. She's all business now and pulls a pair of socks and my boots from the duffle bag she's carrying. She chucks them straight at my face.

I catch them and she scowls.

"Thanks," I say, pulling them on and groaning. It occurs to me she's got her own game of torture to play, she could have given me these on the beach. "Can I have a shirt now? *Please*?" I say through my teeth.

"You may." She pulls a sweater from her bag, hunter-green. Gone are the shaking hands and heavy breaths she had in the woods. She seems totally unaffected by our working relationship as if she's already gotten me out of her system by simply willing it to be so.

I wish I were that strong-willed. I also wish she hadn't somehow managed to flip the power dynamic between us so quickly.

"Shall I grovel at your feet in thanks?" I grumble under my breath as I drag the cozy knit over my head.

"Not necessary. Watching you suffer is enough. Ready, Robbie?"

The cameraman nods.

"Winter, tell us what it's like to be a real prince?" she asks sweetly.

Oh for fuck's sake. My horse grunts her agreement and I take a minute to press my forehead to hers before speaking.

"When you're ready," Robbie prompts.

"Royalty, at least for me, is about loving your country. Denmark's beauty is what I'm in love with. My little town of Skagen has a history of raising artists in a fishing village full of lively people. Hans Christian Anderson spent time there, and my great-grandmother wrote numerous diary entries about that time."

Who knows how long I go on. When I talk about my country, I always lose track of time. Until something catches my eye off camera.

It's Cat, dipping into a basket. "Am I boring you?" I holler so my voice will carry to the back of the barn.

Robbie huffs and turns to Cat, "I think I got enough. You good? I can go run this by Marco."

She's holding the basket with all our cell phones. Rummaging through it, and without a look, she says, "Yeah sure, we've got enough footage of him to last a lifetime. Thanks, Robbie."

I charge toward her. "Going through withdrawal?" I growl.

"Winter, you're mic'd. If I get caught I can't make this post."

"Are you leaking details about the show? It's a picture of me no doubt." I've come to terms with the fact I'm making a mockery of myself on national television. Hell, that's probably the real reason she took this job, to make me look bad. She's beating me at my own game.

She turns on me slowly, still looking at her phone and pecking at keys. "Of course, you think this is about you. Everything is about you, right, pretty man?"

I snag her phone.

"Hey!" she protests in a whisper yell.

Someone fake coughs.

We both freeze and look up. Robbie is watching, but all he does is laugh and walk out of the barn without another word.

When I look at Cat's screen I expect to see a post about me, or one of her doing some sort of silly dance for likes. But it's not. It's a post with a picture of an elderly couple holding up cups of coffee from behind a barista bar.

"What is this?" I ask.

She snatches her phone back. "It's my clients, the Rushmores.

I've handed most my projects off, but they need to up their foot traffic."

"So, you're posting from your account about a coffee shop? This has nothing to do with me?"

She rolls her eyes. "A struggling coffee shop. Their contract is up with Brand Hub, they couldn't afford to renew. So, I'm doing what I can to boost their special this week."

"Their special?" I ask incredulously. "Are we talking about lattes in . . . where is this quaint establishment?"

"They're in L.A. It's a tough market. Yes, we're specifically talking about a sugar cookie latte. Mrs. Rushmore puts sprinkles on top. And not the cheap tasteless kind, the good sugary kind."

"Can I help?" The words are out of my mouth before I can stop them.

Why does that keep happening to me around her?

"What?" she snorts, and her gaze snaps from her phone to meet mine. "You want to help?"

"I do. Is that so hard to believe?" It's hard for me to believe I'm offering to help her. This is not the plan.

"Yes, it is. And you can't, it's against your contract to use your image for any sort of promotion while you're on the show. You can't post on any media outlet while you're filming."

"And you can?"

"I'm not the one being married off by Streamflix." She glares at me and I catch something in the molten chocolate of her eyes, a punishment? She's mad at me, but not for the reasons I thought.

She hits send. I see a flash of the post and then she dumps her phone back in the basket.

I don't like having my hands tied, and I can't unsee those cheerful, wrinkled smiles holding that damn pretty sprinkle latte. The walls needed paint and the counters were scarred beyond charming.

And I can't un-know the fact that Cat Bloomfield is trying to help out of the goodness of her heart, not for personal gain of any kind.

Eleven

CAT

On Sunday, Little Star Lodge is quiet. The crew lazily stretches out in pajamas and hoodies around the bar listening to Marco's three-hour pump-up speech for the first date on *Royal Hearts*. Darcy struggles with sorting ornaments at her desk while watching *How the Grinch Stole Christmas!* on her laptop.

I sit off to the side with a cup of tea while stylists are assigned to get Winter's wardrobe confirmed and delivered to me for each date. Robbie gets instructions to follow Winter's every move, and I'm named the official liaison between Streamflix and Winter. We all pack it in early and with no phone and no doom scrolling, I sleep like a stone in a very fluffy bed.

Today, Little Star Lodge bellmen are back bright-eyed and bushy tailed for Monday morning, all wearing their caps knocked at an angle. Decorating has resumed, and they're in glitter mode, sparkle exploding from every corner the eye can spy. They seem poised to break out into song and dance any minute. I wouldn't put it past Darcy.

Liam takes my breakfast order at The Nook and has some very tart words to say about the skinny, sparkly tie with a grinning snowman he has to wear for the season. Along with my breakfast, he gives me some pages of a script he's writing. I promised to pass it on to a crew member on Streamflix's team who currently has a Hallmark movie deal and an agent. He's a determined kid, and I love him for it, so I swear to beg her for notes and give her his contact information.

"Cat, wait!" I'm headed out the door but double back to the front desk when Darcy calls out.

Holding my bagel in my mouth, I wrap my belt bag filled with oil, lip balm, dental floss, hand sanitizer, a small sewing kit, and a handful of Sharpies that always come in handy around my waist. During yesterday's meeting, we reviewed the promo footage from the beach and Marco doubled down on oil being the secret to any dating show. *Make them shiny whenever possible.*

He's not wrong. The way the light played against Winter's skin on camera, shadows cutting deep under each defined muscle, was something out of one of Willow's romance novels. So, I refilled the bottle and came prepared. I don't expect him to be shirtless on a date making cookies in a bakehouse, but then again with this brand of content, you never know.

Not that I'm looking forward to applying it again, despite a body that must be earned with a rigorous gym schedule, because I'm not—definitely not—looking forward to that.

The whole encounter with Winter in the trees was so awkward, so unnerving, that my hands were shaking the entire time. I hate that he noticed. It doesn't matter how built the man is, how he must torture his body day in and day out to achieve the cuts in his physique, the defined curves, and the hardened Adonis belt that forms a V dipping below his waistband, his personality is a dumpster fire of cocky entitlement.

And that's not hot no matter how you dress it up.

"Cat, I've got something for you," Darcy shouts again.

"Coming," I mumble through my bagel.

"I hid it and now I can't find it," she says when I reach the front desk.

Her laptop is tucked discreetly on a low shelf behind her, playing a movie. Today it's Tom Hanks and Meg Ryan yukking it up in a bookstore, and I give myself a moment to watch.

"Cat, we're loading in five!" Robbie's voice carries from the front door, and I catch a glimpse of his blue mohawk walking out the double doors.

"I'm in a hurry," I mumble through cranberry cream cheese, leaning across the front desk to see the movie better.

"Sorry, it's my ADHD. I had it two seconds ago but then I got distracted by the glitter pens."

"Can I get it later? It's our first full week on set and my mind is already in work mode."

"You've got mail," she says cheerily, clusters of jingle bells dangling from her ears.

"I know," I nod at her laptop, "I love that movie. I watch it every year around the holidays, too. Why don't they make movies like that anymore?" The pine scented candle on her desk only adds to the nostalgia and I breathe deep, thinking of bouquets of sharpened pencils, and stores with holiday trim in the windows.

"That's not what I mean." She rummages through a small pile of mail behind her adorned with pretty holiday stamps. "Well, yes, you caught me. Mornings are usually slow so I sneak in movies while I do office work, but here," she turns back with something in her hand, "you *literally* have mail."

Oh. Maybe from my sister?

She's supposed to be back from a buying trip for the motel

she's opening any day now. I'm pretty sure it's an engagement moon because I helped pick out the ring. The fact I love her boyfriend and I get to spend Christmas with her is the best present I could ask for. My sister is turning into Joanna Gaines, but I hope she doesn't have a hundred kids. I'm not cut out to be the charming aunt of ten. I fear too many sticky fingers and no personal space.

"Thanks," I say, finishing off my bagel and taking the creamy, heavy envelope Darcy hands me. It's got my name written in the most scrolly, rolly red calligraphy. "Did Santa send this himself?"

"No, but I am supposed to show you something else."

"Wha—" she rounds the desk and grips my elbow. "Darcy, I'm gonna be late." Why does she look so excited?

"Come with me." Her eyes light with mischief.

We walk out the doors and into the sunny, but notably colder morning. I rub my palms together and blow as I take in the mountains capped white with snow. "It's cold today."

"This is nothing. You're going to need a bigger coat. Didn't you bring a ski jacket?"

"Er, no. I was in a hurry when I left."

She drags me down the circle drive, past ornate statues of reindeer grazing on the lawn that sparkle with twinkle lights when the sun goes down. We come to a stop under the archway of Little Star Lodge at the end of the cobblestone street. Further down, the road turns a bit more rocky before you go through the pass. A tight squeeze between gargantuan mountains spits you out into two tiny towns below, smashed against each other on the state line of Nevada and California.

"Just a little further," she says with a skip in her step as we round a few trees and come to a small clearing. The sound of skittering animals is faint as pine needles under our feet crunch, and a view of untouched mountains stretches far and wide. It's breathtaking. "Here we are."

I stuff my hands in the pockets of my leather jacket. I really need to find some gloves. "What am I looking at?"

Little flurries of snow I hadn't noticed before are dancing around something that looks like—

"Your new mailbox."

A pretty wooden house stands before me, painted white with a red front door, black shutters bookending all the windows. It's got dormers popping up across the roofline each adorned with tiny wreaths and bows. Easily the size of a community mailbox for an apartment building, or maybe one of those Little Free Libraries Willow loves to troll neighborhoods in the Bay looking for.

"It looks like it could hold all of Santa's mail." I eye the substantial mount it's on, two posts dug deep into the ground with what looks like fresh dirt. "Why did you bring me to see this, albeit charming, mailbox, Darcy?" I check my watch and glance at the running Streamflix van at the top of the hill. It's filling with crew.

"It's from Winter."

"Excuse me? From Winter? For who? Whom?" I stutter, then take a breath to calm a pulse that has suddenly decided to sprint. "For what?"

Darcy pulls on the roof of the house and it creaks open on large brass hinges. The inside is huge and empty.

No, not empty. There's another thick cream envelope inside with my name on it.

I glance back up the cobblestone drive, exhaust spewing from the van while Marco stands outside, tapping a toe. "I don't understand, and I need to get going—"

Tearing open the first envelope from Winter because I want to know what I'm walking into here, I find exactly what I expected: a laundry list of requests, albeit in nice handwriting and I do see the word please, but who knows what's in the second one?

"Don't shoot the messenger," she holds her hands up in response to my short tone. I'm late, and now I'm jealous of her fingerless gloves. Those would be so handy if I still had a phone to peck at. "He said you needed a way to communicate."

I snatch the second envelope from the box and open it. "And this is his solution?"

Bloom,

Perhaps the art of letter writing isn't dead?

Winter

"I think it's kinda romantic. Laurie did this in *Little Women*. I watch that every winter, too."

"You would fit in well with my friends." I slam the box shut and start marching back up the mountain, stuffing both creamy envelopes into my nonexistent pockets.

What is Winter trying to accomplish with this? I stop in my tracks: *has he seen Little Women?* I don't have time to psychoanalyze what that means. I have to get to work.

Clearly, this little stunt is supposed to appear charming, to appear thoughtful, but I know that sort of thing isn't in his DNA. So, what? Is he making fun of me? Is it a joke?

Darcy tries to keep up with my pace. "What sister do you identify with most? I'm a Meg. *Definitely,* a Meg." She rolls her eyes but smiles. "You're a Jo, I think. Which version have you seen?" She trots alongside me, ready to make a case for a classic novel that I do, in fact, love to watch in every film adaptation in existence every holiday season.

"Actually, I'm pretty sure I'm an Amy," I say, my boots crunching harder into the snow as I stomp. "Tell him no thanks. I'll do messages at the desk and that's it."

"But, but," she stammers.

"I don't do letters. I don't do silly little stunts meant to mess with my head." Nope. Whatever he's planning, I am not taking the bait.

"But it's *romantic!*" You'd think I'd told her I don't breathe air, the way she's looking at me.

"I don't do romantic, Darcy."

"We're starting big," Marco's jazz hands and general energy is enviable. "Big set, big, sweeping, romantic dates, all the vibes—until one of them starts to click." The crew and I are getting a talking-to before the contestants arrive, and I hold back vomit just thinking about a woman falling for Winter.

Best of luck, she's gonna need it.

"I thought this was a live stream?" I ask, still not understanding the need for a 'set'.

"It is, but we'll open every shot with a specific date, then we'll follow them for the duration after. We air three days a week, and can cut from time to time. They'll swap in sponsored ads, then right back to live streaming. Got it?"

"Got it, boss." I salute him.

"Where's our mark?" Robbie asks.

"Here, behind the counter. The pots and pans in the background give a real working kitchen look."

It's because we're in a real working kitchen, the bakery of Little Star Lodge. There are a few checkered tables and a pass-through window for ski-up orders. It's at the bottom of the first lift and opens every morning at the crack of dawn with hot peppermint mocha coffee, strudel, and egg sandwiches wrapped in foil for early bird shredders.

If I thought I was freezing at the base of the mountain this morning, I'm a Popsicle up here.

"What are we doing about the staff?" I ask as bakers and servers buzz around the small kitchen all wearing striped red aprons and cheerful, if not a bit sleepy, expressions.

I scoot a little closer to a hot oven behind me to keep warm and inhale the cardamom and cinnamon in the air.

"They're in the shot. We've already gotten approval from the lodge."

The worktable is littered with shiny silver cookie cutters, piles of pre-made sugar dough, and bowls of icing, sprinkles, and edible glitter.

"Where do you want me?" Winter saunters through the front door, kicking his boots on the rug to knock off the snow. These boots are ankle-high and trimmed in fur. If I saw another man wearing boots like these, I'd think he looked ridiculous. Pretty boys, the ones who care more about their hair than I do, are not my type. And that is Winter Larsen. His hair is styled perfectly into a rolling wave that clearly took effort, with caramel streaks running through his sandy blonde locks. Not my type at all.

Except if I'm being honest, those boots, his fitted pants bunching slightly at the ankle, and the thin cashmere sweater stretching across his toned chest somehow work.

Until I see his hands.

"What are you wearing?" Marco asks. I'm guessing he sees what I see.

"Cozy mountain gear," Winter replies without hesitation, as if we're dense and wouldn't know a sweater from swim trunks.

Ass. He's being obtuse on purpose. "But what's on your fingernails?" Marco presses.

"Did you paint your nails?" I say with a raised eyebrow, speaking only to him. This is not part of the preppy prince image the styling team is going for.

He shrugs. "I was feeling a little blue, Bloom."

"Get him in wardrobe," Marco says. "Most of it's fine, but we need some plaid. And, sorry Winter, but lose the blue nail polish. Doesn't track with the image we're going for. More Prince William, less Prince Harry."

His jaw ticks and I can tell he's struggling to maintain his care-free expression. "Have you all turned on my man, Harry?"

Dear God, is he friends with every famous Harry on the planet? When all this is over please let me never forget that my job was once gofering for this idiot. I've stooped as low as I intend to ever go.

"Come with me," I groan.

Winter waggles his eyebrows toward Marco as if to say *what's his problem,* like we're in this together, as he follows me down a tiny hallway.

Twelve

CAT

I spin to face him outside the all-gender bathroom. "Seriously, blue nails?" He smiles, devil may care, but looks away. "You've been briefed by Streamflix, you know what's expected of you."

My words are curt, but this is how I work. Yes, I try to be a bit softer with clients who need it, like the Rushmores, but Winter does not need coddling.

"What's wrong with a man expressing his feminine side?" His gaze finally swings back from an intense study of the all-gender bathroom sign to meet mine.

God, the bravado rolling off him could seduce someone in seconds if they didn't know what a jerk he is. But there's something underneath it that he doesn't want me to see, a vulnerability to his words and actions.

"It's unexpected, I'll give you that." There. That's playing nice.

His smile falters and he bites his lip. "Do we have to remove it?"

Whatever he's trying to hide, his façade is slipping. He's nervous, and something inside me can appreciate the position he's in and how terrifying it must be. He's already mentioned he doesn't like cameras.

But I shrug. This is the job we both signed up for. "You heard Marco. It's not the image we're going for."

He takes my comment as sarcasm, which in this case, it wasn't. "Give me those then, if I'm so repugnant to you." He pulls a plaid vest and scarf off my shoulder that I selected from wardrobe specifically to highlight the intense blue in his eyes.

His shift from arrogant to wounded throws me.

"Winter, wait." I can't say I'm sorry, because I have no idea what's going on here. "Is this all about blue nail polish? Do we need to find a more private place to shoot? Are you," I hedge because I'm not sure how honest he'll be with me. Probably not at all. "Are you that nervous about filming?"

"No." His eyes drop to his boots.

That was a yes. It's odd watching a confident man unravel before my very eyes and before I let any emotion in, I remind myself he's the reason I'm here, carrying his boots and gofering his breakfast. And now I need to find nail polish remover on the top of a mountain.

Still, I stupidly feel sorry for him despite the fact he thinks I'm someone who uses people. Someone who doesn't care. Maybe it's time he realizes how wrong he is.

"I didn't mean to hurt your feelings. Is the polish like, what, a crutch or something?"

"If you must know, it's a visual reminder. Helps me focus. I've been doing little things like this since I was a kid, when I had to make a public appearance."

I've seen pictures on the internet of him as a kid. A sandy-blonde-haired boy yawning and earning glares from his mother, sitting on his grandmother's knee in a velvet coat, stopping to tie his shoe in a parade on the streets of Denmark.

"I'm sorry. I didn't mean to be dismissive about it. I'm sure Marco didn't either."

"You could have fooled me. We can't mess with the brand, now can we?"

"What do you expect?" I throw my arms out wide. "You signed up for this to torture me with lists of demands hidden in secret mailboxes in the middle of a snowy mountain."

"The mailbox is whimsical. Some might even say," he pauses and I swear, if he says romantic— "helpful."

I can't even think about the mailbox right now as he gazes at me, waiting.

"What?" I shake my head, trying to make sense of the energy rolling off him. I thought he was all cocky confidence but, he's more tumultuous than that, deeper than that. Seems I might have misjudged him—*a little*— just like he's wrong about who I am.

"I didn't do this," he wiggles his big hands with long fingers tipped in blue in front of my face, "to make your life difficult this morning. It's my way of dealing with being an object. First, I was a son who had a duty. Now I'm on a reality show to find a wife because the Crown's aggressively selfish team thinks my country hates me."

Blindly, I sink into those intense blue eyes and try to make sense of the words that tumbled so freely from his lips. "That was a lot of personal information."

"I've made a lot of questionable decisions lately, Cat. I thought I could handle this and play the game my way."

"What's changed?"

"That's just it, I don't know." He leans back against the door. "And last night, this was my distraction." He runs a hand through hair that has darkened since he was a boy in those pictures, now with more golden caramel streaks. A muscle in his neck flexes. "I guess I didn't realize how real this was going to be."

I lift my chin and square my shoulders. I've got to pull him out of this spiral, we're filming in minutes. "I think I can help—at least with the nail polish. Getting women to fall in love with you? That's all you."

"You don't believe I can make someone fall in love with me, yet your reputation depends on it."

"If it elevates Brand Hub and gets you out of my hair once and for all, I'll help you any way I can."

"What about long after the show, when your sister's married to my best friend?" he tries.

"Then I'll be more than kind to your wife because I know what she deals with every day."

He chuckles, mostly to himself. "Now that sounds like team spirit. And just think," he stands tall and looks down at me, "what would you be doing without me right now? Dancing for your fans?"

"Nope, you don't get to judge me." I start down the hall to look for some acetone as quickly as possible in a bakehouse full of hot chocolate and frosting.

"Cat, wait." I hate that I stop and turn around.

"What now?" I groan.

"Despite the fact you're trying to help your clients, I think you've got a lot more to offer than selling your soul for fame on the internet. You're commanding, charismatic, and," he shrugs, "people seem to like you."

His words hit me in the face and roll down my body like I've taken a strong drug. He's wrong, of course—fame has nothing to do with it—even if it did, to each their own. And his delivery is one of those double-edged compliments that hurt as much as help. If I could drop off the face of the internet and still do my job, I would.

But his praise, the part where he thinks highly of me, wraps around me like a warm glove. I hate that his opinion of me, given so freely and honestly, affects me the way it does.

My feet move of their own accord and I march right up to him, my heart pumping hard. He pushes his shoulders back, standing tall, matching my energy.

"Of course, that's what you think, but it's not about fame." *Why do I care to set him straight?* "You take one look at me, you stalk me on socials—don't deny it—and you've got me pegged. But let me tell you," I reach behind him and open the door to the restroom. It's a single, and thankfully no one's in there, "You're wrong."

"What are you doing?" he balks but lets me push him a few steps back toward the door.

"I'm coming in there to peel that polish off your fingers. We're out of time and on top of a mountain."

"I'll do it," he says.

I grab his wrist and hold up his hand. "With what nails? You've bitten them down to the quick." That gives us both pause. There's a truth here. The nail polish and nail biting are physical signs of stress and anxiety.

His lips form a firm line, a muscle ticking in his jaw.

"Winter, it's going to be okay." My heart goes out to him while my head is at war with what I know of him. He may come off cocky and confident on the outside, and he may think he's got me all figured out, but I think he's as confused as the rest of us.

"Is it?" he asks, with no hint of sarcasm. An honest question.

"Yes," I say. "Get in there." When he doesn't move I add, "March."

"God, you're so, so fucking—" he says, letting me push him back even more so I can follow him in.

"So fucking what?" I ask over my shoulder while adjusting the tap to warm and pumping a generous amount of peppermint hand soap into my hand.

"*Det er et helvede!*" He slams the door.

But in a short time, I've become accustomed to his moods and I think he's as humored as he is angered in this moment. "Get dressed." I nod for him to put the vest and scarf on while I wait for the water to warm. "I've scrubbed a thousand temporary tattoos, stray marker, and ballpoint pen off my sister. This is going to be right up my alley. Push up your sleeves."

"You are full of surprises, Bloom."

A knock sounds on the bathroom door.

Winter opens it roughly, his features blazing with indignation.

Robbie appears in the doorway, camera on his shoulder. "Marco said to tell you, English only," he says directly to Winter.

"What?"

"You used Danish."

"How do you know?" He seems genuinely surprised and it wipes more of the tension away for both of us. We've been caught sparring, speaking totally unprofessionally to each other.

"Cat's already mic'd."

Oh no, I forgot. Who knows how much they heard? "You did," I offer. "You said something that wasn't English two seconds ago. And the second mic packs are turned on they're recording."

"Tell Marco, apologies. I didn't realize I was doing it. It comes out every now and again."

Robbie merely nods and goes on his way.

"Winter," I soften my voice when he closes the door quietly, "let me do this, and then you can meet us in the kitchen." I can deal with his eccentricities like any other difficult client. "Hands, please."

He pushes up his sleeves and drops his hands to rest on top of mine in the sink.

Our shoulders press together in the tiny bathroom and we glance up at our reflection in the mirror. I tense, smelling clove and citrus and a bit of smoke on him. I wonder if he's got a penchant for burning candles.

He turns his head toward mine, breath hot on the shell of my ear. "Is this what you wanted?"

Unable to tear my eyes away from him in the mirror, I watch

his reflection, taking stock of his strong jawline and the vulnerable twist to his lips.

"You know this isn't what I meant." The moment turns intimite, how do we keep finding ourselves in these tight-knit situations?

"But is it okay?" It's a whisper, and the room shrinks while my stomach bottoms out. He presses his shoulder more firmly into mine, standing at my side, and that seems to help him relax as he releases a long breath.

Is it okay? I hurt his feelings earlier, feelings I didn't know he had. And I feel like a jerk taking his polish off if it is his way of dealing with anxiety. Despite wishing I didn't feel this connection with him, I want to give him a little comfort in return.

"It's fine." The shiver running the length of my spine says otherwise. It's fight or flight, a reaction to being in a small space with a man I thought I hated.

But now, I guess hate is too strong a word. I don't like him, that's for sure, but I don't dislike him so much that I want to see him suffer. See him struggle with worry about what he's signed up for. The show is a big deal. Anyone with a pulse would be nervous.

I take his fingers, letting the warm water wash over our hands, and gently peel at the thick blue polish. It comes off his large thumb easily in one smooth sheet, which is oddly satisfying.

"How many coats did you do?"

"Four."

"Two, Winter. Two is the number."

"Noted."

"Why didn't you want to be in your country? As a kid?" He slipped into Danish so easily, and without realizing it.

"It was hard being ignored all the time, and I was pissed." More truths coming from him faster than I can process his honesty. It's jarring compared to how we've interacted in the past, but not terrible.

"Pissed at . . ."

"My parents, my lot in life, my voice in my head because I was alone all the goddamn time. I had to get out. I was suffocating under the weight of expectation, only to fail over and over and over. Alone. My parents only ever showed up to tell me I'd tied my tie wrong for the benefit, or made a sour face in the photos, or stumbled over a word in my speech. The criticism became paralyzing."

My hands freeze when he leans more heavily into my shoulder, the full length of our arms now pressed together. He seems desperate for connection, for support, and that makes me epically sad for him.

Mentally, I shake myself from thinking about a poor little prince, all alone in a castle, and keep working all the polish off his nails. "That's a lot."

His proximity isn't an advance or a challenge, it's sadness, pouring from his body and raining down onto mine. I'm not even sure he knows what he's doing, much like slipping into another language without meaning to.

He straightens, going still before pulling hands that have been polish-free for some time from mine. "You asked," he says, defensively.

I turn into him, regretting the move instantly because he turns into me at the same time, dropping his hands against either side of the sink. I'm pinned in place with nowhere to hide.

He doesn't step back and my chest presses against his. My heart goes from thumping to outright pounding in my ears when I look up into a pool of sad blue.

"I didn't mean it like that," I say, a little disappointed with myself that his first thought was that I was judging him. "That's a lot for a kid to deal with."

"Thank you."

I shrug and release a breath, "You're welcome."

His shoulders soften, his eyes searching mine with a question he won't ask. Then he takes a step back, releasing me. "Personal space, remember?"

"I think we're well past that." I wiggle my fingers at him, bits of blue nail polish still clinging to my skin. He smiles, a real smile, and it feels like I've been given a gift.

"I'll change, and be out in a minute. Ready to put on a show."

"One more thing." After drying my hands, I dig into my fanny pack and pull out one of my black permanent markers. "Give me your hand."

He hesitates, patting his hands dry on his pants, then gives me his right hand. His palm is heavy in mine and I flip it over, noting calluses and veins that run up his strong forearm as I gently push his sleeve back up to expose the inside of his wrist.

I don't think, I just draw. A tiny black heart.

"What's this?" he asks, pulling his wrist away to inspect the drawing himself. It's not perfect, uneven sides and all, but I colored it in and it's a solid if not permanent tattoo on his skin.

"It's not blue nail polish, but it's something to ground you. If you get nervous, press that spot and remember why you're doing this."

"Why am I doing this?" he rasps without looking up, rubbing the little heart with the pad of his thumb.

"I have no idea."

The bakehouse is busy when Winter strides out with his usual swagger back in place. The women of *Royal Hearts* are here in all their glory, after being primped and polished at the Lodge. They rode the ski lift up the mountain and look positively frozen, but no worse for the wear.

"Ladies," I say, when I realize it's up to me to give them the rundown, "we'll have you line up here behind the counter. You're making cookies with Winter today. It's our first date so just be yourselves. Any questions?"

All five of them yawn and simultaneously shiver. A few reapply lip gloss. One is eyeing Robbie as if he's a peppermint stick she wants to lick.

This should be interesting.

"Quiet on set!" Marco calls when we've got Winter at the counter, polish-less hands already working a snowball's worth of dough with the women at his sides.

Every once in a while, he presses a thumb into the heart on his wrist.

"We're getting a good mix of whimsy and rustic-chic vibes, you know, ski season and life on the mountain," Marco says under his breath. "People are going to be into this for the holidays."

The kitchen ignores us, a server sliding the passthrough window open and taking a hot chocolate order from a cute couple. This is a reality show but Marco seems determined to treat it like a storyboard.

Robbie swings by me along with a few other cameras in the room to get a good shot.

"Hey, Robbie?" I tap on his shoulder and he stops to listen while keeping his camera pointed at Winter. "If you've got any creative connections at Streamflix, I know a guy who's looking to break in as a screenwriter."

"That Liam guy? The waiter at The Nook?"

"You know him? I'm connecting him with that writer on the crew with the Hallmark deal, too."

"I've noticed him, um, yeah. I'll see what I can find out and let you know."

"Thanks, Robbie. You're a gem."

"Do we have any direction for the contestants?" Marco drags an exasperated hand down his five o'clock-shadow. The cookie-making setup is epically boring. Winter looks asleep on his feet and no one is talking much.

Robbie shrugs. "We've been live for a few minutes now."

Winter and the ladies are all standing around the table. "Should we start?" Winter asks.

"It's not that kind of show!" Marco bellows. "We have started!"

Winter shrugs, looks at me. "Oh, I didn't realize we're on—"

"Just . . . Rolling!" Marco says, dragging a hand down his face while clutching a clipboard for dear life.

It's as if a switch is flipped in the women. They start pressing rolling pins across the counter, everyone leans in, and they gasp and giggle though no one has said a word yet.

"What's happening," I whisper, looking up at Robbie, his camera perched on his opposite shoulder now.

"Usually contestants on shows like this are hoping for second place. Aspiring actresses or models or entrepreneurs. You know that, right? This is kinda like an audition."

"Seriously? Is that how it is for all the shows?" I mentally scan through the reality dating shows I've watched on the couch with Willow and Frannie over the years, from the corner of my eye while glued to my phone.

Robbie snorts. "I didn't peg you as a romantic."

"I'm not, but I've watched these shows, and some of the couples make it. Right?"

Winter chuffs a laugh in my direction, making eye contact with me while a blonde whispers in his ear. My chest gets all light and flippy. Was he listening? Why is he watching me, and not looking at the woman next to him?

"So, what brings you all to my little mountain oasis?" he asks the ladies, still looking directly at me instead of them. He sounds nothing like himself, or at least nothing like the guy I spoke at length with in the bathroom.

"I love cookies," a brunette woman on his right purrs.

"Really?" Winter rolls a tiny ball of dough in his hands and holds it up to her glossy mouth.

She opens wide and he drops it on her tongue. "And you are?"

"Mmm," she murmurs. "I'm Mandy."

"I'm Lexi H. Can we go have a chat somewhere a little more private?" The blonde woman on his left takes his arm and before Winter can respond, she's pulled him toward the front door.

But another woman jumps in their path. "I'm Lexi A. from Alabama!"

Lexi H. ignores her, opening the door of the bakehouse and letting a gust of frigid mountain air blow through.

"Things seem to be moving fast, Lexi. I'm not sure I'm that kind of guy." Winter laughs but allows himself to be manhandled out the door.

"Lexi H.," she corrects. She's wearing the most ridiculous blue furry boots that look like that abominable snowman in that old Christmas cartoon. What was that one called? When I look at her feet all I can see is that squirrely cobalt yeti face.

"Where does she think she's going?" I hiss. "We've just started, no one's even used a cookie cutter yet!"

"Follow them," Marco whisper-yells, rushing by me and struggling with his coat.

We all follow Winter and Lexi H. outside to the ski lifts. "Wanna go up?" she asks, wrapping herself around him like a warm pretzel.

"Er. We don't have skis," Winter replies, glancing at Robbie and his camera.

"Yes, you do," I pipe up, then shoot a horrified look at Marco and Robbie, I'm still mic'd and I don't want a guest role on this show. But Marco nods vigorously and shoos me toward the skis and boots we ordered for Winter and all the contestants for exactly this purpose.

Mentally, I pat myself on the back for being prepared while ducking under the camera and waddling toward them in a sort of squat, tossing the boots at their feet.

"What are you doing, Bloom?" Winter asks, eyes wide and full of mirth.

"Staying out of the shot," I hiss.

Winter's gaze cuts to Robbie's camera. "I don't think so."

"Whatever, just, put your boots on and grab your skis over there." I point to a ski rack that's mercifully empty except for Winter's custom skis and a few pairs for the women.

"I'm a size eight." Lexi H. frowns at her size nine rental boots, then shrugs. "Oh well, these'll work." She kicks off the yeti boots in a flourish.

I breathe a sigh of relief, I have an assortment of boots behind me in a bin and I'd guessed at her size in an effort to stay off camera. The thought of appearing in the organic shots as they were described to us is my worst nightmare and I'm trying my best to lay low.

Before I can say 'elf on a shelf,' we're jumping on the lift and following these two nitwits who've popped on skis up the mountain.

"Keep your camera on them," Marco shouts as he drops into the chair with me, and we're whisked off our feet.

We let Robbie take the lift right after Winter and Lexi H. so he has the best shot of the prince on his first official date on *Royal Hearts*.

"What the hell is this woman's angle?" I growl to Marco. I'd rather not be freezing my ass off on a lift right now, we were supposed to be in a cozy bakeshop all day.

"Way to be prepared with Winter's skis, by the way," Marco says.

"Thanks. Is she trying to get frostbite?" I ask, incredulous.

The girl didn't stop to put a coat on. She's wearing a hot pink turtleneck, a bright white puffer vest, and thin leggings.

"She's trying to nab a crown," Marco laughs as if I should know this. "Or maybe a spinoff show as runner-up. Either way, she's already winning. They always go off script, always off set for a *private chat.*"

Marco rubs his palms together, grinning from ear to ear. I wonder if his hands are cold? Or if he's hoping we've struck reality TV gold? Probably both.

But as I watch Winter, backed by snowy mountains, tall emerald green pine trees, and skiers flying down the mountain beneath us, I notice his body language looks off.

Instead of a cocky grin turned toward his impromptu date, instead of dropping an arm around the woman and chatting her up like I'd imagine he would, he's gripping the bar in front of him and looking skyward. Not at the attractive woman next to him, not at all, as she continues to yammer and make eyes at the camera.

Thirteen

WINTER

Breathe, fucker. Breathe. This cannot be the image I project.

My mom and dad know I'm afraid of heights. If they're watching they'll realize I'm on the brink of a melt-down right now. I hope they never watch, because if I have to hear my father say, *mind over matter, Winter,* one more time—

"And then I traveled to Ibiza—" Lexi H. has been talking non-stop, I don't think she's even noticed my freak-out. Good. Hopefully, no one has noticed. I just need to make it off this lift in one piece without screaming.

"I've been thinking about getting my captain's license and sailing to Ibiza," I manage to grunt out, the opposite of dashing while clinging to a safety bar.

"Ooooh, a captain. That's sexy. Ahoy, my matey," she winks.

I offer her a tight smile, the best I can do while I press my thumb into a black heart on my wrist so forcefully that it'll surely leave a bruise.

But it appears I've fallen behind in the conversation because she goes on, "Three kids really is the magic number. People say two, but I think it's three. I have two sisters and when one of us is being a raging bi—, I mean, brat," she smiles sweetly over her shoulder at Robbie and his camera, "there's a tiebreaker sister to say who's right and who's crazy—I mean, shit that word's been canceled, right?" She turns in her chair, rocking the tiny thing precariously enough to make me want to call for Annie. Whimper her name like Mommy, but I haven't got that type of mommy that would come running, so I'd call Annie . . .

"Hey!" she yells to Robbie, about twenty feet behind us. I risk a glance and feel my heart jump into my throat. Bad idea, Winter. Eyes on the sky. "Can you edit that out? I don't want people to hear me say crazy. *Crazy's* been canceled."

This fucking woman.

"Almost there," I breathe, when I see the lift crest the top of the pulley system, the tracks coming into sight under my skis, almost there.

"So, three kids works for you, right? Is that enough for a royal? I mean, heir and a spare plus one has to be good enough, right?"

My skis hit the snow with a crunch, and I push off with my poles heading straight to a cabin dotted with benches and heat lamps where people stop to warm up. My heart races and my stomach is throwing an absolute fit.

I push the tip of my pole into the back of my ski, then the other. And I'm out.

Lexi skis up alongside, pulling an impressive hockey stop that scatters snow across my boots as I drop to a bench. The air is too thin up here.

"Where are you going?" Sun glints off her perfect teeth, nearly blinding me.

"I can't breathe," I rasp, dropping my head in my hands.

"Oh." Reluctantly, she pops her skis off and sits next to me.

Rubs my back. It's nice. "I'm feeling it, too," she says, right into the shell of my ear.

I pull back and try not to vomit all over her. My guts are pushing up my sternum. It's a panic attack I've felt a few times when I've gone too high, my vertigo kicking in and making me wish I was dead. "Wait, um, Lexi."

Desperately, I push up my sleeve and press my thumb so hard into Cat's heart, I have to bite down to bear it. But it grounds me, and the slight pain gives me something to think about other than my queasy stomach and lack of oxygen.

"Lexi H. There are three Lexis here," she says.

Even through my dizzy vision and rolling stomach, I pat myself on the back for getting her name right.

"Lexi—"

"Yes, baby—"

My head snaps up. "Did you just call me baby?"

"How about, you call me baby," she giggles. "Lexi baby, that's what I like to be called. I'm a feminist, we ask for what we want. And you should like that about me, because now you know how to make me—"

"Oh God," I groan, as my throat tightens. I try to gulp down some air, searching for ways to settle my stomach and my mind, but she keeps talking.

"I know. I know," she moans, clocking Robbie as he comes to a stop in front of us—*oh, dear Lord, she's leaning in.*

I lean away but the woman stretches like taffy on the bench, up to her knees and long-necked like a goose on the lake. Her lips are seconds from hitting mine. I can't think how to push her away without looking like a real asshole, but I'm gonna puke if she breathes on me again and—

"Cut!" Cat yells, running up to us.

"Excuse me?" Lexi H. demands, her hands wrapped around both my cheeks and staying put as her eyes swivel slowly to Cat.

"You can't yell cut!" Marco bellows, coming off a lift not far away. "We're streaming!"

"You called action," Cat hurls back at him, then takes a knee, getting on eye level with me and my date. "Lexi, he's about to spew all over you."

"Commercial!" Marco yells to no one in particular, tossing his clipboard in the air. It hits the snow with a smack.

Cat's enjoying this, smirking through her words, eating my embarrassment with a spoon. Still, I'm not mad that she's intervening. In fact, at this moment, Cat Bloomfield feels heaven-sent.

"What?" Lexi rears back.

"Here," Cat chucks a bottle of water in my hand, already open and sloshing over my knuckles as if she's read me like a book and knows there's no time.

"Ohmigodthankyou," I blurt as I dump the thing down my throat. Then I drop my head between my legs and try to breathe.

"What's wrong with him? I seriously doubt you could captain a ship if a ski lift makes you this sick." The disgust in Lexi's voice is so acidic, I realize I'm fucking up the show without even trying.

"He's got vertigo," Cat says calmly. "Give us a minute." She stands, rubbing the arms of her flimsy leather jacket and huffs as if she's got zero patience for the situation.

The commanding tone of Cat's voice sends Lexi H. scurrying.

Water helps. So does the quiet. Also, Cat's fingertips which are currently squeezing my left earlobe give me something to focus on while I try to rein in the spins.

"Heights, huh?" Cat drops onto the bench next to me. "Not so cocky now, are you, pretty man?" She averts her eyes when she sees my thumb still pressing into the heart on my wrist.

"That's helping."

"The ear? Good. It's an old trick."

"One you've used, personally?" I ask.

"Maybe. I don't struggle with anxiety often but I loved skiing when I was little. Sometimes the mountain got to me. The thought of racing down a black diamond was a terrifying challenge that I was obsessed with conquering, despite the thought making me sick—I have an emotional stomach. This helped."

"And you prevailed."

"I did."

"I'm not cocky, by the way. I prefer confident. There's a difference." She makes a sound as if she's begrudgingly agreeing with me and I peek up at her, pressing my forearms to my knees to get a good look at her face.

"My dad has vertigo, too. And when we skied as a family, my mom always pinched his ear when he felt an episode coming on."

"Must be nice, to have someone to lean on like that."

"Yeah," her voice softens, "must be."

My vision stills, no longer blurry, and I watch her watching the lift a few yards off in the distance. When I follow her gaze, I notice Robbie has backed off, his camera still on his shoulder making sweeps of the scene probably for a montage or something.

Still, I know better. "I don't want to talk about this while we're mic'd."

She's shivering and lets out a long sigh through chattering teeth. "You should have put that in your contract: no heights. They're not paying attention to us. The date's over."

I peer at Robbie again. Everyone's mic'd, everyone signed NDAs, they're filming everything and she's lying to herself if she thinks she's going to be excluded for some reason.

"Why'd you get on the lift?" she presses.

"Why don't you have a decent coat?"

"Why are you evading my question?" She turns her chocolate gaze on me and I think of some fancy pots of fondue, dipping strawberries through hot, thick, chocolate and then denying her a taste. "Scared to answer?"

Damn, I'm attracted to her. There's no rationalizing it or denying it.

I shake my head, trying to banish all thoughts of chocolate.

"It's been a while since I've tried and I thought, maybe today was the day I'd conquer the fear. Not quite."

"What else are you afraid of, Winter Larsen?" Whether she knows it or not, she's allowing me to scoot a little closer to her.

I square my shoulders to block the wind. "Not telling unless you give me one of yours. I already endeared myself to you in the bathroom today."

"Now, that's something you don't hear every day," she quips, maybe as uncomfortable as I am with how sincere our conversations seem to be getting every time we speak.

"It's only fair. Otherwise, you hold all the power."

She stops rubbing my ear as if she realized what she was doing. "Power, of course, that's what this is about for you. Every time I think you're not a total monster—"

"It's only natural for me to ask your insecurities if I'm going to bear my own." It's what I want people to see, the Winter she's talking about. And I should let her go on thinking she's right.

"Well, I hate to tell you: I don't have any fears, not since I was a kid. Fears are for weak people." She cups her hands and blows into them, her tiny fingers white with cold.

"No fear, hmm? You better watch out, you're going to get canceled with that kind of talk. Stephen would have a field day with you."

"Stephen?"

"Life coach, and personal trainer."

"Of course," she says sarcastically. "All those muscles bought and paid for."

I ignore her jab and take the compliment, "You like my muscles?" I ask, puffing up my chest a little for her.

She punches me on the shoulder. "Good thing I'm not a contestant and it doesn't matter what I like."

I scoot a touch closer, watching her shiver, desperately wanting to wrap my arms around her—enemy or not. "Good thing. Except, you've revealed your biggest fear anyway."

As much as I'd like to press her about liking my body, and how I keep finding ways to touch her and she keeps letting me, I dig a little deeper. In a shocking turn of events, I sincerely want to know what makes this woman tick.

"What?"

"Weakness. Cat Bloomfield thinks she has to be the strongest person in the room, horribly afraid of appearing weak. I wonder why that is?"

She tries hard to keep her features neutral, but I see it. I've hit the nail on the head.

"Just because you say it out loud, doesn't make it true." She straightens her back and lifts her chin. "You don't know anything about me."

Those deep brown eyes ignite, daring me to argue with her. I'm more than happy to oblige. "I know you're freezing your ass off and even that is a show of strength for you."

She sniffs, unaffected. "I didn't have time to get a winter coat."

I bite down on my molars.

That doesn't track with the prima donna I've made her out to be in my head. That woman would have taken care of herself first, before worrying about posting for a tiny coffee shop in L.A., if the owner of her small agency succeeded, or if her roommate was okay with her being gone over the holiday.

"I'm sorry, you're right. I don't know anything about you, do I?"

She turns to me, little flecks of ice in her hair from the flurries floating around us, "Really? You're admitting you're wrong and I'm right?"

There's still fire in her eyes, but maybe a little curiosity as she regards me, too.

Maybe I'm confusing her as much as she's confusing me.

When I don't respond, at a loss for what to say next, she stands and walks off.

The rest of the women have made it to the top of the mountain, hovering in clusters with steaming cups in mittened hands sporting eager faces. Cat points one of them back to me with a big smile on her face.

Robbie catches on and starts my way.

I drain the last of my water and crunch the bottle in my fist.

Dammit, Bloom.

Fourteen

CAT

Weak?

He doesn't know me at all!

I throw my feather duvet off and sit up in the middle of the night.

Winter's words are plaguing my mind like a trending sound you can't escape—even though he backed off and apologized. Still, I can't unhear him commenting on my personality so decidedly.

Cat Bloomfield is afraid of weakness.

Shit. He was wrong about me wanting fame and attention, but this rings true enough deep down. How did I let that show? That detail about me I keep hidden under layers of black—how did he see it?

He wears his weakness proudly. He'd probably prefer I didn't know about his nail polish and vertigo, but he spoke about them openly, freely, and without embarrassment. It's why I drew that silly heart on his wrist. I did it without thinking, hoping it would replace the polish and help him. Give him something to focus on.

He never stopped touching it, not for a moment throughout the entire day.

Fuzzy slippers are at the foot of my bed and I hastily stuff my feet into them as I wrap the Lodge's soft robe around a silk cami and shorts.

Outside my door, the inn is fast asleep as my slippers sink into thickly carpeted stairs and my fingertips graze over garland with each step I take. Moonlight catches on tiny bulb ornaments sprinkled with glitter that are rough to the touch, but the thick velvet ribbons threaded through the greenery are smooth.

It's hard to remember that Santas and nutcrackers dot every dark corner, and I almost scream twice stumbling into them. Unsure what I'm even looking for, I reach the lobby and spot The Nook. My nerves are all in a jumble, Winter's words and the ghost-like memory of his hands in mine making it hard for me to settle. Maybe I can pop in for a nibble. This place is so homey, and Darcy has said many times to help myself, so I press through the swinging doors of the kitchen and beeline for the industrial-size refrigerator.

The counters are clean with glowing appliances in the dim room, and there's a dish of cookies wrapped in cellophane as if waiting for me. I marvel at Darcy's thoughtfulness while I paw through the fridge to find a jar of milk. After pouring into a Christmas tree mug, I take a bite, the sugar melting on my tongue. God, I miss Frannie. She loves eating cookies in the dark.

I make sure to clean up after myself before I leave, swiping up my crumbs and dumping them in the sink.

On my way back upstairs, I spot a glint of white outside. Then another, and another that pulls me right back downstairs and toward the front doors. Globs of fluffy white dance in front of the moon, floating like heavy chunks of glitter, hitting the ground and sticking already. It's snowing, and I press my nose against the chilled glass, watching my breath make fog. My hand wraps around a chilled brass pull, I'm mesmerized by the sparkle in the dark sky. For a second, I think the door might be locked, but this is a hotel, people come and go at all hours of the night.

And that's why I'm able to hold in yet another scream when I hear a voice. "You're up late."

"Oh, shit." I clutch my throat as if the scream I'm swallowing might still pop out. "Liam! You scared me."

"Sorry, but you looked so moony staring out at the snow, then it looked like you were going outside and you don't have a coat and —" The concern on his face strikes me as odd and in stark contrast to his normal snark.

I think I might have made a friend. *But why is everyone around here so concerned with my lack of snow gear?*

"It's okay. I just want to go out for a second. To taste a snowflake." I sound silly, but I've grown up far closer to beaches than mountains most of my life. I want to feel the snow on my tongue. I've loved the magic and the smell of *snow* since I was a kid.

"I think I should give you this first," he says, handing me a thick cream envelope.

I'm not surprised when I see it. I knew it was coming. As if I knew he was thinking about me, just like I've been thinking about him. But, that's because we're working so closely together, right? It has nothing to do with the fact that every time we speak to each other, someone seems to uncover a secret in the other.

"You're being awfully nice." I quirk a brow at him wondering if he's buttering me up because I gave him an industry connection.

"You caught me at my witching hour. I'm much more at home alone in the dark with my laptop." He points to the computer glowing in front of him. "I'm going over notes from that writer who crews for Streamflix, the one you connected me with."

"She's already read your work? And sent notes? Wow. You must be good."

He sniffs, shifting as if he might open up but thinks twice. "Thanks. Almost makes working back-to-back shifts worth it."

No wonder he's growly in the mornings at The Nook. I can respect someone hustling for their dream, though. Up all night, fueled by *what could be*. "I've asked Robbie, one of the cameramen, for some contacts to send your way, too. You'll probably be famous before the show is over. If you are, reach out to Brand Hub. We'd love to do your PR."

"Will do," he smirks. "Robbie's the guy with the mohawk?" If I'm not mistaken, a touch of pink dusts his cheeks.

"Yuuuup," I say, drawing out the word to try and read his energy.

"Here," he says, his voice going a little rough, "Take your mail."

"It's a little late for mail," I grimace. Usually, I can keep my attitude under control better than this. Something tells me Liam gets it. "I'm sorry. I'm just tired."

The past few days have been long, and I'm starting to feel the weight of hustling for the past ten years culminating and pressing down on me like a dark shadow.

I glance back at the snow. *Enough, already,* my body seems to be saying through tense muscles and a need to breathe fresh air.

"He said, as soon as I see you, I had to give you the letter. And then he dropped a fat tip. So, don't blame me. I'm in the middle of a compelling monologue from an untrustworthy narrator. Take it, I need to focus."

"Ah. Love a good monologue. Carry on, you young Cameron Crowe."

"You like Cameron Crowe? I live for him, '80s, '90s, I'll take all of it."

"Yeah. Me, too."

He's already typing away, his features focused and lit by his screen, but one corner of his mouth twitches with the hint of a smile.

I tuck the envelope under my arm and tote it with me outside. The snow is falling thicker and faster now, flurries catching in my hair. It's easy to admire the Lodge after walking a few feet out on the cobblestones, lit up by red and white lights glowing along the rafters and sprinkled with a fresh dusting of sugar snow.

Ignore the card under your arm, Cat. Ignore it.

But I can't, it's as good as burning a hole through my too-thin-for-this-weather robe.

I give in to temptation and rip the envelope open as wet slush begins to soak my slippers. Even though the scrolly, rolly script tells me exactly who it's from, I'm shaking with anticipation.

A skeleton key falls at my feet and the card reads: *Thank you for today. Check the mailbox.* There's a shoddily sketched black heart, colored in and slightly unbalanced, like the one I drew on his wrist. *Winter.*

"Are the theatrics truly necessary, pretty man?" I ask the stars above me as I bend to retrieve the heavy iron key.

Nice touch. What does he do all day? Where does he find the time to concoct elaborate schemes for his PA—his best friend's soon-to-be-fiancé's sister, and sworn enemy . . .

Don't forget that last part.

What's in the mailbox?

I weigh the key in my hand as I weigh the options. Another list of demands? His dirty laundry? A puppy?

The charming little mailbox, an uninvited link between Winter Larsen and me, sits unassuming and just off the road. It's covered in an inch of snow. When the suspense is almost to the point of killing me, a thrill I find I kinda like, I twist a newly installed lock and lift the top.

But inside, there's not another note. Not another cream envelope with a laundry list of to-do's as I expected. Instead, the mailbox is full to the brim with another box. This one I recognize, the thick font encased in a black triangle.

Prada's branding is iconic, classic, and timeless with a signature geometric shape. The box is large but relatively light. I pull it free, drop into a squat in the snow, and whip off the top.

Tissue paper flutters and my heart races. Excitement makes me laugh out loud as I paw through the wrapping.

But I'm quickly silenced while snowflakes cling to dark tendrils of hair falling into my eyes. Because this isn't funny. Not at all.

Inside the box is a puffy, down-filled coat that goes all the way to my ankles. There's a cream card tucked inside, another hand-drawn black heart, and the words, *For you.*

I shrug it on over my robe and wrap my arms around myself, engulfed by softness and warmth, all black, and all for me.

Fifteen

CAT

"Winter, hold up!"

Tonight's date is a Friday night craft session at the bottom of the mountain in a vintage furniture store. The showrunner suggested wreath making when he spotted an ad for special holiday classes in the Spirit Lake newsletter stocked at the front desk of Little Star Lodge. Now I'm struggling to keep a box of Winter's potential wardrobe options upright while following him down Main Street. It's amazing how much beanies and faux fur vests weigh.

"Mics are hot," Robbie says as we approach an actual line painted across the street, white letters proclaiming State Line in clear, approachable script that my sister has told me all about. We pass Mr. Bears Toys which is indeed next to Smooth Operators.

She thinks it's magical, the ability to be in two places at once. I think it's mere logistics as I step over the line into Clover without a second thought and trot after Winter as we continue down Main

Street, passing a mint-green Victorian with a sign reading Town Hall Clover, Town Hall Novel. They share, how cute. This would be an adorably perfect location to shoot a small-town romcom. Hallmark should know about this place. Maybe Liam's script would be a fit, wouldn't surprise me if the grump had a heart of gold.

"Winter, *hold up,*" I shout again, running toward the furniture store called Revival.

It's no longer snowing but the smell is still in the air. There's a magical feel to Little Star Lodge for sure. I felt it the minute I crossed the threshold, like a relief of some sort. And as I clock passers-by sipping from cups that say Patty's Spicy Nog and little kids in turkey hats riding on parents' shoulders, I wonder if I've wandered into a Christmas movie myself. I swear I just saw someone walking a poodle dyed red and green on a candy cane leash.

"Keep up," Winter hollers without looking back.

"Slow down," I groan, watching his long legs eat up the sidewalk. We pass little shops with frosted windows. One reads Dazzle Paws—no doubt where the poodle got her holiday flair, and a little shop presumably responsible for the cups I've seen called Patty's Pastries.

"Revival's coming up on your right," Robbie says, keeping up much better with Winter than I am.

"I know where it is," Winter bites.

Who peed in his Cheerios this morning? He's been avoiding me all day. I've even left a note in our mailbox but so far, no response.

Marco appears at my side and I swallow a yelp. I'm not nearly as jumpy as my sister is but he's stealthy for an extrovert with a foghorn for a voice box.

"Where did you come from?" I gasp, eyeing the camera. Good, it's trained back on Winter, he's chatting up some townie outside Revival's front door.

"I followed in my jeep."

"You got a jeep?" I raise an eyebrow at him, shifting the box to my opposite hip.

"Rented. Just wanted to feel like a local for a bit. How's our prince?"

"Touchy, with an attitude that won't quit."

"Well, turn that frown upside down. Tonight's date is important. Yesterday's views were low."

"You can tell that? Already?" We both shuffle to the side as a family of five passes us on the sidewalk eating caramel apples on a stick.

He nods. "Streamflix isn't happy." His boots are plaid with red laces as if he was dressed today by wardrobe, fully embracing the aesthetic. "Tell him to turn on the charm, would ya?"

Robbie's camera is on us, the lens sweeping in our direction. It's not that I mind being on camera, I do post videos of myself all the time, but it's under my control when I do it. And it's all for my clients.

No one cares about you on this show.

They're here for him. Winter meets my eyes and comes to stand beside me. Robbie backs up to get us both in the shot.

"Now that you're not running from me, got a minute?" I ask, meeting those deep blue eyes head-on. Then I turn to Marco, "I'll handle it."

"We need sweeping glances and grazing fingertips. We need sweet nothings and stolen touches. We need jingle bells, lots of fur, and I'm working on a spiked cider station from this place called Patty's."

Winter yawns next to us, who knows if he's listening or whether he cares? My bet is he does not.

"I've got this, Marco. Don't worry," I say for Winter's benefit. He needs to know I'm not going anywhere, so he may as well get on board.

"I think I like working with you, Bloomfield."

"If you tell me I've got spunk, or a twinkle in my eye, or chutzpah, or whatever it is men used to say to women in the workplace, I'm going to kick you in the crotch."

Winter glances at the sky and tries to hide a laugh. Definitely listening, and it's all I can do not to elbow him in the chest.

"Is that what you think of me?" Marco deadpans. "But just so you know, in all that black," he waves his hand around at my face, "the shades, the red lips, the cat eye sharp enough to kill a man . . ." He throws in a wink. "You do—have all that stuff, that I won't dare mention."

A gust of truly frigid air blows past us and I pull my jacket tight against my chest, I didn't wear Winter's gift today and I'm trying hard not to think about why.

"Don't worry, this date will be must-see TV." I look up at Winter, who's edged closer and closer. He's pushed up against my side now, his chest bracketing my shoulder, his puffer coat a thin barrier between us. But I no longer feel the wind, so that's one benefit of him being incapable of staying out of my personal space. "Right, Winter?"

Despite being blocked from the cold, I shiver as he holds my gaze, waiting for a response, searching his face for an answer to my question. I'm not about to blink first.

Abruptly, he turns on his heel and strides through the door. *What was that?*

Marco and I barrel in behind him and watch as he bumps fists with two men behind the cash wrap. The store is rustic, clean, and well organized even if it's a bit cluttered. Generations of furniture are staged in little vignettes, Turkish rugs litter the floor, and vintage lamps glow in corners. There's a hideous purple living room set smushed into a corner and I crinkle my nose in its direction.

After dropping the box of wardrobe on a table set up for production, I head to the cash wrap to make introductions. A pumpkin spice candle glows on dark wood next to a stack of business cards fanned out in a brass dish reading *Revival, we've got the diamonds, you make them shine.*

"Nice tagline," I murmur.

"And who's this?" The man asking has a substantial build to him, black skin, and a huge smile.

"Jack, this is Cathy Bloomfield." Winter pins his lips together as if he's about to burst into laughter and motions to me. If it's possible, Jack's smile grows bigger. "Cathy, this is my buddy Jack, two-time Super Bowl champ, and his husband, Wagner, the shop curmudgeon," he finishes, barely keeping a straight face, gesturing to a tall white man wearing a tool belt and a grimace.

"Nobody calls me Cathy," I say sweetly through my teeth.

My elbow meets Winter's hard stomach and his buddies laugh.

"Bloomfield!" Jack booms, "Frannie's sister, right? It's an honor." Jack takes my hand, his covered in huge gold rings, and shakes vigorously with his gentle paw.

The rings and the magnanimous smile trigger a memory. "You were the bachelor, at the club where my sister met John, right?"

"I'm going on break, honey." Wagner cuts in before Jack can answer, he has a beard trimmed to perfection and cut at angles as sharp as his taciturn welcome.

"Camera shy," Jack offers as an apology.

"Believe me, I get it," I say.

Jack goes on. "And I've had to apologize for that night, a lot. Not my finest moment," he rubs his jaw, "but I remember you, too."

"It was your bachelor party. You looked like you were living it up appropriately."

"Thanks," he says sheepishly. He was about ten sheets to the wind, if I remember correctly. "I'm not camera-ready, either," he adds, patting at a meticulously maintained mini-Afro. I think he looks perfectly prepared to dazzle the camera, but I keep my mouth closed. "I'll be in the back working on some inventory. You holler if you need help with anything."

"Thank you," Marco says. "And thanks for opening your shop for us."

"You're welcome. The crafts are ready to go. You guys do your thing. Bro," he directs his attention to Winter with a chagrined smile, "don't be afraid to name-drop." He slaps him on the shoulder.

"I got you, buddy," Winter says easily, confident.

It's time, I know this is my only chance to talk Winter into putting on a happy face for this date. It's not his fault he got vertigo yesterday, but still, I need the guy to turn on the charm.

I pull him to the corner of the shop by the cuff of his coat and decide to kill him with kindness. Not my favorite approach by a long shot, but you gotta do what you gotta do, right?

"I've never seen you be so affable," I say, trying my best to compliment the man even though it feels like crunching rocks with my teeth.

"Are we living in an Austen novel now? Affable?"

"I'm trying to be nice," I grit. "Maybe I'm a little stiff, but I've been like that my whole life. I don't know how to charm. It's not in my nature and yes, I'm self-conscious about it, especially in my line of business."

He slips out of his coat and hands it to me.

"I'm also trying to be nice, and not just for the show. Revival needs the exposure. This whole town can only exist if we get the word out," Winter grumbles. "Most of the shop owners survive on tourism." He's so prickly today, way worse than yesterday even with the whole nail polish debacle. And now he's worried about the town? Towns?

"Why would a prince from Denmark care about the tourism in these tiny towns?" I ask, keeping my eyes averted from his as I fidget with his coat. It smells like him.

"These tiny towns are my home. I love Denmark, but this place is my refuge. I want to give back, and selfishly, I want to preserve them so I've always got a safe place."

Today his nails are clean and color-free, and for some reason, my heart constricts at the sight of them. He might have a clear strengthener on, but who am I to tell a man with phenomenal grooming habits he can't treat his cuticles? The heart I drew on his wrist has been washed away. It makes me sad, though I can't for the life of me think why.

It's messing with my head, hearing him talk about his buddy with the small shop, and how he wants to help. A place that has saved him while I know he still loves his home country, too. That's not the self-absorbed pretty man I know—and love to hate.

"I couldn't agree more," I say, stowing his coat with mine under a table. "Supporting a small business is a good thing."

He's watching my every move, I feel like I'm under a microscope when his eyes are on me. "Right, and I think you can be charming, at times," he agrees and compliments me as if surprised to hear himself say it. "So, I'll plug the store a little," he rambles. *Wait, is he nervous?* "Drop the name a few times."

I sort through a bin of microphone packs the crew has put out. "Listen, Winter. Ratings are down."

"Already?" *Exactly what I thought.* "I guess a man afraid of heights and nearly vomiting on his date doesn't make for good content?" A muscle in his jaw twitches. "I swear, I'm usually better at this."

I smile at him, but keep my lips zipped instead of hurling an insult at him because I think he's being sincere.

"Well, you better give me my armor then."

I glance up from cords I'm untangling with patience I don't naturally have. "Your what?"

He pushes his sleeve up and extends his arm. "Go ahead," he prompts, pointing to his wrist.

He wants me to draw another heart.

While holding his gaze, I drop the microphones, unzip my fanny pack and search for my permanent marker, then pull the cap off with my teeth.

I ask through the side of my mouth, "The usual?"

"Yes, please."

His wrist is warm and my fingertips tingle when I graze his skin, turning his heavy hand palm up in mine. I draw a small, slightly crooked heart, watching the ink bleed into his skin with satisfaction I don't understand.

"Color it in," he demands.

"I know, I know," I murmur around the cap still in my mouth, focusing on my handiwork.

When I'm done I replace my marker and bring his wrist to my lips, and blow.

He swallows a cough, and takes a step closer, always watching me with those intense eyes. "Thank you."

I like the feel of him. But I drop his hand the second I have the thought. "We need you to, uh, turn on the charm. You know, make viewers fall in love with you. As the prince, on the show. You know what I'm saying? Play the part . . ."

His features rearrange instantly. One moment he's soft and sweet, the next his eyes are cold. "Yeah, Bloom. I know exactly what you're saying. I've had a lifetime of what you're saying."

Ugh, why does that gut me?

"That's what you signed up for, right? Why are you fighting it? I don't understand why you're not basking in the attention, rolling around in the adoration. These women want—"

"These women know exactly what they want." He looks directly into my eyes and the room falls away. The women who've just come through the door of Revival that he hasn't even glanced at, the crew organizing crafts at a table near the cash wrap, it all dissolves into nothing.

All I can see are his eyes drilling down into mine. There's so much more there than I ever realized. He looks sad—*again.*

"You want me to be *that guy.* I get it." The hard set of his jaw and the thin line of his mouth make me want to press my fingertips to his lips or massage his shoulders again like in the woods. Anything to force him to relax.

"What's with you today? Where's your *nothing bothers me* swagger you usually throw around by the heaps?" I stammer, suddenly off my footing and confused by the turn in conversation. I thought I knew what he wanted, exactly why he was here, which was to make me miserable.

But now I'm so confused, I almost wish he'd start calling me Cathy again and demanding smoothies.

"Where's your coat?" he spits back.

Is that what this mood is about?

"I'm wearing my coat." I busy myself by getting back on task with the microphones, it's a miracle Marco hasn't come for us. "Didn't you get my note?" I dropped my own hastily scribbled response this morning.

"Yes."

"Well?"

"*Thank you*. That's all it said."

"That's what you call, manners, pretty man."

Finally, he looks away. And dammit if I don't feel the loss. "But you're not thankful because you're not wearing it."

I throw my hands out to my sides. *What does he want?* "You've declared war on me, you promised to make me quit this job—or worse, to fire me!"

Robbie, that ghost of a man, materializes near the cash wrap in the middle of the room. He's got a bird's eye view of everyone, crew setting out wreathes in a row, Marco on his cell phone, me and Winter in our corner struggling with microphones for way too long now.

"No reason to freeze your ass off." My attention snaps back to Winter and I do my best to ignore the blinking red light on the camera.

God, I've got to get a grip.

"Is that supposed to make me swoon? A coat and a, *I don't*

hate you enough that I wish you dead from frostbite, but I do still plan to torture you daily while working as my PA?" I hold up my hand to stop him from interrupting me, "A job which, let me remind you, I'm wholly overqualified for and only doing because your fancy royal name is going to change the trajectory of my company!"

"That's a lot to dissect, Bloom. I don't even know where to start except to say, you're awfully fired up about a coat. A simple gesture. It means nothing except *don't freeze your ass off.*"

Like I wanted it to mean something?

Ugh. He's twisting my words and I decide to ignore him and do my job. I grab two mic packs and two cords I've untangled from knots, one for him, one I'm contractually obligated to wear because who knows why.

"Arms up," I say.

He obeys, and I begin wrapping the mic pack around his torso, both of us ignoring the fact that the past two days we've shot, I've handed him the mic pack and let him put it on himself.

His ribs expand and contract in my hands. He's so wide, all muscle, and so strong as he stands here letting me manhandle him.

"Is this important to you?" he suddenly asks.

"Are you asking about the show?"

"Yes."

I don't glance up to see if he's watching as my hands brush the hard knots of his abs. "It's my job, so yes. If you look good, I, and in turn Brand Hub, look good."

I clip the mic pack to the waistband of his pants, sliding it down the divot in his back where his spine is concave. He shivers at my touch and I try to breathe through my mouth so I don't smell his distinct clove and smoky matches man-smell.

His fingers flex at his sides.

Every time I touch him it affects me. And I think it affects him, too.

I'm not ready to talk about the coat he left in our mailbox. Is it supposed to make me like him? Has he realized he completely misjudged me, and he's apologizing for declaring war between us? Because he's not buying me off with a gift. Even though I loved it, I adore opening presents in general no matter the size or the value, and I wish I were wrapped up in it like a winter's robe right now.

"Temps have dropped below freezing and they say snow is coming tonight," he manages, his tone raspy. Is it hard for him to speak with my hands on him? Because it's becoming harder and harder for me to focus on what he's saying as my fingers glide over smooth, taunt skin. "If you had an emergency, if you got stuck outside, it could mean life or death, Bloom. You're living on a mountain for the winter if you haven't noticed. You're not in the Bay area anymore, Toto."

"Ha," I laugh, more genuinely than I'd like. "You nailed that *Wizard Of Oz* quote."

His lips twist and his eyes light up. "Thank you."

He's a handsome man, infuriatingly so. But he's always been physically attractive, nothing there has changed, and none of it crossed my mind before the way it is now.

I shiver as I snake the cord of the little microphone up his middle, my hands pushing up the front of his shirt and over his pecs to clip to his collar.

His muscles respond, flexing under my fingertips. I want to touch more. "Wear the coat," he says, his eyes moving all over my face.

"I have a coat." I press my palms flat against his broad chest, I shouldn't, but I do.

"You have a flimsy piece of leather. I give my horse more protection than that in this weather. Have you listened to nothing I've said?" he demands.

When his voice drops low like that, and he speaks as if he's more passionate about my warmth than anything else in the world, I cannot for the life of me ignore the way it affects me. Did he notice my shiver? In this warm, cozy antique store? Does he know it's not because I'm cold, far from it, at this exact moment?

"We're on camera right now," I whisper. "We'll talk about this later."

On cue, Robbie takes two steps closer and Winter glances over his shoulder. "Is that a problem for you?" he asks, so low it's a whisper I pray our mics can't hear. "The camera? The public eye?"

Don't look at his mouth!

"I don't love it, and please don't say you're surprised."

He nods, assessing me as my fingers fumble, taking way too long to clip the mic to his collar. His knuckles brush my hip. "You want me to win these women over? Flirt with them? Woo them?"

"That's what you're here for—" Reluctantly, I pull my hands away, mic in place. I'm quickly becoming way too familiar with touching him.

He gives me a funny look. "Not originally, but if that's what you want, I can adjust my plans."

"What does that mean?" I ask, looking up into his eyes, totally confused. He's either a mastermind, a lunatic, or both—jury's still out.

"Bloom, is that what you want?" He presses, inching closer until we're boot to boot. Both hands graze my hips as if he's dying to grip them.

"Yes."

"Fine," he huffs, "*your wish is my command.*"

Is he throwing my words back at me? I said that sarcastically first, and why is everything so epically tense between us?

Head held high, he walks toward the group of contestants who are twittering around a table covered in butcher paper and glitter.

Sixteen

CAT

There are ten hot glue guns for the ten ladies who've all got their eyes glued to Winter. God help us. The whole scene is giving holiday, craft-girlie vibes but everyone's out for their own sequins. The women shift their feet and take in the competition. I'm not sure any of them have formed feelings for him, how could they, we've only just begun. Nevertheless, they want him. He's handsome, yes, epically so with a cut jaw, proud brow, and full lips, unfortunately for his ego. But the castle, which they've all asked to visit, and the crown, which apparently exists and they've all asked to see, is the prize they're after, too.

I slip my mic pack around my waist and snake the cord up my shirt, trying to forget the feeling of his warm skin under my fingertips.

Marco opens his mouth and bellows, "Winter, ladies, let's get crafting!" Then over his shoulder, with the sweetest smile, he shouts at a production assistant who's wheeled in provisions for crew dinner while we film, "Can we get some goddamn Christmas music? Please?"

The guy freezes in place with the cart full of food and looks around. "He's not talking to you," I say, and the kid relaxes.

When did I become the nice guy on this set? Sloan would love to see me now. Everyone at Brand Hub would think I'm going soft. *Maybe I am. Maybe I don't mind being a little soft. Maybe, it's not a weakness.* These thoughts, brought on by sad-boy-eyes, cute little towns, and everyone's obsession with plaid, no doubt.

"I got it," Jack pops his head out. "I'll put on a classics playlist. Thanks again for the promo, Winter. I'm working on the books back here and," he makes a face, "it's not pretty, man."

"Jack, you're on camera, too," I hush him.

"Yeah but nobody's watching me. They're here for him," he points at Winter in a half-zip pullover with a plaid collar poking out—wardrobe I didn't have to fight too hard for, it's all his.

Surprisingly, the prince takes direction well. I wonder if that extends to the bedroom . . .

What? No! Brain, I command you to banish those thoughts. It's because he touches me so reverently, and I'm overworked, and watching single woman salivate over him—it's in the air. It's like an animalistic reaction to try and hunt him, too. Right? He's too beautiful, too tall, his smile is too perfect, and this whole situation is too competitive for thoughts not to naturally move in that direction.

It means nothing, except I need to get a life off this set. I thought the problem was my phone, but maybe it's me. Maybe I sink too much into work. Case in point: fantasizing about a man I hate only because I've been glued to him and am mistaking random touches for affection. Frannie will help. The second she's in town we're going out for a girl's night.

"We've gotten our first few hits on the message boards," Marco says, quietly shouldering up to me. "Winter Larsen is, quote, a dream in tight khaki pants. There are one hundred sixty-one comments on his pants alone so far. We should look into an endorsement deal with JCrew."

I roll my eyes. "You know I'm mic'd."

I know, he mouths back. Everyone's got an agenda.

Winter is in full schmooze mode, handing out wreaths to his ladies and plugging in the glue guns, so I take a walk around the store and drop into a worn leather chair the color of pine needles, pulling a soft plaid blanket with tassels up to my nose. A glance over my shoulder tells me Winter has gone from melancholy to downright magnanimous. He's just said something that has sent the women into bubbling laughter. He's rolled up his sleeves and his forearms flex as he shows the camera his wreath. He's glued on every bobble and bow, and loaded it with glitter. It's so ugly that it's adorable. His grin is sheepish, his eyes shine bright.

My stomach cramps and I look away, sinking further into my own grouchy mood. This is exactly what I wanted. I asked him to charm the camera. *Why is it so annoying to watch?*

I need to see my sister. That's what's wrong with me. She'll help me get my head back in the game. Willow, too. I need to talk to my girls and then I need to focus on my job. This will all be over soon and I can go back to my real life.

"Ow!" a woman screams.

My head snaps toward the craft table but I can't see around Robbie's broad shoulders.

"I'm sorry, sweetie," another woman responds as I run to see if I can help, and I realize we've got a case of crafty sabotage.

Lexi H. is holding her glue gun with a pouty expression on her face. "I swear, I didn't see you leaning in—"

"How the hell do you accidentally glue gun someone's boobs?" the other woman, Mandy, rages. Mandy is the brunette who got left in Lexi H.'s dust in the bakeshop yesterday.

Behind me now, his camera looming over my head, Robbie sucks in a breath looking honestly pained for the glued boobs.

"That's gotta hurt," I murmur.

"I'll get a wet cloth." Winter sprints through the back doors of the shop hollering for Jack and a First Aid kit as he goes.

I watch, wide-eyed as the two women start to passive-aggressively apologize to each other. "Marco, a little direction, please," I yell.

He's nose-deep in the dinner spread that's finally ready, face currently turning white as he eyes the glue gun, thinking about lawsuits no doubt, a ham sandwich in his hand.

"Ladies, language—" I try, motioning with my eyes to the camera, wondering how far Streamflix's language allowance goes.

Winter comes running back to the table causing them both to pull it together.

"Here, let me," he says, dabbing a gob of wet paper towel over Mandy's chest.

The camera zooms in on his hands and Marco gulps, coming to stand beside me and just outside the shot. "This is either great content, or we're toast tomorrow," he whispers.

"Oh God, it burns!" Mandy wails while the first *pums-pums* of Little Drummer Boy float through speakers by a crooning Bing Crosby.

"I'm trying to be gentle," Winter says soft and concerned.

I look away, prop my hands on my hips, and glare at a moose on the wall. We couldn't have written a script better: the damsel is in distress and here comes Prince Charming.

But why am I angry? It's good to know he's a kind, caring, gentle man under all that bravado. And smart-ass-ness. And stupid swagger. And—

"Get it off, get the glue off!" Mandy moans.

Sure, hot glue on skin hurts but I can't quite tell if she's playing it up for the camera as well. She's really drawing this out as she grips Winter's arm and whimpers.

He gives her a concerned look and I put a hand over my nauseated stomach. I must be hungry. "It's kinda stuck on there—"

"Get it off, please," she pleads, holding his gaze, dropping her voice so that it's all soft and lusty, batting her eyes.

Winter asses the problem protectively but also looks slightly uncomfortable, and I tuck all my hair behind my ears, needing to get it off my face because I'm burning up.

"Oh yeah, this is great content." Marco bumps me on the shoulder as if we're buddy cops about to catch the bad guys and win the day, but really, all I want to do is wake up from this nightmare.

"It's okay, let me take care of everything," Winter croons. He uses his pointer finger to push a strand of hair from her face ever so slowly, tracing down her jaw and tipping up her chin so she gets a good long look at all his caring.

Maybe they're both in on this charade; I did tell Winter to up the swoon.

I consider stuffing the icky feeling in my stomach with my own ham sandwich. Maybe I need a snack, and maybe I need to get out of here.

"Should we do this somewhere a little more private?" Mandy's voice turns sultry, no mistaking the huskiness in her tone.

"Let's go find that first aid kit." Robbie's camera swings back to catch Winter lifting her effortlessly. She wraps her legs around him as he strides through the backroom doors, clinging to his neck.

"What are you doing?" Marco hisses to Robbie. "Follow them!" When my feet don't move, he adds, "You too, Cat." He double-takes when he sees I've put my sunnies on, trying desperately to hide.

Seriously, I'm trying to disappear.

The song overhead rings out with the first few notes of Jingle Bell Rock as we all file through the small shop door, squeezing into the tiny breakroom like breakfast sausage. Winter lays Mandy across the counter, her head nearly banging into the cabinets above, but she props her feet up so she can be laid out flat like a fish.

Jack, taking the scene in stride with zero questions, probably because he's seen a lot on a football field, whips readers off his nose and jumps into action. "Here's the first aid kit." He pulls a white box from beneath a sink and hands it to Winter, patting his hair and smiling wide at Robbie's camera. There's a Holiday Hunks calendar pinned to the wall behind him. Mr. November is wearing an apron and nothing else, almost all the days for the month crossed out with a slash.

Winter raps his buddy on the back. "Thanks, Jack. Revival is such a nice place to shop, and good to know you're prepared for any customer emergency." He's a damn good charmer, delivering the ridiculous line with the sincerity of a celebrity heartthrob.

"Glad to be of service, bro." Jack salutes and makes for the door. "I'll, uh, go see if the ladies need any help."

Mandy arches her back like a centerfold laid across a beach and whimpers, effectively drawing Winter's attention. "Does it still burn?" he asks.

"Yes," she confesses all too eagerly.

"I'll get a better angle," Winter says, a bit more stiffly as Robbie's camera presses insanely close. His face is paler than normal, and his hands shake a little as his focus returns to Mandy on the counter.

He's playing the prince in shining armor to a T, absolute perfection. But now I realize, he truly hates it. Before opening the first aid kit, and only for a second, he presses his thumb into the black heart on his wrist.

A little more space in my chest opens up for Winter Larsen. Who knows why he agreed to this show—other than making my life miserable— and who knows what he hopes to gain? I don't think it's attention.

That's when he looks at me, spotting me easily over his

shoulder and to his right as if he knew exactly where I was the whole time.

It's a small room. It means nothing.

I push my sunnies up my nose and hold my features still. He's not getting a reaction out of me.

He smirks at me as I hide behind my sunglasses. Not the *'isn't this a funny turn of events'* kind of smirk, instead it's the *'watch this'* kind of smirk.

"How is it now? Still burning?" He pushes the hair back from Mandy's forehead again and leans over her.

"Yeah," she breathes, her chest heaving even though the glue is gone, leaving angry red traces where it burned her skin.

"Do I have your permission to blow?"

No. I did not just hear that. I refuse to believe it.

I cross my arms and think bad thoughts all involving Winter Larsen. He's taking this whole charade up a notch with that suggestive tone.

I don't like it.

"Wh-what?" She stammers as her eyes turn to pools of pure lust.

"On the burn? Can I blow on it?"

"Please," she gushes, her greedy little hummingbird lashes batting a mile a minute.

"They would have gorgeous babies," Marco whispers in my ear as if reading my mind.

Robbie presses in from behind me again to get a better angle—how is he everywhere?

This is damn good TV, I'll give them that. It's an absolute spectacle. But I'm hot and sweaty, and I'm sick to my stomach. This yucky feeling has been coming on since we started filming and I'm about to crawl out of my skin with nowhere to go, nowhere to put the emotions dragging me down second by second.

I can't move. I can't make it stop because I'm sandwiched

between the camera and Winter while he tends to his date with a chivalry most thought was dead. *If he kisses her . . .*

My vision turns to slow motion as he leans down ever so slowly and blows lightly across her chest. Goose bumps pop all over her skin and I swear to Prada, a blind man could see her press her thighs together, propped up over the tiny sink.

"This'll do it. This is exactly what we needed." Marco is smug now beside me, still munching on his ham sandwich. "This might be the first kiss on *Royal Hearts*," he says excitedly around the meat and cheese in his mouth.

"Dammit, Marco." I glare at him. "This is a spectacle."

"Yeah," he grins and points with his sandwich as the canoodling couple carries on. "A good one."

"Is there such a thing?" He's right and I know it. The flirtation, the attraction, the sparks and *will they, won't they*, happening right before my eyes is exactly what we needed, exactly what this show is all about.

"Whatever you said to him, it worked. He's turned on the charm, I'll say. Even I think it's feeling a bit hot in here. Robbie, get closer."

Robbie glares, pressing his lips together, probably hoping Marco will shush.

"You know what? I could use some air," I spin on my heel, beeline through the store, and duck out the front door.

The cold air is refreshing, cooling my flushed cheeks and frantically beating heart as I brace my hands against my knees. *What is wrong with me?* I've never left a set during a shoot.

Dusk has fully turned to night and the entire street is lit up in multi-colored string lights. Brick buildings glow green, red, and blue. Blinking icicles hang from shop awnings and glittered snowflakes shine in windows. I stand there breathing hard until I start to shiver, apparently long enough to miss the remainder of the scene because by the time I head back in, the girls are streaming outside, and the crew is packing up.

Refusing to even look in Winter's direction, I quickly grab my things.

Marco smiles brightly at me, clearly satisfied by all the drama that unfolded today. "You alright?"

But I have no words. All I can manage are two thumbs up and the fakest smile I've ever produced as I hightail it out the door. I just want to be anywhere but here.

Thank God it's Friday and we don't film on the weekends. I don't have to see Marco, Winter, or Robbie's camera again until Monday.

I reach for my phone as my boots slap against the pavement so I can at least call my sister, but my pocket is empty.

Seventeen

WINTER

The Breakfast Place, my favorite spot on Main Street, is a flurry of activity this morning. Skiers are here in full force as we begin December at the bottom of the mountain, making my favorite diner feel even more quintessential Americana.

Around me, the dudes order, and I mumble something to the waitress about a sausage scramble that I hope is coherent. I grip a mug of Earl Grey, trying to focus on brunch, on seeing the guys, and not on *Royal Hearts*.

I'm on a fucking reality show. It's been two weeks of dating women in groups with cameras following my every move, and my PA taking up all my thoughts. *Why did I agree to this?* I look around waiting for someone to recognize me, to ask if I'm *that guy*. How quickly I gave away my anonymity in this town. Before people knew who I was, but they didn't care about an old rusty European title. Being the bachelor on a dating show is different.

I checked my computer this morning to tend to business things that needed my attention, and I stumbled across a new story highlighting the unorthodox show and the Danish crown's PR team defending their choice to exploit their prince finding his queen. *Royal Hearts is Prince Winter's way of connecting with his people, letting them into his life which has remained uber-private up to this point. He's looking forward to taking a wife, returning to Denmark, and taking the crown when his time comes.* A direct quote from Anker. I slammed my laptop shut.

"Pass the salt?" Jack asks from across the table as our waitress lays a spread of eggs, bacon, grits, and pancakes in front of us. I pass him the salt but push my plate away.

The first few weeks of *Royal Hearts* were a blur of spray tans (I turned orange and scrubbed it off immediately), cheeky comments (I'm not as charming as I thought I was), and awkward dates (all around, I'm not sure anyone was having fun). My hands shook when Robbie's camera pulled in close, my heart raced when I worried about saying the wrong thing, and I often compensated for it all by acting as if I didn't care.

But I do. It was pure ignorance for me to think I could appear on camera for all the world to see and not feel judged, to the point of panic. Because of my history with the media, I do have some coping skills. I breathe deep, I visualize the cameras fading away, and I focus on something to ground me. When I was really little, Annie would take my hand in hers every chance she could. That was the best.

Now, I press my thumb into a little black heart on my wrist, since I no longer have painted fingernails. I think I like the black heart better.

When someone at the table laughs, and the men around me I call my best friends pound the table making water glasses jump, I join in. But I haven't heard a word they've said.

I've worked in the barn as much as I can, mucking out stalls and feeding the horses while cameras recorded. I gave my stable hands some extra time off. Riding in the mornings helps take my mind off the show before we film, and yesterday I assisted Annie with a particularly difficult pot pie recipe that filled the main kitchen of Vikingstrong with savory smells just in time for a tour. But try as I might, thoughts about my feisty PA keep popping into my head.

Later today, on the doorstep of Vikingstrong, I'm supposed to say, and I quote, "I'm sorry, you will not receive the crown," to ten of the fifteen women on the show. Ten.

This is grating on my nerves for a few different reasons, (1.) My entire personality, I've recently learned, revolves around making other people like me. My social anxiety from a childhood spent in front of media makes me want to pull away, but deep down I crave the approval. Stephen says it's all wrapped up in my self-worth, that I desperately want to be close to people, and am also terrified by the thought. Fuck. I can feel my pulse jumping in my neck just thinking about it. Dumping ten women on a live stream doesn't a likable, worthy of your admiration, man make. (2.) I think I'd like my PA to be part of the cast.

Which is a problem, since I've signed on to this show specifically to make her life hell. It's too much fun playing with her, trying to make her crack a smile, and trying to pull down some of her walls. Cat's not quite who I thought she was, and I find myself wondering almost every minute of the day—*then who is she?*

Shit.

"He's being so quiet." Ben Holiday passes syrup across the table. "My mom's worried about you, you know. She noticed you didn't go for seconds at Thanksgiving."

Though I haven't even unrolled my silverware, I say, "Let me eat in peace, Holiday."

"You want me to tell Marion Holiday you no longer love her famous homemade gravy? Or you wanna tell us what's up with you?"

John's home from his trip and the dudes called an emergency

brunch. "Did you guys break him while I was gone?" he asks, flipping his cap backward and digging into a veggie omelet.

Logan just got here but isn't eating with us, something about a fast. "Wasn't us, but something's gotten under his skin," he adds, sipping hot water and lemon.

"Something with dark hair, named after an animal—which is perfect for him—and knows how to put a prince in his place," Ben adds.

I glare at him but don't put full force behind it. "Do you want me to start in on your love life? How you're still hung up on your high school sweetheart, you run every time she calls, knowing full well you get your heart shattered every time?"

He puts his hands up and leans back. "You know what, I'm gonna let Boggs take this one."

"Don't get involved with Francesca's sister," John says matter of fact. "You two do not have good history."

"Bro, you've been gone for two weeks, how do you already know it's Frannie's sister?" Jack asks.

"I happen to be living with one of the Bloomfield sisters. And we caught a few episodes of the live stream before Frannie turned it off and said it was too weird watching Cat on TV."

Ben chews through a grin and says, "The PA he had to have is putting him through his paces. It's poetic."

"I mean," John leans in, "I've never seen tension between two people so thick. They were on the mountain, you know at Little Star, and he was about to puke all over this girl because of vertigo—"

"Oh shit," Jack covers his mouth trying to swallow a laugh.

"And then Cat comes over," John goes on, "shoos the girl away, gives him water, and tells him to pull it together and man up."

"That's not exactly how it went," I interject. "I was sick. It's a condition." These guys are supposed to be on my side.

"Well you should have seen him on the craft-date-thing at Revival, there was a hot glue in cleavage incident, and our boy was

all '*Can I help, can I have your permission to dab at your chest?*'"
Jack laughs raucously and they all join in.

"Man, I need to start streaming this at work," Ben chuckles.

"You all should be ashamed of yourselves." I point around the table. "I'm family. You have to support me."

"Fannie's gonna be my family, too, pretty soon," John's eyes dance and the table sobers, "which means you're gonna have to get along with her sister."

That shakes me out of my complaining. "Did Fran say anything? About me and Cat?"

All four men clap and pound their fists on the table. "Damn, you nailed it. It is the PA that's gotten under his skin. What happens if you two marry sisters?" Ben asks, still grinning ear to ear while packing away his breakfast potatoes. "I did catch a little at my parents' house last night. My sisters had it on, and you could bottle the attraction between you two and use it as bait. I like that they're filming everything. Cutting from shot to shot. Giving us behind-the-scenes footage with the producer and the crew. Feels very artsy," he muses, adjusting the aviators on his head. The guy could have been an actor, I'm not surprised he's into it.

"There's absolutely zero going on there, I promise you. The tension you see is absolute revulsion, coming from both sides. What about you?" I ask Logan. Is everyone watching me make an ass out of myself in front of the world? "Are you watching, too?"

"No." That's all he says while sipping lemon water, his big bear paw wrapped around a cream mug.

"No one's marrying anybody," I go on. Even though I know John's planning on proposing soon, I thought he'd do it on their trip but he hasn't made that announcement so I'm guessing he choked.

"Well, actually, you're marrying someone at the end of this asinine show you signed up for." The brackets around Ben's constant smile pop, and I can see myself reflected in the mirrored glasses propped in his sun-streaked hair. I look miserable.

I groan.

"Don't worry buddy, I'll be right behind you. And then we work on these two chuckle-heads," John says, pointing at Logan and Ben because Jack and Wagner started the whole wedding fever that seems to be working its way through my brunch crew.

The waitress appears over his shoulder with a check she places neatly on the table. "Please fill out the survey on the back of the card for The Breakfast Place if you've enjoyed your meal. I get a gold star," she drones, clearly not as motivated as one might think.

We all throw our credit cards in a pile and Ben shuffles them like a deck of cards. "And the lucky winner is—"

I feel her presence before I hear her voice. "Where the hell have you been?"

"*Uh-oh*," the dudes chorus as one, like a classic sitcom track. I swear, they probably practice when they're supposed to be paying attention at lake committee meetings.

Turning in my chair, I look up to see my PA frowning down at me. She's all in black with lips so red, like an apple I could almost take a bite of. "At brunch?" I motion to the table to make sure I'm right because she's looking at me like I have horns.

"We're supposed to be filming!" She launches forward, grabbing me by the collar and hauling me to my feet.

"I thought we started at four?" *Is it so wrong that I like her jerking me around?* I need to ask Stephen what that means and how I can fix it.

She pulls at my bicep and I take a few steps, letting her think she's got a hold on me.

"That got changed. Didn't you check our mailbox?"

"You two have a mailbox?" Ben plunks his chin on folded hands and bats his eyes at us.

I point at him, "Don't start, Romeo." Out of all of us, he's the biggest ladies' man and the most moony about romance. I turn to Cat and give her my full attention. "You hardly use it, so I didn't think—"

"Well, I'm using it now. And you missed my note."

"I'm sorry," I say. *She's using our mailbox.* A silly thing I got a notion to build out in the barn in the middle of the night. I never thought she'd play along.

Noted, Bloom.

"Is it me, or are we about to witness Winter Larsen's first grovel?" Ben whispers to the table, loud enough I hear it.

I pull my keys from my pocket. Without further protest or apology, I stand and say, "Let's go," and motion for her to lead the way.

"Gentlemen, I'll return him when I'm finished." She nods with a half-smile and a mischievous twinkle in her eye, instantly winning them over. "Hey, John." She waves.

"And that's Ben Holiday," I point him out, "Logan Green," Logan tips his cup, "And you know Jack."

"Hey, Cat." Jack waves. "I've gotten a lot of foot traffic since filming, thanks."

"Nice to meet you guys," she says. "John, give Frannie a hug for me. I can't wait to see her."

"She's dying to see you, too. Can't reach you on your cell but that's because of the show, right?" He turns his baseball hat back around, a tic he picked up when he played pro-ball.

"Right. Tell her to stop by the set today if she's free. We're filming at Vikingstrong all afternoon. The first crown ceremony."

"Ooooh," every single voice at the table unanimously mocks me, "*Crown ceremony,*" the chortle.

"You can all come," Cat laughs. "Just don't sign an NDA if you don't want to be caught in the background."

"No. You cannot all come," I say, looking at her with wide eyes. She's betrayed me already. I thought she had my back.

When did I start thinking that? When she took care of me in the bathroom of the bakeshop? When she found me water on the mountain?

"Sounds like we'll be there," Ben winks.

"Are you committed to being late?" Cat throws her hands out wide when I fail to follow her as she turns.

"So long, fellas." I salute them, deciding to take the high road. The more I beg them not to show up this afternoon, the more determined they'll be to make room in their schedules. "I've got a gaggle of women to date."

John yells, "Glad someone's got you on a leash, Larsen!" as I make my way out of the restaurant. "It's about damn time."

Men's laughter follows me almost all the way to my car, I can see them through the front window, carrying on and saying God knows what about me. My credit card is getting picked for roulette. No doubt.

"Get in," I say to Cat. Surprisingly, she does, slamming the door of my G-Class behind her. "How'd you get here anyway?"

"Darcy dropped me off on her way to yoga."

I raise an eyebrow in her direction as I start the engine and check behind us for traffic on Main Street. "And how'd you know I was here?"

"I used the front desk phone to call Annie. Darcy gave me the number." She tucks a chunk of hair behind her ear, looking satisfied with herself as I gaze at the curve of her cheek. Her profile is positively Roman, perfect and balanced.

"You spoke to Annie?"

"Yup. We had a nice little chat."

"About?" I prompt, straightening in my seat and gripping her headrest as I back out of the space.

"Wouldn't you like to know?" Sure would. I'd also like to know why it lights me up from the inside out thinking of Annie and Cat chatting on the phone—about me.

I floor the gas pedal, something electric and exciting coursing through me as we take the curves in the road at a clip. She lurches back and cracks a smile.

"Where are we headed?" I ask, my head completely foggy with the sight of her in my car, her lavender smell filling the small space.

"We're filming on the front step of Vikingstrong, remember? I reminded you of all of this in the letter."

"Bloom, I can't wait to read your letter. From now on, I check that mailbox first thing every morning. I won't even stop to put on breeches. I'll ride out in my pajamas."

"See that you do."

"Your box is very important to—"

"Winter!" I chuckle, enjoying her feigned shock at innuendo. Is this what we do now? When did we crossover from sparring to bantering?

"Excuse me, let me rephrase: your letters are very important to me." I throw her a half-grin and to my shock, she smiles back fully and laughs out loud.

I've never seen her like this. "Cat Bloomfield, are you flirting with me?"

"You started it," she says, not looking at me and scrolling through my playlist on my monitor.

My brain demands I fill the encroaching silence like it always does. "I'm nervous about today," I admit.

"Really?" she turns in her seat to face me as I follow Main Street's curve toward Paradise Bay and Vikingstrong. "You know, before all of this, I didn't think someone like you got nervous."

"Someone like me?" She's leaning in, over the center console of the car, listening intently to every word I say.

"All the confidence."

"You've certainly seen me struggle, now," I almost swallow the words but push them out anyway.

"But you overcome that struggle, every time," she counters, arguing for me.

"Ah. Well, you see, I can fake it through most things in life. Be whatever it is I need to be. But despite the fact you think I'm evil incarnate, I don't want to hurt anyone's feelings today."

"Oh."

"I didn't think that part of this through. There's a plan I've been chewing on," I hit a blinker and pull the car to the side of the road. "Can I run it by you?"

"Should you call Stephen?" I can't tell if she's joking, or if all our real conversations are starting to add up for her. Are we both beginning to see each other in a different light, as an ally, instead of an enemy?

"I think you can handle it."

"Okay," she shrugs, "proceed."

"I think I should cut all the nice women first."

She makes a face. "Why would you do that?"

"Well, and this may come as a shock, Bloom, brace yourself— my heart really isn't in this. Originally, I was going to be an asshole, piss you off, make you quit. I hadn't thought much past that, I think maybe I was out to piss off my parents, too. For blindly following the Crown's ridiculous PR stunt."

She stills, I know she's thinking about the end game for her in all of this. If I ruined the show by quitting, her business reputation might be at risk. "And now?" she whispers, her voice as light as I've ever heard it.

"Plans have changed, *per your request*. And I figure, if I cut the women who are here for love, I save them from any real heartbreak. Get them back to their lives, and their families. There are plenty of women who are here for their fifteen minutes of fame. I keep them, instead."

"That's surprisingly chivalrous of you."

"See. I can play nice. The other day, I realized you're not exactly who I thought you were. I'm man enough to say it. Maybe the banana splits both ways."

"What?" she makes a face at me.

I glance her way, "Is that not an American saying?"

"No."

I run my hand through my hair and scratch comically at my chin. "Well, it should be."

She leans back in her seat, looking to the roof of the car. "Are you really nervous about today? I thought it might get easier for you, I know you don't like the spotlight, but I figured you'd get used to it. That you *were* used to it."

"Look," I hold one hand up, and yes, it's shaking, "have you ever thought maybe you got a few things about me wrong, too?"

Shocking the hell out of me, she takes my hand and stretches it across the console. "I think we both misjudged each other. You're shaking." Then she digs into her bag, pulls out her marker, and begins drawing a heart.

My armor.

Her fingers grip my wrist with a light touch and I lean toward her, desperate for more warmth, more affection, all of it. My voice is gravelly when I speak. "I'm sorry."

I glance at her then back to the road and wait for what she says next. Traffic moves past us as we idle on the shoulder. We need to get going, but I'm not ready. Not yet. This feels like a pivotal moment between us and I wish I knew which way it was going.

She drops her marker in my cupholder, then intertwines her fingers with mine. "I'm sorry, too, and I hate that this is hard for you."

I'm afraid to say anything, to ruin the moment, the magic in this new world where Cat Bloomfield doesn't hate me.

And I don't hate her.

Not even close.

Maybe all the tension between us from the very start has been because we have a few things in common, perhaps because deep down *we like each other.*

I pull back onto the road, driving with one hand.

On the steps of Vikingstrong, under crossed dragon heads carved by my ancestors, ten women stand in front of me while I hold one of my great-great-great-grandmother's crowns.

My eyes dart to Cat. She looks away.

The crown is heavy, and I'm overwhelmed standing alone on the steps to my house while all eyes are glued to me. Hungry. Waiting. Thankfully, when we arrived, Cat had a chat with Marco and convinced him to let me do the first cut in one fell swoop. My gratitude toward my PA is immense.

"I'm sorry," I shift my feet and try to keep my face neutral. "I've called this group here today because I cannot offer you the crown." The red light on Robbie's camera seems to blink double time, and I'm holding on to the crown with a grip that could bend steel.

The women gasp, some sigh, some give me a little wave goodbye. It's over and I gulp down air. There's not enough of it, even though we're outside with the lake lapping in front of us. The first cut, standing in front of the camera on my own, had been weighing on me. I don't want to waste anyone's time, and I also don't know how long I can keep this up. Filming is affecting me the way being followed by cameras as a kid in Skagen used to affect me.

It's downright paralyzing and I eagerly descend the stairs ready to be done for the day.

"Wait, Winter, stay right there," the producer shouts. I barely hold myself up while a crew member takes the crown from my hands, I was about to have a nice little sit—instead of possibly passing out in front of everyone. Marco doesn't seem to notice. "We need a quick interview with you. Robbie, pull in tight."

"On it," Robbie approaches me and settles for five feet of distance, which I appreciate compared to my first round of interviews when he was damn near in my lap.

Cat's eyes meet mine and she must see something she doesn't like because she yells, "Hold for wardrobe!"

"Doesn't anyone understand we're live?" Robbie asks in a rare verbal moment.

"Hey," I whisper when Cat comes to stand beside me. "Was that okay?"

"Numbers are high," she says, meeting my eyes, "but you're white as a sheet. I thought you could use a minute." She reaches up to brush at my hair, but I'm too tall, so I move down to the step below her, my back to the camera.

Oh. "Thank you."

"You did good," she says, and I fucking preen at those small words of affirmation, some of the pressure to perform fading away.

Instead of responding, I test the new touching policy she instated in my car this morning as my hand wraps lightly around her hip. "Because of you," I murmur. "I feel better when I'm grounded by something, or to something."

"We're both mic'd, and you can't . . ." She makes eyes at my hand, visible to Robbie's camera, and I guess the world.

"Sorry. I don't know what to do with my hands." What I just did took way more of an emotional toll than I thought it would. Even though the women took it well, I'm suddenly struggling with the entire premise of the show.

"You're fidgeting," she says.

"Yeah, Bloom. I'm aware."

"Here." She hooks my pointer fingers in the belt loops of her jeans. There's barely room between us and no one can see. I hold on.

It's a miracle she's being nice to me, and I don't want to fight with her. For a while, since last summer I think, I loved sparring with her. I may have even been looking forward to it when the show started, but now, I crave her praise and her smiles just as much.

She's still running her fingers through my hair, lightly squeezing my earlobes in an effort to calm me, and it's working. I almost purr.

"Cat, what's the holdup?" Marco yells.

"Two more minutes, he needs gel." She pulls a bottle from her belt bag and after rubbing a dot of gel in her palms, begins moving it through my hair. "You good?"

I glance over her shoulder and sure enough, Robbie's camera is trained on us from the bottom of the steps, and he's got this look like he doesn't want to break us up but feels bad about filming, too.

"Any day now. We're at your leisure," Marco yells from a snack table set up for production. "His hair is fine. It's always fine. It's a character of its own at this point, people love it—there's a hashtag, I think."

"Not yet," I say for only her to hear, leaning in a little more so I can inhale her scent. If she notices, she doesn't say anything. Why is she so comforting? Like my own personal brand of bandages.

"I need to check his mic pack," she yells over me, pulling me closer so that I can graze her skin with my cheek. That's a blatant lie, and I love it, chuckling into her neck.

"They're picking all this up, you know. Viewers are probably watching and listening right now," I murmur.

"Let them," she whispers, and I melt a little more. Surrender a little more to her right there on the steps of my home.

Marco groans. "Why don't we call this the Cat and Winter show?"

"I would ship them!" Ben Holiday's voice rings out from somewhere on the beach.

I turn around while she pretends to check my mic pack clipped to the back of my pants and find all the guys in a huddle steps behind Robbie. Though I tried to deter them, it helps a little more, knowing they're all here to watch me make an ass out of myself. They showed up to support me. They always do.

Ben's words embolden me, who knows why, and as quietly as I can while looking past Robbie, past his camera, past the crew, to the lake, I whisper, "Maybe I should just hand you the crown and send everyone else home."

Her fingers still and she goes rigid behind me. "What did you say?" she whispers back, it's more to herself than to me.

I keep my eyes trained on my buddies, on the lake, a tiny smile tipping my lips. My own confusion takes over my nerves, the awkward but giddy feeling is better than almost passing out. And I like her reaction. I've caught her totally off guard.

"What's shipping?" John asks from across the lawn.

"It's being obsessed with a couple. Man, you've got a sister, too. How do you not know this?" Ben responds.

"Guys, if you're not signing NDAs you need to get off my set," Marco yells, exasperated but smiling nonetheless. "What am I running here, a kindergarten? Cat, get out of the shot!" Marco's shouts grow so loud that crew members next to him cover their ears comically.

That catapults her into action, stumbling down the steps and off to the side. Her face is red, her chest is heaving, and she's left me feeling the same if not worse.

Did I mean it?

Maybe?

I could talk to her on dates all day long, our conversation is always easy and real, so much different than I've ever felt with anyone else. It's just natural. The camera fades away when she's next to me. I guess, everything does. When I'm with her, she's got my sole attention.

"Winter?" Marco asks, "Are you ready?"

"Yeah," I say, but my voice is hoarse and dazed.

"Question number one," he says, glancing at Cat curiously, she's frozen behind Robbie at the moment. Tongue-tied. The producer carries on, "You signed on to this show to find a partner. Do you think you can fall in love in a matter of weeks?"

"Uh, sure. Why not?"

He smiles. "So, do you think *the one* is here? We've been filming for almost a month now. Is the woman for you here on *Royal Hearts*?"

What should I say? I could give a flippant answer, or I could say something that would make *Royal Hearts* viewers hopeful. Make Cat believe this show is going to be a success, and therefore, Brand Hub a success. Didn't she say, if I look good, she looks good?

The answer is out of my mouth in a flash, "One hundred percent, yes."

My eyes meet Cat's, now standing with my buddies on the beach as if she's one of them. She looks over her shoulder, out toward the lake and the guys erupt into hoots, hollers, and catcalls.

If it's a battle not to look at me, she loses, dragging her gaze back to mine as I stand on the steps of my castle and add, "She's here."

Eighteen

CAT

"You need me to call a bellman to haul you to your bed?" Liam asks.

I jolt awake in my booth at The Nook, instantly aware and on edge. Thank God he woke me up. Frannie and I finally connected and planned a coffee date.

Shoving my things into a tote, I glare at Liam while he snickers and watches me.

"Remember, you want to be part of this industry, *young screenwriter*. This is what faking it till you make it looks like." I gesture down at myself, an all-black uniform to match the black bags under my eyes. The set schedule has been grueling, and running this show with only a skeleton crew and one foghorn producer is taking its toll. They're not only relying on me to be Winter's PA. Marco, Robbie, and I are basically running this show entirely. And we're being filmed. It's a lot.

I also rolled into this town on an empty tank. I hadn't quite realized how close I was to burnout before I got here. The fresh air and lack of Wi-Fi have done me good. And staring at Winter Larsen day in and day out, dressing him, mic'ing him, watching him—*because it's my job*—has been a nice change of pace.

Digging into him like a piece of coffee cake and getting to know all the layers, he's so much more than I thought he was. He's struggling, he's confident, he's thoughtful, he's so privileged, and he's so sad.

"You look fine." Somehow, coming from Liam, I know that's a high compliment.

"Thanks, but you should see the crew and Robbie. He's constantly pulling at his neck during filming breaks and dropping his camera every chance he gets. We're all a little ragged, honestly."

"Maybe you guys need some time off?" he offers. "I'd like to meet some of, the uh, crew."

With that, he turns on his heel and goes to take an order at the next table.

A bell chimes overhead when I pull the door open to Patty's Pastries on Main Street, across the street from Boggs' Bar and Grill where flying fish flags still adorn the docks. Frannie swears her new boyfriend makes the best margaritas on the lake.

It doesn't look like margarita season around here now as much as it did when I first visited her at the end of last summer. Now, there are paper garlands cut into elves, pink gingerbread houses, candy canes, and sprayed snow in all the windows. Patty has wrapped her shop door like a hot-pink present with a big silver bow.

Inside, I find a cozy table with round cushions on the chairs and wait for Fran.

"Can I get ya something, honey?" A short, stout woman appears at my table while the shop buzzes with more morning traffic than I would have guessed a little lake town like this would get in the winter months.

"Coffee, black, please."

She's got three pens sticking out of a grey bun, one is wrapped in floral tape, a poinsettia sprayed with gold glitter attached to the tip. "No cream? No sugar?"

"Black. But I will take one of those chocolate croissants?" I dig into my bag for my wallet.

"Today's raincheck day for locals." She waves me off.

"Oh, I'm not—"

"You're Fran's sister, aren't you?"

"Um," I look around while skiers that must be heading up the mountain for a late-morning run peruse her merch wall and munch on sticky buns. "Yes, how'd you know?"

"You've got big-city written all over you, girl." She laughs heartily as if I should have known that answer.

Still shivering in my trusty leather jacket, I do stick out like a red tomato in a salad next to all the puffer coats, knit scarves, and unavoidably next to the blinking Christmas tree earrings currently hanging from Patty's lobes.

"That's alright, sugar. I didn't mean to make you feel out of place. Fran'll have some rain checks, and first-time customers are on the house anyway. Company policy."

"That seems bad for the bottom line."

"Ah, but good for morale, don't ya think? And happy people eat lots of sugar."

"What kind of market research have you done on that?" I give her the best smile I've got because I like her already.

She laughs again, her earrings dancing merrily. I'm surprised her sweater, covered in presents with tiny little bows, doesn't start playing a tune. "You really are the opposite of your sister, aren't you? She said you two were like salt and pepper, but I didn't quite believe it. She's such a ball of sunshine."

I can't stop the grumble that comes from my chest. My whole

life, my little sister has been praised for being sweet, cute, utterly adorable, and optimistic. *I just gave Patty my best smile.*

"Don't get me all wrong," she places her hands on the table and leans in real close, "you've got a shine to you all the same. You can't hide the sparkle in those dark eyes."

After a few seconds of eye contact that feels sort of, clandestine, I finally find words to respond. I don't want Patty to feel bad for me. "I understand. Frannie has always been the nice one."

"We all sparkle in our own ways, honey. Some of us shine so bright it's almost hard to look, blinding. For others, you gotta dig a little for the glitter. For the sweetness, and the things that make us special. No harm in being one or the other."

"Uh, thank you?" There's no other way to respond to the dose of kindness she sprinkled over me like cinnamon on a latte, for no reason, asking nothing in return.

I shiver again, but this time, it's not because I'm cold.

The door swings open and a gust of wind blows through the cozy cafe before Frannie pulls it shut, her long blond hair flowing from under a bright red beanie and a mega-watt smile greeting me in the perfect punctuation to Patty's words. "Kitty-Cat! You're here!"

It's only slightly annoying that everything people say about her is true.

I jump to my feet and hug her fiercely over the table. From the corner of my eye, I watch Patty put a hand over her heart. "Aren't you two precious? I'll be back with your order. It's raincheck day, Fran."

"Is that seriously a thing here?" We settle into our seats. Her cheeks are all pink and she smells like the snow that's been falling consistently for a week now.

"Yeah, cute, right?" She pulls two purple glittery pieces of construction paper from her pocket and hands them to me. "The kids make them as school projects and then when something gets canceled, they pass them out around town. I got these when I had a two-for-one coupon at the Tipsy Taco for frozen margarita night, but the frozo machine was on the fritz." She shrugs. "On the rocks did just fine, and now I've got these to cash in with Patty." She wiggles in her seat, trying to get settled. It's been so long since I've seen her, my heart melts.

"You're freezing. Did you walk here?"

Frannie rolls her eyes and for a second, she's twelve and I'm her babysitter all over again. "Yes, Mom." She laughs at me.

"At least you're wearing a hat."

It's a knee-jerk reaction to worry. I practically raised her when we were kids, taking care of someone you love isn't something you can turn off. "John wanted to drop me off, but Boggs' is a few blocks away. We were in the car forever driving home. Even though it's been a few days I still needed to stretch my legs. I cannot believe you're working here for Christmas!" she screams.

"I know, I was hoping to visit, especially with Mom and Dad out of town, and then when Allyn sent me my new job assignment I didn't think I'd be able to. *Then* I got the details and I was shocked."

"How's the lodge? I haven't been up there yet." She takes a bite of the biggest, gooiest cinnamon roll I've ever seen. Patty winks at us as she scurries back to her register to ring a line that's quickly forming.

"The lodge is every Christmas dream I've ever had come to life."

"That good, huh? Well, don't get too invested in Garland. You know you have to be team Clover, with me. Novel has Ben on their side because most of his businesses are on that side of the Stateline. But we have Vikingstrong, Revival, Patty's, and Boggs'."

"This place does well off-season." My coffee is steaming, strong, and perfect.

"Patty's is Clover's claim to fame. I've heard Novel is going to try and get their bookstore to add a coffee bar to compete, but I've also heard Wanda Crosby is retiring and looking to sell. Try that chocolate croissant." She nudges my plate toward me, so I do, picking delicately at the flaky crust covered in smooth, melted chocolate. It dissolves in my mouth like fluffy cotton candy, ridiculously divine.

"Ohmigod," I mumble, taking another sip of my coffee to cut the sweet. "So good."

"Like Dad's cotton candy, but chocolate, right?"

"That's exactly what I was thinking!"

She nods. "Patty's the best. I've gained five pounds since moving here."

"You look amazing," I say, licking chocolate from my fingertips.

"Thank you," she smiles, big and bright.

"You're happy," I add, going to town on the croissant now, it's not long for this world.

"Mhm." She nods. "I am. What a whirlwind summer was, but now we're all settled in and the motel is about to open, and—"

"How's that going?"

"A couple of snags here and there, to be expected, but overall, great. Reno is done. Now I put the finishing touches on all the rooms. Can you post about it? We're opening on Valentine's weekend, trying to draw a couples crowd since that's the most off-season month of the year."

"Good for a soft launch, though."

"Exactly what I was thinking."

"Am I going to see a ring on your finger from lover boy anytime soon?" I know John has a ring stashed somewhere, and I wonder if she's got a clue?

"Oh gosh," her cheeks turn crimson. "We've got so much going on with the bar and the motel. I mean we've talked about it, but there's no rush." I believe her, I know my sister is happy, but I also know she's dying for a ring, and a wedding, and kids. The whole shebang. "I want some reviews and word of mouth for Thistle and Burr by spring."

"Solid plan," I nod. "Of course, I'll post. I should have my phone back and access to socials by then." After my post about Beanie's sugar cookie latte, I got flagged by Streamflix and Marco told me to lay low online or else I'll be bombarded by press trying to get *Royal Hearts* intel.

"You still don't have your phone? Not even on the weekends?" She looks around as if my phone might be walking out the door on its own accord as we speak. "How are you surviving? It's a part of you, like an appendage. Or like something that's grown on you, like that pretty green mold on the trees around here—"

"Frannie," I laugh, "You're spinning. It's not that big of a deal."

She blinks, stunned. "Oh. Weird. Are you like, dying?" She grasps my hand. She's joking, but also, not.

"I get access while we're on set but they've got all these restrictions so we can't intervene with the show. They don't want the media to get to me, I guess."

I realize my sister's reaction means I needed this hiatus from my phone more than I realized. "I haven't watched any of the live streams or replays either. Truthfully, I don't want to see myself, and I'm beginning to understand Winter's aversion to the media."

"Winter?"

"Yeah, that guy in the castle who's the star of the show I'm working on."

"Okay, smartass, I know. But I've never heard you talk about him like he's an actual human and not the monster in your nightmares—never heard you use his actual name and not *pretty man*."

I shift in my seat. "We've kinda gotten to know each other while on set. Enough that I know he struggles with the media, his family . . ."

"Hmm. That's interesting." She looks around the café, keeping her voice light. "I wouldn't know. I haven't watched," she murmurs.

I eye her suspiciously, knowing full well John mentioned she watched a little. "I can't believe you haven't watched?" I test her. "Not at all?"

"Nope—well, okay, a little," she finally admits, unable to stick to the lie. "You're kinda famous, Cat," she gushes, eyes watering with laughter.

"What about John? He must want to watch his buddy—*wait, what?*"

Her eyes go wide and she leans in. "People know who you are, it's weird. But we've been on the road and so busy, so I haven't completely kept up." I know exactly how busy they've been, up to their ears in romantic road trips and cozy hotel rooms. I'm happy for her, if not a tad jealous. "But yes, we've watched. Maybe more than a little," she says through her teeth as if I'm going to scold her.

Instead, I prompt her, realizing in the moment how much I want to know. "And?"

"People like you . . ." she trails off, leading me to believe people don't like me. Exactly what I was afraid of.

"They hate me," I drop my head to the table.

"So," she braces her hands on the table seriously, "in the beginning, it's true, people didn't really like either one of you, I don't think. But also, all the contestants are funny and they were airing their backstories and stuff, so you weren't even on that much. But then, that mountain date when you pinched his earlobe to get him through vertigo . . . and then the wreath date, you drawing that black heart on his wrist . . ."

"They showed all that?"

Maybe I should just hand you the crown, send everyone else home.

"Yeah," she bites down on the straw in her water glass, "you've got some fans saying they wish you guys would hook up." She shakes her head as if the thoughts are her own and she needs to get back to reality. "But you hate Winter Larsen. I've witnessed how much you both squabble, multiple times."

I shrug again, and will my features to stay neutral. "Eh, he's not that bad, actually."

"He's not that bad, *actually*?" she parrots me. "Well, that explains the whole situation with the Rushmores." Her grin is mischievous.

I sit up straight. "What about them?"

"Oh, nothing," she twirls a piece of hair and sips her coffee. "Mom called me because she couldn't get a hold of you. Said that the Rushmores were very grateful to the friend you told to invest in them? Ring any bells yet?"

I'm on the edge of my seat, "I have no idea what you're talking about."

She scrunches her nose, realizing I'm completely in the dark here. "Winter called them and invested in Beanie's. They've already had new countertops installed, a new paint job, a new sign hung above the door, and new espresso machines delivered yesterday. This is all per Mom, but she was rushing to board a plane so I didn't get the details."

"Wait—*what*?" I'm down to two words in my entire vocabulary as I shake my head and try to make sense of what she said. "Winter? Helped the Rushmores? *My Rushmores?*

"What did you do to him, Kitty-Cat?" She blinks innocently but she knows exactly what's going on. "John said he was obsessed with tracking them down and making them an offer they couldn't refuse as a silent partner. He dropped a bucket of cash in their laps without much in return."

"Why did he do that?" I breathe.

"Oh, I think I *know why.*"

"Why?" My eyes are wide open and I'm trying to read her face for clues. It couldn't be because of me . . . because I care about the Rushmore's, and he knows that . . . It couldn't be.

"You know. I'm aware Mom and Dad think you're the smart one," she laughs and holds up a hand to stop me when I'm about to protest. "I'm just saying, when it comes to matters of the heart, you're a real dummy."

How did this happen?

"Oh God, Frannie, now I can't hate his guts for all eternity. Not after he's done something like this." My head falls with a thunk on the table, at least I'm able to inhale the bits of chocolate left on my plate as I let the sounds of the coffee shop soothe me.

I've never in my life been so confused over one human being.

"Noooooo," she says, but enthusiastically, jumping up and down in her chair.

I plug my ears and glare at her, pretty sure she means, *yes*, but the word still rings true to my ears. "Seriously, you can't be saying—"

"I think you like him."

"Noooooo," I groan back, dropping my head again to my crumb-covered plate.

Nineteen

CAT

"Streamflix wants more B-roll." Marco sidles up to me while we watch Winter mimic a Little Star Lodge bartender in a black vest and bowtie, shaking a dirty martini for Lexi A. from Alabama. It's become easier to keep the last two Lexi's left on the show apart if we refer to her that way.

"Okay. I'll let Winter know." He's not going to like it, and I don't relish subjecting him to more exposure either.

"His attitude is improving, but his heart doesn't seem in this. We need him to sell it."

"I'm working on it, but honestly, the women don't seem to care. I think you're right, they're all here to work their platforms." And we've only got a month left to film.

"They don't matter. He matters. Viewers are falling in love with him."

"I'm on it," I say more firmly than I've ever spoken to him before.

He backs off immediately and I love him for it. "I know, you got this, lion woman. I hear you roaring." He waves his hands between us congenially, "I'm on your side, you know."

"Then act like it." I slap him on the shoulder and give him my best smile, my Frannie smile, using all my teeth.

Out of nowhere, I feel—literally feel—Winters's eyes on me and turn around.

Sure enough, he's staring at me while all the ladies sit across the bar, perched on stools, watching him.

He snaps his fingers high in the air. "Bloom, Bloom? I need you." He looks like a smart English gentleman, not to mention his hair perfectly styled away from his face, highlighting a handsome jawline and winsome smile.

Annoyed by the snapping that is surely meant to annoy me, I march over to the bar. I've let my guard down with him too much. Today, it's back to business. I don't care why he helped the Rushmores. Maybe all princes dream of owning a cozy American coffee shop.

"Mandy would like an eggnog martini." He's got a secret in his eyes, all mischievous and boyish, and I don't think it has anything to do with Mandy and her drink order.

"Okay," I wait for him to finish whatever he's getting at and try to stay out of the shot at the same time.

"We don't have any. So let's you and me run out real quick and get some."

"Cat, turn your mic on. You're on camera!" Marco whisper-shouts from behind Robbie.

"Let me," Winter reaches toward my waist where my mic pack is clipped to my back pocket.

"I got it," I say, holding one hand up and using the other to flip the 'on' button by memory. "I don't have a car here, Winter," I manage between clenched teeth while trying to maintain a smile. Robbie's camera blinks a red light in my line of vision and Frannie's words about fans speculating about us ringing in my ears.

"Not much of a personal assistant, is she?" he says to his adoring onlookers. They snicker and sip drinks.

"But it's so cozy. Eggnog, the fire roaring, the tree outside. And our Christmas sweaters. We have to have eggnog, Winter." Mandy, like the other ladies, is dressed in matching Christmas sweaters the show had made for this 'holiday mixology' date. They say *Royal Hearts* with a crown where the O should be.

"We can take the production van, Bloom," he says a little more pleadingly to me.

"I'll go," I say under my breath so hopefully only he can hear.

"I want to come with you," he replies equally low, "Get me out of here, please."

Quickly, I use my hands to cover each of our mics clipped at our collars. "Winter, you're on a date!"

"Not the one I want to be on." No. No, no, no.

Did he say that? Did his mic, or mine, pick up the audio?

This exchange cannot be happening while filming. "What can I do to change your mind? We can't just leave, the two of us, in the middle of your date."

"Then let's all go—"

"Winter, we can't—"

"Take it or leave it, Bloom. If not, I'm throwing you over my shoulder. There's no reason I can't walk out of here."

"You wouldn't."

He leans down and I try to brace myself, all the women lean forward on their barstools in unison trying to catch what he whispers in my ear, "I need to talk to you."

"No, you don't," I say sweetly, uncovering his mic and turning toward the bar. He's not going to let up on this. "Field trip ladies!"

"Where are we going?" Marco asks.

"We need nog," Winter says with a laugh in his voice that I know now is more anxiety than anything. His hands fidget with a bar glass, so I slowly tap his elbow.

He puts the glass down, and then reaches for my hand. We're

behind the bar, what can it hurt? He needs a connection, something to ground him while he's got a camera shoved in his face. If it's not a heart drawn on his wrist, which I wasn't here to do before they started today and I feel bad about, I guess it's holding on to someone who knows he's struggling behind that cocky grin of his.

The cast of women sings, "Road trip!" And as if on cue, every single contestant hops off their bar stool and squeals.

We all follow Winter out into the snow like the classroom full of toddlers I saw holding a rope and marching down Main Street last week, and pile into the production van.

"I don't think this is worth getting my own spinoff," Lexi H. mutters to no one in particular.

"Lexi," I turn in my seat. "This show isn't edited. Remember, everything you say is out there." The girl is not my favorite, but she must know her current attitude will never land her a spinoff.

"Right," she nods as if truly grateful for the advice. "This is a lot."

The van pulls down the long, winding road, heading through the only exit and entrance to the lodge and squeezing through the pass that dumps us, finally, onto Main Street.

"Stop here." Winter taps on the driver's shoulder. He pulls into a spot at Grover's Market. "Everybody out!"

"Can't you just run in?" Mandy demands. She seems pretty over this show. And winning his heart, if that was ever her real intention.

He raises an eyebrow at her. "Sure can, princess." She preens at the nickname, probably picturing herself in his crown. Then he adds, "Bloom, you come with." And her face drops like a hot potato.

"I'm not buying Mandy eggnog," I huff, but Marco gives me wide *this is your job* eyes. "Fine. But so you know, this is insanely humiliating."

"Attagirl," Winter pats my thigh. Despite my trying not to, a big fat ball of warmth explodes in my chest. I've made him happy, which has in turn made me happy.

When the hell did that start happening?

Winter registers my smile and looks pleased as punch. He wanted to talk to me alone, and now through an unscripted field trip, he's gotten exactly that. I glare at him as hard as I can until I feel a vein popping in my forehead and I soften my face when I realize Robbie's camera trained on me with laser focus and only about a foot of space.

Before I can protest his wily ways, he's out the other door and walking toward the grocery store with the camera trotting behind him.

Marco shoos me with his hands. "Go! Follow him!"

"Good luck," Lexi A. says, the only girl I'd grab a drink with in this van.

I have to sprint to catch up with his long, regal-looking stride.

"Will you wait up?" A cramp pops in my side as I hustle toward a quaint market with a waving Santa in a sleigh on the roof.

He pulls open a door with a dancing cartoon Christmas tree painted on the glass, a banner over its head proclaiming *Happy Holidays from Grover's Market.*

"Is everything always storybook-perfect around here?" I huff, not even sure who I'm mad at. The cartoon tree? If so, that's a new low for me.

"After you."

"Thank you," I glance at the blinking red light behind me and stride through. Winter orchestrated this entire moment and I can't even be mad at him about it, because secretly, I've been craving his attention.

I can't ignore the jitters in my stomach when he's around now, and I don't know what to do about it.

"So," he claps his hands. "What sounds good?"

"Eggnog. Isn't that why we're here? Though the thought of creamy, eggy, alcohol makes me want to gag."

He shivers, pulling his bowtie until it hangs loose. "Same. But duty calls. We must procure the finest in all the land for the spoiled brat in the backseat—"

"Winter!" I shush him and make eyes at the camera so he gets the hint.

"Bloom!" He makes wild eyes right back at me. "You need to lighten up."

"I'm light."

"Then loosen up." He pops two buttons on his collar to punctuate his statement.

"I'm loose." I even shake my shoulders out and stretch my neck to prove it.

He raises an eyebrow and turns on his heel, leading me down an aisle full of drinks. It seems we've lost Robbie for the time being, who stopped to grab a Dr. Pepper and ended up fighting with an old-timey refrigerator. "It was suffocating in there. I needed to get out for a minute. And I need to talk to you about something."

He reaches for my hand but I move away, unsure where the camera is. I pull a bottle of eggnog off the shelf, but when I turn around, Winter is there, all chest and shoulders like I knew he would be.

"Did you know," he gulps and I watch the cords in his neck flex, "that we have fans?"

"You and me?" I do know, Frannie told me but . . .

"They think we're secretly attracted to each other. The Prince and the PA."

We stand there in the beverage aisle, under fluorescents with music softly flowing overhead. Judy Garland sweetly suggests we have ourselves a merry little Christmas, and we just sort of orbit around each other. The heat coming off him makes me want to snuggle in but I know if Robbie hasn't found us yet, he will, and soon.

"But that would be crazy," I murmur, it takes all my strength to get the words out.

"It would," he confirms, but halfheartedly, I'm not sure he believes it.

He takes a step forward and I shiver. "Wear. The. Coat."

I laugh, a gaspy thing because that's not what I expected him to say. *What did I expect him to say?* I shake my head at him, "What are we doing?"

"If I told you that the fans are right, I am attracted to you," he gulps, "Very attracted, Cat." His eyes roam my face, "Would that make you uncomfortable?"

My hands, clutching a bottle of eggnog, come between us as he steps closer. Citrus, clove, and the smell of matches making me dizzy. "Honestly, everything about you makes me uncomfortable," I gasp. The venom that's usually in my voice isn't there, much as I try.

"See, here's the thing, Bloom," He takes another step, pressing me into shelves as bottles rattle and clang. "I don't believe you anymore."

He pulls a marker from his back pocket, it's red. "I couldn't find black," he says.

"We can't do this, you and me. We can't be feeling like this, or standing like this, or—"

"But you feel it, too?" he asks, placing the bottle back on the shelf and turning my wrist up to face him. He draws a red heart on the tender skin. "I thought, this might help you with whatever you're feeling nervous about, like it helps me."

A throat clears and Winter drags his gaze to where Robbie's camera appears in the aisle, then back to me.

I look down at the heart on my wrist, frozen in the moment, but then something inside me warms, softens. Like I've been cracked down the center and all of me comes pouring out.

I look up and plead with him, using only my eyes, knowing full well the camera is pulling in tighter and tighter. Both of us are breathing fast, I can see him becoming more and more uncomfortable as Robbie steps closer.

This is my job. We cannot be caught on camera. What would Streamflix even do at this point? We're halfway through filming the show.

Winter seems to understand, stepping around me and shielding us for one last moment, giving the camera his back.

He presses his thumb into the red heart on my wrist before begrudgingly retreating. Everything he's feeling is written across his face: want, need, and a surprisingly sweet determination. I guess that's what he needed to talk to me about, but for the life of me, I can't make sense of anything he said.

"Cat found the eggnog," he says roughly, keeping his eyes on mine.

I grab the bottle off the shelf behind me and hold it up, stupidly, for Robbie and his camera. "Here it is."

Robbie laughs at us, breaking some of the tension and pulling me back to reality. *Thank you, Robbie.*

The three of us wrap back around to the front of the store. Winter pulls the bottle of eggnog from my tight grasp and plops it on the sole checkout.

"Well, well, Winter Larsen. Fancy seeing you in my establishment."

"Hello, Grover," he drawls without missing a beat. On the other hand, I'm still an emotional puddle next to him, trying to hold myself together.

"And this is?"

"Cathy Bloomfield," Winter's large hand waves over my person, then gestures elegantly across the conveyor as if we're being introduced in a fancy restaurant, "Grover Stockton." Grover adjusts a corduroy hat with an embroidered fish that says Holiday Bait, Boat, and Tackle in a happy font, shaggy brown hair pouring out the sides.

"Am I going to be on TV?" Grover adjusts his hat and pushes some shaggy hair behind his ears.

"It's streaming, live, so as long as you sign a waiver, yes," I reply.

"So now would be a good time to tell all the viewers about how Winter and his buddies glitter-bombed my family's goat farm back in high school, right?" He's got a shit-eating grin as he waits for Winter's reaction.

"You snitched on John's senior year prank!" Winter says, taking the bait. "What did you expect?"

"Ah hell, it's just 'cause I thought you guys were cool."

"We think you're cool, Grover. No harm, no foul. We're even, yeah? Water under the bridge."

The two men shake hands and I can't help it, I give the camera a WTF look. "Okay, then. If we're done with the walk down memory lane, boys. I've got a prince to marry off." I hand Grover a debit card Streamflix supplied for expenses like this and he swipes it.

He hands the card back to me. "Winter getting married? I never thought we'd see the day. Damn, first Boggs buys a ring, now you?"

Immediately, I cover the camera lens with my hand. "Wait, how do you know he's got a ring? He hasn't proposed yet—"

"Nah, the whole town knows he's got a ring. We're rootin' for him."

"If you don't keep it down, Frannie's going to know he's got a ring, Grover," Winter winces and nods toward the camera.

"Oh, geez. Shoot. I didn't mean—"

"Hands off the lens, Cat." Oh shit, Robbie is not playing right now. I've never heard him so stern, his voice dropped ten octaves.

"Sorry," I mouth to him, removing my hand gently. "Winter's here to find true love," I tell Grover, mostly for the camera's sake, trying to get us back on track.

"For fuck's sake, Bloom," Winter says, dejected. "They're here for the crown, the castle, and the inheritance. Can we drop the act of this being about a love match? That's never what it was about and everyone but you knows it."

My jaw drops. I look at Grover who shrugs. Then, I look into the camera, frozen, while Winter stomps out the door.

Back in the van, he's still in a mood and suddenly announces, "We're not going back to the lodge stuffed in here like rabbits in a hutch. Take us to my place. I've got a better idea."

"Are we finally going to see the castle?" Lexi H. asks.

Twenty

WINTER

We pull off the main road to the public parking above Vikingstrong and I jump out of the van and into the cold.

"There's no good way to get everyone down," Cat says, knowing good and well what kind of hike it is and that the ladies in heels will never make it. "Especially with the snow starting to accumulate." She peels off the group and comes to stand next to me while I gaze at the lake below. "Are you okay?"

"I want to check on the horses." I don't know how to tell her that I can't articulate what's wrong with me. Suddenly, faking it on this show is excruciatingly painful, the last thing on earth I want to do. I'd almost rather move back to Denmark if I have to keep playing this game and that gives me pause. Abdication is an option, but I want to be a part of the crown, just my way.

Could I have both? Do I have the nerve to try?

It's nearing five o'clock now, the temps are dropping, and the wind is picking up. Water crashes more than normal on the beach below. There's a storm coming.

"Um," Mandy pipes up, "We aren't dressed for a hike, Cat."

"Aren't we going to make drinks?" Lexi A. from Alabama holds up the eggnog.

"I just," I drag a hand down my face, unsure how I got here. Not *here*, as in Vikingstrong, but *here*, as in this mess with a show I'm finding out I want nothing to do with. "I'm sorry, I want to check on a few things before the weather turns."

I want to show up for my country, and make them proud, but not like this.

I don't know what I'm doing anymore. I've completely lost track of why I'm here. Did I really want to punish Cat? Was I really that pissed? She did nothing wrong other than telling a little fib. Why did I seek her out like this? Why did I insert myself into her business? Why was I so obsessed with making her pay?

We had sparks from the start, and as I've come to know her, I've realized perhaps we got off on the wrong foot. How different things might have been if I hadn't overreacted at the game? Now, I know she cares deeply for others, including her sister. It explains everything.

I could never have predicted the way she'd support me. She's taken care of me with an unspoken understanding of my struggles with anxiety, media, the Crown—all of it.

The thought rocks inside my chest, crashing like the water in the lake on the beach below. I don't want to know this about myself, to know that I went way overboard, because I was scared of my own shortcomings. Scared to be taken advantage of, believing that everyone wanted something from me. And then of all people to prove me wrong, it's Cat Bloomfield.

What the fuck?

"Take them back in the van. I'll meet you there," I command no one in particular.

Marco opens his mouth to protest but Cat interjects. "He needs a minute, Marco. We can give him a minute."

"Fine." Marco nods, motioning for the ladies to get back in the van. They all groan thankfully. "But stay with him, we'll send the van right back for you." Robbie and Cat trek down the mountain after me, snowfall making it slick. I glance over my shoulder, gauging my distance from Cat in case she slips.

"Hey, excuse me, sir. I am not dressed for a hike down a mountain in the dead of winter, either!" Cat hollers.

"You have a suitable coat, but you're too stubborn to wear it," I holler back.

I'm pissed. Mad at her for *not wanting anything from me* to the point of not taking my help, refusing to let me in. Mad at myself for wanting in so badly.

They struggle to keep up as I wrap around the castle, skirting the lake and finally come to large stable doors with wrought iron pulls.

"Winter, hold up," Cat says. But I'm on a mission, making my way down the row of stalls.

"Here they are." I pull apples from a bag on the wall and feed one to Daylight, and one to her colt, Destiny. Instantly, I feel better. Grounded.

"They're both beautiful. Can I?" Cat comes to stand at my side, raising her hand to pet Destiny's pink nose.

"Sure, let her see your hand first." I flatten her palm out while the horse investigates, sniffing and snorting, then gently place a red apple in her hand. It's gone in a flash of fat teeth.

Destiny tosses her head a little. "Her nose is so soft," Cat says.

I hand her another apple.

The horse greedily gobbles the treat and slobbers generously on Cat's palm. If she minds, she doesn't show it.

"What happened back there? What's happening with you today, in general?" she asks.

How do I explain what's happening to me when I don't know

myself? "You're a natural. Animals can sense who you are, what you want, how you feel. She likes you."

"Does she?" She holds my gaze. "Do you? Really? After everything?"

I told her I was attracted to her, but just because I've had a change of heart doesn't mean she has. "Do you want to talk about it?"

She bites her lip. "Winter, you know we can't do anything more than *like each other*, right?"

"Come on, then." It's not what I want to hear, but also, I'm not a quitter. I grab her hand and pull her further down the hall, rounding a corner into my small office with all sorts of horsey things on the walls.

I plop into a well-worn leather chair on a swivel and pick up an ancient landline covered with dust and dirt. Space heaters litter the room, the smell of oats and particles in the air. I unbutton my stupid bartender vest from the lodge and toss it to a corner of the room.

"Hey," I say into the phone to one of the guys who works my horses when I can't, "Can you get the draft horses ready? It's about time we get the sleigh up to the lodge. I'll take it for a test spin or two over the next week before showtime."

"Showtime?" Cat asks from the doorway, her eyes casting all over the room but her feet stuck outside. It's as if she doesn't want to step fully into my world. She's hesitant, and I don't blame her. I'm freaking out, no idea where things lie with us.

"The kids from the grade school in town come up to the lodge every year on Christmas Eve for a sleigh ride around the mountains. I'm a sleigh-driving Santa. Are you shocked?"

"No. A month ago I would have been, but I can see it," she says, idly dusting her fingers over old bridles tacked to the wall. "You're surprisingly sweet under all your sad puppy eyes and porcupine quills." She can't meet my gaze when she says it.

Still, I watch her touch everything, memorizing her in my space.

"Hmm." I flip through some paperwork on the desk. "Annie says something very similar." I stand, trying to hide my new delight at the decision I've just made. "Okay, ready?"

"For what?"

"To ride back?" I need to get this girl on a horse. I don't know why, I just do.

"But you sent the van back to the Lodge. We'll have to wait a while for it to circle back for us."

"Nope. We're taking Daylight."

"We? What about Robbie?"

Shit, I forgot all about Robbie and his eagle-eye-long lens. He's hovering a few feet outside the doorway. "Can you ride a horse with that thing on your shoulder?"

He shakes his blue mohawk no, an incredulous look on his face.

"We can't go without him," Cat protests.

"Who's going to stop us, Bloom?"

"Winter, I, about earlier . . ." It's in her eyes, there's a warmth that wasn't there before, her guard is coming down and her walls are crumbling whether she likes it or not.

But she's struggling with the choice, I can see that. "Come on, Robbie, follow me. I've already arranged a suitable ride." I pull on an old sweater I left at some point in the barn, and a spare coat off a hook for her.

Cat and I mount Daylight, with a small boost from me first to get her in the saddle. It takes some serious debating with Robbie to get the man awkwardly on the back of the sleigh, his camera aimed at my horse. But we're finally all making our way through a snow-dusted town. It's quiet, most shop owners have closed up due to the weather. Twisting lake roads are nothing to mess with covered in ice. Robbie rocks from side to side on the back of the sleigh while it's drawn by my horses and my wrangler as they head up the mountain.

He doesn't look happy, but he does look funny.

When I check on Cat behind me, snowflakes dot strands of her hair and dust the tip of her nose. Her lips are crimson and positively kissable against the white background and I mentally chastise myself for even going there.

I'm torturing myself on purpose now.

Riding on horseback with Cat gripping me around my middle, despite the fact Robbie is facing us with his damn camera, is kind of perfect. I can't quite put my finger on what it's making me feel. Not long ago I would have hated it—feeling her all pressed up behind me in the saddle and feeling every shift of our torsos as we ride—because I thought she was awful and I thought I hated her.

Now, not only has all that misplaced anger melted away, but I find myself past the point of curious about Cat Bloomfield. I find I'm obsessed with figuring out what makes her tick. I want to know her, in any way she'll let me.

I don't want this time between us to end. We've been around each other nonstop the past month and as each day progresses, I'm more and more sad when it ends. When she goes her way, and I go mine.

I steal another glance over my shoulder. "You look good on a horse. Feel good." I transfer the reins to one hand and squeeze her hands where they're clasped around me. "Let's try to lose them."

"What? No, we can't!"

"You know, contrary to what everyone believes, I'm not a puppet. I'm not a dog to be trotted out for show. I'm sick of the cameras and sick of doing what everyone else wants me to do."

"I know, but it's only a few more weeks."

"It's been my entire life, Cat, and I'm exhausted."

She drops her forehead between my shoulder blades as if giving in. I think she's tired, too.

"A lot of people would kill to be in your shoes," she whispers.

"Are you sure you want to give it up so easily, to give up looking for someone on the show? We could go back, finish the date . . ."

"Are you really asking me that question?" I laugh. Absurd. She knows there's no one on the show I'm interested in.

I think she knows who I want.

But she keeps pushing, determined as ever. "Yes. To have a chance at finding love handed to them on a platter? It's a privilege."

"Are you speaking personally?"

"God, no."

"See? So why am I supposed to love opening my life, myself, for everyone to see but you'd have nothing to do with it?"

She shakes her head. "It's not in the cards for me."

"Going on a reality show to nab a Prince Charming?"

"Nabbing anyone. I don't do relationships, never have. I would never give someone that kind of power over me."

"Never?"

"I mean, the few times I've let things get a little serious they never worked out. And then I got hurt. And then I felt—"

"Weak."

She takes in a slow controlled breath, contemplating her response. "I can take care of myself, I always have. It's easier that way."

"Turn your mic off."

"What?"

"You're wearing a mic," I remind her.

"Oh, yeah. Why?"

"Bloom" I groan. I'm trying to be spontaneous. And it might land me in a tub of hot water with her, but I can't care about the risk right now. All I can do is get away from all of this, and fuck if I'm not going to take her with me. She needs a break as much as I do. She needs a soft place to land. "Aren't you tired of all this?"

I've hit a nerve because she relaxes behind me and says, "Okay,

okay," and reaches around her back while keeping one arm wrapped around my waist to turn her mic off.

"Mine too, please."

Without hesitating, she pushes my sweater up in the back. "Shit, Bloom, your hands are cold."

She lets her fingers graze bare skin, enjoying my torture a little too much. "Done. They're both off. Marco is going to have an aneurysm."

Ahead, Robbie's face drops instantly when he realizes he has no audio. Somewhere, I imagine Marco has gone nuclear, but neither of us has a phone and there's no way for him to communicate with us.

"Now, hold on tight."

"Why?"

I kick Daylight firmly with my heels and pull her reins to turn her.

The horse pivots on a dime, and we take off like a shot.

The snow falls heavier and heavier with every second we ride. We cut through trees, taking hiking trails off the road. There's only a short way to go before we make it back to Main Street, then we can slow our pace and wind back to Vikingstrong.

But for now, I let the horse run.

"Hold on tight," I shout with another quick glance over my shoulder.

The pounding of hooves against the ground rings out as we ride. Cat's hands squeeze right in the center of my chest as she holds on. Equestrian riding usually requires holding the reins with two hands, but this horse can neck rein so I grip both in one hand and reach up to press my palm over her hands.

"Do you like going fast?" I shout over my shoulder.

"I love it!"

She's beaming. But that doesn't last long, because when I look back, there's a low hanging branch headed straight for us. There's no time to turn, so I drop the reins and swing one leg over the horse's neck to make a moving dismount. I've never done this with someone else in the saddle, but I manage to grab Cat around the waist and take her with me.

She screams as we land and the horse continues galloping right under the enormous branch that would have taken us out.

I hit the ground on solid footing, but the force of both our bodies propelling off the horse is too much to stabilize, and we go rolling in the snow. Both my hands wrap instinctually around her head, trying to save her from serious injury.

"Holyfuckshit," I gasp as we tumble through deep snow that most definitely broke our fall. I land on top of her, bracing my weight immediately, my eyes searching her stunned face.

"What the hell was that, cowboy?" Her lips are blue, her face is white, but her humor is still intact. A good sign for sure. My hands search her face, no cuts, no gashes anywhere I can see. Another good sign.

"There was a branch, and no time," I'm breathing heavily all over her, surveying her from head, to neck, to torso. My hair falls in my face and I push it back, I need to see every inch of her unharmed before I'll be satisfied.

"Winter, relax. I'm okay. Are you okay?"

"Don't worry about me, is anything broken?" Continuing with my assessment, I open the coat she's wearing to gingerly run my figers over her ribcage checking for breaks or pain. She sucks in a breath. "Tender?"

"No." She looks up at me through her lashes and shakes her head.

I bend one arm and then the other. Run my hands down her legs, bending both her knees, checking one ankle, and then rotating the other.

"Ouch, shit, don't do that," she breathes.

"Does it hurt?"

"Yes, Winter." She sits up more in the snow, her clothes soaked but there's no blood to be seen. Thank God. "It hurts."

"Cat, I didn't think, I just jumped and took you with me."

"It's fine, I'm fine."

"You're not. Your ankle's sprained, I think."

I shove a handful of snow in her boot and she yelps. "What are you doing?"

"Putting snow on your ankle, in case it swells up like a balloon. Do you want me to take your boot off first? I'm not sure if I'm supposed to do that?"

"No, I don't want you to take my boot off," she answers, incredulous. "How are we going to get back?" Towering trees rise above us and she looks up to the sky.

"I'll go after the horse. You sit tight, I'll be right back."

She groans, "That's what they say in slasher movies! Don't say that!"

"Worried about me?" I joke, anything to make light of our situation, of how scared I was that I'd gotten her hurt.

"I'm worried about me," she says, then adds, "And maybe I'm worried about you just a little. I'm glad you're not hurt." She pats at her hair and looks around the forest. "There's so much white."

"That makes two of us, Bloom. And yeah, this is a lot of snow. We need to get out of here."

"Then be safe," she gestures with her chin as if shooing me off, "but only because you're my ride home, cowboy."

"Ma'am. I will return."

"Winter, I'm serious. Be careful." A cracking branch echoes nearby and she jumps.

"Just trees bending under the weight of snowfall," I say, grasping her around the waist and lifting her into my arms.

There's more coming down around us. It seems to be picking up. She's scared, and I get it. We nearly broke our necks and now I've got to go find this horse if we want to make it home without getting frostbite.

"What are you doing?"

Though I relish the feel of her in my arms, I set her gently against a tree and check her coat pockets. An old beanie I wear when I ride is there and I plunk it on her head. "I swear it, I'll get you home safe."

"You should wear your hat," she says, but pulls it low over her ears as she shivers. That makes me smile.

I press a light kiss to the top of her head as I stand. If she thinks anything of it, she doesn't say a word. "It's going to be okay, Cat. Trust me."

She nods, and I head off into the trees praying our horse hasn't gone far.

Twenty-One

CAT

He stomps his boots at the back door of Vikingstrong. Snow clings to both of us as he enters the mudroom off the side of the rustic castle—me leaning against the doorjamb to catch my breath because I refuse to lean on him.

"This snow really came out of nowhere." He's smiling, bigger, wider than I've seen to date. He's glad we're still alive, I guess? "Doesn't usually fall so heavy in town or on the lake, it's got to be a record. Did you bring the chill along with the drama, Bloom?"

The snark that used to riddle his tone is no longer there. After falling off a horse and almost losing him in a snowstorm, we're both awake in a way we weren't before. Now, he's playing with me. "I'm from the Bay Area, you ninny," I say to his retreating back.

The rafters and the eaves above the door are all carved wood. I can feel the history, the charm, and the warmth of the place seeping from the mudroom inside, beckoning me to enter.

He spins, catching me off guard with a direct look. "Why

aren't you wearing the coat I gave you? Why won't you let me help you instead of hobbling on one foot in a snowstorm?" When I don't respond, he huffs a disgruntled breath. "Ignore that it's me offering the help if you must. The coat is *Prada*. And as for the ankle, if you don't let me help you I'm afraid you're only going to make it worse!"

That makes me laugh. No one has ever worried about me this much.

"You can't buy people with gifts, Winter." The words burst from my mouth, I can't stuff them back in and I can't help hating the way his face falls when he hears them. "Sorry, that was mean about the coat. Maybe I thought that's what you were doing at first . . ."

"But not now?"

Slowly, I shake my head. "It's not what I think now," I say, looking up at him. "And my ankle is fine. It's just twisted. I'll walk it off here in a minute when it stops throbbing."

"You'll do no such thing."

"I shouldn't even be here," I counter. "We have to get back up the mountain."

"Why not?" His bottom lip puffs out and I've got an unrealistic urge to stroke my thumb across it. The way he helped me when I slipped from the horse, the way he worried. *The way I worried for him when he went into the trees and didn't come back for what felt like a very long time.* "Let me take care of you, like you've taken care of me."

It's possible gifts are how he shows his affection—like the coat, the mailbox, and the sweet little key. I guess that does track, in general gift gift-giving terms of endearment.

But if I let him take care of me in that way . . . A tiny voice inside me is screaming to be careful, tread lightly. I don't *need* anyone to take care of me. Even with a bum ankle and a snow storm on the way.

"Cat, I'm serious," he presses.

"It's not that easy for me," I blurt, even though my mind is swimming and I honestly don't know how I feel about him anymore. "To let someone in."

"Can't you elaborate?" he asks, pushing two hands through his hair. It slicks back with the wet snow, away from his face so there's no hiding from his searching eyes. "If it's because I was such an ass to you before, I'm sorry. I was so wrong about who you are."

The request feels like a challenge, even though part of me knows it's not. "I carry my own bags. I cook my own dinner. I don't depend on anyone." I throw my arms out wide and catch myself on the doorjam when I wobble on my bad ankle.

"But, why?" He stomps through the hall, back toward the doorway where I lean, and scoops me up.

"Hey, you can't just do that!" He carries me over the threshold and toward a cozy cream and blue kitchen with lots of warm wood.

"Yes, I can. When you need help, Bloom, I'll give it." I scoff but I don't fight him further. I'm about done fighting him, I think.

He notices my letting him manhandle me, and he gazes into my eyes. "Where I'm from, we take care of each other. Maybe not my immediate family, but my people, my culture."

When he plops me unceremoniously on a counter, he opens his mouth again as if he's going to launch into another scolding, or another lesson, or maybe even another question as to why I am the way I am, but Annie comes running in with fluffy slippers on her feet, knitting needles poking from a bun in her hair.

"I told him to leave," she gasps, out of breath. "I was in my cottage, minding my own business with Penny Lane and my knitting, and saw the cars on the streetside monitors. We really should have security for this—hello, Ms. Bloomfield."

"Cat," I correct her, remembering our friendly conversation over the phone a few weeks ago. She smiles warmly at me.

"Who's here?" Winter demands, paying no attention to her

and fussing with removing my coat that's soaked through from my roll in the snow.

My eyes slide over the room, a mix of creams and whites with dark wood furniture. On a carved table near a large window, there's a stack of cream stationary and red calligraphy pen.

"Anker, in the living room. Little menace, he's got the team with him." While she is worrying with her hands, the look on her face is all determination.

"Who's Anker?" I ask.

"My parents' PR, and his team of lackeys. He's the reason they got on board with *Royal Hearts*. It was all his idea, no matter he's known me since I was three and is aware how much I hate cameras invading my life." He takes a deep breath and turns back to Annie who's pulling tea cups off a shelf. "I didn't see any vehicles—my parents?" I watch his hands fidget and without thinking, reach for his arm, squeezing once to ground him.

"No, they're still in Demark," Under Annie's gaze, Winter laces his fingers through mine, but if she thinks anything of it she doesn't say. "I think the team parked down the road so they wouldn't get stuck down here, storm coming and all. Seems Anker has been sent with a message to deliver."

My head snaps from Annie to Winter, and I watch as all the color drains from his face.

"Wait here," he says grimly. "Annie, can you make tea? She took a spill."

"Poor dear." She's already rummaging in cabinets and filling a kettle.

I start to push off the counter but he holds firm in front of me, "I'll come with you," I insist.

"You don't need to see this, Cat. They're not a pleasant group." He almost looks embarrassed. "I have no idea why he's here. No one notified me of his visit." His shoulders stretch as he leans over the counter, a hand braced on either side of my thighs. He breathes deep, as if inhaling me. "You should go."

My back stiffens like a rod. "Right, like I said, I shouldn't be here. I'll—" There's no way for me to get back to the lodge on my own, I've got no plan. Still, I try and push myself off the counter. Expecting him to move.

He doesn't budge. "No. I mean, you should go up to my room. Get dried off, and Annie will bring you tea and dry clothes. When I'm finished with this, I'll come to you."

"I'm really good with unpleasant people," I say, pushing him back so I can gingerly hop off the counter. But he's there, with hands around my waist to brace my landing. "Lead the way." I motion to the door Annie came from. Winter eyes me to confirm this is what I want, so I say, "Please."

"Anker, team," Winter strides into the room, knowing good and well I'm hobbling with my head up behind him. I tuck into a stuffed chair quickly and watch him face a small man with long, slick hair, still wearing a thick wool coat, his soggy boots melting into the carpets.

"Thank you for seeing us."

"You didn't give me a choice, did you?" That venom I used to think was reserved only for me is back in full force, even more so than I've ever heard from him. It's becoming clearer by the second how he's grown up, and why he's been so guarded.

"True, on request of the king and queen. So, I'll get to it." He eyes me over Winter's shoulder, Winter takes a step to obstruct his view. The rest of the team sits as Annie comes through the doorway with a silver tea tray.

"Would you like a cup?" Winter gestures to a tray.

"No."

The tray goes untouched as the people in the room look anywhere but at the two men standing toe to toe in front of the large stone fireplace decked with red poinsettias, and long, skinny, green velvet bows.

"You requested your own PR for this project after refusing to work with the Crown team. However, we've become aware of a personal relationship and the Crown cannot abide it—your people do not like it."

"Nothing you've just said matters to me," Winter responds easily. "Is that all?"

"Not quite. It's come to our attention you adjusted the fee we're paying the little American company. You insisted on paying them much more than the going rate for their services. Why is that?"

I sit up and listen harder.

"The king and queen can afford to be generous," Winter deadpans. "What of it?"

"We also know you've personally invested in a new project with some new writer and a little screenplay. Do you actually plan to make a film?"

"This is all none of your business." Winter waves him off again. "These are my personal investments."

"Doesn't sound like a prince who's looking for a bride to bring back to Denmark and take the crown, does it? Add that to the fact you're canoodling with your PA for the world to see. This is a warning. Save your image and make our people feel comfortable with a prince willing to take a wife and settle down. Right now, they don't trust you. According to our polls, they don't even like you."

My heart breaks for Winter as he stands there, head high, and takes this abuse.

"Is that all?" But he weathers it, keeps his cool and his composure.

"Yes, that is all."

"See yourself out, Anker," Winter says, his face neutral though we can all hear the anger in his voice. "And if you can't make it out of town, don't come back here. Sleep in your car, for all I care, you weasel."

When they've left the room and I've found my voice, I manage, "Is that who's been running your life?"

He exhales, long and dejected. Then rearranges his face, as if he's been dealing with this kind of torment for years.

"Did he say, you paid Allyn—"

"I paid for services your company is well known for providing. If I padded the number a little, it's only because I'd heard you once, saying the company was struggling."

"So, it's not all about getting back at me, tormenting me?"

"Ah, hell." He smiles sheepishly and crosses his arms over his wide chest, "You're Frannie's sister. You're going to be family in a way when John finally proposes. And you love your job, so much so, you've dedicated your life to it. I saw a way to help. To apologize for misinterpreting you. So, I did."

"And Liam's screenplay?"

"How did you know?" Now he's caught red-handed, but he holds his stance and comes clean. "He's a nice kid. He's worked for Ben renting boats most summers, and I heard you were floating his screenplay to a few crew members. Ben and I made some inquiries, then some calls. Holiday tries new businesses like he tries on hats. That's all."

"You're going to make a movie with your buddy?"

"Maybe. Or we'll help him find the right partners. Money doesn't create happiness, Cat, but it does open doors."

"But you're the bad guy!"

"Am I?"

"You let me believe you were. You're making his dreams come true," I breathe, seeing Winter Larsen morph before my eyes from my nemesis to the most selfless, generous, thoughtful man I've ever known.

"I'm sorry, too. About how I treated you before," I blurt.

"Come on, Bloom. Let me find you something dry to wear."

Before I can decide whether or not to follow him, there's a clamoring of paws and I'm accosted by a furry bear.

"Lola, down!" A shaggy dog the size of a minicar jumps up and plants her paws on my chest. "Off," he shouts again.

"She's missed you," Annie says, poking her head in. "Nibbles to get you through the night are on the counter. I'm off to the cottage before I can't even leave on foot."

"You want me to walk you?" Winter scratches his head. "I know it's just by the barn, but still."

"You stay put. If I can't make it I'll come back and bunk with you two."

He looks stricken but tries to smile back at her and she laughs down the hallway until we hear the door snick shut.

Lola's paws are knocking me off balance since I only have one leg to stand on and I try to plant my feet. I get a gigantic lick to the face. "Well, hi."

"Now, she's trying to warm you up."

"By eating me?"

"Lola, come." The dog immediately turns and runs for Winter. She plops her big bottom at his feet and looks up at him with the biggest, sweetest eyes. "This is my girl, Lola. She had a litter of puppies a few months ago and we're weaning. She's needy right now, aren't you, girl?" He drops to a crouch and smothers the dog with kisses and cuddles. It's disarming, knowing what I know about him now.

I shake my head to snap out of it, but I can't not look at him. Lola licks his cheek and Winter turns to mush. He hugs, scratches, and kisses her all over.

His eyes cut to mine, but I don't look away. I let myself take him in like this. His big hands, his full lips, his blue eyes, and how easy he is in his cozy home with his dog.

"Robbie's not showing up anytime soon," he says, watching me watch him with curiosity. "It's just as well. I prefer giving Lola her dinner."

I follow him to the kitche, Lola under our feet, and watch as he drops a scoop of dog food in a blue toile bowl and throws a few pieces of steak on top from a bag in the refrigerator. Lola wastes no time and gets right to it, tail wagging.

"You're a good dog dad." He gives me a shocked look in response to my unfiltered compliment. I shrug. "You're sure no one's coming for us?"

"It's a tight road up the mountain, they can't turn and head back down in a sleigh like you can on a horse. No way the van could make it on icy roads. I guarantee, they got through the pass, turned around at the lodge, and found they couldn't get back down. This snow is intense and you don't mess around with that while traveling through the pass."

"It can't be that bad outside, it just started coming down. Your team got out, it seems."

"Thank fuck for that," he says. "That's why they parked at the top of the mountain. Like it or not—" The lights in the house blink, stutter like a sentence ending in ellipses, and then wink out. "I can't take credit for making that happen, but it does punctuate my point nicely." He pats Lola on the head before she curls up in a plaid dog bed by the kitchen door. "It's you and me tonight. Don't worry, a backup generator will kick in by morning."

"Morning? We'll freeze."

"I'll keep you warm, Bloom. If you'll let me."

Twenty-Two

CAT

There's nothing to do but follow him, is there?

"See ya, Lola," I say over my shoulder, but she's already snoring. "Where are we going?" I pant a little catching up to him using tiny hops to save my ankle. I've never done a stair master or a gym routine in my life, and this winding, dark staircase is giving me a run for my money.

"Up to my apartment to get us dry clothes. You should wait downstairs for me." Even in the dark, I can make out his grimace when he turns to see me struggling up the stairs. "Cat, you stubborn woman, wait—"

Sure enough, I miss one and bang my shin, catching my toe just shy of clearing the tread, and crash to my hands with an unceremonious shriek.

I hear him rush toward me and drop to his knees. "Shit, are you okay?" He gropes for me in the dark. "From now on, I don't care if you don't like being taken care of. I knew you were going to hurt yourself. Now I'm calling the shots." He stands, taking me with him by the waist with one arm, and continues up the stairs.

"You don't have to carry me, again," I grumble, but my legs wrap around him and I hang on.

"Trust me, Bloom, I know this house like the back of my arm. Relax—"

"It's back of your hand, and . . . I don't even have it in me to fight you. *Fine*," I groan, "carry on."

I motion forward, waving my hand in the dark, then wincing as my elbow bends and burns.

"Where are you hurt?" he asks again, moving down the hall, his strong arms carrying me like I'm nothing.

"Both my elbows," I seethe. I'm not sure if I'm angry at him or at myself. This is not something I do: let myself get hurt, put myself in the position of being helpless. I've done it twice now in as many hours.

"I'm so sorry," he says, absentmindedly dropping a kiss at my elbow and wrapping my hand back around his neck.

As much as I hate the feeling of being helpless, I can't fault him for being so sweet with me. "I'm fine."

He moves into a room that smells like cloves and incense and sits me in a fluffy chair next to a table nestled like a bird's nest in a bay window. "Wait here."

I do, using the light from the window to survey my surroundings as best I can. Club chairs are situated around a small table littered with a few books, a pair of reading glasses, and a stack of mail. Outside, the moon is high now, cut in a sliver while stars pop around it, snow cascading from the sky in lumpy puffs of white. There's more cream stationary stacked neatly and to the side, clumps of balled-up sheets under the table, too.

He walks back in the room holding two candles, and a box under one arm. The light jumps and cuts across his face. Strong cheekbones, proud nose, sultry smile.

He's laughing at me.

"What?" I demand.

"Easy. I'm taking in the view."

I look around. "Of what?"

"You," he kneels next to me, setting both candles on the table, the box in my lap. "In the moonlight, you look almost sweet, Bloom."

If I were my sister or Willow, I'd swoon right now. *He's on his knees for me.* But I'm not, and I'm not about to forget Winter Larsen is off limits, despite the way my body reacts to him, or how far we've come since this new mutual burying of the hatchet.

"I'm not sweet, and I'm fine. I don't need any of this."

Matches lay on the table, so I make use of them and light a cedar-scented candle. I wish I still hated him. I didn't know it then, but this was all a lot easier before we became friends. If that's what we are now...

I hold my features still and firm and look away.

"Fair enough," he murmurs. "I realize this is hard for you. Roll up your sleeves, let me see."

I do as I'm told and he sucks in a breath. "Cat." The way he says my name is full of worry. "You might need stitches. You've got gashes in both your elbows. This flimsy sweater didn't help."

"It's cashmere," I mumble, watching the snow out the window, willing myself not to get used to someone taking care of me.

Willing myself not to feel his touch as if it's fire.

"I didn't say I didn't like it, but I'm afraid it's toast. Soaked with blood. Do you want to try and get to a doctor? We can take Daylight, she can make it into town—"

"It's not that bad. They're only elbows." I glance down and while there's a lot of blood, it seems to have stopped. "I don't care about scars."

He's got both hands wrapped around my upper arms as if he thinks I'm going to slide right out of my chair. He squeezes twice. "It's okay to be hurt—to need help."

"Don't you have something in there that'll do?" I nod to the kit, keeping the rest of my body still.

All I can think about are his big hands and strong fingers wrapped around my arms, keeping me in place as if I'll disappear at any moment. I hope he doesn't notice how uncomfortable I am. *I know he does.*

"I've got a couple of butterfly bandages. But you will have scars if it's not tended to properly."

"I told you. I don't care about that."

"Funny, I would have pegged you differently." He shakes his head.

I lift my chin.

"That wasn't an insult, Bloom." He applies a bandage to each arm gingerly, as if the last thing on earth he wants to do is hurt me. Even a little.

"It felt like one." And maybe that's on me. "What did you mean?"

"You know," he looks closely at one arm and begins to clean the wound. "You're so concerned with image."

"Oh my God," I burst, pulling his cheeks with my hands so we're eye to eye. He freezes in my grasp and I think he's holding his breath. "Can you let my social media history go? It's my job, and not even close to my favorite part. I couldn't care less about a few scars."

His eyes heat, like he's listening to my words as hard as he can. He's hearing them as loudly as I need him to. "It's a button for me, but I believe you. I shouldn't have judged you so harshly when we met."

"And I should say the same—you helped the Rushmores." It's easy to say, because I know it's hard for him to hear—he likes to hide his good deeds. He's not the only one who's judged too harshly, and I still I don't understand why he did it. "Why?"

The candle flickers as I wait for his answer.

"Because I knew you cared," he whispers.

Both of our vulnerabilities fade into the dark room as he presses his cheek into my hand.

I let my fingers fall and clasp my hands in my lap before I do something silly. "Winter?"

He looks up. "Yes?"

"That was a good thing you did. I'll forever be indebted to you. The Rushmores, Brand Hub, Liam." It makes me feel uneasy, entrusting all that happiness to someone else.

"It was my pleasure." He wants to say more, I see it in his eyes, but I'm afraid of what it will mean.

So I do what I do best, deflect and keep myself safe. "So, how are we going to fight Anker? How do we get rid of him? Because that guy has to go."

"Okay, okay, Rocky," he laughs, getting back to cleaning and bandaging the cuts on my arms.

"Rocky?" My smile cracks and I wonder if he can make it out in the dim light, still kneeling in front of me. "My dad used to watch those movies. Rocky the boxer, right? Workout montages, running upstairs and cheering. That Rocky?"

"Yeah."

"God, I haven't thought about them in forever. Mike Bloomfield lived on those in the old days. I think they inspired him and my mom when they were building their business, following their dreams."

"The guys made sure I got a strong dose of American culture when I was kid. It involved *Rocky*, *Lord of the Rings*, *Sesame Street*, and *Friends* on repeat till I thought I'd pass out. I know I still get a lot of the sayings wrong."

I bite my lip to stop from laughing. "It's cute."

"Cute?" He raises an eyebrow sky high, creating little crinkles in his brow that I'm tempted to count.

"Endearing," I confirm.

He falls back on his heels clutching his chest. "Is that . . . Could that be another compliment?"

It's easy to laugh at him, but I don't miss how he gulps down praise as if he's been waiting for it his whole life. Maybe he has. "Don't get too worked up."

"I was keeping a mental tally but there's too many to count, now. It's official—*you like me.*" It's true. I know it, and now he knows it, too.

"No comment."

He barks a laugh at that, clearly enjoying getting under my skin. My chest warms to know that I'm making him happy, especially after seeing him torn down by Anker. If that's what he's dealt with on the regular, I don't blame him for escaping to the States.

"You need something to wear. You're soaked, you're bloody, and now you're buttering me up so I'm not going to give you something horrible from my ancestor's closets."

"You've got that kind of stuff around here?"

"Oh yeah, Vikingstrong is chock-full of antiques. You should see the furs. PETA would have a fit, and frankly so would I, but they're old and useful in the winter. I would never condone it now, but a hundred years ago, that was still a way of life in the mountains."

He moves around the room, shucking his own sweater off, revealing a plain white t-shirt. He digs through a chest of drawers near his bed and then tosses a lump through the dark at me.

"Hey!" I barely manage to get my hands up to catch the soft material.

"It's cashmere." The joke floats in the dark, a lightness to his voice, playfulness in his tone.

"I'm not wearing your clothes."

"Suit yourself. Naked is acceptable."

"Winter!"

"I'll use the bathroom down the hall. Can you see this doorway? Here." A match strikes with a flare of fire. He sets a candle inside a bathroom, black and white tiles shimmer. "You can change in mine. Don't go through my medicine cabinet."

The room is glowing and I let my head tip back to rest on his soft leather chair. "Are we really snowed in?" We both hear it, the stress, the cares, and the worries rolling off me.

If we're stuck, there's no fighting it, right?

His clothes are soft in my hands, and he waits, watching me. When I say nothing else, no sarcasm or complaints, he says, "You're welcome, Bloom."

Twenty-Three

WINTER

Standing in the window, she's surrounded by moonlight in a shirt of mine and some soft wool sweatpants that I accidentally washed and shrunk about ten sizes. She turns, still cinching them at the waist with the drawstring pulled tight, and gasps when she sees me watching her from the doorway.

"Sorry, didn't mean to spook you." The way her hair cuts under her jaw makes me want to drag my fingertips up the expanse of her long neck, press my thumb into the divot in her top lip.

"It's so quiet here. And with the snow, it feels like we're getting buried alive in this little castle," she says. "Frozen in a snow globe."

After changing into sweatpants with what I thought was a matching hoodie, but is actually an old argyle sweater with a V-neck, I step back into my candlelit bedroom.

"So morbid, Bloom. And if I wasn't secure in my manhood, I might take offense to your use of the term *little*."

My intention is humor, but her face drops and her fingers pull at the too-long cuffs on my shirt, looking everywhere around the room except at me.

"Are you alright?" I ask. "Sure you're not lightheaded? Maybe you need something to eat?"

"I'm just, I don't know." She wraps her arms around her middle, clutching at her elbows. "I'm not sure what I need, and I can't think of a smartass retort to what you said. Honestly, I'm exhausted."

I know what happened between us while I patched up her wounds has thrown her off guard. What happened between us in the woods the first day we filmed. What's happened since in secret, stolen touches. And now she knows I spend my gold coins like Robin Hood, trying to help people who cross my path and need it. It's not because I'm such a good guy, it's simply because I can, and it'd be a sin not to.

But she doesn't know how to act if she's not sparring with me, that's clear, and that makes two of us.

"Sure. Yeah." I scrub my hands through my hair and drag my palms down my cheeks. "I just thought, that's what we do. That's how we talk. I didn't mean anything—"

"You think Annie made it okay? I'm worried about her."

"She lives in a cottage by the barn, a little carriage house tricked out with her every desire. She made sure of it when she agreed to relocate with me years ago, didn't want to let go of Danish culture, a true believer in *hygge*. She's got a claw foot tub, baskets of her favorite knitting yarns, a tea assortment that would make all of England jealous, and she commandeered three of my favorite tabbies: Mr. Bingley, Ross, and Penny Lane. They used to be barn cats and now they eat cheese from her palm and get groomed at Dazzle Paws monthly. And I made her adopt one of Lola's pups. I promise, she's good and cozy under lumps of purring, panting, perfumed fur. We can check on her tomorrow."

"Then, feed me, now."

"Demanding little thing, aren't you? Follow me." When I look over my shoulder, moving down the hall candle in hand, she's still favoring her ankle but following and I can't quite tamp down my satisfaction at having her all to myself tonight. "And mind your step."

We find more candles stuffed in an eighteenth-century buffet in the formal dining room. Embroidered draperies keep the whistling cold from breaching the old walls and I hope she feels it —the comfort, the warmth my ancestors built into the place. Every carving has a story: the flowers from Denmark's springs, the dragon renderings taken from Viking ships in history books, textiles that tell the story of where I come from. I've only had Christmases here with Annie so all the lovingly placed holly, wreaths, ribbons, bows, and crystal snowflakes on a big tree in the living room are infused with good childhood memories.

Damn, I'm feeling nostalgic and I don't even know why as I grab a pair of fresh tapers and stuff them into the antlers of silver, stag-shaped candlesticks.

She walks around with a box of matches, striking and lighting as if she were at home. A queen in a castle. I should have known she'd assimilate to any surroundings, to any problem, or circumstance. She always does. I've seen her adjust, defend, and take control in so many situations—since the night I met her in a club, since I saw her take control of an entire baseball stadium, since she's wrangled a room of fame-hungry women and industry men, she's a formidable force to be reckoned with.

She catches me staring and I quickly look away, focusing on the charcuterie I'm piece-mealing together in the kitchen off the living area. Olives, tapenade, some pretzels, a particularly stinky cheese I'm quite fond of, some chocolate-covered raisins, and an almost too crusty baguette that I found on the counter—probably staged for the last tour that came through.

I rummage through some cabinets and drawers until I find old metal kabob skewers, add them to a basket of crackers, and truck the whole thing into the living room so I can get a fire going.

"Are we eating in here?" she asks. "On the floor?"

"Are you averse to a carpet picnic?"

"No, it's a little drafty down here," she shivers.

The main floor of an old Viking chalet is maybe not as cozy as I thought it was, especially now that we've got no power. The rose-colored glasses I've got for this place might be to blame. "Not to worry. Lola, come."

My girl is at my feet in a flash, panting and looking up at me with sweet brown eyes.

"She loves you," Cat surmises.

"Sit." I point Lola to Cat's feet. "See, foot warmer and best friend. We've got plenty of firewood thanks to Logan. He keeps me stocked during the winter, and I know how to get this beast going."

"It really is a beast," she says, admiring the gargantuan stone fireplace.

"Built by hand." I pat a fat chunk of river rock, shaking off the memory of facing off with Anker here only an hour ago. I'll deal with him later. "My ancestors liked to stay warm."

"It's almost as tall as I am. Anker looked like an ant next to it. He was awful, by the way, to you. I wanted to punch his teeth out. And you know he's lying." She motions at me. "There's no way your people hate you, not if they've seen what I've seen."

I've experienced her anger, to be sure, but the fact she's angry on my behalf does something to my gut that makes me feel like I'm way too high up and I might fall. I've only cried once, and of course, it was in front of Annie. It was the first time my parents came to visit after I moved here. They stayed three days and then left early one morning, a note on my mother's royal stationery slipped under my door to say farewell.

"Let's not talk about all that. I'll get us some blankets." I pad down the hall before I say something stupid. Something soft, and raw of my own, because I feel like I can do all those things with her.

By the time I get back from ransacking the closets, she's inched close to a fire that's matured to roaring and Lola has abandoned us for her dog bed.

Her face is glowing. In my room she was cut in moonlight, her features sharp and striking. But now her skin is golden, her cheeks dusted with a rosy shine. The tree Annie and I decorated nights before sits fat in a corner and the wreaths on the windows outside are covered in snow.

She looks up at me, locks of raven hair falling softly around her face before she tucks it behind both ears. "Well, you sharing the wealth, or what?"

I startle, because I'm staring. I've been staring, and because I'm enormously embarrassed at being caught, I dump the contents of my arms on her head.

"Winter! You ass!" She pushes her way out of all the blankets, a tiny fur avalanche she didn't see coming. Lola groans at our antics and rolls over on her featherbed.

"You asked for it."

"What is all this?" She's tangled in a bundle of twinkle lights that must have been at the bottom of the box and jumps to her feet. Lola, to her credit, doesn't move. She's out like a lightbulb.

"Hold still." A rumble of laughter builds in my chest, she's gotten herself thoroughly tangled up in the lights in a matter of seconds. I pull her back to my front and wrap my arms around her as I struggle to get her untangled. "Pulling away is making it worse," I whisper in her ear, letting my hands drag over her waist and her hips, taking a knee so I can untangle a knot at her feet.

She turns and braces her hands on my shoulders. "Sorry, my ankle's still sore."

"I'm glad it's just a twist and not sprained. Though I'd be happy to carry you around the set next time we film, viewers would have a field day with that." She pushes up on her toes, trying to step out of the lights, my thick socks I wear under my riding boots pulled up to her knees over the knit sweats I gave her.

It should not be sexy. These are not sexy socks, they're dirt brown.

Why is the sight of her in my socks turning me on?

"You are not carrying me around set, I'm fine. Where did you get all these lights?"

I shrug. "Forgot they were in the box. I can't sleep at night and shop online buying things I don't need like everyone else. Annie vetoed them because they blink and give her a headache."

When I've untangled her feet and am confident she won't fall, I rise to meet her face, tangling the lights still around our chests even more. She watches, letting her hands drag from my shoulders down my front. Breath catches in my throat when she fists her hands in my sweater as if she doesn't want to let go.

I click a button, and multi-colored lights blink around us.

Her eyes are hooded, gazing at her hands as she holds me in place. I bite my tongue, afraid to say the wrong thing, waiting for I don't know what, but she steps back, trying to pull free of the final strands around her upper body.

"You're a menace," she quips, but her words don't match her actions. I don't think she wanted to step away from me, not this time. "Are you trying to tie me up and take me to your dungeon? Death by twinkle lights?"

My eyes catch hers and I raise an eyebrow, pulling lightly on a strand wrapped around her back and making her stumble back to me.

"You like it. You like me," I press, damn my fear. She needs to aknowledge what's happening between us.

She high-steps like a pony, still favoring her ankle, but manages to extract herself from the knotted string and steps back again. Her breath is ragged as she stares at me in my living room.

Push and pull, fire and ice. I gather the lights that fall at my feet, dropping them back into the box.

"Relax, Bloom," I soothe her as we sit in the nest of blankets and take in our bounty for the night. "You need to eat." I gesture at our spread. "Limburger cheese, some nuts, crackers, raisins. And I've got this baguette that's past its prime but I'm hoping we can toast it in the fire." I rip off a piece and pierce it with my skewer, resting it over a flame. After a moment, I hand it to her.

She runs the warm bread over a hunk of cheese and takes a bite. "Yum," is all she says.

"Good," is my reply.

"You're different tonight." She meets my gaze and I do my best to give her my honest regard, no hiding, no jokes, and no smart comments.

"You are, too. I never thought I'd hear you admit a weakness. After all, you're determined to be the strongest woman alive."

Her chin tips up. "What weakness—oh, you mean when I said I'm tired?"

I nod.

To my surprise, her shoulders relax and she leans back against an ottoman behind her. "God, I am. I think I have been for a while now. Something about being forced to unplug here, I mean, I'm still having to deal with you and that's been no walk in the park, but getting out of the grind, the constant posting, the tracking, worrying over things like algorithms and analytics. It's been freeing."

"Isn't there another way? A way you can accomplish your goals without draining yourself?"

"Like a fancy benefactor to invest in all my clients?"

I smirk at that. Did I like showing off for her? Saving the day the only way I know how? A little. But when I looked at Beanie's coffee, they did decent business with good foot traffic. I even had Holiday assess everything before I made the move. Cat doesn't even know the details of making Liam's movie. All the dudes in my crew invested. The people in our town have a way of supporting their own. And overpaying Brand Hub because I knew they needed it, well, that one was personal. I can admit that.

Finally, I shrug. There's no defending my actions here. I'm

guilty of all she's said. And I'd do it again, because I like her. And it's time she knows it. "Might as well jump out of the pot and into the oven—"

"What?"

"What? I'm trying to tell you—"

"No, the saying. You got it all wrong." She swipes cheese from her bottom lip and sucks on her thumb. I hold in a whimper—my God, she's gorgeous even in my old clothes with cheese on her chin. "It's *out of the frying pan and into the fire.*"

"What the hell did I say?" I'm bewitched, that's what this has to be. Cat Bloomfield has me under her spell, she's turned the tables and now, I'm at her beck and call. I think I'd do just about anything to please her.

"I don't know, something about a pot," she laughs so hard she doubles over.

Bewitched by the snow and the near-perilous ride, the smell of pine invading my senses from all the garlands Annie has draped through the house. The roar of the fire lighting Cat up in front of me. Cat lighting me up inside when I thought I'd burnt out for good.

"Well, what I'm trying to say is, you're right. I wanted to help, in my own twisted way," I eat a bit of gooey cheese on toasted bread, pushing through the sudden urge to kiss her. "It makes me feel better. Like I'm in control. I can't be used by people who only want me for the crown, if I'm the one making the deals."

"Winter Larsen—what the hell?" she yells.

I can't tell if she's mad at me, or at herself. "What?"

"You are royally screwing with my brain right now!" While laughing, she pushes at both my shoulders. I'm not ready for it, and we tumble backward. Quite ungracefully.

"Oof." My breath hitches as I catch her waist and brace her weight since she's lost all balance, her hands grasp my upper arms as she hovers above me, hair falling in her face.

"Sorry," she gasps, her laughter mingling now with mine.

Suddenly kissing her is the only thing on my mind. My body begs me to do it, my chest heaving as my hands grip her hips. I struggle to cut through the haze and make a clear decision. Maybe it wouldn't ruin me. Maybe it would be like any other kiss.

Lies, Larsen. Pure lies.

Instead, I bench press her twice, grunting more than is necessary.

Shrieks and laughter fall from her lips, "Winter!" She weighs nothing compared to what I lift in the gym, and she's soft, and she smells so good. "Stop!" she screams, but her face is lit up like a Christmas tree.

"Can't, trying to break the mood because all I want to do is kiss you. I'm willing myself not to lower you all the way down. Not to settle you right between my—"

"So do it." Abruptly, I look up into her eyes.

She blinks above me, a small, challenging smile playing on her lips.

Slowly, I use every ounce of strength in my arms to lower her until her chest presses into mine. Her hips do exactly what I was fantasizing about, lock gently in place, notching into mine. "You are mesmerizing, you know that?" I say, using both hands to push the hair back from her face so I can take her in.

We fit so well. *I knew we would.*

"You are the surprise of a lifetime." I don't know if that's a good thing or not but she brings her lips to mine, hesitates.

"Cat," I whisper. "I want you." She knows this, but I say it anyway. Encouraging her. "Kiss me."

"Let's pretend we're in a little snow globe," she murmurs, her gaze roaming my face as the fire crackles. "This can't happen," she continues, "Just so you know, this isn't happening. I'll deny everything if Marco finds out." She closes her eyes and lightly dusts her lips over mine. Testing. Grazing.

I hold very still and let her do with me what she will.

But I can't hold my composure long. The weight of her body

on mine is too much, the brush of her lips against mine—it's too right. My hands flex in her hair as a groan escapes me, turning her head so I can get the angle I've been desperate for, and I kiss her deeply in return for taking a chance on me.

Her lips open and she lets me in. Our tongues mingle and test, and then take. "Cat," I breathe her name like I'm about to suffocate with need. Our kiss is a crash. It's pent-up frustration, it's want, and I can't get enough as I growl her name into her mouth again.

"I know," she says back, letting me kiss down her neck as my hands grip her hips, then her ribcage, my palms grazing the sides of her breasts.

"It's so good," I say, when her hot mouth finds my neck, too. She kisses sweetly across my collarbone, and it's bliss experiencing this soft side of her. Instinct causes me to flex my hips, and her thighs press wider, opening for me.

"Wait, Winter, we can't do this." She pops up. The soft heat of her mouth gone in a flash and way too soon.

"Why the hell not?" I demand, sitting up on my elbows. She's still straddling me but I don't hold her in place, I think it'd make her freak out more. No, she needs to be in control right now.

But we both want this, of that I'm sure.

"Forget it happened," she stammers, bringing her fingers to her swollen lips and breathing hard. "I thought it could just be once. A quick thing to get out of our systems." The words tumble from her, but she stays put in my lap. She doesn't want to stop any more than I do.

My resolve crumbles and I grip her thighs. "Don't disappear on me." She's only just begining to let me in.

"We have to stop."

The last thing I want this woman to do is shut down, and I will myself to stop getting hard beneath her. "Is that really what you want?"

"No. But that's what has to happen. There's an entire show

dedicated to finding you a wife. My job is to get you to the finish line."

Fuck. My hands are itching to be all over her because, no, I don't think I can ignore how much I want her any longer.

She considers me as she pushes off my lap and I let her go.

With the fire at her back, she pulls her knees into her chest. "You're nothing like who I thought you were, Winter Larsen." She's still breathing heavily, smiling despite the fact neither of us are satisfied, "Are you?"

She touches her lips as if she can't believe she let me thoroughly kiss them seconds ago.

She's asking me to confirm it, looking into my eyes now. I know I keep most people at arm's length. The only people who've seen the real me are the men I call brothers, and Annie, and sometimes I even feel I have to perform for them. It's a monumental task, to always have a smile, a quip, a joke and a dashing retort to keep people on your side. To make sure they *like you.*

But Cat hated me from the beginning and because of that, I've never felt that pressure with her. I wasn't trying to win her over in the beginning, nor was she trying to charm me. Somehow I think we've accidentally done both.

"No, I'm not. And I don't want this to stop. I don't care about the show. I care about you." The truth is what I give her.

She reaches across blankets and pillows and pushes a lock of hair from my forehead. Her words echo in my mind, when we were covered in snow and first realized we were stranded here: *I don't need anyone to take care of me.*

"You hide a lot from people, don't you?" She lets her hand slide to my cheek.

I think she needs me to be vulnerable, and hopefully, that helps her feel safe enough to do the same. "Yes."

"Since you were a kid?"

I lean into her touch. "Yes."

"That's . . . sad."

"Come here," I pull her toward me, and to my surprise, she lets me. It's as if she's removed a sandbag from my chest as I let out a long pent-up sigh. We recline back. I stretch an arm under my head, the other under hers, and gaze at the beams in the ceiling. "Yes, it is sad."

Her hand snakes over my middle and I startle as she leans into me. "Winter?"

I meet her gaze. "Yes, *sod bloomst*?" She gives me a quizzical look. "What did you just say?"

"Don't ask, it just slipped. Like your lips just now. I hope you slip again, Bloom."

She swallows a scoff. "Don't count on it. And, I'm not what you think I am, either."

I know.

Gold flecks shine in her eyes and I try to count them as I tuck a lock of hair behind her ear, lightly dragging my thumb across high cheekbones. I'm dying to pull her closer, for her lips to meet mine again. "What are we going to do about this?"

Her gaze roams my features in return, on the edge of a thought I wish I was privy to.

She has a strong nose, delicate chin, and smoldering eyes. A thousand flecks of gold.

I lie still, giving her all the control as she watches me watch her, neither of us trying to hide the fact we're both memorizing features, breathing heavy, weighing our options and the turn we've taken. This snow globe could break any minute.

"Like I said, nothing can happen between us." She moves away on cue, fluffing a pillow beside me, pulling blankets around us in our little nest.

"Something is already happening between us, Cat. But I can wait until you're ready to deal with it."

"Winter." She eyes me shrewdly, that pretty face gearing up for a debate, no doubt.

"You know I'm right."

"Fine. Let's talk about us . . . another time."

It's not a no. I turn on my side and she does the same. We're almost nose to nose.

"You are a comfort I've never known." The words spill from my lips and she grasps my hand and laces her fingers with mine in return.

"Yeah, I feel that, too." It's a small step, a hint of trust. Loads of truths and understanding, unlike anything I've experienced.

She yawns, and my chest tightens with emotion as I bring our intertwined hands up and graze her knuckles with my lips, something like longing tugging at my heart.

She closes her eyes and sighs. "Tell me a story about your home, about when you were a little prince. I'd love to see Denmark someday."

"Your wish is my command."

Twenty-Four

WINTER

I've woken up five times already. It's the light.

In my room, velvet curtains keep the sun out as long as I wish, but here on the floor with a fire smoldering in the grate, Lola's snores, and a headstrong woman wrapped around me, I can't sleep. The sun highlights her cupids-bow and it's calling my name.

The first time I wake, I smile.

The second, I chuckle.

The third, I risk it all and wrap my arm tighter around her. She hums in her sleep and rolls into me, nuzzling her cheek against my chest and I've never wished I was naked more. Wished that her skin was on mine, not this ridiculous argyle V-neck that I pulled from the back of a drawer.

The fourth time, I lean into her and inhale, wondering if I could let my fingertip rest in that sweet divot on her upper lip if only for a second. She smells so good, like expensive lavender. It's penetrated my clothes, the pillows, and I hope it lasts forever.

The fifth, I wonder if I'm being a weirdo, and as I'm pulling my numb arm from beneath her head to try and sneak off in the direction of the French press, a phone rings.

The house phone has a shrill, earsplitting tone and I wince.

Her eyes crack. "Is that a phone?" She pulls away. "I've got to call Marco. He's probably had two heart attacks and an aneurysm by now."

Still sloppy and off my footing from sleeping next to a gorgeous woman with chocolate eyes, I stumble to the house phone attached to a wall near the pantry. "Hello? Larsen house of pain," I grunt, perturbed I've been cheated out of whatever she might have said to me first thing in the morning if reality hadn't come bashing down on us.

"Oh, thank God," shrieks a voice, so loud I have to pull the receiver from my ear. "Winter, put my sister on the phone!"

Cat's eyes pop open, "Is that Fran?" She's still curled up on the floor surrounded by old family furs, patting Lola's sleeping head.

The twinkle lights strung across the mantle are no longer shining bright. Everything looks different in the daylight, including the sour look on Cat's face. Not a morning person, then.

"Do you have owl hearing?" I ask as she snatches the phone from me.

She wraps the cord around her finger, dancing nervously in my socks. "Hello?" She gives me a face while covering the receiver and mouthing, *why didn't we use this phone to call Marco last night?* She rolls her eyes at me.

Good morning, Bloom, let's not go losing our heads and all the common ground we've gained, my returning gaze says.

Maybe I wanted to be snowed in, away from the cameras. Deep down, I think she did, too. And the kiss... Seems like we're going to ignore that little detail, and for now I'll let her get away with it. But not for long.

"Cat!" Fran says, as I dig for coffee in the kitchen to give her a bit of privacy.

Twisting the cord around her little finger, then her arm, looking adorably playful like her namesake with a ball of string, Cat chats idly in the corner, leaning against the wall, popping one foot on her knee so she's standing like a sloppy ballerina.

She's oddly comfortable in my clothes and in my space, the visual hits me in the gut, striking me as surprisingly delicious.

It was one kiss, man. I shake my head at myself, pour coffee grounds into a glass press, and heat water in a kettle on the gas range.

"We're fine," Cat says into the phone, then goes on to relay the events of last night.

A peek outside the window proves the sun has melted a good amount of the snow already. It usually doesn't last long down on Main Street, as opposed to the top of the mountain. We might still have trouble getting back up to the lodge, but that's a problem for future Winter to worry about.

Nonchalantly listening to her conversation while pressing our coffee, I pull two mugs with tiny blue birds from a cupboard.

"I don't care what we do for my birthday. I probably have to work all week anyway. Maybe this weekend?"

It's her fucking birthday?

"Dinner at your place sounds great. How's the motel coming along? Have you installed all the furniture you bought on your trip?"

She catches my eye and mouths, *do you think he proposed?* I roll my eyes. If Frannie and John got engaged, we'd both know within minutes.

When I don't answer, she stomps her foot and makes a face but continues chatting away. And I get an idea.

By the time I return from a guest room that's tricked out with heirlooms under glass for the tour, her conversation has turned heated.

"We lost power, or I would have called you, *Marco*." She glares at me and I wince, "Sorry! I was, I was," she stutters and finally resorts to the truth, "I was distracted."

That one word, that little slip. My chest constricts and all the blood in my body suddenly rushes south. *Distracted.*

Indeed, I can't argue that I slipped into my own fantasy world in front of that fire with her, all night long I dreamed of doing things to her. Soft things. Hard things. And everything in between. The kiss we shared was just enough to kick off a myriad of fantasies about what I would do to Cat Bloomfield, if only she'd let me.

Passing by her to get to the cupboard with the sugar bowl, I press my chest against her as I stretch to reach. Her cheeks turn Saint Nick red.

Does she feel the same? She no longer thinks of me as the boogey monster, and I know she's not a wicked witch, but I think we're both unsure where that leaves us. On the other hand, her cheeks are telling me at least physically, we're on the same page.

"Yes, I understand it's my job to wrangle him." She points at me when I back off and fill our mugs. "Yes, I understand it's my future career on the line."

So, there's an obvious problem. It's the show.

I hold my hands up in surrender and gesture to a chair at the breakfast table. The wide window is bookended by Wedgwood blue curtains that make me think of a Denmark sky in spring. They've got embroidered floral trim and were shipped straight from Skagen years ago when my mom gave the place a refresh.

Cat hangs up the phone. "What's all this?"

"I'm sorry if work is . . . not happy about yesterday, and last night." I slide her chair out and gesture for her to sit. Surprisingly, she doesn't have a smart comment, or balk, or flat-out refuse.

"It's fine," she says, in a tone that says she can handle it. I know she can, still, I feel a little guilty.

Once she's seated, her back to me, I grab my surprise.

"Happy birthday," I say, dropping to a knee in front of her.

She takes one look and then pins me with a glare. "That crown's for your future wife."

I feel my own cheeks heat. "On loan for breakfast," I say, the rubies glinting in the sun coming through the window. I will my hands to still. "My grandmother gave it to me when she passed and it's on loan to the museum, on display in one of the first-floor bedrooms—and yes, what we've agreed to use for the show."

She speaks slowly. "It's the crown you'll use in the finale of *Royal Hearts*."

Is this a mistake? I don't know why I'm kneeling. I didn't plan to kneel, I wanted to do something special for her on her birthday. *Fuck, I'm kneeling.* I'm holding a crown out to her with shaking hands. Never in my life have I been on my knees for someone, yet I find myself in this position—for this woman—constantly.

Take it. I will her to take it. If she doesn't, my heart races, *what if she doesn't want—*

"So this is what all those women are vying for?" she says, assessing the hundred-plus-year-old jewels in my hands. That comment hurts more than it should.

I think I've made a monumental mistake, a sharp jab rises up my throat, but her features soften and she looks me in the eyes. "Thank you." She takes it from my hands. "I'll take it for a test drive, it's not every day a girl gets to wear a real royal crown."

"Yes, please. That was the plan. I don't have a breakfast fit for a queen, but the jewelry, that I have in clubs."

"In spades."

"Whatever." I wave a hand and enjoy her exasperation.

"You have this stuff lying around?" The crown shifts precariously on her head and she steadies it.

I pull two ruby earrings from behind her ears, an old trick my uncle Erik taught me. I've been thinking more and more about him lately, rest his soul. Elias is a good kid. Maybe he and I can help each other. I need to reach out. I always had an affection for him and I promised Erik I'd look after him. Elias could be the solution I've been looking for.

The earrings clip on but I drop them on the plate in front of her, afraid to try and put them on her myself. "Did you forget you spent the night in a castle? With a prince? And had the best make out of your life?"

A laugh bursts from her chest. "Are you for real, Larsen? What else do you have hidden up your sleeve?"

"It's nice to hear you laugh." It seems we did make progress last night if she's still laughing.

"Instead of bark orders?"

"No. I like that you're in control of the show. You're always professional on set. I like hearing you laugh, too. We laughed a lot last night. You can be strong and still let your guard down, Cat. You can trust me."

"We did—and I know." She smiles down at the rubies, sparkling on a breakfast plate, trimmed in green holly leaves with red berries and a gold edge. "I think you like being the one to make me drop my guard, pretty man." Her words don't have their usual edge, the self-protection I may have misconstrued this whole time as venom. "Still, last night stays in the snow globe. Okay?"

For now. If she needs time, I can give her that.

I nod to the earrings. "Put them on. They're generations old. Many a Larsen woman has passed these down, so, mind the clasp. My mom always said they were too tight."

She raises her hand to tuck her hair behind her ears, but I beat her to it, gently using my pointer finger to push her hair back, dragging the pads of my fingers lightly around the shell of her ear.

We both shiver, and we both notice.

The silence isn't awkward. It's more telling as we size each other up. The shift from hating each other to wanting each other, happening in real time. In this kitchen where my relatives used to summer, and laugh, and love. This is the only place I ever remember feeling like I had a real family as a kid, a thought that shoots through me like a racehorse.

I want this. I want warm fires, waking up with someone, and that elusive feeling of familiar comfort I've only tasted with her.

"I'll go find us breakfast." I stand abruptly and pull mugs off the counter, handing one to her and taking a sip from mine.

She wraps her hands around the steaming cup, in my grandmother's crown and fat ruby earrings fit for a queen.

"Shit," I shake my head to dislodge the thoughts bounding around my ridiculous brain.

"Are you okay?" she asks. Except for my brothers, and Annie, no one asks me that question.

"You look like a queen." I can't help myself from telling her the truth.

"Thank you, Winter," she says softly. "I'll never forget this birthday, that's for sure."

The phone on the wall rings again, ripping my attention regrettably away. "I'll, uh . . ."

"Get it." She stands and heads to the door. "Can I borrow your coat? I want to take this coffee for a stroll. The lake looks really beautiful surrounded by all the snow out there."

I pick up the receiver as she grins at me, "Knock yourself out. Your boots are by the door."

"Winter?" John's voice asks.

"Hey, man. I just talked to your girl, what's up?"

"Oh, you know, she's freaking out because her sister spent the night with you and now, I'm on a recon mission."

"Frannie wants you to get intel on me and Cat?"

"Pretty much. Is there a 'you and Cat'?"

"Well, I'm not sure." I push my hair away from my face as I try to think of the right words to explain. There's rustling in the background and the slamming of a door. "Where are you?"

"In my truck, in my driveway. I've got about five seconds

before Francesca will want to hear what I got out of you. So, let me give you some advice, like you did for me one day not too long ago."

"You mean, lady advice."

"Exactly—you want her so bad."

"Wow," I deadpan, wiping a smile off my face with my hand. "That's it? I already know that—wait—*how do you know?*" I stand a little straighter because while I've realized I've got growing feelings for Cat, I hadn't realized it was so obvious.

"We watched the stream last night, *Royal Hearts*," he chuckles and I mumble *dick*, under my breath. "It's weird seeing you on TV. And then you were speeding away with Cat on the back of a horse —wait—did you just say, you know you want her so bad?"

Right. The show, the fans.

"Yup. I've worked it all out in my pretty little head. Call it self-sabotage, or wish fulfillment, it's an odd mix of both, I think. I'm hopelessly enamored with a ball-busting goddess."

"What are you even saying right now?"

"In layman's terms, I know I've got a thing for your girlfriend's sister."

"And you're fine with that? Cool as a cucumber? Goodbye single Winter? It's that easy?" he stammers. I've shocked him.

A grin spreads wide across my face and I roll my eyes when Lola comes to sit at my feet. "Boss is such a caveman," I say while scratching her ear.

"Are you talking to your dog about me?"

"Yup, and I really like her, man. Cat," I add, but he already knows how much I love Lola. "The show is a problem. . . ."

He grunts at my antics. "Well, shit. I guess you wait it out?"

"I think that's the plan."

"Who would have thought Winter Larsen would fall so easily for a woman? If you figured everything out all on your own, what do you need me for?"

"Oh, plenty," I confess, wrapping the cord around my finger

like Cat did. Thinking of her lips on mine, thinking about her lips wrapped around something else.

"Like? Leave it to you to get yourself in this kind of pickle." His chuckle rolls through the line.

"I need an invite to a birthday dinner. Oh, and let me bring the cake—I've got a woman to woo."

CAT

"Well, well, well. Look what the abominable snowman dragged in," Liam drawls, while folding silverware at the hostess station of The Nook. If it's possible, they've added more Christmas decorations, and he's wearing an elf's hat.

"It's like Santa's workshop threw up in here," I say.

"I love you," Liam responds, giving me fake moony eyes while also gagging on said Christmas décor as if he's a cat with a hairball. If he were straight and I wasn't lusting over a prince I have no right to, we'd make a beautiful, sarcastic pair.

"I didn't say I didn't like it. Big congrats are in order I hear, *young screenwriter!*" I clap him on the back and the tips of his ears turn pink.

"Cat's out of the bag, huh?" I narrow my eyes at him. He sobers. "I'll never say that again."

"Thank you," I respond primly. "And you're using Brand Hub for your PR."

"Of course," he confirms with a hand over his heart.

"What a charmer, this one," Winter deadpans, casually coming to stand beside me and shaking Liam's hand, because, well they're sort of in business together now.

While the men do the gruff chit-chat thing, I look nervously around hoping I don't catch a glimpse of Marco.

We tried to enter the lodge separately in case a camera was around. We both know we look awful. Me, still in Winter's shirt because he threw my bloody sweater in the trash, deeming it unsalvageable. Him, with a five o'clock shadow he insisted on keeping and a little black heart on his wrist he insisted on me drawing after breakfast. My red heart is still on my wrist, too, maybe I can take a bubble bath without getting it wet.

Then I spot a blue mohawk. *Shit.*

"Where have you two been?" Robbie asks, trotting up to us with his camera on his shoulder. "Hey, Liam." He nods and Liam's ears go from berry pink to Santa red. Robbie's grinning ear to ear at him and it seems like a real effort to stay on task and turn to me and Winter. "Marco's pissed. Brace yourselves, he's right behind me, and put these on." He thrusts mic packs at both of us.

"I've already talked to him," I say, then shove the mic packs back at him. "We're not scheduled to shoot for another few hours." And I need to change out of Winter's shirt.

"Dammit, Cat!" Marco skids to a stop after bursting from an elevator off the side of the restaurant and barreling toward us on his short legs, led by an enormous puppy on a needlepoint leash adorned with snowflakes.

Winter drops to his knees and coos sweetly in the dog's ear, giving pets and accepting sloppy kisses. "Who's a good boy?" he purrs, "You are. We miss you, buddy. You look good in a bowtie, bro." The bowtie matches the leash, of course.

"You got a dog?" I ask incredulously.

"Last one of Lola's puppies that needed a forever home," Winter says, scratching the dog behind its ears while nuzzling noses.

"How many deals can you possibly be making during the eight hours a day I'm not at your side?" I throw my arms out, but I'm not annoyed, not even close. I'm becoming more and more enamored with this man by the second, and my internal alarm bells are screaming.

"You better be filming," Marco says to Robbie, pointing at Winter while he continues cooing at the puppy. Robbie flips a button on his camera.

A little part of me hates Marco for it, for trotting Winter out like a prize pony. But then I'd have to hate me for it, too, because I signed up to do the same damn thing. It's become clear Winter is a whole person, with layers and thoughts and feelings, and this show is hurting him. It's not where he should be, or what he should be doing. It can't be over fast enough, for all of us.

As if he can feel me tensing beside him, Winter says, "Relax, Bloom. Pet the puppy. Isn't he the most handsome man you've ever seen?"

Dropping into a crouch, I let my hand roam soft, fluffy fur. "A close second." My stomach drops at my blatant flirting. The memory of the kiss we shared has been in my head since I woke up this morning. I can't stop thinking about his mouth on mine, so possessive, so needy as if I was the only thing in the world he wanted.

Winter bumps my shoulder with a chuckle. "Noted."

"How is this going to work in your apartment in L.A.?" I ask Marco. Are we all just assimilating and melting into this place like Stepford Wives?

"You never know. Maybe I'm over L.A."

Oh my God.

We're causing a scene in the middle of the cafe now as guests sip from fat, clay mugs stamped with the Little Star logo, all eyes trained on our odd quartet and the camera. They simultaneously reach for their cell phones. News has traveled fast that the show is filming here, and I've heard numerous people chatting about the latest episodes every morning in my own little nook at The Nook.

Winter stands, noticing we've got an audience, and takes a step closer to me as if he might be able to shield my body from onlookers and their cell phones.

"Why isn't he mic'd? Cat, you are seriously dropping the ball. Don't make me cut you from this production—"

"Easy," Winter commands, low and slow and directly at my producer. "Let's take it down a notch, shall we? I'll put on the mic." He takes it from Robbie's outstretched hand, then hands it to me.

"I don't work for Streamflix, Marco."

Winter doesn't need my assistance, he knows exactly what to do with a mic pack at this point. Still, I snake the long cord with the clip-on microphone up his front, feeling every ridge and ab as I go, and attach it by memory when my fingertips reach his collar.

I slept on those abs last night.

He leans into me as I do it, and I want to wrap my arms around him. Tell him this is all going to be over soon, and then we can, we can . . .

I cut that thread of thought off—we can't do anything. Last night's kiss was a one-time thing, a total loss of control on my part and while I don't regret it, I can't let it happen again.

Patrons around us continue filming with phones propped against salt shakers and creamers, aimed in our direction, carrying on fake conversations as if we're none the wiser.

"Sorry, Cat, it's your ass on the line as much as mine," Marco huffs. He stoops to pat his puppy on the head.

Maybe I need a cuddly pet? I did love listening to Lola snore all night. It was almost like a sound machine but more snuggly. She kept inching her way closer until she was covering my feet with her furry body.

"Watch your tone and your words when speaking to a lady." My head snaps up. Winter Larsen is defending me. From a curse word? "At least, that's what I was always taught," he finishes, looking directly at the camera.

No passive-aggressive cursing at my PA allowed. His face and his words deliver the message clear as a jingle bell and I love him for it, even though I can out-curse a sailor when I want to.

I've been working my whole life. I'm not new to salty, strong, and demanding bosses— Allyn is one of the worst, in the best ways. But I don't stop him because God help me, it feels luxurious. It's like dropping a heavy tote bag after lugging it through multiple airports all day or being toted around merely because you've got a sore ankle. That is to say, sublime, cared for, and coddled in the most specific way.

Am I this hard up for affection, these days? Waiting for someone ballsy enough to take care of me even when I say I can take care of myself?

Clearly, yes.

Marco puts his hands up. "Apologies, all." He glances at the camera and to his credit, looks authentically sheepish. "But the blogs and socials had a fit yesterday when we lost track of you. We had to fill the remaining hours with ads and that did not go over well with fans. The speculation, *your fandom*, has really kicked up a notch." He motions around the room, case in point, as people continue to film, no longer hiding it.

"That's all a misunderstanding, Marco. We had no idea we'd get snowed in overnight and not make it back to finish, um, Winter's date."

"All is not lost. Now that I've seen the dashing prince on a horse, I think we need to see him ride again, don't you? But instead of galloping away from viewers, we film him on a date with a woman on the show, a *contestant*." He puts inflection in his last few words as a warning.

"Would make for great content," I agree, but the thought

makes me sick. I've got to get ahold of myself, I cannot have feelings for Winter Larsen, no matter how much I might want—

Don't finish that thought.

"We've got another week of group dates, a crown ceremony Friday night, then we'll start next week with our first one on one—a romantic horseback ride through the mountains. This is where things get serious, Winter. We'll be down to three hopeful women."

My stomach turns at his words. This is all moving too fast. Friday's ceremony kinda snuck up on me, and while I haven't loved watching groups of women vie for Winter's attention, I'm not sure I can stomach what will happen on one one-on-one dates. The kissing will start—I'm surprised it hasn't already—then the groping, the doors closing while the camera fades to black but the microphones stay on a minute longer and all you can hear is . . .

Winter glances at me. "You okay? Your face turned green."

"I'm fine." My tone is not convincing.

Winter considers me a moment longer, then drags his gaze to Marco. "Nothing says romance like putting a novice rider on a four-hundred-pound animal on a snowy mountain trail."

Marco ignores him. "The viewers will love it. You two painted quite the picture on that ride yesterday."

A muscle in Winter's jaw flexes as he shifts in snow boots, looking out the window at the mountains outside. He seems to be getting more and more put out by filming, and I don't think he likes the idea of a one-on-one any more than I do.

"Are we sure this is a good idea?" I hedge. "Not because I don't want the storybook date to happen," I rush on, and shit, I think everyone is on to me because all three men, even Robbie, give me looks of concern. "Nothing halts romance like falling off a horse. That's all I'm saying!"

My pulse is racing and I touch two fingers to my neck. Can they see it? Because I am lying. While terrifying, falling off a horse and rolling through snow cradled in Winter's arms is the most romantic thing that's ever happened to me. He took care of me. Before, during, and after the fall, I was his priority. It felt good to mean that much to someone.

Winter pulls his beanie off his head, the black one I gave him on the beach on our first day filming that he's refused to give back, and runs a hand through his hair. "Fresh, soft powder is difficult for some horses to maneuver . . ." He drops his gaze to me and it's full of longing, full of apologies he doesn't need to give. This is what he signed up for, what we both signed up for. "It might not be the best idea." His voice cracks.

Robbie moves around us, switching up his angle. Winter presses his thumb into his wrist and bites down.

Marco shakes his head. "But you rode with Cat yesterday. Viewers got an eyeful of the two of you, on one horse. Looked plenty safe to me."

"It wasn't," Winter whispers, eyes on my throat. "It was reckless."

I gulp at his words and stare at his mouth.

Marco looks back and forth between us, I know he's reading the room, the tension. He clears his throat. "Two horses then. You'll make it work. I know you will."

"So, we're headed back to Vikingstrong?" Winter asks, still holding my gaze and saying a thousand other things as a muscle ticks in his jaw.

"Oh no," Marco wags a finger in our face, and finally, the spell is broken. I glance at Robbie's camera. "Don't think you two are going to sneak away from us again." He looks over his shoulder and winks at the camera for effect.

Without thinking, I turn away and press into Winter's side so I can hide my face in his shoulder. His hand finds mine and our fingers lace together, hidden from the camera against my hip. How much of me did the audience see yesterday? The entire grocery store run? Us sneaking away on horseback with snow coming down as if we'd been shaken in a globe?

"Call whoever you need to call," Marco says, "and get the horses scheduled. After Friday's cut, the first one-on-one will open with Winter and his love interest on horseback. The snow, the trees, the final three," he waves a hand as if painting a picture. "I can smell the romance! The *snow-mance!*"

"I can't wait," Winter finally agrees. There's no way out of this. But his voice is thin, his heart isn't in it. And neither is mine.

He pulls me close. I don't even care what it all looks like on camera. A weak PA, a melancholy prince who isn't nearly as bad as I thought he was. Two people who got into this for all the wrong reasons, and now we're stuck—together, but not.

CAT

The week flies by in a handful of minutes that slip through my fingers. Winter is everywhere: standing by my side, whispering in my ear, and starring in my dreams. We draw hearts on each other's wrists daily, probably feeding the rumors about us for internet sleuths to find, but I just don't care. It'll be my job to disregard it in the media via press releases and PR statements when this is all over, anyway. Still, I hold on to the tiny looks he gives me as if my oxygen is running out. We haven't spoken about what happened between us the night we were snowed in, but the kiss is constantly on my mind. His mouth on mine is all I can think about, I'm addicted to the memory, grasping for the details.

And the letters. Every day there's been a letter in our mailbox.

He tells me he's going to have my heart tattooed permanently on his wrist when this is all over. When I tell him he's crazy, he tells me crazy's been canceled—as if that's supposed to make me laugh and soften the blow of the most romantic things any man has ever said to me.

In a hastily scrawled response on the back of his letter against the very mailbox, I slip and tell him I dreamed about him. About his mouth on mine, about his mouth in other places. I can't believe my fearlessness. I drop it in and then run so I don't second guess it, but I trust him with my truth regardless of it being impossible for us to act on it.

He tells me he's dreaming of me, too, and then he tells me all the reasons he wishes I were a contestant on the show instead of acting as his PA. *Wouldn't that be the perfect solution?* he asks. *I could date you, pick you, and give my people what they want—a responsible man with a remarkable woman on his arm to support him. Would you let me? In this dream world scenario where we never got off on the wrong foot and understood each other from the start, would you let me have you?*

I only wish I could have him, keep him.

The crew is grumpy when I make it downstairs Monday afternoon. Like a bonafide princess, I took breakfast and my coffee in my room this morning. I didn't want to run into Winter before we started filming the first one on one and have to face my confused bundle of feelings and insanely distracting attraction to him head-on.

Liam is at the front desk and I give him a questioning look, *any mail?*

He shakes his head no, but of course, that doesn't include our mailbox. I spin on my heel and run outside. I am addicted to his letters, to him really, and I've got to figure out how to turn back time and make it not so. Still, I crave the letter that's waiting for me like a Christmas present that's been sitting under the tree for a month. Waiting for you to unwrap it and gobble it down.

When I reach the pretty house on posts nestled in the tall trees, I pull on the top, making snow slide off and fall with a satisfying plop.

Inside, two heart-shaped ruby earrings shine up at me. I gasp. I left the earrings at Vikingstrong after our slumber party of course, but here they are, heavy in my palm, glinting in the sunlight, blood red against the snowy white backdrop of the mountains.

My head tells me no, not to accept them and leave them here for him to find. But my heart, my heart tells me yes.

There's no turning back when I clip them to my ears and open a cream envelope, heart in my throat.

Sod Bloomst,

Wear these and think of me. I'm always thinking of you.

Yours,

Winter

P.S.

I'm trying to wait patiently but, please, for the love of Pete, whoever he is, put me out of my misery and say you'll be mine.

A squeal peels out of me, everything inside me begging to let go, so I do. I sound like Frannie when anything good happens to her, or Willow when she's reading a book she really loves. And it's euphoric. But then there's a loud crack high in the mountains. It echoes around the tall trees and think randomly of avalanches, the tumbling snow, the power, *the fall.*

That's exactly what I feel like when I think of him. My heart is falling, it's been underway and unstoppable for weeks already. I plaster my hand to my mouth, breathing hard against my own palm.

"You ready, Bloom."

A messy table is piled high with equipment, the production team is tired, and I can tell everyone is ready to wrap this project for Christmas break. I untangle two mic packs from a knot of cords as Winter strides by me and down a hallway leading to a back patio. Nonchalant, casual as if he didn't just drop a bomb on me in the shape of ruby hearts and love notes.

"Are *you* ready, pretty man?" I toss his words back at him playfully, but my heart's not in it. Instead, my heart is thumping a million miles a minute and I can't feel my feet. Suddenly, his cut jaw and intense blue eyes are all I can think about as he pushes dark blonde hair from his handsome face.

He wants me, the feeling is so foreign. *Say you'll be mine.*

He tips his head, assessing me. "Hey," he whispers, coming to stand by my side while I pet a Christmas tree in the entryway, looking for anything to do with my hands so I don't find a silly excuse to touch him. "Everything okay?"

"Sure, yeah. Yes." I can't meet his eyes.

"Bloom." He pulls my hand from the tree. "Did you check our mailbox?" I watch as he sneaks a red marker from his back pocket and begins marking me with his heart.

"Maybe." My hair is down, hiding the earrings from him but more importantly, from everyone else.

His voice drops three octaves. "I wish it were you with me out there." He nods out the door behind me where snowmobiles have lined up and horses are being saddled by Winter's trainers.

"We both know that's impossible."

But he plows on as if he's on a mission. "It wasn't one thing that changed my mind about you, Cat. It was so many little things and now they've all piled up. And," he replaces the marker cap and pushes two hands through his hair while I blow on my wrist. I don't want it to smudge. "And why can't it be you? I feel comfortable with you. You're all I've thought about for weeks, invading my senses, and then I have to go out there and pretend . . . *Fuck.*"

I open my mouth to say . . . I have no idea what. But my throat is tight with feeling, with words I want to say back to him if I could only find them, if I could only rationalize everything that's happening.

Marco sticks his head through the door, letting a swift gust of cold wind hit my face, snapping me out of the moment. "You two coming, or not? Shall I get up on that horse and go on a date with this woman myself?"

My hand finds his, our fingers lace together, and that's the best I can do as we follow Marco out the door.

Our hands pull apart when he's motioned to take his place next to the horses, and when Winter glances back at me, a yearning in his eyes for a response he never got, I tuck my hair behind my ears—watching him, watch the rubies catch the light.

"Thank God the sun is shining. It's fucking freezing out here," Mandy grumbles. "When I get my show, I'm filming inside on a cute, homey set with nineties vibes and walls full of string art."

"Okay, everyone listen up." Marco's boots crunch in new snow as we all huddle, waiting for his direction to kick off this date. "Winter and Mandy will saddle up while crew follows on snow-mobiles—"

Winter interjects looking directly at me, "Can you drive a snowmobile?" Everyone's head turns on a swivel toward me.

"I'll figure it out," I say, pulling my sunnies from my bag to hide my reaction to his concern.

Marco adjusts his sunglasses. "We'll keep a good distance behind so the motor doesn't interfere with sound. Turn your mic packs on, you two." He points at Winter and Mandy, who's fluffing her hair.

The two of them move toward the horses, Winter taking the reins from his trainers. We're on the side of the mountain now, ski lifts and the lodge complete with smoking chimneys off to our right making a very pretty holiday picture for the backdrop.

I straddle a snowmobile and wish I had my phone so I could

search a quick tutorial—the internet does have its charms. Robbie gives me a few quick instructions, and that'll have to do.

"Would you mind?" Mandy shrugs out of her coat and pulls her shirt up her back so her mic pack is exposed. She looks over her shoulder at Winter, "And warm up those hands, please."

Clocking them out of the corner of my eye as I start my motor and sit on the rumbly seat, Winter hesitates for a beat, or am I hallucinating? Then he cups his hands and blows into them. Marco, Robbie, and I watch from snowmobiles, rapt, as Winter's fingertips graze her exposed skin, moving slowly and making their way to the mic pack clipped to the band of her bra.

"Damn, this is good TV," Robbie murmurs.

Marco nods and shouts, "We're picking up your sound now, Mandy. Winter, turn yours on, too."

Mandy turns, "I got you."

"Uh, thanks." Winter glances in my direction and my head snaps up to admire the mountains. Then he says loudly, projecting as if he *wants* me to hear, "But I can do it myself."

Robbie coughs next to me. "He lets you put his mic pack on."

He lobs that accusation at me but I'm ready, it's perfectly normal that I put his mic pack on. "Only because I'm his PA," I respond as the horses' whinny and nicker. *It's not because I have a secret crush on a prince who's supposed to marry someone on this show in a matter of weeks.*

"Alright, let's do this," Marco shouts.

Winter walks toward his horse, but Mandy whines, "I don't know how to ride a horse."

"Aren't you from Texas, raised on a cattle farm, right?" Winter asks.

My head swims and I'm dizzy, I chug water because, altitude— it's not his proximity to another woman making me want to lose my breakfast over the side of my snowmobile. I don't want to see any of this, I also can't bear to tear my eyes away.

"You wrote on your questionnaire you were comfortable with

riding," Marco shouts. "We prescreened everyone for optimal safety before we planned dates. Streamflix is not liable!"

"Oh, I'm *totally* comfortable," Mandy rephrases, "but I can't jump in the saddle all by myself. Plus, this is one of those fancy English saddles, no pommel."

"I got her," Winter hollers and my back goes rigid. It's on the tip of my tongue to tell Mandy where to shove her foot.

It's hard to watch him wrap his big hands around her waist and whisper in her ear. Make her laugh. I know exactly what a whisper from those lips feels like. I gulp and lift my face to the sun.

Marco pulls a laptop from his backpack and fires it up.

"Is that the show?" I lean over to view his screen as his snow-mobile rumbles.

"Yeah, there's a bit of a lag but we can check audio, visual, make sure we're getting the shots we need."

Now I have the pleasure of honing in on every detail, all zoomed in with what I now realize is absolutely a hawk-eye lens in Robbie's camera.

Damn, that thing can really pick up details from a distance. No wonder we have a shipping situation. If his camera has been on us like this, viewers have seen *everything*.

Winter whispers in Mandy's ear. "On the count of three, okay?" Oh God, now I can hear them perfectly, too. "Bounce a little with me, keep your knees soft, and on three you jump."

She leans back into him, stretching her neck and twisting to look up. "Okay, thanks Win."

Win? Who the hell is Win? Does she think she's on a nickname basis with him?

"You got it," he says, strong and sturdy. "Ready, one, two," they bend their knees together, Robbie's camera zooming in on Winter's grip around her hips, "three."

She jumps and he lifts her easily into the seat. His hand slides down to check the saddle, dangerously close to her ass as he says, "You on?"

"I'm on," she breathes. "This is amazing. The power between my legs . . ." Her eyes glitter as she looks down at him, "You know?"

Oh, fucking hell.

He grabs the reins and hands them to her. "Are you comfortable using these?"

She shakes her pretty head up and down, brunette hair laced with highlights flowing to her waist. She's already refused a helmet. Winter refused, too, of course, stating he's fallen off horses plenty of times and another knock to his head would be a drop in the bucket.

At least we agree on that.

Winter places the leather reins in her hands. "When you ride English, you generally hold the reins in two hands." He fits each leather strap around her fingers. "Pull in the direction you want him to go, gently. Let the reins drop and push a bit on his neck—don't choke up on them too much—and he'll know exactly what you want."

"And how do I stay on? It feels real high up." I'm not buying any of this as Robbie's camera zooms in on her ass, again.

I look up from the laptop. "Robbie!"

He shrugs. That's the job on a show like this.

Winter's hand drops to her thigh. "Squeeze here, as hard as you can."

"I think I'm gonna puke," I make a gagging noise for comedic effect, like come on, this is grade A crap we're filming here. Right? But no one pays attention to me. They're all glued to the scene unfolding with fresh snow on the ground, the smell of horses and nature in the air, the lodge's massive Christmas tree adding holiday whimsy to the shot.

"Like this?" She lifts and flexes in the sleek black saddle, her thighs actively squeezing.

Days ago, it was me in that saddle, squeezing my thighs and riding behind Winter. Holding on to his middle, his muscles hard under my hands as we flew, somehow naturally in synch in the saddle. He took me home. He fed me, and I slept in his clothes, and he kissed me like I've never been kissed. Like I was his world. Why did I stop him?

He ran away from all of this with me, just him, and me, and one horse.

As if she's read my mind from yards away, Mandy says, "I'm not sure I'm steady. Maybe I should ride with you?"

Oh, hell, no. "Hey guys, we're losing light here!" I shout.

Marco covers his ears. "Cat! You wanna cause an avalanche?"

Robbie sniffs and holds in a laugh.

"Sorry, but we need to get this show on the road. Or rather, on the trail," I'm trying to keep it light for Marco, *just doing my job, smiley face!* "Right, Robbie?" I'm unhinged and I pray they don't know it.

Why didn't I let him kiss me all night long?

Robbie grins at me. "Yeah. Can't lose the light." It's one in the afternoon and I dare him with my eyes to comment.

The last thing I see on Marco's screen, all zoomed in so I can't miss it, is Winter's Larsen's knowing smirk, aimed straight at the camera.

Possibly, aimed straight at me.

Twenty-Seven

CAT

"I've been looking for you everywhere." Winter appears at my side before I make it to the winding staircase that will take me safely to my room where I can freak out in peace. There's a happy hour going on with a cast of Dickens carolers singing a cappella by the bar.

The smell of clove, snow, and outdoors is still on him. "Hi," I say weakly, letting him pull me by the elbow to a corner off the entry.

Torture. The entire date was absolute torture to watch. And I'm frozen. You'd think all the heat coming off Mandy would have kept us warm in the mountains; the woman was a blaze of flirtatious glory. But while she smoldered and batted her eyelashes, somehow simultaneously sneaking in a tutorial on wall stenciling because she's vying for a show on HGTV, I got colder and colder. My heart sank. Even though I know Winter has no intentions, it was still hard to watch.

"You're wearing the earrings." He swallows hard, his eyes roaming my face, always assessing. "What's next?"

"The next date is scheduled to shoot in two days. Tomorrow's just some B-roll and filming everyday moments. It's—"

"No, I didn't mean with the dates. I meant, tonight?" His hands move to my waist, fingers barely grazing my hips.

"Tonight?"

My chest aches with cold and an empty feeling I've been trying for a long time to fill. I can no longer ignore it—fill it with work, with emails, videos, and graphics. What I need, is a night off, but instead I'm heading to Frannie's for my birthday dinner.

"What are you doing, tonight?" Winter presses.

Robbie's camera appears in the corner of my eye, sitting on his broad muscular shoulder. That red light's blinking.

"Tonight?" I repeat, gulping and gazing at what I can't have. But his letter . . . *Put me out of my misery and say you'll be mine.*

Before I can answer Mandy appears. "Great shoot today, Win. I'm headed to the hot tub to soak. Sore thighs." She rubs the tops of her quads and I will my eyes not to roll. "Join me?"

"Uh." He glances at me and I know he clocks the camera that's on us, too. "It's been a long day."

"No problem. I mean, they're not scheduled to film anyway, so what's the point, right?" She smiles.

I hollered so loud at one point during their date, there was another echoing crack from the snow-packed mountains and I caught myself wishing we'd have another storm, or maybe even a teeny, tiny avalanche that didn't hurt anyone but buried the lodge indefinitely. I'd never go back to my pink apartment in the Marina District, never get my phone back, and live on Christmas cookies, sleeping in my four-poster bed and taking lavender baths with Winter Larsen for the rest of my days.

Frozen, in a holiday snow globe, forever. That could be nice . . .

The coat, the weight of the heirloom crown, the heart-shaped earrings in my ears that I swear I'll give back are all weighing heavily on my mind. Peeling blue polish. Hearts drawn on skin. French press coffee, sleeping in his arms with Lola snoring beside us, the fire smoldering in the grate. Snuggled in his clothes and his cozy socks—which let's be honest—I've slept in all week.

If he thinks he's getting his ugly, brown socks back, he's got another thing coming. And honestly, I love the coat he gave me, and I've decided I'm going to wear it.

Why the hell have I been refusing to wear it?

But aside from all of that, being wrapped up in the comfort of *him*, his soft gaze and his soft words, were a gift I didn't know I needed. Suddenly, I want to make the sad parts of him that he shows me, happy. And I want to take all his masks off myself and burn them. Show him he doesn't need them, he's lovable the way he is.

"See you guys later, I guess," Mandy finally says, after watching me stand awkwardly next to Winter for too long. "I'm filming a tutorial in my room tonight for candy canes made from braided yarn. Wish me luck, my views have been down—"

"You're online? How?" I demand. Marco would not be happy to hear this.

"My laptop," she says as if I'm a three-year-old.

"Mandy, if Streamflix catches you online promoting anything other than the show before we finish filming, there'll be blowback—"

"They won't. And even if they do, the shitstorm bad publicity stirs up is usually worth it. Have a good night." She winks.

"I think she's in love," Winter deadpans. "Alas, another influencer looking for her big break."

I smack him in the arm and then wince, I've got to stop finding silly reasons to touch him. "You keep laying on the charm, and she might just fall for you for real."

He gives me a quizzical, lopsided smile and a boatload of scrutiny. "You think so, huh?"

"Let me help you into the saddle, bounce with me," I mock,

though something like my pride—my heart—still smarts from the interaction.

"Somebody's jealous," he says, taking a determined step forward. "This show is a farce, I'm done with it. I'll finish," he adds when my eyes go so wide I feel them about to pop out of my head, "but I'm only doing it for you."

"What about the Crown?" I throw my hands out wide in exasperation.

"Maybe I'm working on a new deal." He takes another step and my feet inch back, afraid of what he'll say next. "Maybe I have a plan, but I want to keep this crazy, infuriating, terrifying feeling all to myself for a little while longer."

He takes a final step, and I retreat as far as I can so that our chests don't touch. Not yet.

"Haven't you heard? Crazy's been canceled." My back hits the wall behind us. "When you figure out a plan, you'll tell me, won't you?" I could use a plan, right now I'm floundering.

"You'll be the first to know," he looks at me intently, burrowing right past all my walls, like he always does.

The front desk is cluttered with people checking in and out. Robbie has surprisingly put his camera down on the bar across the room and is chatting up Liam who must be covering a shift tonight, looking dapper in his vest and cap. No doubt, he's happy to be rid of the snowman tie. "Winter, we can't—"

"What are you scared of?" he asks, licking his lips, his shoulders crowding me in.

"I'm afraid of what happens next, if I admit I want you to be mine," I breathe.

Time to be brave.

He gulps and I watch the Adam's apple in his throat move, straining the cords in his neck. "The night we spent together, talking by the fire, that was real. The way my body reacts when you're merely in the room—that's real. We are real. You can't stop what's happening between us, Bloom. I know you're strong, but not strong enough to fight this. You'll be okay, I'll see to it."

I put my hands on his chest, planning to push him away but I forget to push. "Sharing a few secrets, a few truths, one kiss . . . Does that mean there's something between us?" My words get lost in his chest, in the warmth that's radiating off him, and then I make the fatal mistake of looking up into his burning gaze.

My hands slide to his neck, my thumb dragging across his jaw.

He groans. "I've thought about you every night since I had my mouth on you, wished for you in my bed," he whispers, coaxing me gently.

My gaze shoots over his shoulder to where Robbie is now sitting, elbows perched on the bar with a sloppy puppy-dog grin on his face, hanging on every word coming from Liam's mouth. "We can't. Nothing about our situation has changed."

"I say we can," he murmurs while closing the distance, face buried in my neck, breathing me in.

I grab his cheeks and force him to focus, "I say, and your Streamflix contract says, we can't, and it's my birthday week, so you have to do what I say."

"You get a day, Bloom. Your birthday was one day, and I got to wake up with you and wish you merry first."

I'm not sure why this comes to me, or why I have to say it. "I can't keep the earrings."

He rubs his thumb over a red ruby in my ear, then under my jaw. "You'll keep them. They were a birthday present. I like seeing them on you."

I fight him, "I don't want to owe anyone anything." There's a knot of emotion in my throat. *Why is it so hard for me to surrender?*

"You owe me nothing. Except for admitting that your birthday is one day, and you spent it with me."

"I get a week. It's Bloomfield tradition."

"Says who?"

"Says Mike Bloomfield, and my dinner plans tonight to celebrate with my sister."

"Hmm," he muses mysteriously, rubbing at his strong jaw, "I may know something about that. Do you always get your way?"

"Mostly."

"Fine. But now it's my turn. Get in that closet, birthday girl." He motions with a head nod.

"What?" I look behind me and sure enough, my back isn't against a wall. It's against a door. A little plaque that says *maintenance* in gold lettering to the side of my head. I've watched Darcy dip in here a hundred times. "No."

"Listen to me for once and get in that goddamn closet, Bloom."

I tip my chin up. Who does he think he is? "Why?"

"Because Robbie isn't a moron, and while he's put his camera down to flirt with Liam, it's still aimed right at us and the red light is blinking. I don't think I want what happens next on film. No one needs audio to know what I'm dying to do to you right now."

My heart stutters at his words. "What's going to happen next?"

"If I give you a kiss for your birthday, you can't give it back—"

A laugh bursts from my chest, then I sober when his expression only darkens. "Another birthday present? But you just said—"

"Get. In. The. Closet." If I get in the closet with him looking at me like that, things are going to seriously change between us.

"Okay." Surrendering to him is terrifying but it is getting easier, or I'm getting weaker, but I'm not mad about it.

Turns out, it feels good to let go with someone you trust.

My pulse gallops as I turn my back to his chest and he hovers over me, hands circling my waist under my sweater. The contact of his skin on mine spikes my adrenaline, want rolling through me.

How do doorknobs work again?

We both fall into the dark and he's on me in a flash of hungry lips and warm skin—hands, just everywhere. And for the first time in my life, I can't follow the rules, *because I don't want to.*

The kiss is ferocious. It's greedy, and I love it. Our tongues clash, and his hand grips my neck, angling my jaw with a firm press from his thumbs. He has waited like a good boy, and he's ready to take what he wants.

"Is this happening?" I wonder aloud, breathy, awestruck, off my footing and out of my element.

"You shouldn't have come in here with me if you didn't want my hands all over you, Bloom. I thought you were smart." He mocks me with a chuckle and a challenge, warm breath, and the whisper of lips on my neck as his hands push under my sweater to grip my ribcage roughly.

"I thought you were a vapid pool of entitlement." I fist my hands in his shirt and he props me on a countertop, lifting me easily like a feather.

My knees spread and he grabs my ass, pulling me flush so he can grind into me. I feel every single inch of him—of which, oh God, there are many. "I thought you were an advantageous, greedy, little narcissist."

"Winter!" He laughs hard and I love the sound falling from his lips as his thumb brushes under my jawbone and tips my chin up the way I like it, but I turn my cheek.

It's fun defying him, even though I'm allowing his hands to be all over me, allowing him to press between my legs as we both pretend we might get enough from this alone. "Don't you dare pretend you missed the past tense part of my words. I thought you'd never want anything to do with me."

"No." I breathe.

"No?"

My head falls back and he takes the note, running his mouth from my collarbone to my ear, until he clamps down on that soft spot under my jaw. His tongue is warm and needy as he sucks at my skin.

I hiss as he palms both my breasts. "I thought, *I think* we're playing with fire. Someone's going to get hurt."

"I won't hold back with you, if you don't hold back from me." That promise is more comforting than he knows. He pulls away and I take a full breath for the first time since we've been alone and frantic for each other in the dark.

"But what if—"

"Do you want to stop?"

"No." I reach for the pockets of his pants and pull him back in.

"No?"

"Wait, yes." My head is spinning, thoughts of what I want to do and what I should do clashing. "I can't have you." He pulls my wrist to his mouth and sucks at my pulse point, right over his red heart. "Winter, *I can't have you*." I'm telling myself as much as I'm telling him. I can't. He's not for me. He's not mine.

"I want you so bad, it hurts." His other hand moves to push a lock of hair behind my ear. I whine at his touch, the intimacy, hating myself for wanting more. The heat that pools between my thighs is shocking, I don't think I've ever been this high off of someone's mere touch.

"Winter . . ." He hums in response to his name, pressing his length harder into my center while I press right back into him. Trying to find a release, trying to make this enough.

"I'm trying, baby." He knows what I want and his mouth lands on mine again, slow, steady, hot. I gulp him down with a groan while my fingertips dip below his waistband.

"More?" he asks, because I'm moaning and really, it's clear I want more. I think this is Winter Larsen trying to be a gentleman in a closet full of hot breath, and frantic touch.

"Can't." It takes everything I've got to pull away.

"Why?" he pleads, and it puts a crack right down the center of me. If he only knew how much I want him. I'm soaked between my legs.

"I can't have you," I repeat, contradicting my words and gripping his shoulders, pulling him close again. I'm determined to enjoy this to the last moment until we leave this closet and go back to reality.

He growls, pressing me back into cabinets. "Do, do you want me?" He almost covers his uncertainty. "I've told you I want you to be mine but . . ."

He can't imagine I'd want him? Like really want him, for more than just this. Is that what he's asking? He is so want-able it's funny. I have to swallow a laugh. How could anyone not want this enigmatic, melancholy, endearingly strong for everyone but himself man?

But I shake my head. "It doesn't matter what I want."

"It does," he whispers in my ear, wrapping my hand around his neck, and securing it there. "Because I crave you, sod bloomst."

A thrill runs the length of my body, from the tip of my head to the toe of my boot, settling heavily in my belly, then sinking between my thighs where he's still pressing and I'm so close to firing off.

Could we hide it? "You're theirs," I whisper in the dark. "One of them is going to win you, and there's nothing I can do about it."

This is the truth. This is reality.

He scoffs at the ridiculousness of my statement. "I'm yours," he growls as if the truth doesn't exist.

"Winter—oh my God." Something inside me pops, like a balloon filled with wanting. I combust for him, mewling into his ear while he rocks into me, whispering and encouraging me.

"That's right, that's exactly what you needed."

I can't believe that just happened, through my jeans. I've never been this affected by anyone. My hands still in his hair, and I look into his eyes. It's dark, but I can make out the blue with flecks of grey surrounded by lashes three shades darker than his hair. His eyes smolder and hold mine while I unabashedly drink him in.

Could he be mine? If only for a short time? Even if it's a secret?

I bite my lip as my heart pounds with indecision in my ears. My core still throbbing for him. I've never put myself first. It's been what Frannie needs, what my parents need, what Brand Hub needs, but never what I need. Never me first.

"It would never work." I shake my head but really, I'm nuzzling into his neck again and clinging to him as I come down from my orgasm. "I've promised to hate you forever. I've promised to marry you off and never think of you again. It's in our contract that production is not to fraternize with the cast. The Crown wants nothing to do with me."

Give him up, before it's too hard, before it hurts too much.

He laughs lightly against my cheek and pulls back to look at me seriously. "You read our contract? Like, start to finish?" He presses a finger into the divot in my top lip. I hold my breath and look into his eyes.

His mouth is everywhere again, and despite my trying not to, I open for him. My shoulders push back, my neck stretches long, my knees open wide. He's still hard as steel between my legs.

"Of course I did, and you're forbidden," I say into his mouth when his lips come back to mine.

"Fuck, that's hot. Say it again." I reach for the button on his pants, but he swats me away, making quick work of undoing it himself.

His nose nudges mine, and I'm barely able to ask, "Which part?"

"How you can't have me," he breathes, his hand plunging into his pants as he grips himself.

"Why?"

"So I can tell you forever and a day that you can, until you believe me."· I watch his hand work and it's the sexiest thing. "Fuck, Cat. How did you do this to me? I'm gonna come right now like a teenager." And he does, and the sounds of pleasure he makes are perfect. And they're all mine.

"Winter . . ." I say to the darkness, the last bits of my resolve fading into his touch, his smell, his want.

He collapses against me, panting, pressing his forehead to mine. And then he says the four little words that—for better or worse—seal the deal. "We can hide it." Then adds as if for extra insurance, "No one has to know."

Twenty-Eight

WINTER

Later that evening, when I've got her snug in my passenger seat, she asks, "Why did we drive together?"

After my seven minutes in heaven with Cat—forget football, *this* is my new favorite American game—she went to get changed for dinner and I promised I'd be back to pick her up. An uncommunicated *we'll-deal-with-whatever-happened-between-us* later.

"Because John invited me, and Fran invited you, and it made sense."

"For you to go home, get cleaned up, drive back up the mountain in the opposite direction to pick me up, and then back down the mountain in snowy, uncertain road conditions, to Fran and John's?"

"Well, when you put it like that, it sounds advantageous," I quip. "You're going to have to let me take care of you a little, Bloom. It's in my nature."

She crosses her arms and hugs her elbows, she's wrestling with the idea. "And how did you come by an invite, and the birthday cake?"

"What cake?" I ask quizzically, looking this way and that in the car, everywhere but at the enormous cakebox in her lap. The smell of sugar mixing with the leather interior and Cat's lavender scent proving to be an intoxicating combo.

"This cake," she taps the top of the box, and I glance at her sideways, I could get used to her in my car. Like, on the regular. I'll drive her everywhere she needs to go.

It's decided, I'm a chauffeur now, for one very demanding woman.

"When I asked John if I could crash your birthday dinner," I wink at her, "He was getting ready to call in the order—I guess Frannie's given him a to-do list a mile long before the motel opens. So, I offered to sweet talk Patty for something custom—"

She drops a hand to her chest and gasps, "Custom? You?"

"Shut up, I wanted you to have something special. Now deal with it," I reach over the console and squeeze her thigh twice.

She knows exactly why I drove up the mountain, why I procured myself a dinner invite, why I took the liberty of ordering her a cake, and why I've discovered a penchant for writing love letters.

The jig is up—I'm infatuated with her. Obsessed. Besotted, and smitten as hell. My thumb taps nervously on the steering wheel just thinking about the hold she's got on me and my gut reaction to take care of her..

"You sure are going to a lot of trouble for your PA," she says, looking out the window in thought.

Yeah, there's that. *My PA. Not the Crown's choice, and technically against the rules of production.*

But I think, what's best for me.

"I got to Patty's before she closed early tonight. They're calling for more bad weather, it's the snowiest winter in decades. Which means road conditions might prevent us from making it back up the mountain to the lodge. You could be stuck with me, again," I shrug and steal another glance at how she's taking all this, "but I also might be saving your life. PA or not, it's the right thing to do."

"Even trade, then," she smiles deviously in my direction, taking my concern for her safety better than I'd guessed she would.

"I think so."

"I could stay with Fran and John—"

"The new power couple? You want to cramp their style when they've just started living together, building a new business together, and he's planning to propose any minute?"

She lifts her chin. "When is he going to do it already?"

"Boss has more patience than a rooster. He'll bide his time till he's good and ready. And it's only because he's probably got something very specific and thoughtful planned."

"I don't think roosters are known for their patience. You really need to work on your American sayings," she laughs, nudging my leg with her hand, so I snag that hand and hold on. My thumb dips over the red heart I drew on her wrist today. "Did you shower with one hand?"

"Bath. I miss it when it washes off, so kind of yes."

"Bloom," I hesitate only because I'm not sure she's ready for the conversation I'd like to have. It would start with me begging, *more kisses in the closet, please.* And probably end with, *be mine, in whatever way you're comfortable, but say you're mine—not just while we hide it on the show, but after too.*

She looks out the window before I can go on. "You respect him —John."

"Am I supposed to be embarrassed?" That wasn't implied in her words at all, but I still enjoy needling her when I can. "We shoot straight with each other, always have. I appreciate his honesty and his loyalty."

"I feel the same about my sister and Willow. So," she hesitates, nervously as I pull up John and Fran's drive. Christmas lights string across the roofline and rafters of the big house, the fancy white kind. "Do you mind if we don't tell them just yet what's going on? With us?"

"They might have an inkling, Bloom."

"I know, but it's still new to us and we don't have to confirm it. They can speculate all they want, but no PDA. No funny business while we're there. That's all I'm saying." Her cheeks flush.

"We'll tell them when we know what's what." I'm not ready to leave our little bubble, but I open the door. "Ready Freddy? It is Freddy, right?" I ask, hopping out of the car before she can answer, and making my way around to open her door.

"Yes, or spaghetti, but that might be a Bloomfield thing." She takes my hand, and I pull her to me. "You're going to struggle with no PDA, aren't you, Winter?"

"Who, me?" I take the cake box and wrap my free arm around her so we can make our way up an icy drive.

She laughs, gesturing at the hand that's snaked into the back pocket of her black jeans as we walk *oh so slowly* to a front door with a cherry red wreath covered in candy canes and pink-cheeked Santas.

I school my features intentionally blank, batting my eyes at her.

"Yes, you," she says, her words silken and laced with innuendo.

Minding the ice so we don't fall, I whisk us to the side of the entry before she can push the doorbell. My mouth falls hungrily to hers as if I haven't eaten a bite in weeks. A wolfish sort of sound comes from my chest unbidden, and I'm thankful for my ability to balance a cake box while feeling her curves with my free hand.

This whole thing, *us*, is new and out of my control. I swear I didn't see my insane attraction to her coming, and I have no power to stop it now. Nor do I want to.

"Winter?" The way she says my name is suddenly sweet, and it's pleading, which makes my dick twitch and my heart pound.

"Yes?" My mouth is at her neck and I suck on the hollow under her jaw in that tender little spot she seems to like. When all she does is whimper, I breathe into the shell of her ear, "Cat got your tongue?"

"I hate it," she moans, long and slow as my hand slides down the curve of her hip and slips between her denim-clad thighs, "when people say that."

She can barely get the words out as she bites back at me, my neck, my chin, my bottom lip, as all her panting breath turns to little puffs of smoke on the cold air.

So I'm not the only one who still enjoys sparring. Good. I wouldn't have her any other way.

"Apologies." My fingers gently pop the buttons on her puffer coat, the black one that I gave her. The one that goes all the way to her ankles because it pains me to think of her being cold. She's finally wearing it and maybe I'm insane, but that means something. To her. To me. To us.

I've let her in, and she's letting me in a little, too.

She pushes her hands under my sweater, and I flinch. "Sorry," she murmurs.

"You need mittens."

"Mittens are for babies."

"My baby needs a pair of nice, warm mittens," I chastise playfully.

The woman giggles, and nothing has ever pleased me more.

"I love it when you laugh. When it's me that makes you. Cat, I . . ." I trail off unsure how to finish my thought, tugging her sweater away and pushing my hand down the front of her jeans, over the slope of her belly, and quickly past the silk edge of her panties.

There's a chair near the door and I dump the cake, carefully, then give her all my attention as I brace one hand above her head, the other sliding to her core. "Is this okay?"

"Yeah, yes," she responds quickly, her back arching as she presses into my hand. So wet. She's been waiting for me, and I've been dying to touch her here since our time in the closet.

"You're drenched, Bloom." I slip two fingers inside her, there's no time to waste and I fully intend to make her fall apart, relax, and moan my name before her birthday dinner.

"Winter, is there a camera out here?" she gasps, speaking into my mouth as I kiss her through her words, through her building orgasm that is happening even faster than I could have hoped.

For a second, I think of our blue-mohawked friend, but then I realize she's talking about the house. "No, Boss is old school and this used to be his dad's place. I doubt he's thought of all that." I find her clit with my thumb and rub slow circles, and she grips my arms tighter. My girl needs to get off. All she does is work. Well, now it's time to play. "Know what?"

"What?" My fingers push and curl into her. She widens her stance a little as I apply more pressure to her clit with my thumb. Pick up speed.

"I'm pretty sure you officially don't—" Her hands grip my neck.

"Don't—oh—hate . . ." she trails off, her words coming high and breathy as she rocks against my hand. Her core tightens around my fingers and when she falls apart, I apply more pressure, pumping into her, kissing her, and panting right along with her as she falls apart.

"You don't hate me anymore." I finish the full sentence in her ear, holding her up against the wall, swirling my thumb as she comes down, milking every last drop of her orgasm from her body.

"Nooooope," she says, long and lazy while her body shudders under my touch. "At this exact moment, I really, really like you."

"Good." I punctuate my point by slipping my fingers into my mouth and sucking them clean.

We both jump.

Frannie pulls the front door open, "I thought I heard a car —Oh!"

Cat's cheeks are rosy on pale skin that somehow matches mine. She probably has some Scandinavian in her somewhere even though her sister is tan and brown as a berry from the sun even in December.

Shielding her in an unavoidably conspicuous way with my body, I give her time to button her jeans in a flash. She steps around me, picking up the cake box, her chest moving rapidly as she tries to control her breath. There's visible pleasure and contentment written all over her face, and a little bit of sweat on her forehead even though we're standing out in the cold.

I put that there. I did that to her, and I can't help it, my chest puffs with pride.

"Hey, Frannie-Bananie!" she says, her voice ridiculously saccharine.

I only half try to cover up what Fran might have seen, pushing my hair back and attempting a natural stance, because I really don't care if her sister knows what we were doing on her porch.

"Heeeey, Kitty Cat" Fran hugs Cat as she steps across the threshold. "What were you two doing out here? It's freezing," Fran says, eyeing me curiously over her sister's puffy coat. As our eyes meet, I can't tell if she's playing along or honestly didn't see that we were face-deep in each other's necks, my hands all over her sister.

Cat has a mark above her clavicle, easily visible in her deep-V-neck sweater.

Shit. I'm going to have to make a mental note not to suck so hard. It would be helpful if I had my phone to make a real note. I have a feeling I'll need it. The sooner I can be done with *Royal Hearts* the better.

"We were..." She works to find words.

"Fighting," I supply smoothly, rolling back on my heels and

holding the box waist-high with both hands. I am one hundred percent trying to hide a hard-on tenting my pants.

"Yeah, fighting," Cat repeats, her cheeks redden even more.

"We fight. A lot," I add for good measure, finally moving inside and closing the door.

Cat narrows her gaze on me as she hands Fran her coat.

"Riiight, I remember." Frannie's eyes are bopping back and forth between us, but she takes pity on our little charade and invites us in without pressing us more.

"Babe, are they here?" My best friend's voice travels from the kitchen where I'm sure he's hard at work in something appropriately wholesome like a *kiss the cook* apron.

"Honey, I'm home," I say, sneaking up behind him while he's stirring a pot, clapping him on the back. "Plan is in motion, but we're playing it cool," I whisper in his ear.

"Dude—Winter. You almost made me drop my ladle." But he gives me a firm nod, he heard me.

"Heaven forbid. Damn, you domesticated him fast," I say laughing and looking at the blonde who makes my best friend glow like a sparkler. I remember when John lived like a nomad, in sleeping bags, and his truck.

I was a fan of Frannie from the start. Boggs was gone for her almost the second they met, though she made the man work to get out of the friend zone, and I'll take a little credit for encouraging him to woo her.

Fran beams with her own huge smile and hands wine to her sister and then to me. John claps me on the back, a little harder while laughing. "Sounds like you're ready to let someone do the same for you. I gotta say, I didn't see that coming."

I choke on red wine and will my hand to stay steady. "Excuse me?"

Cat steps in quickly, "The show. You're going to pick someone to marry, in two weeks."

We meet eyes over our wine glasses, and I gulp another large sip. "Right, the show," I manage.

Cat checks the buttons on her jeans, but I think I'm the only one who notices. "Have you guys been watching?" Her question is all high and pitchy as if she's afraid of the answer.

"Yeah, we gave in and caught a little here and there in the past few days." Fran's eyes tick-tock between the two of us. "Anything you need to tell me, Kitty-Cat?"

"No, not unless you want me to blow your Christmas present —" And that's why she gets paid the big bucks—nice deflection, Bloom.

"Don't you dare!" Fran squeals, taking the bait. Or maybe, she wants to drop the awkward subject as much as Fran does.

"Soup's on in ten," John announces from a gas range. "Make yourselves at home. Cat, it's nice to have you here. I know Francesca's happy not to be talking through a phone screen."

He does a really bad job at winking, trying to hide the fact they spent a day shopping for rings a few months ago in the Bay Area. He's an adorable jock and I do love him.

"So," Fran says when we all sit down to a cozy table off the kitchen of their rustic home. "How are things going with you two?"

Cat freezes at my side, a spoonful of chili halfway to her mouth.

Easy, Bloom. I take a bite and answer, "She's a great PA," then give her a look. *Relax, they don't know anything.*

"She's a professional, that's for sure." Fran smiles at her sister. "She seriously took one for the team with this assignment, you know she usually manages a laundry list of clients. And relocating, living at Little Star for the holiday. Glad she's here, though. Do you guys get a break from filming for Christmas?"

"We do, one week," Cat pipes up.

"We do?" I had no idea and I gaze at her with a thousand ideas in my mind.

"You," she points at me with her chili spoon, "should read your contracts."

"So, we get a little downtime." I raise my glass in her direction. "Nice. Merry Christmas to us."

"Yeah, Merry Christmas to us," she clinks her glass against mine. And there it is, a smile that says she's thinking the same. We get a whole week to be together without cameras, without filming, without Marco constantly shouting at us.

"And how are you doing with all the ladies?" John chimes in, eating his chili, oblivious to the conversation Cat and I are having with our eyes.

Could your timing be worse, Boggs? My hand slips under the table to find Cat's thigh. "Hey, I'm no womanizer, that's more Holiday's style."

"That's just what he wants us to believe, you and I both know he's still hung up on Lucy Lark."

Cat pipes up, looking at her sister. "Lucy Lark? Like, the fallen popstar, Lucy Lark?"

"Yup," Fran pops her lips for emphasis. "Lives not far from Little Star Lodge, I hear. On the lower part of the mountain."

"So she really is living off the grid like a homesteader? That's the last I heard of her," Cat muses.

"Holiday checks in on her, the guy who really likes flirting," I say, glaring at my best friend. "They were Homecoming king and queen at Clover High."

"Dude—I just meant, I bet you don't hate a bunch of women vying for you. How am I in trouble for that?" he looks around the table.

"It's surprisingly stressful if you must know. I don't mind a crowd at the bar, or in town, but all those cameras pointing directly at me," I say with a shiver.

Cat touches the heart on her wrist and sips her wine.

"And what's the point," I press. "None of these women are there for me, or to make any sort of real connection."

"Come on, that can't be true. Some of those shows work, some of them have babies and second generations now," Fran points out.

"True, but I promise you. *Royal Hearts* is not going to be one of them. One woman is trying to get a show on HGTV, one is launching a makeup line. I kid you not, she put lip gloss on me on one of our dates to get some product placement."

"What did you do?" John laughs.

"I don't mind trying new products. Everyone can benefit from soft lips."

Cat chokes on a bite of chili. "Hot," she says.

"Look, I applaud her hustle," I go on, squeezing her leg and letting my fingers inch their way higher. I've had one small sample of her, and it wasn't nearly enough. "I was totally fine with it, but a romantic connection is not in the cards."

"I heard there's cake!" Cat cuts in, awkwardly draining her wine, while her other hand squeezes mine under the table.

"That cake has been calling my name." Fran jumps up and grabs the box on the counter. "Wedding cake is my favorite, but Patty makes amazing cakes and I've been thinking about it all day."

"I'll help," I offer, giving Cat a small smile. I'm pretty sure we both just passed a test we were wholly unprepared for. Though if I have it my way, after the show, we'll tell them everything.

We leave Cat with a freshly filled wine glass and Fran gets plates, forks, and a knife. John pulls candles from a drawer.

This is the kind of thing I only ever saw on TV as a kid, never witnessed in real time. I went to some of the guys' parties in high school, but by then it was always baseball fields with John, fishing with Ben, and a campout with Logan. Never this warm, cozy, family vibe in a kitchen with matches and frosting, dimming the lights and—

"This can't be right," Fran tries to hide her words, speaking through the side of her mouth to me and John, but fails epically.

"What?" Cat asks.

"Nothing." Fran and John reply too quickly.

Cat's cake says, *Happy Retirement Wanda* written in gold icing across a cake shaped like a fat leather-bound book. "This is not what I ordered," I say, stating the obvious.

"They gave you the wrong cake," Fran groans. "Probably because they were closing early for the storm? Did Patty hand it to you herself?"

"It was crazy in there. I saw Mayor Troutwine get in a fight over the last cinnamon roll. Everyone was stocking up in case we can't get out tomorrow."

"Virgil Troutwine is on my last nerve. He's all over me about the new signage at Thistle and Burr being against town colors policy," Fran groans. "How was I supposed to know there's a set of colors banned in Clover?"

"You guys, whatever it is, it's fine," Cat says from the table. But she likes nice things, pretty things, and this will not do.

"I bet poor Wanda got your cake," Fran says. "Should we cut it and sing anyway?"

John tugs at the brim of his hat. "I heard about her retirement party. She still hasn't found a buyer for the store, but she's pooped. Ready to be done. Talking about closing the place and donating all the books. This cake definitely got mixed up."

It's important to me Cat has her own cake, something just for her. Hasn't she told me her childhood was all about making do, taking care of Frannie, and helping out her parents where help was needed? And don't I know plenty about ruined childhood memories? "We'll go down there and swap them. It's my fault. I should have checked."

"I'll go." John pulls keys off the counter.

"Dude, do you see the snow coming down out there?" We all turn and watch out the sliding door as fat snow sparkling like glitter falls over the lake outside.

"Dude, have you seen my truck?" he retorts.

It's true, his truck can eat up snow.

"Cat and I will go. I'll feed her the cake with candles." I swipe the box from Frannie's hand. "I promise. We'll be lucky if we make it back to Vikingstrong as is. We should get going."

I trust my car. No reason to wait for the roads to get worse. And this means I get Cat all to myself with her birthday cake.

"My truck is as good as your G-Class."

"Buddy," I clap him on the shoulder. "Not a pissing contest. Yeah?"

My best friend grins at me. "If it was, I'd win. Drive safe."

Twenty-Nine

CAT

The way he maneuvers through the snow into town is commendable. We pull up outside Wanda Crosby's old bookstore shortly after promising Frannie we'd call when we got home safe. Tattered paperbacks are stacked in the window in the shape of a cheery Christmas tree with a bow at the top.

I guess I'm going home to Winter's castle on the lake, again. With a birthday cake. And a man I find I want more than I've wanted any job, any title, or any present.

"Willow would love this," I tell him as we make our way to a worn, green front door. Whatever the name once was has worn away on the glass, only *Bookstore*, remaining. She'd love the courier lettering, the fat plaid ribbon tied with bells around the handle that jingles when I twist.

Inside it's like a little cottage made of paperback and leather-bound walls. Books line shelves floor to ceiling, stacked on every surface. There are even classic book covers painted on the ceiling tiles. If I were branding for book lovers, trying to sell coffee, bookmarks, stickers, journals, or anything cozy-bookworm-related, I'd build a brand that looked exactly like this.

A woman curled up in a green velvet chair by the window is reading, one leg tucked under the other, biting her nails as she turns pages and ignoring the store around her. Behind the cash wrap, there are more books, some behind a lock and glass. An elegant wooden ladder is attached to brass rails for easy access. If I had my phone, I'd take a picture and send it to Willow. This is the first time I'm genuinely sad I can't do exactly that when I reach into the pocket of my coat on instinct and find it empty.

Winter and I slide into the crowd, stealth like the cake burglars we are—but we're stealing for good of course. Shoppers mingle in cheery corners: some stoop to pursue half-off bins, others drag their fingers lovingly down spines on new-release shelves. The smell of spice and burning candles is all around us, the heavy scent of musty paper, too, and two young girls are sitting on the floor cross-legged with books in their laps, trading paperbacks back and forth as they chat. To the side, near a children's corner, there's a round table painted green with a Patty's Pastries cake box, my birthday cake inside, presumably.

I shift Patty's box containing the retirement cake in my arms. "What should we do? Swap them? That way no one has to know, and Patty's saved from a bad review. It doesn't look like they've gotten to the cake part of the party yet."

Winter's front is pressed close to my back. "Look at you, looking out for people you hardly know. You're a real softy, Bloom."

"I know Patty. We're buds, we go way back," I quip. "She gave me a rain check."

"You're assimilating into this town better than I thought you would. It sort of, sucks you in, doesn't it?"

"Maybe," I shrug, then steady my hand when the box tips precariously.

"Look!" he shouts excitedly tugging at my elbow, shocking me but not drawing any attention. Pretty sure a bottle of champagne just popped, everyone drawing around Wanda, an old afghan draping her shoulders. These bookish types can really party when they want to—I've seen Willow literally swing from chandeliers, but you'd never guess it when she's curled up in her cardigan and glasses with a novel.

"What?" I ask, confused by his excitement.

"Mittens! Black ones."

"You're not serious?"

"Swap that cake, Bloom," he points to the table that is probably the next stop after the champagne toast. I need to do it now if we don't want to explain ourselves. "And meet me over there."

I do, slipping the box gently off the table and replacing mine in almost the same motion, like a magician pulling a tablecloth trick. Honestly, I'm a little impressed with myself.

When I meet Winter, triumphant and smiling ear to ear by a spinning rack of trinkets and toys, he swaps the cake box from my hands for a pair of knit mittens.

"They're so cute." My voice sounds foreign to even my ears, but I can't help it. I've been awfully mushy lately. Almost sweet. Most of my colleagues back in the office at Brand Hub wouldn't recognize me.

"Annie makes them."

"Really? But they're black. Annie is all nature colors, sage greens, Nordic blues, and burnt oranges that make me think of teatime, old lady buns, and purring kittens. Black doesn't seem like her style."

"You've branded Annie," he says, twinkling eyes moving fast over my features, laughing at me but admirably, I think. "You're good at your job."

I shrug. "It's how my mind works."

"Well, I'm wondering if maybe she made them with someone in mine? Perhaps, she's been influenced." His eyebrows wiggle.

"No, me?"

"Yeah, but she's shy and probably lost the nerve to give them to you. I think she misses home, Danish people, Skagen. And there's a pretty efficient entrepreneur hidden under all that yarn—she likes selling them here to earn her *mad money*, though I'd happily pay for anything she wants."

"Good for her. A woman has to have something of her own, always. A smart woman told me that once—I love them." They're soft, light, and I can't resist slipping them on.

"Of course, you like them because they're black, but the little white hearts and snowflakes make them appropriately *hygge*."

"That word."

"It means cozy, soft, comfortable, and safe . . ." He trails off, unknowingly tapping into my innermost desires. Or maybe he knows he's tempting me with something my life has always lacked. Something I've always yearned for but never knew how to access, much less to accept.

That all seems to be changing with him.

His hand grasps mine, and he presses against the little red heart on my wrist. "I want you to feel cozy and safe when you're with me, Bloom. You're so strong, and I adore that about you. It does things to me," he raises one eyebrow this time, and I get the message. He likes it when I take care of him. "But I'd really like to be the person that gives you that feeling, too. We all need to feel cared for by someone."

It's so hard for me to accept his words, to accept what he wants to give me. But I try by responding as unguarded and grateful as I can. "I love them!" I yell, no longer caring that I'm excited over a pair of mittens in a little shop, in the middle of a lake town, in the middle of a blizzard. "A little hard, a little soft."

I can be that, I'm beginning to realize. I can have weaknesses, and need others, and still be strong.

"I think this is the first time you've ever squealed—like a girl."

"As opposed to?"

"Oh no, I'm not falling for that, boss lady. But I like your assessment, a little hard, a little soft. It's the perfect description for my new favorite person." He steps into me at the register, the party still going strong in the corner, the right cake unveiled and properly cheered for, and grasps my chin to tilt my head up. "But I'm not letting you off that easy. What about everything I said?"

"You do make me feel safe, Winter. You do." I can admit it because it's true, and he's proven ten times over he's someone I can trust. "I think it's because you lean on me, you're honest about your fears. It makes me feel like I can do the same, you know?"

"Maybe we could use each other to test our fears. You let me take care of you, just a little. I let you see all the ugly parts of me." Soft lips dust mine and I grasp his arms with mittened hands. "I'm buying you the mittens, and then we're going home to demolish that cake."

Cared for, cozy, and falling fast.

I laugh when I stomp my boots on the mudroom rug at Vikingstrong, placing them next to Winter's in a sweet little row. Lola's leash hangs on a hook on the wall. God, I'm getting silly. It must be a trick of the eye, but our boots look right together. Like a pair. And I had an odd flash-forward, a vision, of *me* walking Lola around the lake in the summer. Maybe on my way to Boggs' to say hi to Frannie and indulge in a margarita before five p.m.

Oh, no. This town, or this man, really is sucking me in. It's magical what I feel for him, or insane, maybe a little bit of both.

We take our cake upstairs to Winter's room and I plop it on the round table in the sitting area while he totes plates. He's got a jug of milk under his arm, too. I'm sinking into this moment, this room— this man— with a purr like a cat who needs a scratch.

"Kitchen's stocked. Let me know what you require, princess."

I shake my head at him and almost choke on my scoff. "Nope, definitely do not call me that, ever again. Is that like, a line? I mean, I get it if it usually works on . . . women you've . . . you know."

"Women I've . . . ?" Sparkling eyes watch me wrestle with our situation.

Fine, if he wants to watch me struggle, I'll come out and ask him. "Why don't you have a girlfriend, again?"

"Aside from the three women I'm currently dating?" His tone is mocking, a joke. Still, it stings.

"Right," I force myself to smile and not make a big deal of it, not to let the jealousy that's been brewing for weeks now show because I know he's not interested in them. "Aside from them." The cool, aloof, in-control Cat has left the building. I barely get the words out without my voice cracking.

Smooth, Bloomfield.

"Isn't it obvious?"

"No, Winter, it's not." It was, when I thought he was a royal ass, but now that I know him, I wonder why he's all alone in this half castle, half museum.

He uses a sterling cake knife with a crystal handle to slice into a beautiful birthday cake. Of course, he has crystal serving utensils. "It's not easy, dating in a small town while trying to maintain my privacy. You may have noticed that I don't have security around twenty-four seven. I like to live as normal a life as possible. But that means keeping a low profile and aside from a few discreet . . . relationships, I've kept to myself."

"Hmm." Letting his words digest, I focus on the cake he hands me. The very custom cake he bought just for me. "I can't believe you ordered this, by the way."

"What's wrong with it?" He intentionally plays dumb, scratching his temple and propping a hand on his hip.

I swipe some frosting and lick my fingertips. "It's the Prada logo, but with my name instead of Prada. This screams Winter Larsen."

"Damn. I thought it screamed Cat Bloomfield."

I laugh. "It does." Another swipe of frosting on my finger lands on my tongue, sky blue and sugar-sweet.

He shrugs. "You appreciate nice things, and I appreciate that about you. And, I thought it was *punny*."

"You're such a nerd, and I don't think that's how you make a pun," I say. "Back to your lack of love interest—"

"Why is the lady so obsessed with the gentleman's dance card, I wonder?" I wait him out as he takes a bite of his cake, giving him time. Finally, he drops the act. "It was never a focus, a real relationship that was more than physically scratching an itch. But I do want something, serious . . . now, I think."

Eyeing him and balancing my plate in my lap, I say, "I get it. I've never had the time, or the desire to invest in anything serious. Yes, I've loved, but you know what it got me." I look up at him pointedly.

"A whole lot of unkept promises? Thwarted expectations?"

We agree on this, at least.

"Mhmm." I nod, letting myself sink into thought without feeling the need to spin the truth. "The hard part of me," I go on, "the tough part, the part that can't be taken care of or let her guard down because that's all I've ever known, can't set herself up for the letdown. I've only ever known my parents saying they'd make it home for dinner, then call to say a meeting came up, or the toilet at their new office overflowed and can I please make my little sister some dinner, brush her teeth, and get her into bed?"

Winter nods vigorously. "I was so used to being alone that often," he takes my empty plate and his, and stacks them on a tray on a dresser across the room, "whenever someone wanted more, I knew they'd realize I'm a lot more work than they bargained for, and I knew it would be over before it even started. So usually, I didn't even try. Fuck, that didn't sound nearly so terrible in my head."

I snort through a mouth of buttercream, one last taste stolen from the cake box. "But you have Annie."

"You think she's responsible for all this?" He motions at himself, puffing up his chest, then chuckles under his breath and looks out the window at the snow-covered beach below, the lake unfrozen and still lapping at the shore. "No. It's true. She's the only person, other than the dudes, I trust. If you won't take me up on my offer, I'll just live here forever with my nanny. That's not weird."

What exactly is his offer? He wants me, yes, and I want him. But we still haven't determined what happens after that. "I was doing just fine until you."

The unknown is so scary, depending on someone is so out of my comfort zone, but I want to risk it with him.

There's a peachy low light from the single lamp he turned on, and the fact that once again, I have nothing to sleep in floats unsaid around us. No way to brush my teeth—at least my breath will smell like sugar. I'm in his space again, with no idea where to go, if I should avert my eyes, if I can get away with snooping because I find myself inexplicably curious, or if I should let go of all of it.

Just be me.

"Bloom, you have nothing to worry about. What I'm feeling," he rubs the base of his palm over his heart, "it's all for you."

What's hanging in the air is the bed in the middle of the room. My cheeks heat when I glance at it, no more cake to hide behind, no more banter, we're putting it all on the table. He clocks my gaze and raises a knowing brow.

The pleasure he pulled from my body in the closet, and only hours ago on a doorstep in the falling snow, is suddenly all I can think about.

And I want more.

Maybe we could use each other to test our fears. You let me take care of you, just a little. I let you see all the ugly parts of me.

"What's happening in that mind right now?" He waves an extra fork that he's plucked off the table at me in a circular motion.

I exhale, "Nothing."

He cuts a bite of cake from the box and brings it to my lips. "Work?"

I take the bite, sliding my lips over the fork, letting the icing hit my tongue as he watches me smile. "Surprisingly, maybe for the first time in a long time, no," I manage, licking my lips. "I think it's this place."

He drops the fork back into the box, sitting across from me, leaning on his elbows. "The rustic castle built for cozy indulgence and arrogant wealth that most only dream of? It has a way of romancing people, making them forget the real world. Work. Responsibility. Maybe this is what you needed, maybe you were meant to find yourself here all along. For generations, my family has come here over the summers to pretend just that."

"Every summer?"

"Yeah, they came and went. I stayed."

"So you don't want it, the crown? Wouldn't care if you woke up tomorrow morning and it was all gone?"

"Not one little bit. But I would miss Denmark, my people, and I'd hate to think they'd feel abandoned or like I didn't want them. That's a terrible feeling. I've been wrestling with how I can have it both ways. I don't want the crown, Cat, but I do want my country."

"Hmm," is all I have to offer him. I'm not sure what this means for the show, or us, but I feel deeply for him and his difficult situation with his family.

"PJs?" he asks, looking more than ready to change the subject, even though I know he'd answer any question I asked him.

My heart skips a beat, heat spreading down my sternum. "Yes

please," I answer more quickly than I'd like and hope he doesn't notice, but I know he does. Winter notices everything.

He moves around the room to the chest of drawers in the corner and pulls out a set of pajamas. He tosses me the top, then steals into the bathroom, letting the door snick closed behind him without a word.

I look down at the nightshirt. Large. Traditional. His. Plain blue cotton with buttons and white ticking stripes.

When he emerges I've done exactly as he silently commanded. "You only gave me the top." My heart pounds in my ears, my clothes piled at my feet.

"Yes." He stalks toward me in matching pajama bottoms with the drawstring loose, the waist slung low, and stops at the edge of the bed.

I meet him toe to toe, allowing myself the pleasure of admiring him up close in the soft light. His skin is soft to the touch, his chest hard with muscle, and his pecs jump as I run my hands down his front and to his waistband. My fingers play with the drawstrings. No cameras waiting to catch us.

Just him. Just me.

My fingers dust over the ink around his ribcage that I discovered on our first day shooting on the lake, that feels like a hundred years ago, and also as if only minutes have passed. This is the last time I'll press him, if he wants to test each other's fears, there's no time like the present.

"What does it say?" I ask.

He doesn't hesitate. "Heavy is the head that wears the crown," he murmurs, with eyes so sad I could take a swim in the blue.

"Winter," I say softly, cupping his strong jaw dappled with scruff with my hands. "Of all the tattoos, of all the quotes?"

"It rings true enough."

I run my fingers over his chest, and his pecs jump again as if my touch is electric. My journey continues down and around his ribcage as I inspect the script that wraps around his right side. "A formidable bear, a stately stag, sure. An elegant dragon breathing fire, that's you. But this? It makes me *hurt* for you, for that little boy that wanted love and some attention." It hurts because I recognize it so well.

I drag a finger over the ink in his skin, thinking how both of us grew up so lonely while surrounded by people and responsibility.

"You know," he says, sniffing and using that beguiling tone I've noticed he saves for charming a crowd, "It's meant to be funny."

"But it's not." I can't let him off that easily as I meet his eyes. "And you know it. Don't wear one of your masks with me."

"My masks?"

"You know, put on a show and hide your feelings. It's clearly what you're doing, and I don't want you to do that with me. You said you'd let me see the ugly parts of you, but I don't think they're ugly Winter. I think you're beautiful."

"Cat." His hand snakes over my shoulder and up my neck, gripping me as if he needs to hold me in place. "My family issues go deep. I'm well aware I use coping mechanisms to survive it. You, being one of them... I've spent my entire life in my head, and compartmentalizing is working. I am trying," he exhales, "this damn show."

He grasps my nape firmer, pulling my head back and a little to the right. "I can't stand the cameras constantly hovering, getting in the way of what I really want. Do you want to do this?"

He cups my chin and exhales, waiting for me to speak.

"If you're not interested in the women on the show, and they know your intentions are only to honor the contract, and you believe we can keep it hidden, then . . ."

"Then I can have you?" Both hands grip my hips.

"Don't break me," I whisper.

One sharp nod.

Our affair will be over when the show is over, we haven't promised any more than that. But no one has ever looked at me with eyes quite so hungry, so needy, and so desperate as Winter

Larsen. We're already playing with fire, and if I were smart, I'd put a stop to it right now, but at the moment, everything fades out into skin, and touch, and racing hearts.

I can do this. *We* can do this.

"Your mind is working hard, baby, I can see it all over your pretty face. Are you sure, no more back and forth. Last chance, Bloom, I can have you?"

Thirty

CAT

"Have me," I yelp.

He spins, flipping me around faster than I can say Prada, and pins both my hands above my head with my back pressing against a cold, frosty window.

I've got an idea of what Winter truly thinks of himself under his mask of constant confidence, and only a glimmer of what I think he might need. In so many ways, we're the worst two people to fall into bed together, forbidden to be together by a legally binding contract that he is not to fraternize with crew. Both of us devastatingly lonely in our crowded lives. But both of us are willing to try and be what the other needs for the time we have together, and no one has ever given me that kind of gift.

None of that stops me from pulling my hands free as he attacks my neck and gripping him through thin cotton pants probably spun on a Danish spinning wheel in a tower somewhere. He gasps and I lower my lashes, licking my lips, I'm not above doing my best in the bedroom like I do in the boardroom.

Dropping unceremoniously to my knees, I tug at his pants until his commanding length is in my hands. So strong, so big, and so ready. I grip him at the base and waste zero time as I drag my tongue up his shaft.

"Cat," he grits, both hands gently cupping my cheeks.

"You're perfect," I sigh. "I think I've wanted you since the first day on set, when I had my hands all over you but couldn't taste you." I paint my lips with his tip, then stare up at him as I lick at the salty precum left behind like lipgloss.

"How did I get so lucky," he breathes looking at me with awe and reverence that only encourages me to please him more. I take him in my mouth to the hilt and enjoy the sound of that gasp, too.

I drag my lips over him, hollowing out my mouth, until he pops free."You taste so good."

"You think you wanted me then? I was dying for you already." He groans, stroking my cheek. "Fuck, Cat, your mouth. I knew it would be good, but—" He whimpers in the dark as if I've struck him right in the heart. That's exactly where he's struck me, and I suck him hard into my mouth to prove it. To prove I'm his.

"Shh." My lips pop as I release him again, stroking him a few times with my fist around his hot flesh. The veins protrude from his length and his perfectly pink tip presses toward my lips as if he's eager for more.

And I'm willing to give more. I'm willing to give him so much while he's mine. I take him deep into my mouth again using my tongue to feel every ridge, sucking hard, and he begins to rock, hitting the back of my throat.

My eyes water as he looks down at me.

"God, you're so beautiful, and you're mine." I hum my agreement as he moves in my mouth, hardening even more as he picks up the pace and I meet him thrust for thrust. "Can I paint your body? Can I—"

He doesn't have to finish his sentence because I undo the top buttons on his shirt and press my breasts together in my black bra. He rubs the back of my head while he continues to thrust into my mouth and it's not long before he pulls back, fisting himself as I arch my back and watch as he paints my chest with his release. Ropes and ropes of warmth arcing across my skin.

I've never felt so claimed in my life.

"You are such a good girl," he praises me revrently, grabbing a few tissues from his nightstand and cleaning me up as best he can, then scoops me up and tosses me on the bed, tumbling down on top of me and covering me like a heavy blanket. "You are going to be the death of me. I know it, and I don't even care. I can't save myself. What sort of witchcraft are you weaving? You know what? Don't answer that. I don't want to know."

"It's the same for me," I breathe. "I blame Marco and his stupid but very sexy oil."

Yes, I usually like having the power in a relationship and the bedroom, but I know in my gut he needs to hear how much he affects me. It's both freeing and scary to admit how badly I want him, to be vulnerable. But his reaction, his pleasure in hearing me say it out loud is worth the risk.

"Don't stop doing that," he gasps as I grip him again. I want more. And he's ready. "Fuck your hands are magic. You are a witch. I know it now."

I'm dying for him as wet coats my thighs and my nightshirt rucks up over my hips. I let out a strangled scream along with a stream of pleas when he rolls on top of me and pins both my wrists above my head.

"That's two! Two Cat Bloomfield squeals in one day. What's happening to you?"

"I'm still dark and broody," I say, as he kisses his way up my jaw. "I'm just in a better mood with your lips on mine, instead of yammering away."

He squeezes me, his strong hand wrapped around my wrists

like a vise while pumping his hips against me to punctuate his point with a serious hard-on. "I-don't-yammer," he responds.

"Winter," I whine, because the teasing is too much, the ache between my legs getting more demanding. My black silk panties and his thin cotton pants are the only scraps of fabric between us. And I've already had quite the preview of what's beneath.

He sobers, drilling into me with a serious expression as he grips my chin, squeezing lightly with his thumb and pointer fingers right at my jaw so that my mouth opens to him. I noticed him doing this when he bridled his horse but I don't even care, heat racing up my chest and exploding when his tongue dives into my mouth, hungry, demanding, and needy. I expected him to be nothing less in bed: unpredictable, at times soft, and at others commanding.

Tonight, he wants to lead. Maybe because I asked him for it. Maybe because the first time we kissed in a closet, I was the one who made the move? But not tonight. Tonight I'm willing to follow his lead, to let him take me anywhere he wants to go.

"More?" he asks. "What exactly do you want from me, Cat?" My shirt is long gone, my bra cups hastily pulled down, and his mouth is at my breast. He's teasing me with wet flicks of his tongue, then he sucks at my nipple while he massages and pinches the other.

"More," I answer with a groan, pushing into him anywhere, everywhere I can find purchase.

He flips me onto my stomach, rising to his knees behind me and pulling my hips back, reverently massaging my ass, sliding his thumbs under black lace. Gripping with the pads of his fingertips under my hip bones, he pulls me hard against him and curses in my ear.

"I'm going to have your handprints on me in the morning," I gasp as he squeezes hard.

"Good," he growls, assessing me with his eyes when I peek over my shoulder. I think he could do this all day but I'm impatient. I've never been good at waiting.

I whine in response, pressing my ass into his hands. I'm begging.

"I'm at your command, *sod bloomst*, but you have to follow directions, too." He nudges each of my knees further apart with his thigh. "On your elbows now. Good girl. Let me look at you."

Those fucking words shoot through me and I preen, pushing back against him. No one has ever said that to me before and I didn't know how much I needed to hear it. "You think I'm good?"

"I know you're going to be *fucking good for me*."

"Then do something," I rasp.

"What do you want?" He's toying with me, fully knowing what I want.

"Winter," I mewl, pressing against him. This is getting embarrassing.

"Okay, okay, enough play time." He peels my favorite pair of black lace panties down, tugs so I can lift one knee and then the other, and leans over to open his bedside drawer to drop them in. His fingers glide through the slick wetness of my center and I shiver, gasping so loud I'm almost embarrassed. "Damn, Cat. All this for me? And here I thought you wanted me to jump off a cliff since we met."

"No." I shake my head into the soft feather pillow beneath my cheek, pushing against his fingers, trying to find friction he's deftly holding just out of reach.

"No?"

Fingertips brush the tight bud of nerves at my core and I groan, completely unguarded, as his middle finger sinks into me. The tension builds faster than I expected with his thumb circling, finger thrusting, and then he adds another and I clench around him. He's still grinding into me from behind, the hard length of him under thin cotton simulating something I wish was real but for now, I'll have to be grateful for his hands.

It's been a long time since someone has taken so much time with me. Usually, it's get in and get out, hoping everyone gets off. Business only, and that's all been fine and good. That's all I've needed. I prefer not to get all emotional and weepy—but this is different. Feeling Winter's hot, determined touch, his breath on my back, his whispered praise is so much more than that. Rocking into me in synch with his hand, I can almost pretend it's him inside me.

"Tell me what you want," he rasps in my ear.

Should I tell him this is all I wanted, to feel as if I'm connected to someone else, someone who knows all the pieces of me, even the soft breakable bits? What do these feelings mean?

"Don't stop," I gasp, gripping for something but there's nothing to hang on to, only thin sheets that don't offer what I need. He's made it so I can't get my claws into him, face down with one hand on my center and one pressing into the small of my back.

I'm at his mercy and it's so good, my skin sings in response to his touch. Thoughts of how we're going to hide this, and how this going to end, threaten to distract me but I banish them. We have all the time in the world to talk about what this means. After. At some point. I promise, right after I—

Abruptly, he removes his hands and sits back, leaving nothing but cold air in his wake to sting my skin. Just as I'm about to whine, he says, "You are every dream I've ever had come to life." I can hear the fascination in his voice.

"Are you trying to kill me?" I pant, glaring at him.

"Turn over." I do, scrambling back against the headboard and pulling my knees to my chest. He's still kneeling, towering over me, all tight pecs and commanding shoulders. "It's in my best interest to make this memorable." He grips one ankle, pulling my leg straight, then does the same with the other. "And I want to see your face when you come."

"I want..."

"Say it, anything, all you have to do is tell me."

"I want your mouth. On me." He pulls me by the ankles to the edge of the bed.

His abs flex and his pecs jump as he slowly bows, holding my eyes as he rubs his chin above the spot I need him to hit.

Whispered demands I'm not proud of spill from me. He pushes my legs wide and I wish he was inside me so much I almost change my mind, but then his mouth drops and he sucks my clit into his mouth. His name escapes my throat in an embarrassing plea.

He holds my gaze as he works me, the sounds of his fingers filling me again echoing off the walls but I don't even care. I feel an absolute connection with him, we both seem to read it in each other's eyes, *even ground.*

Want plus want. Power. Attraction. Trust.

He's spending time on me, torturing me in the best way.

"I think I'll keep you," I laugh, as I press my heels into his back and relish the feel of his free hand gripping my thigh so hard I know it'll leave marks. I'm going to have his marks everywhere, on my neck, my thighs, my ass.

He leans in, whispering in my ear while his hands continue to work me up, and up, and up. "And I think I'll let you . . . *Keep me, sod bloomst.*" To punctuate his point, he sucks a nipple into his mouth and gently squeezes the other.

I burst into a thousand pieces. The orgasm rips through me while he mutters praise, *good girl,* and *so proud,* sweetly against my chest, fingers still inside me, his thumb pressing hard against the tight bud where his mouth was.

"God, I fucking love you," he murmurs, his words winding together and trailing across my skin.

I don't know what to say to that, and I pull a fluffy feather pillow over my face to hide my euphoric smile. The pillow also comes in handy to hide my third squeal and not get shit about it. My body is wrung out, bits of stress rolling off me as the orgasm holds, throbbing in my core, refusing to give up its claim on me, before finally fading into the moonlight in the room.

My eyes are wide open now. Winter's room is dark and quiet, the cake box on his little table makes me laugh and I don't know why, because I can't believe what we just did. The things I did to him and the pleasure he gave me feels strong, transcendental, like starting over and I stretch like a cat, tangled up in sheets. This is like nothing I've ever felt because it was raw and real and I can't wait to see what we do next.

"Sorry, I made that weird." He drops his feet over the side of the bed, hanging his head, shoulders tense and muscles twitching. "That was so stupid—what I said. Obviously."

What does he mean? He said a lot of unbelievable, amazing, perfect things. Unless he means saying . . .

All I can see is the back of his head and he braces his elbows on his knees and gazes out the window. Snow is still falling.

Oh. "No—yeah. It was just, in the moment. A turn of phrase. You laughed." His laugh was beautiful, it pushed me over the edge because I loved the sound, because I was the one who brought it out of him. Pure, unmasked, happy Winter.

And hearing someone say it . . . We're not on that level, I know that, he explained everything to me clearly. I'm a coping mechanism, I'm helping him through this show, but after telling myself my entire life that I don't need anyone to love me. It was still nice to hear.

"I know you didn't mean it," I say, rolling to drape myself over him, wrapping my arms around his shoulders, pressing my cheek against the warm skin of his shoulder, hanging on. Willing him back to me. "Winter, I don't want to stop."

He's gone stoic and cold. "I'm sorry. Let's forget it."

"Seriously?" I sit back on my heels, stunned at the turn we've taken, still throbbing from his touch.

I've never heard my voice sound so small.

And I've never seen this side of him.

Singing wakes me up. Bad singing. The room is bright, curtains that I remember stumbling across Winter's room in the middle of the night to pull closed, now wide open. There's a note on the nightstand, his riding helmet and a crop next to it.

Cat,

These are for you. You can punish me when you wake up.

-Winter

P.S. I'm sorry about last night.

I already knew he felt bad about how last night ended, but the man just dropped a horse whip on me. And yes, he freaked out over using a turn of phrase. I was upset and confused in the moment, but when he turned off the light, he didn't turn away from me in bed.

He turned into me. And I held him. And he held me right back. And he whispered some of his fears in my ear. Fears about growing up alone, not hearing those three little words he longed for most from his parents, hating himself for all of it. Blaming himself for all of it.

It was easy to forgive the sad prince in my arms. Brushing his hair back, hushing him till he felt calm, kissing him—and only kissing him—until both our lips went numb and we drifted off holding on to one another.

I've got a choice to make here and I reach instinctively for my phone. I'd love to text this over with Willow and Fran, if anything, to get it out of my head so I know how I feel and what I want. Instead, I hop out of bed. Maybe we are what we are, the damage is done, and now all we can do is try and mend ourselves as we grow and evolve.

Still, I want him to know I appreciate the sentiment. This is Winter Larsen being raw and real, showing me his ugly parts. He's trying. So, I grab his helmet from a chair, secure the latch under my chin, take his crop in hand, and pad down the hall.

He's singing, alright.

The song has changed by the time I hover in a pair of heavy socks and his sleep shirt in the doorway. The Kinks sing "Lola" blasting through old school speakers set into a wall. Winter bends, apron unfortunately covering his defined chest but showing off his broad back, and hands Lola a batter-covered spoon to lick.

His smooth shoulder blades flex and his ribcage expands and contracts as he belts out lyrics to his dog. I bite my lip.

"Think she's gonna like our attempt at an apology? We acted like an ass last night."

When the dog pauses mid-lick to assess the man in front of her, gives him her big droopy dog look of indignation, and resumes licking her treat he says, "You're right. It was me. I shouldn't drag you into these things, I'm sorry, Lo. See? I can apologize when I'm wrong."

She slops at the spoon and looks up at him again, this time the spoon caught in her jaws. *More?* Her big droopy eyes say.

"Greedy girl. No more, I have to save some for the apology pancakes, remember? This face will only get me so far." He waves his palm around his head.

My heart constricts and I sprint down the hall because I don't want to ruin whatever he's got planned. But I'm wearing slick, thick wool socks probably darned? Knitted? Crocheted? By Annie herself. I go flailing, knocking into a small table and sending a vase crashing to the ground.

"Shit!"

"Cat? Are you okay?" He catches up to his voice and skids to a stop at the bottom of the staircase where I'm in a heap.

"Please tell me that's not an ancient, Scandinavian, Larsen family heirloom?" I gesture at the vase.

"Is it this specific set of stairs that trips you up? Or are you like this around all staircases? Good thing you were wearing a helmet and carrying a big stick."

I cover my mouth to hide a grin, hanging my head. "You're a punny prince, I'll give you that."

His head tips back, and this beautiful man lets out a huge laugh at my expense. "Seriously, you okay?" He pulls me up by my elbows. "Don't step in it, I'll get a broom," he adds, lifting me effortlessly off my feet and placing me gently on the first stair. Absentmindedly, he kisses my forehead while surveying the wreckage.

"I'm fine. I didn't want to ruin the surprise," I nod with my chin toward the kitchen he's abandoned, then steady my Helmut as it wobbles on my head. "Apology pancakes sound good."

"Ah. Well. I'll make you a deal. You get your ass back in my bed, keep my gear on, and I'll feed you all the apologies you want."

WINTER

Am I all bluster and bullshit?

God, I hope not. I just told a gorgeous woman to wait for me in my bed and now I'm not sure I've got the nerve to back it up. Last night, I just said it. The L word.

And fuck if that isn't the road I'm on. I told her it was a mistake, a slip, but isn't that what they say about people who drink too much wine and then spill the truth? My high was coming straight from the smell of lavender on her skin, from the way she gripped my fingers when I slipped them inside her, the way she looked right at me and told me she wanted my mouth on her. I have never been so affected by a woman. It's because I've had too many intimate days with Cat, surrounded by her wit and determination, charmed by her, enamored with the secrets she tells me in the dark, and the truths she elicits from me in return.

Am I on my way to loving her? Do I love her already? Like a long walk off a short pier, I'm going, almost gone . . .

I've got to get my head straight before I go back to her.

The barn is my happy place, so that's where I head for a quick check on the horses and to sort out my thoughts while a French press sits on the kitchen counter and a stack of pancakes warm in the oven. Snow crunches under my boots and I relish the feeling of sun on my face. The quiet.

I spoke to her as if I've got it all figured out. Like I didn't choke last night. And fucking bless her, she seems happy to forgive me. To continue whatever it is we're starting with no inclination of how it will end, or how invested I, albeit stupidly, already am.

Except, I have a sneaking suspicion loving Cat Bloomfield would be the smartest thing I've ever done.

Truth is, I got scared. I'm a coward. I pulled away and instantly regretted it, then didn't know how to fix it and now, I've got to pull myself up by the short hairs and make-up for it. We'll figure out all the *Royal Hearts* contract bullshit and how we'll finish the show later. Even if I'm falling for someone behind the camera, I know I've got to finish—for my people and for Cat.

Something matters to me for the first time in a long time and I'm smart enough to apologize and pivot before I fuck it up for certain.

It's the words that came out of my mouth unbidden and yes, technically in jest, that scare me. I've never told anyone I love them, other than Annie, or the dudes when we were half-popped on a bottle of scotch, and of course, Lola. But she's a dog.

I tell all my animals I love them constantly. That doesn't count.

Do I even know what those three little words mean? What they entail? What I'll need to do to back them up if I tell Cat, much, much, later that I mean them?

I shake my head and slide open thick, cedar barn doors. I'm getting off track.

The stalls are mucked out, piled high with clean bedding and hay, and I march down the row pouring oats into feedbags. The horses whinny and nicker at the sight and smell of me, and the feeling is mutual. Just being in here, my safe space, surrounded by soft pungent smells that take me right back to childhood and the only place I was happy, is enough for me to allow myself a deep breath.

Destiny, the newest pony in my barn who is now quite steady on her feet, nudges me with her nose. "Hello, girl. I see you." I pat her neck and feel my body calm, let her take worry and dissolve it in a way only an animal can.

God, I'm a fool. As if priding myself my entire thirty-plus years up to this point on my intelligence, my ability to control a room, to charm a crowd, has led me to the moment I'd royally fuck up the one thing I really wanted. I didn't charm Cat last night—I almost hurt her. Even after I blew it last night, *she stayed.* She didn't leave. The things I told her, things I've never told anyone—not even the dudes—about what scares me, and about who I am deep down. Things about still hoping for my family's love, I didn't even know it until the words left me, coaxed by her calm voice, her firm hand gently rubbing my arm from shoulder to elbow until I'd gotten it all out.

Brave, selfless, ballsy girl.

Faintly, from across the property, the sound of crunching snow bounces off the lake and surrounding trees. But when I exit the barn, it's not Cat, disregarding my request to stay in bed and wait for me, it's a town car. With tiny royal flags flying proudly from the hood.

I dust my hands off on my thighs and brush oats from the t-shirt I threw on.

Eerily familiar voices waft across the property as I stomp toward my back door.

My fucking parents.

No one informed me they were in the country, but I catch a glimpse of them coming up the walk, heading toward the front door, and I call out for them to stop.

Annie pops out of her cheery yellow carriage house door adorned with a skinny Scandinavian Christmas wreath as I'm passing. "Did you see? On the monitors, it's your parents. You really need some security, Winter. Anyone could show up willy-nilly. I think you'd rather they didn't! Most of all, your parents."

"I saw them. Go back to your tea, Annie. I can handle it."

"Better hurry."

I holler out to try and get their attention as I jog toward the house but my attempts at catching them go unanswered. My jog turns into a sprint and exactly fifty-four seconds later, because yes, I'm counting with the beat of my heart as I race through the house and up the stairs, a regal queen walks through my bedroom door before I can stop her.

I make it to the threshold in time to hear Cat scream.

"Oh my God!" She scrambles to cover her naked body.

Well, not all naked. My riding helmet falls to the ground and I see her throw my crop across the room as if it had suddenly burst into flames.

Damn, I would have liked to get a good look at her holding my gear while wearing nothing else. *Fucking parents.* "Mom, I yelled for you to stop. You had to hear me—"

I put a hand on my dad's chest to stop him from entering. He gives me a look, catching on that there's an indecent woman in my room. *Which supermodel is it this week?* his eyes ask, even though I haven't been that guy in some time.

Cat grasps at sheets to cover herself and I push past my parents. Dad, dutifully hovering in the hallway with his hands over his eyes for good measure.

With rushed steps, I cross the floor and chuck an afghan Annie knit me for Christmas last year at the stunning woman in my bed, the woman who's surely going to roast my balls on a stick for this.

Pancakes, which are probably dry as hay at this point, are not going to cut it.

"I, I can explain Mrs. . . ." Cat's voice trails off, speechless. Which is a sight to see but I tell myself not to dwell on that right now and help her out instead.

I open my mouth, but Mom interjects before I can get a word out. "Let's all put our clothes on and meet downstairs." Her tone is judgmental, to say the least. They know Cat is my PA, and they know she's supposed to be here helping me find a woman to marry on the show. They know finding her in my bed is classic Winter-the-royal-fuck-up material.

I hate them for lumping her into an already low opinion of me.

"This is all a misunderstanding, I can explain . . ." I trail off, speechless myself because, how do I explain what this is? I don't even know what this is, and if I tell them what I think this is, they'll surely laugh me all the way to the lake where I'll swiftly drown in embarrassment.

"I have all my clothes on." My father, clearing his throat, offers primly from the hall.

I grimace. He always thought I made terrible decisions and never understood my need to get out of a loveless family and live in America. Even though I'm a grown man with every right to have a woman in my bed, I can feel them judging me for straying from the plan their team set in motion with *Royal Hearts*.

"Mom," I gesture with a sweep of my arm toward the door. "Please, excuse us. I'll be down in a minute."

The Queen of Denmark turns on her heel and I hear her murmuring for my father to follow. Their footsteps echo on the wood floor until Cat and I are in silence, staring at each other with wide eyes.

"I can't imagine what they must think of me," she says.

"I can't imagine a world where you care." The flippant statement is out of my mouth before I can think twice about it—because it's true, the Cat I know wouldn't care a wink.

"Winter! This isn't a game. Of course, I care what your parents think of me," she yells, jumping from my bed and scrambling to grab her clothes off my chest of drawers where I'd left them folded.

She nips into the bathroom, leaving the door cracked while she changes. I avert my gaze, though it's a struggle. "I didn't mean it like that. I meant, it doesn't matter what they think. I don't care, and neither should you."

"Fine," she says, emerging from the bathroom, finger-combing her hair behind her ears. "What do you suggest we say?"

"We say nothing. We go down there, and I hear them out. Their opinion of us doesn't matter to me. But I know they're here for a reason, and I'd like to have it so I can send them on their way. If you want to go—"

"Go?"

"You don't have to endure—"

"And leave you to the firing squad? I don't think so."

My heart swells and I tell it to stand down. I can't deal with my parents and my growing feelings for Cat at the same time.

We trudge down the stairs together, hand in hand which makes me feel some kind of wild for her, and find my parents sitting in the living room. Annie appears in a beautiful knit sweatered with turtle doves that she's been working on all year, and she's made a neat pot of tea with all the accoutrements. She serves my parents and pours a cup for Cat and me without asking.

After handing us the tea, she leaves the room, but not before giving me a gentle squeeze on my forearm. She also pauses to push her shoulders back, and prop her chin up, all while looking at Cat, who gets the message and does the same.

A grandfather clock ticks away while Christmas decorations glitter in the morning light.

"May we speak freely in front of your guest?" Mom asks, sipping her tea.

"Yes," I grit, lifting my steaming cup to my lips so it might soothe the nerves rolling around in my belly.

They've got an announcement. I can smell it.

"Do you want to tell him, Frederik?" My mom says.

Dad takes a deep breath and meets my eyes. "We came to tell you the Crown is pulling out of the show. The theatrics aren't becoming, and it's clear none of the ladies," he says ladies as if he's speaking about vermin under his shoe, "are adequate, anyway."

My mother's hands bunch in her lap. "Anker is trying to protect the brand. He says the people do not like this version of you." Everyone has a fucking brand, even royals.

"There are so many ways to elevate and reinvigorate your brand, as a family, as a united force for your people. Likability shouldn't fall solely on one person." Cat speaks directly to my mom, comfortable talking shop. I wonder if the passion in her voice will make it through their thick skulls.

"You should hire her," I say, smug while my parents realize in real time how smart and savvy Cat Bloomfield is. Formidable. I also hope they finally fire Anker.

"Frederik, maybe she's right—" Mom is stepping out on a limb here, trying to intervene and it hits me right in the chest.

"You've been released from your contract," my dad finishes firmly, ignoring my mom, ignoring Cat, and ignoring me.

"Released?" I repeat.

"From the show?" Cat clarifies.

"And from the monarchy," Dad confirms, ruthless thin lips forming a line to signal there's to be no discussion, no outburst, no emotion. "Until you come home and live by our standards."

I set my cup and saucer on a silver platter, it clatters and Cat sucks in a sharp breath next to me. "You're releasing me from *the family?*"

Dad straightens in his seat. "Stop fucking around, Winter. You, your insolence, reclusive habits, and bad behavior has tainted our family name. Return to Denmark, assume your rightful position, and all will be restored as it should be. This is my final offer." He's bluffing. I am his only son.

"You're willing to risk it all on a threat, Freddy? You're so sure you've got that strong a hold on me?" I ask, not caring that he hates when I address him this way. "You know Elias would be a good fit—"

"My own son, suggesting my brother's offspring take the crown. Do you not have an ounce of backbone?"

"Maybe there's a way," my mom offers. She's being brave today, for me. She and I both know in this moment, this might be our last chance at anything that looks like a family.

"Unfortunately, no, because he's all we've got and goddammit," his cup clatters on a side table, "you're a disappoint-ment. I cannot look at you, much less wait one moment longer for you to fall in line. You disgrace me, you disgrace your mother."

Cat points at my dad with her teacup, a little liquid sloshing over the side. "Wait just a minute your, your royal—Frederik."

"Don't," I say, low and almost in a growl. The last thing I want is for her to be touched by the ugly that is my family.

"But someone has to tell them how magnanimous you are. Don't you realize what a gem you've got on your hands? A man who can stand up for what he wants, who is a solid friend, and who, despite your toxic family, can stand on his own two feet and be confident in who he is? He would be the perfect leader: strong, compassionate, generous. Maybe you should listen to his ideas."

"You," my mother interrupts, gently placing her teacup on the table, "are part of the problem. He was going to play by the rules, before you. He agreed to this show to bolster his image and take a wife so we could at the very least, move toward a possible passing of the crown the country could support."

My dad cuts in, his anger building with my mom's words. "Now, all anyone can talk about is the two of you. The prince and the PA? I think not."

"She's a talented—"

"She's an internet trollop, Winter, honestly," he says with all the righteous pride of the Crown behind his words.

"Don't speak to her like that," I say, standing in a show to my parents that their time here is up. "I'll pack my things, and move out." Make no mistake, I've played out this possibility in my mind before, a reality where I walk away. Hearing them bad mouth Cat puts me over the edge.

The only thing I cannot leave behind is my animals, but I've planned for this all along and have a stable lined up to board already. It never seemed like a long shot, but I also realize in this moment, I never thought I'd do it either. It will be hard to leave Vikingstrong, the only home I've ever had.

"You're refusing to return to Denmark?" The King cannot believe I've called his bluff. *How do you like my backbone, now?*

I try to keep my voice in control when I say, "You've disowned me. In name. In home. In title."

"Exactly what you've always wanted, son. You're welcome."

It's both true, and not. But all thoughts of family drain away when I look at Cat.

She's staring at the carpet, a look of pure dread on her face. But before I can say anything, she pulls her chin up with determination. "It's your choice if you want to disown your son, but let's get one thing straight: he," she points her finger at me without breaking eye contact with my parents, "is a solid man who loves his country, and deep down I know he loves you. He craves your love in return. You break him like this, and you may never get a chance to fix it."

"Why? Because you'll be the one fixing him?" my mother asks. I can't honestly tell what answer she wants from Cat. A part of me hopes my mom is happy that I've at least got someone to lean on while I get cast out of everything I've ever known.

I have no clue what Cat will say next. No one has ever stood up for me, to them, the way she is right now.

Cat stands and smooths her wrinkled clothes with the inherent dignity of a queen. Pointedly as if on stage while my parents' eyes remain glued to her, she tucks her hair behind both ears. The ruby earrings, recognizable Larsen family heirlooms, glint and sparkle against her raven hair.

She holds their gaze until we're all on the edge of our seats and the tension in the room is filling like a balloon about to pop. "There's nothing wrong with him, and while I'm here for whatever he needs, he's strong enough to mend himself."

Thirty-Two

CAT

Winter insisted on continuing to film *Royal Hearts*, and Streamflix was more than happy to sign a new contract even without an actual prince. Who cares about the fine print when the show is eighty percent finished? Everyone's convinced if it leaks to the press it will drum up even more interest in the show, which is great for syndication. I'm not convinced, but this isn't my project and I'm not running this team. I'm just the PA.

He had every reason to walk away.

It's been over a week of watching Winter on dates with Lexi H. And Lexi A. from Alabama. We've actually come to be friends, they're both on this show for reasons that have nothing to do with Winter, and I think they're both realizing most of the rumors about the prince and the PA are true.

Mandy did get quietly removed from the show for breach of contract to no one's surprise and to the delight of internet trolls

314

everywhere. All the while Winter's been pulling me into closets, or into my room at the lodge every chance he gets. My new favorite thing is sneaking kisses behind Christmas trees. But he's sad and even more introverted on set most days, likely because his parents wrote him off over a cup of tea.

Tonight is our first official night on vacation. We won't pick up filming again until after Christmas, and I'm ready to put it all out of my mind. Winter needs a break, too. He's close to burning out from all the interviews, filming, and unavoidable scrutiny—I know the signs.

It doesn't take long for me to slip into a thin, black knit dress with long sleeves after a soak in a cranberry tub. The dress is tight and goes all the way to my ankles with Prada boots. I toss on my puffer coat after dabbing lavender oil behind my ears, the one Winter got me. It feels like being eaten by a cloud and I love it.

At the door where I'm meeting a car sent from Vikingstrong to pick me up, I pull Annie's mittens on my hands and take a look around the lodge. The room is glowing with holiday cheer, families making their way to The Nook for dinner, couples perched at the bar for their après-ski. The room is filled with one-week-till-Christmas-cheer. Everyone is settled. And I think I am, too. For the first time in my life I feel very much like I belong here. Funny, I can't live in a hotel the rest of my life, but I could see myself moving here to be close to Frannie. Working remote when *Royal Hearts* wraps. Hell, Willow could move here, too. We could get a place. I could be close to—

Wait—what am I thinking? The city girl moving to the small town for a man? Could I get more cliché?

Do I care?

The car ride is soft and quiet and leather-scented. Tonight Winter is throwing a Christmas crew party. What everyone else doesn't know is it's also his farewell to Vikingstrong. He's moving out in a few days.

Annie answers the door with knitting in her hands, as if she's a mom welcoming a few classmates to a basement party.

"Hello dear, he's downstairs," she says kindly.

"Thanks, Annie."

"I'll miss him with my whole heart, you know," she adds, closing the door softly behind me. "But I miss Skagen, my family, my culture."

Something about her face, the love in her eyes, makes it impossible not to believe her. Still, I'm a little disappointed in her for abandoning him now. Even if she's been wishing to move on with her life, which would be completely acceptable, but does it have to be now, when the Crown has abandoned him?

"You know, it's because of you," she says, maybe reading the look on my face.

Me?

"We're not—" I start to wave my mitten-covered hand then stop in my tracks, the visual halting my words. We are, I just need to be strong enough to see it through.

"He loves you."

"No. He doesn't." I shake my head vigorously as if her words might tumble out of my ears and I won't have heard them.

But maybe he could?

"Oh, dear. I see this won't be easy for you. But I wouldn't leave if I didn't believe you'd take good care of him. Go on now, go find our boy and make sure he's alright. It's been a tough few weeks for both of you, I know."

"Wait, how do you know I'm right for him? You don't even know me, not really, not enough to make that statement." For once in my life I wish I could be the kind of girl who accepted kind words, but I can't, not when the logical side of me is screaming not to believe them. They can't possibly be true.

"I heard what you said to the family, to the Crown. Wish I had it on recording," she laughs and slaps a hand over her mouth and quickly sobers as if she's afraid the Crown might be listening, maybe they are. "I promise, he's on his way to being the happiest he's ever been. It's just taken him a little work—and finding you—to get there. That's all I need to know. And you'll come to visit," she winks.

"Annie," I hesitate because I'm not yet sure what I want to ask her. "What . . . what does he need?"

A slow smile crosses her face. "Love. Love is all he needs." Humming a tune, she returns to the living room and kicks up her feet with her knitting. A mom, waiting patiently upstairs in case the basement party gets too rowdy.

My head is spinning as I follow glowing lights built into a winding staircase that takes me a few levels down to the basement. When I turn a corner, I realize why, this isn't a normal basement. Not the rec rooms filled with ping-pong tables and hand-me-down couches I remember from parties as a kid, or even the grimy studio hangouts in the Bay Area from my twenties.

The ceilings are vaulted, dotted with numerous chandeliers turned down low. There are an uncountable number of Christmas trees in solid jewel tones clustered in corners and sleek, low-profile furniture for chatting with speckled fur throws. A long stone bar runs the length of one wall with keg pulls and shiny glasses.

And then I see him, backed by colored lights bouncing somehow in sync while Brenda Lee encourages us to rock around the Christmas tree. He's wearing a fur coat, bare chest, leather pants, black nails.

And he's smoking?

So he's still sad, or in revenge mode. Well, I'm not having it.

I stomp toward him, happy to be in boots in case he needs a swift kick in the ass.

"It's not mine, Mom, I swear," he jokes, as he no doubt clocks my mood. I hate that he can read my expression so easily, but I'm also not trying to hide it.

"I don't care if it is." Lie. "Still, getting back at your parents with lung cancer is a slow route to revenge." He huffs and looks away as smoke curls toward the ceiling between us.

Is this what real intimacy is? Knowing the good, the bad, and the ugly in someone, and loving them anyway? Because I do love him. I know it in this second, oddly. It's impossible for all this caring and worry not to be love. This exact moment might not be the most romantic, but it is real.

He may no longer be a prince, but he's the epitome of entitlement standing in front of me. He may have lost his title, but the man will never lose his edge, his essence, that thing that makes everyone in the room want to stare at him. It's a shine, glowing even when he's in a dark mood.

But I can't stand letting their rejection eat away at him. And I won't let him sink into his sadness.

He hands the cigarette to a buddy who was bent over tying his boot. "Thanks, man," he says, before wandering into the crowd.

"Don't hate me because I care about your health," I say, chin up. I don't care if he knows how much I care about him. In fact, I decide at this moment to tell him everything.

"I don't hate you, Bloom."

"No?" I smile despite myself, "Good. Because I happen to care about a lot of things regarding you these days."

He returns my smile and I'm pleased I put it there. "And I'm finding I care quite a bit about you, too."

"Do you want to talk? Or are you going to sulk bare-chested in fur all night?"

His lips tip up, curling into a wide grin. "You gonna do something about it?" he smiles, eager for my comeback.

"I'm not afraid to tell it how it is, pretty man." Whatever game we're playing, I think I like it, and if it cheers him up I like it even more. "Be careful what you wish for."

Something in my chest twists as he drags his fingertips down my cheek and tips my chin up. "You mean, like when you told my parents where they could shove it? I think they're still in shock. I talked to my cousin, he said my mom can't stop talking about a feisty American PA that's stolen me away from the Crown. "

"You liked that, huh?"

"I like everything that goes on inside that head of yours." He gulps and presses on, "I love everything about you."

"That's a big thing to say to a girl in the middle of a crowded room." I drag my thumb across his bottom lip as it pouts.

"The crowd part, I can remedy." Tugging me gently by the elbow through clumps of people, we both give our friends in a corner a wave. Along with the cast, everyone is ignoring us. Giving us space. I think they all know what's going on, and I think they all know we need some time before we explain ourselves.

Off hours are off hours.

We turn a corner by the bar and move at a clip down a dark hall. The music fades, and it gets quieter and quieter as we disappear from the party.

"Where are we going? I came here for a basement party and to see two dudes fall for each other in real time," I tease, almost tripping over my boots to keep up with him.

"Robbie and Liam, right? They're already in the guest room." He winks at me over his shoulder.

"Where are we going if the guest room is occupied?" He's pulling me so excitedly now, as if he doesn't want to waist a second.

He pushes through a heavy door and flips a switch. The room glows around the edges with track lighting, our dark reflections appear in mirrors along with a bunch of fitness equipment. We're in a gym.

"I just want to be with you, I don't care where. Do you?" he asks honestly.

"No."

It happens quick, he pushes me up against a mirror and I turn my head instinctually, my breath foggy on the glass, giving him access as he licks across my jawbone, tugging at the sleeves of my long dress.

"What are you wearing?"

"It's a dress—" As much as I want this, he doesn't quite seem himself.

"I hate this dress," he groans, pulling at the high neckline, tugging at the long sleeves.

I push him back. "Winter, wait."

He stumbles a few feet and drops to a weight bench behind him. I'm momentarily stunned, cold from the loss of his touch. I only meant to say—

"It's too heavy," he shouts at the floor.

"The weights?" I look around, already breathing hard from the knowledge of what we were about to do, knowing he's not talking about a workout. It was a stupid thing to say, to try and break the tension.

"I thought the weight of the Crown was too much, heavy is the head and all." He rubs at his ribcage and I bite down on my lip so my eyes don't turn glassy from emotion. "But now, it's gone. I got exactly what I wanted. Instead of feeling light, it's heavier than ever before." He looks up at me with searching eyes. "I thought I was alone then, and now, I've really got nothing. I am nothing."

"You don't have nothing," I breathe. "You have me." It's a risk, saying those words. We've never talked past hiding our relationship from the show. But it feels right, and I keep pushing myself to open up fully to him. "And you are not nothing without the Crown."

"But that's all I ever was to them. Now that it's gone, what worth do I have?"

"Winter," I want to go to him but I stay where I am, back against the mirror. I'm not sure how to help him right now, but I search for the right words anyway. "I think you should quit the show." This is not in my best interest, that's for sure, but it's in his.

I can weather the storm of the show not going well. Brand Hub could weather the storm.

He laughs darkly. "The last thing I would do is quit the show, quit on you. Not when we're a week from the finale. I would *never* do that to you, or my country. They need to see me finish what I started."

"I don't care about that," I gulp, my throat dry, realizing my words are truth. Brand Hub would get over it; if we got a bad rep in the industry for not fulfilling a contract, I'd find a way to fix it. "I care about you. Tell your parents you'll quit filming, and talk to them. Maybe you can't mend it completely. I know your history with the Crown runs deep, but maybe you could come to an understanding you could live with?"

"No," he shakes his head at the floor, "I don't want to be their puppet anymore." He snorts. "I was not raised the same way you were. We're not a democracy in my family."

"Then make them see where you're coming from. Give them a chance to see it your way, and if it doesn't work out, we'll figure it out."

"We?"

"We."

He looks up at me with hooded eyes. "Cat, you and I both know when the show is over, you'll be gone. There is no we." His thumb presses into his wrist. There's no heart there. I haven't drawn one recently because we haven't been filming, but still, he presses lightly on the exact spot.

I take a deep breath and swallow the queasiness and fear that his words mean he doesn't want me. "Only if that's what you want." Annie's words ring in my ears, *all he needs is love*. I love him. I just don't know if he's ready to hear it.

"What are you saying?"

It takes everything I've got to tell him the truth once and for all. "I want to try. To be with you. Now, and after the show. If that's what . . ."

He looks up at me with eyes so full of desire it stalls my words.
Then I watch, as he slides slowly off the bench onto his knees.

Thirty-Three

WINTER

This gym has seen me in some rough moments. All those years, pounding away at weights and the treadmill, sweat pouring off me in an effort to hold off tears. And now, here I am, on my knees in this room in front of the one thing I've always needed.

Someone willing to stay. To fight my battles with me.

"You'd do that?" My hands glide up her smooth legs under her dress, her skin so soft I shiver.

"If you mean, secretly be with you while you date other women, and stay with you after you pick a wife, then, against my better judgment and the fact it sounds insane outside of context, yes."

"We'll have a plan." I lean in and inhale her. "Finish the show, then after the dust settles, we can tell everyone. *It's you I want, Cat.* You must know that." My forehead dips and I press against her stomach, rolling my head from side to side and gripping her hips in my hands. It's like I'm praying, and maybe I am.

"I want you back," she says simply, running her fingers through my hair.

"We're together, you and me." I have to say it out loud to believe it. "After the show, it will be you and me. Whatever that looks like. Cat, I'll come to you, anywhere you are. I'll support you, in whatever you want to accomplish. I'm free of the Crown, I can be that for you."

She pulls my chin up so I look into her eyes from the floor of my gym, a place I've always found comfort. "Okay."

Slowly, I nod, and untie her right boot, pulling it gently from her foot along with a thick sock that I realize is mine.

She's going to trust me, and that's more valuable than any jewel in this castle.

My eyes meet hers and she sniffs. "I like your socks, they're so soft."

As I untie her left boot, I chuckle to myself. "I'll shower you in cashmere socks, Bloom." I need to be inside her, make love to her, fuck her good and hard until she knows she's mine and she's safe with me.

Quickly I stand, rucking her dress up around her thighs, and grasping the backs of her legs so she can wrap them around me. "Now you've got me where you want me, what are you going to do with me?" she taunts, draping her arms around my neck, letting me hold her but still having the higher ground.

Silently I walk to my weight bench, I'll never look at this room the same again after tonight. Then again, I'm moving in a few days, but I banish that thought. I'll deal with that later.

Laying her gently down on the bench, I pull her hands up above her head. "Hold on to the bar."

"Okay."

"Who knew you'd be so easy to boss around," I smirk, dragging a fingertip down the bridge of her nose, over the divot in her lip, down her neck and all the way down her stomach as I come to the end of the bench, pressing her knees apart with mine to make room. She's laid out in front of me like a present. I've never cared much for presents, myself. I prefer giving them. But this one I very much want to unwrap.

"Why would I fight you when you're giving me what I want," she laughs, then sucks in a breath when I drop to the floor again, pushing her dress up to her waist this time, shouldering myself between her thighs to make room for what I want.

My hands wrap around her hips and I lick my lips. "You're so beautiful, like a rare thing I can't get enough of." My palm lays flat across her stomach as my other hand brushes across her black silk panties. I've noticed she's got a thing for French silk, and I'll shower her in that, too. She drops her hands, but I growl, "Put them back." And she does.

"Atta girl." I praise her for following my directions, which is hard for her when she's usually the one in charge, but I think she likes it. The flip of power, back and forth, back and forth. It's always been like this between us.

"Winter," she squirms on the bench, needy and drenched already. I can feel how wet she is through the silk. "I need you to do something."

"But making you wait is a pleasure I never thought I'd enjoy quite so much." So, so demanding, my girl.

It is fun to make her wait, to make her want, and to listen to her beg even if her begging sounds more like an order. Knowing it's me she wants makes me glow on the inside. Her needing me, her craving me when she knows me better than anyone, is like a soft bandage on an old wound.

Still, it's torture for me, too. My dick is painfully hard.

Pulling her panties to the side, I slowly slide two fingers inside her. She's so ready for me and she gasps, her hips bucking off the bench, trying to meet my hand, trying to get deeper and find the release she knows is coming. "You're very responsive," I whisper, rising to my knees.

I drag my mouth up the inside of one thigh, delighting in the moans I'm rewarded with, and blow a long, slow breath over her core while I work her with my fingers.

I add another. "Winter, now," she demands.

Toying with her is fun, but I'm willing to comply. My mouth seals over her clit as she screams, her voice echoing off the gym's mirrored walls.

"Turn your head and look at us," I command. I can't always let her be in control. We are give and take, she and I.

She follows my direction, and we make eye contact in the mirror, soft light around us. We eat up our reflection, her laid out on the bench, covered in black with her hands gripping the bar of my bench press, the rest of her naked with my face and fingers between her legs.

The image is erotic as fuck and almost makes me spill in my pants. My dick is begging for my hand, or better, to push inside her. *Almost there.* I grit my teeth and hold on.

She gasps, "I'm going to—"

"Let go, *sod bloomst.*"

"Almost, almost—*what does that mean?*" Even on the edge of orgasm, she's demanding and I can't help letting a breathy laugh slip from my lips while working her and working myself up even further.

"It means," I grit, barely getting the words out, "my little flower."

"Oh, oh, *yes,*" she says, falling apart all over my hand. Whether it's my fingers inside her, my mouth, my words, or all of it combined, my own fucking heart melts at the way she comes undone for me. I let go of the silk and give in, palming myself through my pants. It hurts how much I want her. "Get up here," she says with a shaky voice.

Dragging my tongue up her thigh as I go, noticing she's got

faint bruising from the last time I was here, I sit on the bench and wedge my legs under hers, pulling her to straddle my lap.

"You're bruised."

"I don't care, I like every way you mark me." She turns her head and takes in our new position in the mirror. "Do you have anything? I've tested recently, and I haven't been with anyone since . . . I work too much and I—"

"Shh." I put a finger to her lips. "I'm good, but are you sure?"

"Yes. I'm on the pill, and I'm exceptionally strict about it."

"I have no doubts, but, I can have you bare?" I ask in wonder, the thought of feeling her with nothing between us pushing me almost to the brink, but I have to hold on. This is a first for me. I was always taught to use protection, not to trust my future to someone else's promise. But I trust her. And I think she trusts me.

"Yes," she breathes again, another one-word answer, but the astonishment comes through. Well, that makes fucking two of us, Bloom.

"Cat," I take a breath, watching her face. "I've never been bare with anyone."

Her hands scramble at my waist, making quick work of my button and zipper, and then she takes me in hand.

"I've never needed anyone like this, Winter," she whines, working her hand up and down my shaft like she's desperate for me. "I can't wait, I want you to be mine and I . . ."

"Yes, *please*," I hear myself plead, if she thinks I've got any ability to hold back now, she's got no clue what's going on inside me. I am seconds from coming, but I will satisfy her before I allow myself a lick of pleasure. "Look at you," I turn my head and hers follows. "I'll never forget this moment, with you. You're more than I've allowed myself to wish for." This is a damn good way to say goodbye to Vikingstrong.

Deep breaths. Clear my thoughts. I want to last for her. I want it to be good.

In the mirror, I watch as she pushes up. Her shins brace on my thighs while she lines up the glistening head of my dick, shining with precum, with her entrance. Now I'm the one who can't wait, who can't stand any hesitation, "If you're sure," I rasp, "please put me out of my fucking misery."

She does, sliding down my shaft, inch by inch. Oh. So. Slowly, but not because she's being timid. My girl is not the timid kind, no, it's because she's savoring every second she watches in the mirror.

When she's seated, taking me inside to the hilt, we both drag our gazes back to one another, touching noses and breathing each other's air.

"Damn, baby." She's so tight, I'm filling her up inside as I tentatively tip my hips to go a little deeper.

Slowly and with a whimper, she rises, as if she doesn't want to lose me. I wrap a hand around the back of her neck and she mirrors the move as we slam together. "You're so much, you're so perfect for me," she gasps.

"Fuuuuuuck."

"No one's ever been this deep," she whines, holding on to my shoulders with both hands now while I grip her hips. Feeling each other, testing each other.

Bare and seated inside her tight core, I almost black out for a second. I've never felt anything like it, anything like her. But I force myself to focus, *focus on her.* Check on her first before I let myself dissolve into pleasure.

"Does it hurt?"

"God, no," she gasps, dropping her head back and moving a little more fluidly, up and down. "I'm so close already, Win. *Again.*"

Leaning back slightly, I pump my hips into her, making her bounce. The top of her dress is cutting off my view of her body, so I pull it up quickly with both hands. She raises her arms without question, and I whip it off completely.

Black lace shines in the low light, tight nipples peeking

through silk, begging to be touched. I palm both her breasts, groaning, dragging my hands down her ribcage as she rides me, then up her smooth back, relishing the feeling of every notch on her spine. "You are everything. Do you know you have complete power over me? Had it, from the start?"

"Yes," she gasps.

That makes me laugh. I'm not surprised. My girl knows she holds the reins, and I'm fine with that.

Dropping my mouth to one silk-covered breast, I suck as I buck my hips up harder. She is my favorite thing to suck on, my little flower. My balls tighten and my pulse kicks up a hundred notches. It's too much with her breast in my mouth. I pull away and see the wet spot spreading into the silk and for some reason, that pushes me even further to the edge. "I'm gonna—"

"Me, too."

I give one final hard push with my hips, gripping her waist with both hands and holding her down, trying my best to reach as deep as I can and hit the spot I know she needs me to find.

And my effort is rewarded, because as I explode into her, feeling myself gush hard and wondering if I'll ever stop, she screams my name.

I whip a hand over her mouth when there's a knock at the door.

Her eyes meet mine, wide and excited. Both of us shuddering through our orgasm with sweaty brows as she pants against my hand and wiggles in my lap. I'm still inside her and the motion makes me groan, wringing the last of my orgasm from my spent body. No amount of weight lifting or running has ever wiped me out like this.

When I remove my hand and the knock comes again, she whisper-giggles, answering in a falsetto, "Who is it?"

A laugh tumbles freely from my chest, I love seeing her undone and let loose like this.

"Ocupado," I say in an equally high tone, or as high as I can make my voice go.

There's no way we're fooling whoever is on the other side of the door, but it's fun.

"Marco called. It's about the show!" Robbie's voice booms through the thick door.

"Oh shit!" She jumps from my lap and scrambles for her dress, pulling it quickly over her head and pushing it down over her hips. Then she hops around shoving her boots on and folding her socks into a little ball.

"Hide in the corner. Let me take care of it."

"You're hiding me?" she asks incredulously.

"Never, shut up," I fling back at her, letting her know I'm insulted by her even suggesting I'd like to do anything but shout about her from the rooftops. "*What if he has a camera?* Unless you're ready to take a spot as a cast member, which I would more than welcome—"

"No, you're right." She waves me on to open the door.

"I don't have all night," Robbie shouts again. "This'll only take a minute, and then you can get back to—"

I fling open the door, my pants on but unbuttoned, fly gaping. Nothing is going to slow me down for round two after I close this door.

"This better be good, or I'm gonna shave your mohawk when you inevitably pass out on my couch tonight." I'm kidding, of course. I wouldn't do that. And judging by Robbie's clear eyes, and the arm he's got draped over Liam's shoulder, I don't think either of them are drinking heavily tonight. I think they had, and judging by the goofy-happy look on Liam's face *still have*, better things to do.

Good for them. Glad we're all enjoying ourselves. I sure as hell am.

"Marco called," Robbie says again.

Cat appears at my side, unable to stay out of it but there's no camera to catch us, anyway. "But you don't have a phone?"

Glancing down at her I give her a look because, couldn't she relinquish control for two seconds?

Robbie and Liam are unfazed by her appearance. I think they've been watching us just as much as we've been watching them.

"Marco asked Darcy to call me," Liam says. "And pass the message on to Robbie, so he could get the message to the crew and you two."

Cat and I look at each other and back at the two lovebirds at the door. This is either going to be epically bad news or—

"Spit it out," Cat says.

"The finale has been postponed. We get not one," he holds up a finger with a shit-eating grin, "but two weeks off for Christmas break. All expenses paid, motherfucker!"

We look at each other again, "But why would they do that?" she asks.

Robbie goes on, "Fans are rabid, and they've decided to milk it. The finale will air January first."

"New Year's Day," Cat says, and I can hear the wheels turning in her head.

This means the show will be more drawn out, which means we have to keep this ruse going even longer. *Not great.* But . . . "We get a two-week holiday off? Away from all the cameras and bullshit?" I ask again, already thinking of all the things I want to do with Cat between now and then.

"That's right. Merry Christmas, you filthy animals," Robbie says, then pulls Liam away while both of them snicker about us.

Cat looks up at me, a fresh hickey blooming on her neck, I really need to learn to suck softer. She wraps her arms around me and I turn into her, my body responding to hers naturally. "I think," she whispers, "this is good news."

"This is great news, Bloom. For the next two weeks, you're mine."

Thirty-Four

CAT

"Let's tell them, already," Winter groans.

"What if someone leaks to the press?" I'm so stupid in love with a prince and keeping the secret from my sister. Winter's keeping it from his buddies, per my request, which is a problem because we're headed to Fran and John's house and can't keep our hands off each other. And it's Christmas Eve.

And I hate secrets.

Rumors or not, Frannie is going to come unglued when I admit I'm dating Winter Larsen. While he's dating a handful of other women. But that's semantics! And almost over!

Since Winter and I made love in his gym—I will never get the visuals of watching him do erotic things to me in mirrors out of my head as long as I live—we've continued to do it in every space we can find for a week straight. All over Vikingstrong castle before I helped him move out, at Little Star Lodge in my four-poster bed while he stayed with me for a few days, even in his car outside the

Tipsy Taco after we met Fran and John for two-for-one margarita night.

"Cat," Winter shuts the door to the hunting cabin we've been shacking up in on John and Fran's property—or what will be 'John and Fran's' if the man ever proposes. "They probably already know."

"No way, we've been very stealthy." Plus, we haven't talked about what we will mean to each other after the show. I want to stay in our Gingerbread cottage forever, in our snow globe forever, and we could possibly have that. *City-girl-moves-to-small-town-for-prince* has a ring to it.

He snorts, "*The Tipsy Taco?*"

Well, he's got me there. Anyone could have seen us, I guess. But it was fun.

Streamflix's presence has been wiped away, and while I miss Robbie, Marco, and the crew who all flew home to their families after we were awarded more time off, I don't miss hiding from the camera, and despite the risk, I don't want to hide anymore from our friends.

"Don't drop that one!" I yell as we crunch through snow to the main house. We pass snowmen with beanie hats and carrot noses that John and Fran built yesterday. "It's breakable."

"What is it?" Winter catches a large box with his chin before it tumbles from his stack and hits the ground, a tag hanging off it marked for Fran.

"It's a coffee mug for Frannie. We try to repulse each other with corny mugs every year for Christmas, except we secretly love corny mugs, the cornier, the better."

"And this is a corny coffee mug?" He gestures to a massive box wrapped in plaid paper with a shiny red bow. "It's the size of a coffee *maker*."

"I like to throw her off. She'll think I got her a new pair of boots or something."

"But you always get each other mugs."

"You don't have to get it, just carry the boxes!" I direct him.

He's got presents stacked above his head and so do I. It took me all afternoon to wrap them with no help from Win, who spent his day giving sleigh rides to grade schoolers. When John and Frannie offered him the small but cozy hunting cabin on their property, Lola came with him, of course, but the horses are still in his barn until he arranges transportation to a small stable in Clover.

My room at the lodge has been empty most nights. I wouldn't say I moved in with Winter, but most of my stuff has made its way over to the cabin and neither one of us has mentioned any of it going back. I think I could live happily in that little gingerbread house with lattice trim and a red front door for the rest of my life. Working remotely with a cup of tea, after all, internet life has its perks—like living wherever you please.

We both tromp across the lawn, hugging the lakeshore as it gently laps at smooth rocks accustomed to the area and reflecting a high winter moon. "We need to tell them. They'll keep the secret through the last few days of filming. It's all basically over, Cat. Let's enjoy tonight, together, as a real couple."

"You're right." I can tell he's shocked to hear me admit it.

"Good," he says, and kisses me reverently on the forehead before we push through sliding glass doors into the kitchen. It's pretty handy living in my sister's backyard. I don't hate being close to her again.

"Merry Christmas, Kitty-Cat!" Fran runs and jumps into my arms as I set presents on a large marble counter. The main house is nice, hence the acreage and the cabin they had just sitting around to offer us. "How was the commute, neighbor?"

It feels right to be close again. I've hated the past few months being away from her in San Francisco when she was here. Something about all of this, this night, and this place feels right.

"Merry Christmas, Frannie-Bananie. Hey, we have to call Mom and Dad."

"They're in Mallorca now, right?"

"I think so? Isn't that near Ibiza?"

She shrugs and pulls her phone from a drawer. "I have no idea."

"I'm going to step out and call Elias. It's Christmas morning in Denmark and he's one of those uber productive early risers. And Mallorca is near Ibiza. Be right back, Bloom," Winter says, his gaze soft and happy.

I love seeing him this way, and I nod. "Okay."

"And then it's time," he adds, mockingly stern.

"*Okaaaaay.*"

"Time for what?" Frannie asks, eyes wide no doubt expecting a Christmas surprise, but I wave her off for now.

"What is with all the international calls?" John quips, "I've already wished Ricky and Patty a Merry Christmas when I saw them this morning at Bargain Barn picking up a last-minute singing penguin for Patty's yard. The woman has a thing for lawn ornaments." He begins laying out an assortment of glasses, swizzle sticks sporting fish with Santa hats, and cocktail mixers.

When the call connects, and they confirm they are in Mallorca, we catch the Bloomfields up on our lives and exchange Christmas wishes—a Bloomfield tradition. Dad wishes for his old comfy recliner because he's ready to hang up his travel boots and go home, Mom wishes for new luggage because hers has a tear, Frannie wishes for a solid opening week at Thistle and Burr Motel, and I wish for things to stay exactly as they are in this moment in time. Christmas Eve in this pretty house with Fran and friends, on a loop, forever.

The doorbell rings in the background and a crew of men walk in with presents wrapped in everything from newspaper to black trash bags.

"Gotta go. The guys are here and we're doing an exchange. I'm dying to give Cat her present."

"You girls have fun," Mom says.

"We're proud of you," Dad adds. "We haven't seen much but we've heard that show of yours is doing well in the States," Dad says to me. "Is the guy going to get the girl in the end?" Mike Bloomfield will be a hopeless romantic till the day he dies.

Frannie snorts a laugh. "Oh yeah, I think you can safely say the guy is going to get the girl."

I punch her in the thigh. "Ow, Cat!"

"Enjoy yourselves," I say into the camera. "And then get back here, we miss you!" Our parents have fought hard through raising kids, building a business, and falling back in love with each other while starting their retirement. They're not just a love story, they're a *real* love story. One I know my sister hopes to emulate, and one I'm beginning to think I'd like a taste of as well.

Frannie pulls me into the living room. "Present time!"

"Let me at least get everyone drinks," John says, ever the caretaker, while he grins at her from the kitchen.

"You do drinks, I'm going to give Cat the first present." She makes big eyes at John, then turns to a massive, and I mean enormous, present in front of an equally huge fireplace with a roaring fire going. They strung real popcorn and cranberries to weave into their garlands together and I'm swooning right along with them.

"Did you waste that much paper wrapping a coffee mug?" I ask her, as she pushes me to the box. It comes up to my shoulders. "Or did you spring for a bigger refrigerator for the cabin, because—"

"Open it," she squeals jumping on her toes, a Christmas tree scrunchie bobbing on her head.

"Wait, I want to give you mine, too." I run to the counter to grab Frannie's present while she groans and drops to the sofa in the living room.

"Why don't you open your gift?" Winter says softly. "Put your sister out of her misery."

My eyes bob between the two of them and the room goes silent. "Wait, are you two up to something?"

"In cahoots with Winter Larsen? Never," Fran deadpans. "Open it!"

John passes out more drinks, handing a tall glass of dark beer to Logan who takes it and mumbles, "Please, *put us all* out of our misery."

"What could it be, any guesses?" Ben asks and they all glare at him.

"Does everyone know what it is but me?"

"Yes," Logan says.

John punches his grumpy friend playfully in the arm, but the lumberjack does not budge. Come to think of it, he does resemble a tree, big, strong, unmoving, and stoic. But there's also a calmness to him, almost like he knows something the rest of us don't—not just about the present, but life in general.

"Logan, shhhhhh." Fran hushes him and kicks him good-naturedly with a reindeer-socked foot.

"I've got a surprise for you all, too, you know. Maybe I should do mine first?" Winter gives me two thumbs up, but the entire room groans. They seriously want me to open my present.

Fine, our announcement can wait. Because declaring out loud I'm part of a couple, especially after Winter and I have gone to such lengths to hide, still feels a little terrifying.

"Okay, okay." I pull back shiny, snowflake-covered paper and easily find a long piece of packing tape to tug on top. When I pull the first flap, the whole box begins to rustle and move.

I slap the top of the box closed and turn to Winter and my sister, who are both on the edges of their seats, "If you got me a pony . . ."

But a shriek from the box in front of me cuts me off.

"*Merry surprise Christmas!*" Willow pops out of the box, hands above her head in a ta-da pose. "It's really hot in there, by the way. I thought I was going to suffocate." She's wearing a cherry red sweater that compliments her strawberry hair, leggings, and a hunter-green beanie with a pink pom-pom.

The room erupts into applause and my heart grows ten sizes.

"Wills," I yell right into her face. "Oh my God, you're here!"

"I know!" she yells back, trying to hop from the tall box but her knee catches the edge and she goes flying face-first toward a huge glass coffee table.

My body twists at an odd angle, and I try to turn to catch her, but strong arms nudge me out of the way to sweep her off her feet before she face-plants into glass.

The room lets out an audible gasp as Logan's long legs step safely around the sharp edge of the coffee table with Willow in his arms. He slowly sets her back on her feet but keeps both hands wrapped around her tiny waist, making her ample curves even more prominent while she grips his shoulders for dear life. He steadies her, giving her a moment to find her balance.

"Uh, thanks." She looks up as he towers over her petite frame, her cheeks turning Rudolph red as he glares down at her. "Hey."

"Hello, again."

"Willow, you did it!" Fran breathes. "Logan, how'd you catch her?"

He says nothing, steps back, pulls his drink from the mantel where he'd set it, and only nods.

Fran throws her arms around the three of us and we all nuzzle into each other like only old friends can. Willow sighs deeply and I realize it's been a while since I've checked in with her, so wrapped up with *Royal Hearts*, and Winter.

She gives me a sweet grin, as if she knows exactly what I'm thinking and has already forgiven me. "The band's back together. Finally. But what's your announcement? I was kinda dying listening in the box. Do you know how long I was in there? Could you guys have waited to call your parents?"

"Sorry, Wills." Frannie winces. "Okay, Christmas surprise number two," Fran motions to me mischievously. "Out with it already."

I eye her. "Do you know?" I murmur under my breath as the

three of us stand in front of a warm fire in the grate, the guys all watching from the couch now as if we're on stage doing a comedy routine.

"Yes, of course I know," she speaks even lower through her teeth, leaning in mysteriously and giving me a twitchy eye that I think is supposed to be a wink.

"Know what? What are you two talking about?" Willow demands, pouting a little.

Winter stands up. "Cat and I are dating. We're together. God, Jul!"

"What?" I ask, looking up at his goofy grin.

"Merry Christmas!" The men chorus back at him.

"Danish," Winter supplies. "You're probably going to need to learn some, I mean, if you're willing—"

"Ah! Knew it!" Frannie bounces on her toes and claps her hands and the guys go back to talking about fly fishing with Ben leading a very rigorous casting tutorial.

"Wait—" Willow demands. "He's about to propose on *Royal Hearts*! I've been on a book binge so I'm a little behind, but I've been rooting for Lexi A."

"Um, Wills," I hedge apologetically. "I have a lot to catch you up on, but seriously, you guys can't tell a soul."

The night goes on in a frenzy of tearing paper, grilling steaks, glasses of cabernet, and bottles of stout beer, all topped off with hot chocolate spiked with peppermint schnapps sloshing from matching reindeer mugs as Winter and I stumble home.

Beautifully unburdened. Like a real couple.

We both kick snow off our boots in unison at the front door and fall into fits of laughter.

"Oh no, you don't," Winter says as I start to cross the threshold.

Instead, he sweeps me into his arms and attacks my neck with his mouth, slamming the door behind him with a socked foot.

"I can't see!" It's pitch black in the cabin, though moonlight pouring through windows highlights knotty pine kitchen cabinets with iron pulls and some old but serene wilderness art on the walls.

"Freeze, Bloom," Winter says, delight in his voice as he rummages in a kitchen drawer. He finds what he's after and strikes a match, lights a candle.

"The lights work, you know."

"But this is so much more romantic. Very *hygge* on Christmas Eve, I'll make you some sleepy time tea and wrap you in blankets like a *smørrebrød*."

"What's that?"

"Thick Danish toast, usually rye bread, with anything your heart desires on top."

Now that I can see, I move to a small-ish tree in the corner that we barely had time to put up after he moved out of Vikingstrong. Annie packed up all his ornaments and sent them with us. Hanging them one by one, both of us sharing stories about Christmases as kids, was the sweetest thing I've ever done with a man.

"I have a surprise for you," he whispers in my ear. "It's outside."

"We barely made it inside." My small buzz has worn-off but I'm still warm from time spent with family and friends.

"Here," he scoots me around an old leather sofa covered in nubby throws, across the worn wood floors covered in threadbare carpets to a window beside our Christmas tree. "See," he points to the end of a slim drive, paved around the big house toward the cabin and the lake.

"It's our mailbox," I say, fogging up the glass.

"It is."

"When did you have time to do this?"

"After I finished sleigh rides earlier today, you were so focused on wrapping presents. I can't believe you didn't see me. It took a good twenty minutes to dig and cement the posts into frozen earth."

"Winter," I turn into him, his face lit with the glow of colorful lights coming off our tree.

"This might be home base for a while . . ." he trails off.

I swear, my heart grows ten sizes.

"It's perfect, I'm so glad it's here. Might make watching you propose to another woman next week a little less pride-crushing."

This is home base. Maybe this could be a base for both of us, because I have no desire to leave anytime soon. Does he feel the same? Is that why he's made sure our mailbox is here, and that we have a Christmas tree while our boots are lined up at the door, boot tray catching the melting snow?

"Don't let it bother you, please. The show has nothing to do with what's between you and me. We have a plan."

"Yes, a plan, and the sweetest little mailbox outside the cutest gingerbread cabin."

"Have you named the cabin?"

"Maybe."

"Feeling sentimental?" He's teasing me, hanging my coat on a hook, shrugging off his sweater so he's in only a t-shirt.

"Maybe the time we've spent here has been some of the best in my life," I offer up honestly and with zero hesitation. A Christmas present for him, and for me.

After the show, we'll talk about the logistics of making us work. Right now, I just want to enjoy the moment. I want to give us both that gift.

"All the more reason to stay." He comes to stand beside me again and I let my head drop to his shoulder as we watch fluffy snow fall and melt into the lake.

We're on the same page. We both want this. It's a freaking Christmas miracle.

I hum in response, enjoying the snuggle, wrapping my arms around his waist and breathing his scent deep as if it might all slip through my fingers by morning. "You're almost finished with the show." I'll tell him I love him the second it's over.

He wraps an arm around me. "Yes," he confirms.

"And then it's just us."

He turns me by the shoulders to look at him and holds my gaze. "Take this moment, and times it by millions. That's how many moments like this I want with you. So many moments, they make up forever. I believe in us."

"Me too." I close my eyes and try to ignore a tiny voice inside whispering, *when we figure out how this works in the real world, I'll really believe it.*

Thirty-Five

CAT

One week later, New Year's Day.

"Do we know if they'll be sitting? Or standing?" I shield my eyes from the sun-on-snow glare and ask a stylist, sent here to help me orchestrate wardrobe for the proposal episode.

We're on top of the mountain in Garland, past Little Star Lodge, past the Whoville tree that is currently being deconstructed in the most depressing of visuals, past the ski lifts, and to the right of parked snowmobiles where the crew is building the finale set for *Royal Hearts*. There's a clearing dotted with trees where Streamflix has set up a production tent and Winter is currently getting ready. Massive viewership is predicted for the finale, and I can't help thinking about my boyfriend preparing a proposal speech for another woman. Not a good feeling.

Stick with the plan. He loves you—not that we've said that, of course, but he cares. I know he cares. Stick. To. The. Plan. My head commands, though my heart is ringing with warning bells and waving red flags.

"I think it best to be prepared for all scenarios. Anything can happen on these shows." He shrugs and walks away. Did they fly him here just for that bit of sage advice? Our budget must be flush since the ratings skyrocketed.

"We're adding log benches here, if that helps," a young woman with a toolbelt around her waist and a work coat zipped up to her chin offers. "I'm Emily," she sticks out her hand and I shake it.

"Are you crew?" I ask.

"God no, I run a small construction business in Novel. I think you know my brother, he friends with Winter, Ben Holiday?"

"Oh my gosh, you're his sister?"

"One of three, yeah. I'm almost finished building the igloo with faux snow that's supposed to blend in with the real snow under our feet." She stomps her boot. "Then I think they're headed that way, to the arch." She points off in the distance. "Are you headed up there?"

"Yeah," I nod, pulling my sunglasses from my bag. This day started early and it's going to end late, but we're in the final stretch.

"Do me a huge favor, take this box with you?" She points at a box full of blankets, a bucket of roses tucked inside. "I'm drowning over here, and no one else on crew seems to know how to use a power drill. Throw the blankets out and sprinkle the roses around a little. Thanks so much!"

The igloo structure they've assembled with Styrofoam and fake snow spray is perfect, and from what I can see, the proposal set is going to be interesting as well.

I glance at my watch. Technically, I've got time before I check on Winter. "I can do that." I can get behind a woman with power tools.

This is my last day as a PA working on a set like this. When I go back to Brand Hub, I'm making some big changes. I'll still give every last drop of my creativity and passion to my projects, but not all of me. I can no longer allow work to be the thing that defines me, I have to live my life for that. I have to find my passions, my loves, and the things that make me excited. And I have to slow down. I can't wear all the hats. If I've learned nothing else from being forced to get cozy on a mountain for the holidays, I have to rest and recharge from time to time.

My cozy Christmas with Winter, unwrapping presents in matching pajamas, a brunch spread still in our pajamas with his crew, and giving myself a minute to enjoy it all has changed everything.

The towns of Clover and Novel rallied around us over Christmas break, that's the only way we could keep our little secret while living out in the open. There was a meeting at the shared town hall, and a newsletter circulated instructing everyone not to take pictures of us, film us on their phones, or post any details about us on the internet. I heard the Lake Committee held a super-secret gathering at Holiday Bait, Boat, and Tackle to organize a plan for hunting paparazzi should there be a need.

And they listened. It's all anyone can talk about. A Christmas miracle that Clover and Novel could put their small-town rivalry aside for love and band together to hide us in our little snow globe come to life.

My phone buzzes in my pocket, I've already got it back which is making communication all around much easier, though I'm not letting socials take over my life like they used to. Winter's name pops on the screen, *pretty-man-boyfriend*. Adding that to my contacts made my heart thump and the silliest giggle fall from my lips.

> Pretty Man Boyfriend: What's it gonna be, Bloom? Tux, or townie?

There's a photo attached, Winter in the production tent next to a snack table holding a chic black tuxedo in one hand, and a puffy plaid vest with a beanie in the other.

Me: Tux. You're gonna stun, Win.

Pretty Man Boyfriend: Coming home to you, Bloom, with tux ON.

The feeling that tumbles through me is what I think is referred to as butterflies in the tummy, and even though it's scary to be vulnerable like this, I love it. This is the kind of joy that work just can't deliver. This is personal, and it's real. Winter fuels me instead of draining me, I want to be the best version of myself for him.

It's ironic I have to watch him propose to another woman, which is going to gut me from the inside out—I'm only human! But the show must go on. We have a plan. We're almost to the finish line. Then Winter and I can be together, whatever that looks like. Life with a sometimes melancholy, always charming, magnanimous, and entertaining prince (or rather, former prince) will surely keep me on my toes.

It'll still be a risk. I don't know that I'll ever shake the feeling that it's me against the world, but Winter understands that part of me, and it's a risk I'm prepared to take.

I lug the box of blankets to the next set and go about laying them out. A sense of foreboding washes over me as I reach for the bucket of romantic red roses. I can't believe I'm laying out a bed of literal roses for the man I love to propose to another woman, but I push the ugly feeling penetrating my happy bubble away.

"Who made this thing?" I grumble, a guy next to me surveying the structure. The arch is the size of a truck, wood, and in the shape of a heart.

"It's going to burst into flame. Some woodworking-pyro-townie guy dropped it off. You should have seen the circus it took to get it up here."

"Logan Green?" I ask. I know way too much about Main

Street and the people in the towns at the bottom of the mountain already.

He snaps his fingers, "I think that's his name. It's a good set piece, should frame the guy taking a knee nicely. You know, a lot of these reality couples make it. I've got a buddy who was on 'Bachelor Island Tiki Getaway' about ten years ago, he's got three kids now—one in braces."

His words, so nonchalant and friendly make my head swim and my stomach cramp.

"Excuse me," I blurt.

"You alright?"

Jolting to my feet, I run for a secluded spot in the trees. My insides heave, not butterflies this time, and my entire breakfast with the sting of acidic coffee comes back to greet me. I have the presence of mind to be grateful I'm not hurling in front of cameras —they're filming everything today.

"Miss, are you ok?" the guy calls, covering his mouth and nose even though he's at least fifty feet away.

"What's going on?" Oh God, that's Marco's voice.

"I'm fine," I wave them off with a hand behind me. I can't turn my head because I'm still retching into the trees, dry heaving until there's nothing left.

I'm literally lovesick. My body is saying no. No to all of this. The thought of Winter proposing to another woman, marrying her, having kids with braces and ridiculously beautiful hair, has made me physically ill.

Because I'm stupid in love with him.

This show cannot be over soon enough.

My morning doesn't get much better after that. I can't eat and I have to force a bottle of water down so I don't succumb to altitude sickness. Twenty minutes of listening to Marco yammer in my ear about real estate and how he's dying to be a mountain man later, he calls the crew in for a meeting. I still haven't gotten to check on Winter.

My fingers wiggle at my side and I bite down on my lip.

"Final date, quiet everyone," Marco yells. Someone is a jokester and got the man a megaphone.

"Who's tempting an avalanche now?" I holler back. My voice cracks with nerves.

The crew glares at me. I forgot you're not supposed to yell avalanche on a snowy mountain. "Sorry," I offer.

This date isn't streaming live and much more has gone into production, preparing for the producers to cut into the film and splice it together to make it the most gripping content possible.

"Hey, Cat," Lexi A. from Alabama says.

"You look so beautiful," I say when I see her. She's in a white knit gown laced with beads and sequins that shimmer in the light, like little drops of snowy glitter. The perfect almost-wedding-sweater-dress to get proposed to on top of a mountain.

"Thanks. My stylist picked it out, it's from her line. She's still pretty small, but I insisted on wearing it. She could use a boost and I want to do that for her. I heard they're projecting Super Bowl numbers in terms of viewership."

"The fact you're even thinking about that means you're one of the good guys," I smile, trying to reassure her, wringing my hands out and pressing my thumb into my wrist where I wish Winter's heart was. I think I want a tattoo, too.

"Let's keep in touch after all this. You run a PR business, right?"

"Digital, branding, marketing, whatever you need," I answer, my head on a swivel looking for Winter. I don't know where he is but I'm praying he's still in the tent getting dressed so I can catch him before he comes out. I need to tell him I love him. That's the only way I'm going to get through this shoot.

"I'll probably need help after all this." She looks concerned, but not for herself. She pauses, then goes on, "Cat, I know you and Winter have some sort of understanding. We all do."

I suck in a breath, my skin going cold, my empty stomach hallowing out.

"It's okay," she puts a hand on my arm to steady me. Am I swaying on my feet? "The world is rooting for you to swoop in and steal the show," she laughs. "Just so you know, I'm one hundred percent cool with that." She winks.

Is she telling me to sabotage the finale? Jump in front of cameras and profess my love in front of millions? "Streamflix needs an ending." I shake my head, warring with my thoughts. My heart in my throat.

"Thing is," she gently grips my hand, as if she really wants me to hear her, "I'm not so sure I'm the one the viewers want to see him propose to." She smiles.

I tuck my hair behind my ears and pull my mittens from my back pockets. The temperature is dipping quickly up here. "I have to ask, it's crazy I know, but I have to ask if I'm going to watch him get down on one knee—"

"Did I fall for him after three dates with a camera following us around and the world watching?"

I laugh but it's strained. "Yeah."

"Not even close. Cat, we've all seen the way he looks at you."

"How does he look at me?" What have they all seen while I've been swirling around in my own little snow globe?

"Like he's hopelessly devoted." She puts a hand over her heart, swooning, for me. "Maybe not from day one, but even on day one, there was fire between you, no?"

"I guess we didn't hide it as well as I thought."

"I'm rooting for you both." She gives me one last squeeze and walks away when Marco calls her name.

Once she takes her place perched on a log outside the igloo, Marco hollers again, "We need Winter on set! Cat, that's you!"

Right. Winter is my job, for about two more hours.

I turn on my heel and stomp toward a makeshift wardrobe

tent but Robbie pushes through as I'm about to enter. "You ready for this?"

"I don't know what you're talking about." I fake innocent.

"Cat. *We all know.* I could smell the lust coming off you two from the jump. Liam and I want to plan a couples trip when this is all over."

"You got it." I am clearly a terrible actress. "And I'm happy for you, *LiRob.* I've been rooting for my own ship on this show." I push through the heavy canvas flap of the tent, and there he is. His back turned to me, in a tuxedo and snow boots.

My heart stops at the sight of him, his hair brushed back from his handsome face, the scruff I've gotten beard burn from the past few weeks gone. He looks almost too pretty, I want to ruffle his hair and demand he put on sweatpants.

"Are you ready?" I ask.

The air in the little room littered with camera equipment feels thick, despite the fact we're at a high altitude. "Why can't it be you?"

Oh, thank God.

"Winter," I breathe out, putting a hand to my head to make sure I'm not dreaming. I'm not the only one going through an emotional crisis of the heart today, and that makes me feel better. Merely seeing him after missing him all morning makes me feel better. I want to tell him I love him, but . . . "Of course, it can't be me."

"I'm doing this for you, and for Lexi. She deserves an ending that sets her up for success. And Brand Hub needs to fulfill the contract. And, so many reasons. But," he picks something up, then turns back to me and I see what's in his hands: the crown. "I want this to be yours. It doesn't feel right to give it to anyone else. It might not even be mine anymore," he laughs grimly. "Not sure where family jewels fall when you divorce your parents and your inheritance."

"Win," I put my hand on his wrist and press with my thumb. "You know I don't care about that." Deep blue eyes asses me.

"At least everyone will see once and for all that I'm not still a dumb kid, acting out, and uninterested in representing my people. That I'm not a joke. I'm responsible, and I finish what I start. Anker said my people don't like me, but I'm determined to prove myself. To them, to you, to everyone."

The walkie on my hip buzzes, Marco's voice streaming through crackled but clear. "Get your asses out here!"

"Chin up, Win. They're going to love you."

He cups my face with both his hands and looks me over intently, searching my face for any hesitation. The rest of my life with this man is so close. I can wait a few more hours. When it's all over, I'll scream how much I adore him and whisper all his best qualities in his ear until his cheeks turn red.

"Then we stick to the plan," he says.

"We stick to the plan," I repeat.

Winter and I hold hands almost all the way to the igloo, but I pull my hand from his at the last second, right before Robbie's camera comes into view. Out of habit, or because I can't stomach the moment, I don't know.

Almost there.

"Everyone, the happy couple will enjoy their last date in the igloo, then we'll pan to the arch. They hit their marks, Winter will take a knee, and we let it burn. Since we're all freezing our asses off up here, let's get a move on."

Cameras roll, not only Robbie's, they're everywhere today. The sun begins to set turning the glare on the snow into a pinkish golden hour mountain glow. He's charming without being overly sexual; she's sweet and devastatingly beautiful without flirting at all. It's like watching two nice people with zero chemistry on a date. They even feed each other strawberries at Marco's command, rolling their eyes, laughing at each other, and it's not romantic in the least. At least, to my eyes.

When they've hit all their marks at the igloo and she shivers with cold from over an hour of filming already, Winter drapes a blanket over Lexi's shoulders as they walk toward the arch. There's a lot of dialogue that I block out.

A heart made of fire ignites, burning brightly against the snowy landscape, mountains in the background. The visual is passionate and majestic, I can't ignore that.

Winter takes a knee and his great-great-great-grandmother's crown is in his hands as he looks up at Lexi, his eyes cutting only once to me.

I nod, chin up. *Always chin up.*

A hand lands on my shoulder, comforting me, some crew member who probably knows everything—do they all know everything? My pride rears its head, but I stuff it down. Just a little longer. I can take it, then we'll be home in our gingerbread cabin and this will all be over.

The happy couple embraces, Winter kisses her chastely on the cheek. The crew cheers, we've done it, show over.

"So you two, what's next?" Someone from Streamflix begins interviewing them as they both shiver, a few flurries of snow begin to fall and I'm grinning ear to ear.

He's mine.

This is the final part of the plan. The part where he says they'll stay in Garland for another few weeks, getting to know each other without cameras. Then they'll figure out their next steps. And when that time comes, they'll announce an amicable breakup.

"I'm headed to Denmark soon, actually," Winter says, wide smile, bright eyes, and as happy as I've ever seen him.

Wait—what?

His words register slowly. I count the snowflakes that land on my black boots as I look to the ground and try to decipher what he just said. *He's going to Denmark?*

"Really?" the Streamflix rep asks, looking sharply to Lexi.

She waves his confusion away. "We've talked about it, all good with me."

They've talked about it?

This can't be true.

But really, Winter and I never talked about what would happen after we stuck to the plan. We never said we'd continue living together in the cabin, or if I'd go back to San Francisco, or if he wanted to stay in the States forever or eventually return to Europe. He made me no promises.

And I didn't press for them. Possibly, because I knew this exact moment was coming. One way, or another. The inevitable moment where I have to take care of myself.

Everything spins, my world shifting abruptly. I can't hear anything but ringing in my ears and I can't see past the water in my eyes, cascading down my cheeks, turning cold as I soak them up with my mittens.

Chin up, Bloomfield. Don't make a scene. Don't fall to pieces.

He didn't tell me. He has a plan all his own that I'm not part of. This is why I don't let myself love, it always hurts in the end.

He places the crown on her head and it's all a blur as I make my way through snow that feels like quicksand toward the snowmobiles, my feet heavier and heavier with each step.

Against my better judgment, I glance over my shoulder.

Two cameras pull in tight as the happy couple are handed champagne. One of the cameras is Robbie, and I'm grateful he doesn't spare me a backward glance. Winter and Lexi are pink-cheeked with excitement and cold as people cheer around them, answering more questions being tossed their way.

He's going back to Denmark and I can't even be mad. I'm crushed, of course, but this is a positive choice for him. He's going back to a country I know he loves, probably to sort things out with his family.

"Now, get a shot of them kissing! We haven't had a kiss yet,"

Marco says through the megaphone. "Winter, you're supposed to be in love, man—"

"Cat! Where are you going?" Winter's voice, loud and clear, rings across the outdoor set.

He's going back to Denmark. For how long? Forever? And he never thought to speak to me about it?

Everything inside me is screaming to protect myself. That somehow, all of this is going to blow up in my face. That I've gotten it all wrong and I need to retreat, regroup, prepare, and above all, *save myself.*

Maybe I am mad.

"Cat, stop!" I knew he'd follow, but it does nothing to stop me from straddling the snowmobile and firing up the motor.

His hand lands on my thigh. "What happened?" he yells over the roar of the machine.

"You have interviews to do, the press tour, the spinoff they're going to beg you for—"

"Of course, I'll say no! Lexi will say no!"

I shake my head, reaching for a helmet. "You're going to Denmark?"

"I'm abdicating. Elias is fully supportive. I made the decision a few days ago but logistics—"

"That's really great, Winter. I'm happy for you." There's no life in my voice as it trails off. I can't look at him.

I let myself go numb, and it's so much better than feeling.

"Don't do that," he demands. "Tell me what's going on, Cat."

"I've told you everything, and you kept this from me."

"I wanted to surprise you. I wanted to do this for myself, make the choice, and stop hiding. *With you by my side.*"

"You didn't trust me enough to tell me any of this, Winter. How do you think that makes me feel?"

"You know more than my entire country at this point. I've only just decided to support Elias. He's scheduling an announcement with his team and sending me travel details today. Of course, I was going to talk to you about it."

Maybe so, but it's too late. It hurts too much.

"I just need some time, okay? Let's just take some time to think. Regroup. I need to think." I shake my head. My instincts screaming to protect myself.

"I don't want you to leave this way. Don't leave, Cat."

"Winter! We need you on set for interviews!" Marco's voice rings across snow, the entire crew is staring at us from up the mountain. "This heart isn't going to burn forever!"

I push him away and force myself to look him in the eyes when I say, "Go, finish what you started."

With that, I press on the gas, and I'm gone.

The snowmobile gets me as far as Little Star Lodge. I pull it right up to the post where Winter tied his horse the first day we started this whole mess of a show.

Inside, Darcy is at the front desk and I march up to her, shoulders back, head up, unabashed tear-stained cheeks and puffy eyes on full display. "I need a car."

"What's wrong?" She drops everything and rounds the desk to pull me into her petite frame.

"I'm not okay." I shake my head and sniff as she rubs my back. "I'm bad. I'm terrible, I'm—" but I can't finish because I'm sobbing. I'm not sure what I just did was strong. Maybe it was weak. Maybe I'm the weakest person I know and all my fears are coming to a head.

Even if he was going to spring this on me tonight, *Denmark?* No, we were destined for this end from the start, I just didn't want to see it.

Guests in the lodge stare.

"I got you, honey. Liam!" Darcy yells, across the entry and through the bar. She doesn't seem to care that we're causing a scene in her inn and that thaws my frozen insides a little. I'm leaning on her right now, physically, because I have to. If I don't, I'm going to crash and burn right here at the front desk.

"What's up?" Liam comes running from The Nook, black tie swinging as he jogs toward us. I guess it's all over, isn't it? No more fancy tree outside, no more Christmas cookies, no more snowman tie. No more show. No more Winter. "Cat, are you okay?"

"She's not okay, Einstein." I've never heard Darcy utter a sarcastic word, I must really be scaring her. "Said she needs a car."

"I want to go to Frannie's," I sniff and hiccup. This is why I don't cry. It's downright demoralizing. "Can I borrow yours?"

"I'll drive you," Liam says firmly. "Someone will need to help out in the restaurant," he says to Darcy but she waves him away.

"Don't worry about that, just go. Get our girl there safe and sound. And don't speed, the roads are bad."

He nods once, and I'm gently transferred from Darcy's shoulder to Liam's.

He pulls me out into the cold.

Thirty-Six

WINTER

"Winter, we need to finish. There's reaction shots to get on the mountain, and then an interview down at the lodge."

"I need to follow her—"

"After," Marco urges. "Please, man, don't do this to me. This is my job on the line."

Deep in my chest, under this fucking restrictive tux that's suffocating me, I'm buzzing with weight and worry. It's like the snowmobile is still idling next to me. If I shut my eyes and pretend, I can almost feel her face in my hands, her eyes looking up at me and not believing a word coming from my mouth.

I need to follow her. Nothing feels right, everything is upside down, my heart starts to pound and I feel an anxiety attack coming on, but I push it down with a gulp.

"Winter, man, come on. You can go after her once we wrap."

Marco's hand is on my forearm and I let him drag me back up the mountain. A heart is smoldering against the backdrop of a night sky, cameras are everywhere, stage lights they hauled up here not giving enough light.

Lexi wraps her arms around her middle in a white dress, "What happened?" The words barely register.

"I," I run my hands through my hair, searching for the answer I barely understand myself. "She didn't know about Denmark . . ."

"Oh, so she heard Denmark and that equaled—"

"I don't know? She'd mentioned wanting to see Denmark. I just assumed she'd come with me." Lexi doesn't have the answers I'm looking for, but she offers me a kind smile while cameras snap pictures of us in front of a burning heart.

I didn't have the chance to talk through what I'm planning with Elias, because it's all still up in the air. But she has to know, it all includes her.

She feels blindsided—I should have seen that coming. She needs solid, she needs safe, I'm such a fucking moron . . .

Still.

I cannot believe she left.

"Hey," Lexi's voice is closer now and I blink, realizing we're seated next to each other on a log in front of the igloo where we faked the worst romance in history. I'm on autopilot, hardly registering what's going on around me, moving through the motions asleep on my feet. Caught in a nightmare. "They're going to ask us more questions. What do you want to say?"

"What?" I'm stunned and I can't snap out of it. I cannot accept that this is reality. This is not how things were supposed to end. I've envisioned our life together, I was building toward everything I want, and so close to finally getting it.

"Do you want to stick with the plan?"

The plan was to let the media have their heyday. Let my people, those watching in Demark who were hoping I'd turn into an upstanding gentleman follow through on a promise. Then going to Denmark to give a formal speech announcing my abdication, my full support and mentorship of Elias, and spending the rest of my life with Cat Bloomfield—wherever that life may take us.

I can only hope I can still convince her to do just that.

"Yeah. Let's, uh, stick with the plan." I don't know what else to do. If I throw a fit now, let my heart shred right here in the snow, I ruin this show and the livelihoods of a lot of people.

"Shit," Marco says, from somewhere far away, or maybe he's right next to me. "There's not enough light. We need to move the interview people!"

The crew makes their way to the bottom of the mountain and we all convene in the tight space that is The Elk Room for interviews. I look everywhere as I'm ushered in by Streamflix people, but I don't see her.

Liam is at the front desk, sees my face, and immediately grimaces. "Denmark? You should have told her, man." Seems I'm on his shit list now, too. Cat must have been here and have left already.

Stupidly, I pray she's not. Maybe she's in her room and I can run to her the second this circus lets go of me. The second I'm released from this final cage. What will I say?

Why did you leave me when I needed you most? We're so close to having it all . . .

"Winter?" Marco says. "This is Madison from Entertainment Now. She'd like to ask you some questions that'll post to all their media outlets once the finale airs."

Boom mics lower over our heads as Lexi and I take a seat at the conference table, covered in a red tablecloth and flowers, a leftover Christmas arrangement.

"Sure," I look into the lights trying to make out the face in front of me, but the cameras are pulled in tight now and the room is suffocating. I rub my eyes, willing them to adjust, willing them not to appear glassy, and press my thumb into the spot where Cat's heart should be.

We stopped drawing them weeks ago because I'd grown so accustomed to having her by my side, I'd reach out and hold her hand when I needed her. We'd evolved, we'd grown together, I didn't need that crutch anymore but . . .

I need her now.

I can't believe she walked away.

The next day, I check our mailbox, now with a little plaque that reads *Gingerbread Cottage*, but it's empty. I'm trying to give Cat the space she asked for, the time to think she needs, but every minute that ticks by makes me feel more and more like I'm losing her for real. Indefintely.

I think of writing to her. I have so many questions.

The guys watched me pace the floors of the cabin most of last night, and I know Fran took care of Cat, saying they needed a sister night and she'd talk to me in the morning.

Not telling her about Denmark was a mistake. I realize it might not mean much to someone else, but it means a lot to her. She has to give me a chance to explain. I need her to let me in.

Stubborn girl.

I know she can see me loading my car, and I bite back anxiety over boarding a plane before I get to speak with her. I leave for Denmark in mere hours. The little log house we lived in for over a month together feels like a fever dream. Did any of it even happen?

My gaze pulls back to the back door of John and Fran's house. Faintly, I can make out two silhouettes. Cat and Fran, both in leggings and socked feet. I think Cat is holding a mug of tea.

The door cracks and my prayers are answered when she comes running out in her black puffer coat and boots.

"Winter, wait," she yells, slowing to a stop with a weary look on her face. "I wanted to say goodbye."

"Have you gotten my texts? I don't want to board this plane Cat, but Elias is depending on me. My travel details came through late yesterday, and my speech is scheduled. I have to go but I don't want to go without you."

I look past her at the lake. It hurts too much to see the disappointment on her face.

She follows my gaze, and considers her words as she chews on her lip. I want to press my fingertip into her cupids bow. "Listen, the show was a lot. My life is here. I know you've got things to clean up with your family, and I wanted to wish you luck. I want nothing but the best for you, Winter." She's so calm, as if we're sitting in an office meeting.

"Cat," my voice cracks with emotion as I reach out to her. But she's shut down completely. My hand drops, empty, but I still try. "Come with me."

"I can't," she shakes her head and shifts on her feet. "I can't just up and leave, Winter."

"You could if you wanted to." I want to rage, I want to sob, yet I can do nothing but stand here in the snow and plead with her.

"That's not fair. We helped each other a lot, you and me, let's be grateful for that. Be safe, okay? Take care of yourself." And then, she's gone. Back into John's house.

I stand there, willing her to open the door again. But a curtain falls closed and I lose sight of her.

I take one last look at our mailbox on the lawn with about three inches of snow packed on the roof since I last checked it. There's a letter in my pocket I've been debating leaving for her. Somehow reverting to our old way of communication, all the way back to square one is too much to bear.

She's right, it hurts too damn much. It feels like defeat, like one more failed attempt at loving something, only to find it doesn't love me back.

The letter stays where it is, and I slide into the driver's seat. If she wanted to come with me, she could. There's nothing holding her back.

But I have a country waiting for me.

So, I'm going back to where I came from.

I'm going back to where I belong.

Thirty-Seven

CAT

"Why are you doing this to yourself, Kitty-Cat?" Frannie brings me yet another cup of tea. Packages are arriving almost daily: fuzzy socks that say *girls run the world*, a Twining's Tea assortment in a woven basket with matching jams, face masks, and tube of NARS Dragon Girl red lip stain—because she gets me.

I turn to her and sniff, a box of extra soft, extra lotion-infused tissues in my lap. "I can't look away." We've been through eight boxes, already. Yes, I'm counting.

"Here," she hands me a jar of Vaseline fresh from a delivery bag, "You've got clown nose."

"Gee, thanks," I groan, but I slather the stuff on my nose and cracked lips gratefully.

Winter has a monumental speech to give. I had to tell him to go, and I couldn't sort through my feelings fast enough to give him anything other than a goodbye. But it hurts.

"So, what is BBC saying?"

"That he's the prodigal son returned. Even after being basically forced to abdicate, he's chosen to return and his people are applauding him. I don't believe they ever hated him. I think that was the work of some really shitty PR on the Crown's team with ulterior motives."

"Anything about . . . um . . . you?" Fran dances on her toes in fuzzy socks and a t-shirt of John's, asking the hard question like the good sister she is, but afraid of me a little, too. I have not been pleasant these past few days.

I snort a laugh. "The American who shall not be named that," I use my fingers sarcastically to make angry air quotes, "*broke his heart and wasn't even a contestant*, has not been mentioned. Allyn says the Danes were rooting for us."

"There's still rumblings of a *Wincat* reunion," she mutters and when I glare at her she adds, "Just saying. Let's turn this off and go for a walk or something." Frannie swipes at the remote but I hold it close to my chest.

"Shhh," I say dramatically, my tea sloshing in my cup, "It's starting!"

Winter takes the stage somewhere in Demark, a royal flag behind him, and begins a scheduled speech to his people. "Thank you all for joining me today." He speaks in Danish then clears his throat, looking dashing in a navy pea coat and button down, gray sky behind him, clouds bracketing him like bookends. "There's been much speculation as to my intentions on the throne," he pauses, "for years now." He goes on in English because this is airing internationally. The crowd chuckles, a mix of locals and media who've watched him grow up most likely. "This," he waves a hand, "the part where I speak to you publicly, has never been my forte." He clears his throat again and I watch his thumb graze a bandage on his wrist under the sleeve of his coat.

It's wrapped with a thin piece of gauze, and I wonder . . .

"Oh my God," I whisper, dropping my tea to the table,

knowing full well what that bandage must be covering. It's in the exact spot where I always drew a heart to give him something to focus on when he got nervous. Did he actually tattoo it permanently?

Come with me . . .

"What?" Frannie puts a hand on my thigh as I sit rapt, criss-cross-applesauce, listening to a prince who stole my heart make a speech about what he wants to do with the rest of his life.

Tears stream down my cheeks. I've never cried like this. *When is dehydration going to kick in, already?*

"So, today I'll keep it short and sweet. Many of you have heard rumors of my abdication, or *forced* abdication. While it is true my parents and I have never seen eye to eye, I'm willing to admit my part in not—" he pauses, searching for words or courage, and I suck in a breath. I wish I was there. "Not being exactly what the crown needs." He glances down at his wrist, touches the gauze ever so slightly, and looks back up. Determination crosses his handsome face. "It's you, the people, and the country that I'm passionate about. You are important to me. So important, in fact, that I've risked quite a bit to be here today. It is therefore my pleasure to announce I will act as advisor and mentor to my cousin, Elias. He will be good for our country. And I will be right behind him, supporting him every step of the way. I will not waiver, and I will not leave."

A wracking sob moves through my chest. This is how it was meant to be. This is how he was meant to be a part of his heritage without it eating away at who he is and what he wants. He's found a way to be both, and I am so happy for him.

He looks so strong up there.

"Cat." Fran wraps an arm around my shoulders as I draw a jagged breath. "What can I do?"

Tears continue to fall. There's so much left unsaid between us and I wonder if we'll ever get to say it. I wonder if he hadn't had a plane to catch, would he have stayed? Would I have heard him out? I've already risked my heart for him once, but *Come with me . . .* echoes in my ears.

WINTER

There's no way I'm moving to Denmark without my animals, so here I am, initiating the paperwork involved in transporting them internationally. Visits have been promised, regularly and often, to the men I love who have supported me since I moved here. I will miss them fiercely, more my family than the blood relations in Denmark, but it's what's meant to be. Elias needs me, and I need to be in the country I love at least part-time to support him, I understand that.

But being back in Clover, so close to Garland and Little Star Lodge where it all started and where it all ended so abruptly, still smarts.

Who am I fucking kidding? It's devastating, I scoff at myself darkly. This is why I can't live here. I can't be constantly running into Fran, and inevitably, Cat. I'm simply not strong enough, and at least I can admit it.

To make matters even more torturous, I've got a surprise

proposal in about an hour where my best friend plans to take a knee for the love of his life. Not exactly where you want to be when you're nursing your own broken heart.

Staying at Thistle and Burr has been a treat. Cat's living in our cabin I hear, and that makes my chest ache. Thinking of her in our bed, making coffee in our little kitchen is too much to bear, so I press it from my mind as best I can. Fran and John have done a great job with the motel, I'm pretty sure Holiday is trying to convince them to franchise it. But John has bigger things on his mind than expanding a motel business.

He's got a ring burning a hole in his pocket.

"Here's how it's going to go," he explains as the guys huddle, but really, he's working himself up. I haven't seen him this nervous since his last major league game. "I'm going to walk in," he points to the entrance of Boggs' Bar and Grill while we all stand like dopes on the sidewalk on Main Street, "and she's going to say, *oh hey, I didn't expect you in today . . .*"

"Why isn't she expecting to see you in your own bar today?" I ask. It's my job as Best Friend to poke holes in his plan.

"Because I said I'm helping Holiday winterize his boats for the season."

Ben shrugs. "I got a lotta boats, boys."

"But you've already winterized the boats," Jack says.

"Ah," John plays with his baseball cap nervously, "but Francesca doesn't know that."

"And I've brought a few out for today, so technically, we've been un-winterizing boats, and therefore, not a total lie." Ben Holiday has a way of making things work out his way. He is the local golden boy after all. Former homecoming king and owner of almost half the town of Novel despite barely being thirty.

"Because they're picking everyone up so we can motor in after she says yes, right?" Jack says, Wagner at his side doing his best to keep up with the plan like the rest of us.

"Yep." John nods. "I'll pull her to the dock out back and waste a little time before I propose so you guys can get everything inside ready. Patty's on her way with Ricky—I couldn't propose without my dad, and he's going to take video to send to my sister at school. Patty's bringing a bunch of food, and I've got the alcohol covered. Cat and all of you are in charge of decorations. You all sneak out when you're finished and she's said yes."

"How will we know when she's said yes?" Wagner asks.

"She'll be jumping around and going nuts, you know Frannie," Jack answers him, lovingly wrapping an arm around his shoulder. "Have you already forgotten the giddy feeling of being proposed to?"

John ignores the two men having a moment and goes on, "The boats pull up with all our friends and family, and everyone cheers."

"Easy enough," Logan puts in, cracking his knuckles and eyeing the boxes we're about to haul at the speed of light into John's bar.

John nods, again, more to himself than to us. "Okay. Okay, I think this is going to work." He paces the sidewalk, flipping his baseball cap around backward then forward again. "I've been trying to come up with the right way to do it, at Oracle Field, at home while we're cooking, but the dock feels right." He's nodding, convincing himself and I hate to see the guy go through so much stress.

"It's gonna be great, buddy. The woman adores you, and you've known she's the one since you first laid eyes on her. Right?"

"Yeah, right," he nods.

"She'll love it because it's very you, and very her. You nailed the plan, bro," Logan says, he pays attention to the important stuff more than any of us.

"And celebrating with everyone at Boggs' after is a good reason to throw a party. Right?" Ben chimes in. "Why own a bar and grill if you can't throw your own engagement party?" Once a home-coming king, always a homecoming king—ready for a bash.

"You're sort of splitting nails. He didn't re-open his dad's bar just so he could host his own engagement party," I say.

"I swear to God, you like to mess with us—*it's splitting hairs*," John laughs, pointing a finger at me.

At least I broke the tension for him. "How would you even begin to split a hair?"

"That's the point," they chorus at me.

We all pat him on the back and watch him walk into his bar to get his girl. Fran gets tugged out to the lake, and the dudes and I jump into action.

As we're hauling the last of the boxes of decorations inside Boggs', Patty's pickup truck rolls up with John's dad, Ricky, in the passenger seat, Cat riding in the bed.

My heart stops beating in my chest at the sight of her. "What the hell are you doing in the bed of a truck in February?" I shout as they pull up.

It's a gut reaction, not a great hello after she stomped on my heart and drove over it with a snowmobile, but the girl has to be frozen stiff riding in the back of a truck in this cold.

She ignores me and it's infuriating, so I press her, wrapping my way around the truck while Patty cuts the engine. "I'm serious. This isn't safe, Cat."

"Can you honestly tell me you've never ridden in the back of a pickup, pretty man?" A new black beanie is pulled low over her ears, and her cheeks are pink with cold as she clutches a to-go coffee.

She is wearing the coat I gave her. She didn't burn it, so that's something.

"You think the guys haven't thrown me in the bed of a truck before? We've all done it, but that's when we were idiot teens. The roads are slick. Patty," I holler toward the driver's side where she's ambling out of the truck, "you know better."

"There was no room in the cab," she says sweetly, "that's where the engagement cake sat. Ricky was in charge of making sure it didn't slide around the bench seat and get smushed."

Ricky drops a hand on my shoulder and I snap out of my staring contest with Cat Bloomfield. Her eyes were burning into me, mine roaming all over her. "We kept an eye on her out the window."

I bluster and huff back at him, incredulous. "Dammit, Ricky. I expected better from you."

"Nah, just a little fun. And she's tough. You boys got everything inside?" He claps me on the shoulder as we watch Patty and Cat deftly maneuver an enormous cake box out of the truck.

"We got it all. Let's go watch your boy get engaged."

It's impossible to ignore her presence at my side as we walk through thick front doors, the name Boggs' burned into the wood.

"Cat," I murmur, looking down at her. It's pathetic, the pleading in my voice is audible to everyone as Ricky takes the cake from Patty and they move quickly past us. "How are you?"

She hesitates in the entry, a Boggs' Bar and Grille sign with a colorful fish above a vacant hostess station. The lake committee circulated the hush-hush message that Boggs' is closed today for a proposal.

"I'm okay." She lifts her chin and gives me a small smile. "How are you?" Her eyes swim with emotion that makes my chest feel tight, I rub over my heart with the palm of my hand.

"Not great, Bloom." Elias, and the move to Denmark, have taken up every spare second of my time, but I miss her desperately and in this moment, I let myself hope that she's missed me, too.

Her eyes drop to her boots, and when she looks back up there's one single tear running down her cheek. She dashes it away with the back of her hand. "Saw your speech, you did good."

The words hit me like a Mack truck squeezing down Main Street, a lump forming in my throat. "Thanks, it was, tough . . . without you."

The emotion on her face gives me even more hope. Maybe I've

missed my chance to beg her again to be with me, even if that means long distance and video calls and whatever else people do when they're in love but torn apart by distance.

But maybe she'd still have me. I hadn't even considered it because she'd closed herself up so tightly, thrown her walls up so quickly. But if there's a chance . . .

She glances at my wrist. I don't try to hide it, a tattoo of her heart peeking out from the cuff of my coat. I took pictures of many of the ones she'd drawn, and an artist in Skagen layered them in a computer program and tattooed the heart on my wrist the day after I landed in Denmark, the day of my speech.

She sniffs. "Yeah, it's been tough without you, too. But we've got a proposal to get to." She plasters on a smile and pushes her shoulders back.

So strong, this woman.

"Not mine," I quip, and the joke falls flat.

She doesn't look back when she leaves me standing there, walking into the bar as if she didn't just give me hope.

It's been tough for her, too.

Inside, we have about five minutes while John pretends to show Frannie something that needs fixing on the dock, all part of the plan. Then he'll profess his love, take a knee, and that's our cue to walk out and cheer for the happy couple.

However, twisting streamers in all shades of pink and red, hanging flying cherubs above the bar because it's fitting for a Valentine's proposal, and laying out the custom *Frannie and John 4 Eva* napkins I ordered takes longer than one might think.

"Put them on the side of the bar," Cat says as she passes me with a cardboard cutout of Cupid shooting arrows. Her elbow grazes my hip and I feel fire. That fire that's always between us.

Does she still feel it?

"I like them spread out down the bar, ready for drinks. Easier than passing them out one by one."

She tucks a chunk of hair behind her ear and speaks to me

through the mirror behind the bar. "Easier. Well, I guess that makes sense."

Ignoring her barb, I continue sliding the napkins down the wood bar I know John polishes daily—my way. I even go so far as to start dropping them at each seat at all the tables around the cozy dining room. There's a fireplace on the back wall and Logan is already poking at a roaring fire.

"Hey," Cat yells, hands on hips, "you're making it worse. We don't need napkins all over—"

Continuing with my plan, steadfastly ignoring her direction, I respond over my shoulder "This was the plan. I was put on napkin duty, and on napkin duty, I'll stay." If I'm not mistaken, she's sparring with me. And it feels so good.

"Winter," I swear, there's a hint of a smile on her lips. I think she's missed this as much as I have. "Sometimes plans need adjusting."

I drop another napkin. "This plan doesn't need adjusting. This plan is perfect the way it is. Stay. The. Course. Bloom." Drop, drop, drop.

What I'm really saying is *I love you like crazy and we can make this work, Bloom.*

"I tried." She throws her arms out wide, her words echoing off wooden beams in the high ceiling. Ricky and Patty both pull themselves a draft beer as if they're getting settled with popcorn for a movie.

"Come outside and talk to me in private. We both know this is not about fucking napkins." I bite down on my last few words, the tension in my jaw so tight I feel like I could break a tooth. I'm dying to get my hands on her, even if she bats me away, I have to try.

I've regretted not fighting harder for her since the day I left. But since then, I've cleaned up my life, gotten things sorted with the Crown, and I feel more than ready to fight for her now. *If she'll have me . . .*

Ben clears his throat, coming to stand right in between us, his hands up in peace. "Uh, guys, looks like it's show time." He points out the window, pulling his aviators off his head, and walking out into the sunny winter day on the lake.

We all file out behind him, Cat falling into step beside Patty and Ricky, me forming a huddle on the beach with the dudes. Cat and I end up next to each other, our hands grazing at our sides as we silently watch our two best friends get the happily ever after they deserve.

The electricity between us is impossible to ignore. I thought being away from her these past weeks would kill me, but it's this, being right next to her and not being able to touch her. This will be my end.

"She said yes!" John yells from the dock, waving his hat as the cue for boaters to come from around a cove.

Fran screams and jumps into his arms. "We're getting married!"

Cat covers her mouth, smiling happily into her palms.

For a second, it looks as if he's going to take a step back and fall straight into the lake.

All the guys and I shout at once, a cacophony of *don't fall in! Watch it!* And *that lake is gonna be freezing!*

But John pulls his girl in tight and swings her around in a circle on the dock as boats begin pulling in across clear glassy water, cheering, blaring music from speakers, honking horns, and flying *John and Fran 4 Eva* flags from their boats.

Cat's eyes cut to mine. "I was put on flag duty, too."

Thirty-Nine

CAT

"Where's the champagne?" I call out from behind the bar. Of all the jobs I've had, of all the hats I've worn, bartender has never been one of them.

"We're out," Patty says, holding up a sad, empty cardboard box stamped with Veuve.

"Nah," Ricky says, wrapping an arm around her. "I'm sure there's more. Want me to check?"

"I'll go look in the kitchen. You guys stay here and man the bar," I offer, not a huge fan of sticky mixers and the even stickier floor.

"Probably in one of the storage closets," Ricky hollers as I make my way through swinging doors.

But I stop in my tracks. Winter is sitting on a shiny metal table, hands clasped, head down. "What are you doing?"

His gaze snaps to mine. Whatever he was doing in here all

alone, he was deep in thought if he didn't hear me come through the doors.

"I'm happy for them, I am, but it's hard to watch." He shrugs, eyes downcast, all shoulders, perfect hair, and five o'clock shadow. "I needed to get away."

"You have gotten away, Winter. Denmark is about as away as you could get." I wince a little at my biting words. I'm not mad at him anymore, I'm just sad—for us. The room is full of shiny metal and large appliances, I look around for a storage closet and spot one behind him.

He slips off the table. I take a step back.

"Wait," he says on a breath.

Seeing him today has been the hardest thing I've endured in my life. Seeing him, and knowing he's not mine. *Wondering if he still wants to be.*

Behind me, I can still hear the party going on, muffled by industrial kitchen walls. My sister's smile was so big, and when we called our parents their tears were so happy, I convinced myself it was enough. I don't need anyone. My parents are happy, and Frannie is happy. And as much as I still want him, Winter is living his life. And I'm fine.

That's enough.

"Please, *sod bloomst*. Don't leave. Again." But then he goes and says that—those words make my bandaged heart I've only barely been holding together, crack freshly into pieces. "I simply don't think I'll live through it. Who will give Lola her dinner? Do you want that on your conscience?"

"I didn't leave you," I try to hold my voice steady so he doesn't hear the rattle in my words.

This conversation was inevitable, it has to happen if we both plan to be in John and Fran's life. I've been preparing for it, but I wasn't prepared for him. For his sad smile aimed directly at me.

Those blue eyes watching my every move.

"How can you say that? I was there. You. Left," he presses.

"You made me feel like it was all in my head," I throw my arms out wide, shouting more than I should and breathing heavily, holding my ground and lifting my chin as he stalks slowly toward me. "Not telling me what your plans were made me feel like I was stupid to believe I'd be a part of your future." He told me I was wrong, back on that mountain. I didn't believe him.

But I don't know if I can look him in the eyes and tell him I don't need him, again. I don't know if I can say goodbye, again.

Because I don't want to.

How long am I going to lie to myself?

"I begged you to come with me."

"I was freaking out, confused, and you gave me zero time to think any of it through."

He searches my face, his gaze roaming the curve of my cheeks, the pout in my lips, the water in my eyes. "And the regret I feel is something I'll live with forever—I thought I was doing it all for you. Pulling myself together, getting things sorted with my life, my family, my future, so I could be worthy of you."

"You thought you were doing the best thing for *you*," I whisper because I can't let go of how much it hurt to be left out. Blindsided in such a vulnerable moment. "You were saving face, for your people. Proving something to your parents. And I'm glad it worked out for you, honestly, I am. The world loves you, Winter."

He drags an exasperated hand through his hair. "And it means *nothing* without you. Maybe I did want to save face. Be a good little boy who does as he's told—that's deep inside me, Cat, for better or worse. But I should have told you everything so you knew without a shadow of a doubt—it was all for you. I should have followed you down that mountain."

"Yes."

"Yes," he breathes, wrapping one hand around my hip, drawing me in. "Fact remains, you were a part of all my plans. You are the center of everything to me."

My walls are crumbling. I don't think I have the strength to board myself up anymore. Not from him.

And I don't want to.

"Can I believe you? I asked you once not to break me, turns out, I'm very fragile." I shrug. "That's just me." My voice cracks and I suck in a ragged breath. I do have weaknesses, I am fragile, and that's okay.

"It's my fault. We could have avoided all of this if I'd been open with you," he confesses, tucking my hair behind my ear. His eyes search mine, quizzical now. "Are you going to forgive me? Do I need to beg? Because I will."

"You will?" A laugh bubbles out of me in sputters, starts and stops that are escalating with the emotion of the past month.

I've missed him desperately.

"For as long as it takes. I'm yours, Cat. Nothing you can do can shake me. We'll figure out the logistics—*together*. I want you to feel safe." He drags a hand across his face as if he's lost, and tired. And I finally notice his cheeks are gaunt, he's lost weight, and he's sadder than I've ever seen him, and an avalanche of protectiveness courses through me. "I'm sorry I hurt you."

"Winter." I wrap both my hands around his handsome face, forcing him to hear me.

"Bloom." His voice breaks as he grips my arms as if he's afraid I'm not really here. *As if he's afraid I'll walk away . . .*

Voices, louder than the hum of the party outside approach the kitchen doors and we both startle. "It sounds like Jack and Wagner," he says, breathing heavily. "Fuck, I can't do this right now. I don't want to talk to anyone before we've finished this conversation."

"Probably been sent on a champagne hunt. Here, come with me." I take him by the wrist and drag him toward a closet door. And I see it, the heart, my heart just under my fingertips, slightly red but healed with time passed.

My grip tightens and I pull him into the closet as the swinging doors to the kitchen open. Sure enough, the muffled voices of Jack and Wagner talking about the cost of a case of champagne versus what a good prosecco might run trickling through from the other side. I hope they find nothing fast like I did, and go on their merry way back to the party.

I need to be alone with this man.

Winter and I breathe in the darkness, both of us trying desperately to stay silent.

"I'm so, so sorry, Win," I whisper when it's been quiet for a moment. Because I am. I hurt him while protecting myself and erecting my walls. Self-preservation and all that.

"You have nothing to apologize for. I'd make a joke about always running into you like this, but I don't care. While I have fond memories of us sneaking into closets, I'm just so happy to breathe the same air as you again. Even if you tell me it's still over."

"It was never over for me." Fisting my hands in his shirt, I let myself inhale his scent and it feels like coming home. It feels safe. "I wish I could have stayed for you."

"I should have left for you. Explained everything even if I had to chase you down a mountain, made you listen, smashed through your walls. Will you forgive me?"

"Forgiven." The pads of his thumbs wipe tears from my cheeks as he tips my chin up and drops his mouth to mine. Featherlight, he brushes one reverent kiss across my lips.

"I hated every moment away from you, I wanted to crawl out of my skin. Hated not knowing what you were thinking. I have so much to tell you," he murmurs through kisses.

"I want to tattoo your heart on my wrist, too. I've missed it. God, Winter, I've missed you," I say into his mouth, sharing breath.

"Shh," he hushes, and I melt. "I'm here now."

"We'll tell each other everything from now on? Open, no surprises?"

"Of course, you're my best friend, Bloom."

"Yes," I breathe, realizing *that's* the most romantic thing a man has ever said to me.

"You'll never need to miss me again if that's what you want. Cat, you must know how badly in love with you I am—"

"*Madly*," I say, smiling against his lips. "And me, too."

He nods, "Have been, for a while now."

And then his mouth is hungry, starving, but not as much as mine. It's been weeks of fantasizing about him coming to me like this, about running to him like this. About his hands roaming my body, his mouth sucking at all the sweet spots. The heat that slicks through me is instant, wet pooling between my thighs, and I reach for him through his pants, dragging his zipper down.

"But you live in another country." He moans and doesn't stop me as I free him from his pants. Our last episode of sneaky closet kisses never got this far, and I'm wondering if it's a fantasy we've both been holding onto.

Making short work of it, he unbuttons my jeans and pushes them down my thighs. "I live wherever you live. I'll figure it out."

I kick one boot off and manage to free myself from one pant leg—that's all we have time for and as if he's on the exact same page, he picks me up and whirls me around until my back is against the closet door. With zero warning, he presses deep inside me in one fast thrust.

"You—*yes, Win*. I want you, like this, right now, always." I kiss his neck, clutching at his shoulders as he moves fast inside me, stretching me from the inside out. Filling up all the emptiness.

"Good, because I intend for you to have all of me, *sod bloomst*. All of forever. Forever and a day."

"Forever and a day," I repeat, wrapping my arms around him and hanging on, running my hands through his hair, gripping him with my thighs.

"Let me come back? Live with you until . . . whatever."

"Yes, I'm still in the cabin," I sigh heavily into his ear, "I couldn't leave, I don't know why. Allyn's thrilled because I'm not making her hunt for fancy new offices. Maybe I've been waiting for you this whole time. I can work from wherever so . . ."

"Perfect. I was hoping you'd say that," he grunts, pushing into me relentlessly, no mercy, no slowing down. "I'm never watching you walk away again." He's ratcheting me up so quickly, I'm going to come and promise him anything. Everything.

"Yes, yes that's so good. Just like that," I praise him and the man grins so wide, all the cocky confidence back and in full effect.

"Say please, princess—"

"I told you not to call me that—" but he tilts his hips up in the most delicious way. "Please, Winter. *Please.*"

"Good girl." And that does it for both of us I think. Whether we've both been waiting so long to have the other, or needing to heal this wound between us, coming together like this does it. Or we're just that right together. Or we've learned and grown through these past few months together and we can fully trust the other in ways we both needed.

When we find that exquisite release together, him sucking at my throat and whispering through his climax, I know this is it for me.

"There's one more thing—" I drop my head to his shoulder, breathing heavily, sated.

"What else could there possibly be? I got the girl. Fuck, I'm living the American dream right now, aren't I?" He's breathing heavily, holding me up easily against the door as I flex and squeeze my thighs around him, not ready to let go. "Sixteen-year-old Winter would not believe me if I told him Boggs and I would marry sisters and live in each other's backyards."

"Marry?" I press my hands to his chest and pull back. "Did you say—"

But he puts a finger to my lips. "Later. We have forever to discuss it. Whatever you want, whenever you want, it's yours as long as you'll keep me."

"Winter, I need to tell you something—there's one more thing you need to know—"

He straightens, gripping me tighter, a funny little smirk tipping his lips up and one eyebrow raises sky high. "Cat Bloom-field, are you trying to tell me . . . you're not . . . pregnant?"

"Oh my God, no!" I drop both my hands on his chest and smack him.

"Ow," he yelps. "Then what is it?"

"When I was sad, and you were gone, I missed Lola and needed something to snuggle. So, I adopted a kitten."

There's a knock at the door. "Are you guys done yet? Or can you slip a box of champagne out and then you can finish jumping each other's bones, or writing sonnets, or whatever it is you two are doing in there?"

"Have you guys been out there this whole time?" I yell.

"Well, we took a walk down to the docks to give you guys a minute, but we're back now and tired of waiting."

Winter pulls a string dangling over my head and the room goes from dim to bright. We're surrounded by giant cans of tomatoes, dried pasta, simple syrups, and bar mixers. There's a case of cham-pagne on the floor.

Ignoring Jack's voice on the other side of the door, he looks directly into my eyes. "Tell me everything," he demands. "What color is he? She? How old?"

My grin is slow and my chest bubbles with delight. "He's black, twelve weeks old, and has two little white mittens on his front paws. Found in the walls of an old, condemned record store in Novel. It was Fran's idea. She saw the listing in the Spirit Lake newsletter. The vet is getting him ready to go home tomorrow."

"I'll need to get all the records so we can take him to Denmark with us. Have you named him—"

I laugh at his extreme excitement and lower my voice. "We can't do this right now." I rearrange my disheveled sweater and finger-comb my hair.

"Why not?" he drops his voice to match my whisper.

"Because you're still inside me!"

"But I'm a new cat daddy, I'm excited!" He squeezes me.

"Hey guys, thirsty party people out here!" Jack hollers again.

"Well bring it out, just a minute!" Winter replies, rolling his eyes.

"Keep your pants on, we're coming," I holler, already sliding down Winter's front and struggling to get *my pants* back on.

Winter's head tips back and he roars with delighted laughter while I listen to two equally childish men on the other side of the door fall into a fit of giggles.

"What's gotten into you?" Frannie sidles up beside me, a salty margarita in her hand made exactly the way she likes it.

"My sister's getting married! What do you mean? I'm having a great time at your party."

"You've been all slumped shoulders and gray faced and *woe is me* for weeks, and now you're shining like a freaking diamond from the inside out—what's this?"

The collar of my sweater is a bit stretched out at the neck from Winter pushing it over my head and behind my neck. "It's nothing." My hand goes to cover whatever she sees but I'm too late.

"That is a love bite, Kitty-Cat," she hisses, keeping a smile on her face and looking around the bar as if there's nothing to see here. "Have you been getting it on at my engagement party?" she whispers.

"No. No, no," I stammer.

"Is it Winter? Did you forgive him? Did he realize he's a huge idiot?" she squeals, trying to keep her face neutral. "Please tell me it's Winter, you two are perfect—"

"Don't you dare start jumping up and—"

Too late. "Oh my God! Are you back together? I'm totally

making you guys walk down the aisle as best man and maid of honor now."

Winter and John make their way to the bar, drawn by Frannie's freak out, no doubt.

"What's gotten my wife-to-be to be so excited all of a sudden?" John asks.

"You young people, always hanging by the bar without a care in the world. Do you know what kind of hangover I get from one glass of wine these days?" Patty joins our circle, followed quickly by Ricky, who's got a hand on her curvy hip.

"Just a happy bride!" I say, with so much unnatural enthusiasm, it's as if a record scratches. They all turn to stare at me: all of Winter's friends, most of the town, except Mayor Troutwine and the mayor of Novel who are arguing near a bowl of potato chips.

"Tell them what's going on, or I will!" Frannie shouts. "I get a whole year to be a bride."

"We're waiting a year?" John's lips form a pout.

"We'll talk about it." Frannie wraps her arms around his middle and presses up on her toes to kiss his cheek.

"Well, out with it." Logan startles us as he crosses his arms. "What?" he asks, looking around, clearly trying to school his features into something less grumpy. "The mystery is killing me?"

Winter gives me a nod, and I know, we're about to let the cat out of the bag in a big way. Pun intended.

"Winter and I are back together and we're adopting a kitten." It comes out of me in one long gush and the entire bar is frozen still.

Then there's an eruption of *aww* from around the entire room and everyone's eyes go googly.

"And she's coming with me to Denmark for a visit while I take care of some business."

The dudes form a huddle around Winter and bear hug him all at once.

Frannie kisses me on the cheeks. Then she picks up a party

popper off the bar and yells, "Bon voyage to the happy couple, but Winter, you better bring my sister back for my wedding or I'll come for you!"

The party popper explodes in strands of little streamers and a burst of glitter.

Winter wraps both arms around my neck, pulling me out of the crowd enough so that it's the two of us in a little corner.

"Are you happy?"

"Um, hold on—"

"Bloom?"

"I can't believe this, I've got glitter in my eye," I laugh, looking up and blinking at him like a madman. "Yes, I'm happy—but do I look like a pirate?"

"Here, let me." His thumb brushes gently under my eye. "I see it, hold on."

In this moment, I realize I have someone to take care of me. And that hits harder than any tangible gift or romantic gesture could.

"It doesn't hurt, get in there," I say, opening my eyes wide and pushing up on my tiptoes.

He pokes a bit harder and I feel it when he swipes the chunk of glitter away. "Better? I think I got it."

"Yeah, Win. I'm much better. You definitely got it."

THE END

Epilogue

CAT

Three months later, Marselisborg Palace, Aarhus, Denmark.

"When is Elias getting back?" Winter asks, pouring tea from a flowered china pot into a dainty cup and handing it to me. I notice our matching heart tattoos on our wrists and the sight makes me giddy.

The tea service arrived moments ago at our door. Winter wasted no time loading an assortment of Danish treats all over the coffee table in front of him. He's been making me taste-test new things for weeks.

"He's in Copenhagen for another week. A few more press events to attend, and then we'll move into phase two when he gets back." My laptop is under a stack of newspapers and magazines that get delivered to our rooms in the castle weekly. But I'm done working for today.

Off hours are off hours.

"Did you see this?" I hold up the New York Times. A headline screams across the front page, under the fold, that fallen popstar Lucy Lark is recording a new album. "They're speculating that she's recording grassroots style, in Clover. It's a pretty public leak for a girl trying to hide and live off the grid. Not sure what it could mean for the town or for . . ."

"Ben. He's going to be worried sick. We keep telling him to let her go, but he's been taking care of her the whole time she's been up on that mountain. Dropping supplies, fixing fence, and broken porch steps. We've all known her since high school, but I hate her a little for taking advantage of him like that."

I push away from the pretty round table next to a window overlooking the grounds and join Winter on a down-filled striped sofa, marveling again at paintings of his ancestors on cheery yellow walls. "I'm sorry. Tell him I'm here if she needs help."

"You and that soft heart of yours."

"Yeah well, it's not like I'm suffering. I've never been so happy, and I don't like seeing others struggle." This is about as fancy an office as I ever wished for, and Brand Hub's budget is thankful. Instead of new offices, Allyn and I agreed to put that money toward some pro-bono accounts. I feel good about that, the Rushmores have referred friends in the graphic t-shirt business.

He wraps an arm around me and pulls me in. "Back to me. I'm you're priority—"

"Of course," I confirm, a laugh falling from my lips.

"Phase two?"

"Meet the new royal family."

Winter's parents are here in Aarhus, staying in Marselisborg Palace along with Winter, Elias, and me for the spring. It's quaint for a castle, and I love it. The gardens are closed to the public while the family is here, and I've had cobblestone walks attended by armed guards with tall fur hats with Winter every single day.

"We have a photo opp on the front steps scheduled when Elias is back, but I'll hold your hand the whole way. You're almost done, Win. This new arrangement is going to be good, it's going to work." It's a whole new world and I love sinking into his culture, his country, and everything he loves and has missed for so long.

"As long as you continue to clock out every night, eat dinner with me in bed, wake me up with kisses in the morning. I can't thank you enough for sticking by my side as I transition through the announcement of my abdication." He pulls my feet into his lap.

"What's on the agenda for tonight?" Things aren't perfect, and I don't think I'll ever truly forgive Frederik for the way he treated Winter, but this is our new normal. His mom is trying. Elias is turning out to be the brother I never had: strong, determined, and ready to take on the world with Winter as his most trusted advisor. We hit it off instantly. His parents were slow to accept me, but Elias gave them no choice.

"Dinner out, it's time to leave the love nest. I made reservations, and Annie is joining us. They're closing for us, no paparazzi, no cameras. But first, look what I got you—

"More socks?" I laugh as he pulls a pair of black socks with pink flowers from between couch cushions.

"I can't help it. They made me think of you." He slips them on my bare feet and I groan when he gives me a little foot rub, too. He drops a kiss on one ankle, and then the other.

"Let's have desert first." I crawl like a cat across the sofa and climb into his lap.

But he pulls me up before I've even gotten his shirt unbuttoned. I protest, but he shushes me, "You have to see this. You can have your way with me after," he smirks.

We walk into the bedroom portion of our living quarters. This room is painted the palest pink with fresh floral arrangements on the dresser and famous oil paintings on the wall. Sunlight spills through soldered glass doors that lead to a small Juliet balcony and just beside them, next to our bed covered in soft linen sheets and silk blankets, are Lola and my black kitten, Mittens. Snoring away on a cushion in the sun.

"That's probably the cutest thing I've ever seen." Mittens has brought out maternal instincts in me that I never knew I had.

"They're so happy together. Who saw that coming?" He pushes open the doors and pulls me outside while we let our fur babies sleep. A light breeze swirls through my hair and he tucks it behind my ear. "And I'm so happy with you, too. But I need to ask you, Cat, you have to be honest with me . . ."

After a long pause, I stomp my socked foot and prompt him, "Spit it out."

"Can you be happy living like this? I don't want to lose you, but I know this life is demanding. I'll have to be in Denmark for a good portion of my time every year, and I know you miss your sister."

"And you miss all the guys."

"I do."

"So we split time, live here half the year, the other half in our little gingerbread cabin."

"We'll renovate, add on, whatever you want. I'll call John today and ask to buy it. His house will still have a few acres attached to it, I don't think he'll mind."

"And Frannie will love it."

"And so will I," he murmurs, dropping his lips to my neck. Rubbing a thumb across a ruby in my ear.

I look out across the palace grounds, a few fans are faintly visible beyond the gates holding signs that say, *We love the prince and his PA.*

"And so will I."

Also by Margaret Rose

Sink Or Sell

Kissing Bandit (Love At The Lake Book One)

On Holiday, (Spring'25)

Love Bug, (Fall '25)

Acknowledgments

Thank you, thank you, thank you to my cutie-pie family. When publishing feels daunting, and when imposter syndrome strikes, you remind me how lucky I am to have you. Everything else in life is gravy, ya know?

Bringing a book into the world takes a village. To my editors Annie, Jen, and Dani, thank you for reeling me in, pushing me to sink in, and telling me when I've nailed it. To my Beta readers Lainey Lawson, Bianca Miller, JR Boles, Libby Frazier-Nelson, and Kelli Cooke, this book would not shine without you.

And to my sweet friends, bloggers, readers, reviewers, and influencers: none of this happens without you. Being an indie author means being a writer and a business owner. It's not easy, and I wouldn't make it without you cheering me along, spreading the word, and consuming my books.

And finally, to my assistant Alex. You make me feel like it's not just me against the world!

About the Author

Margaret Rose is a true Gemini and the most extroverted introvert you'll ever meet. Before becoming an author, she worked as a personal stylist, secretly drafting novels and begging her friends to read them. Now, she enjoys wearing sweatpants just as much as sequins and watching her kids chase their dreams while she chases her own. You can find her online at Margaretrosebooks.Com.